"YOU NEED TO PAI
head, Marie-Claire, or Professor Dixon said bluntly. **"Leave your comfort zone and follow your heart."**

When American Marie-Claire Wentworth lands a spot at London's most prestigious art school, it's the opportunity of a lifetime. As a watercolor painter, she specializes in the beauty and solemnity of waterfowl. But her professors say her work is too boring and static, and that she needs to loosen up and learn to be spontaneous. That's an impossible task for someone like Marie-Claire.

Until she meets Mick Carr.

Athletic and determined, Premier League footballer Mick Carr is a player out to win, both on the pitch and off. Nothing is refused him. He gets what he wants—when he wants it.

Until he meets Marie-Clair.

When Mick sees her paintings in a restaurant, he's captivated. After searching for her, he loses his heart, and the cocky player is now questioning everything. Together, Marie-Claire and Mick wade through the rocky waters of building a relationship while an ex-girlfriend is determined to destroy them to further her career.

Fighting the pressures of art school and the pushy paparazzi, they battle the world's scrutiny. Can they win a future together, or will they lose everything?

Books by Marina Reznor

Fiction

Fowled
Kingsbury Town Football Club Romance, Book One
Booked
Kingsbury Town Football Club Romance, Book Two
Cup-Tied
Kingsbury Town Football Club Romance, Book Three

Non-Fiction

Dad's War
An army photographer, Lady Chatterley, and the story of
how whole blood helped win World War II

FOWLED

Kingsbury Town Football Club Romance
— Book One —

Marina Reznor

KINGSBURY TOWN PRESS
BIRMINGHAM ALABAMA

FOWLED

Kingsbury Town Football Club Romance Series, Book 1

ISBN: 979-8-9850984-1-9 (eBook)

ISBN: 978-0-9994297-1-6 (Paperback)

Editor: Denise McInerney, Stonewall Editing

Proofreading: Jessica Snyder, Jessica Snyder Edits

Cover design: UpdateDiva Design

PUBLISHED BY KINGSBURY TOWN PRESS LLC

BIRMINGHAM, ALABAMA - KINGSBURYTOWNPRESS.COM

For Joe

Chapter One

MICK CARR WAS having a hell of a time concentrating on the woman sitting across the table in the swank restaurant Sunday night. As Fanta nattered on about some fashion show, his gaze kept drifting upwards to the painting hanging on the wall above her head. It was a swan in flight, its wings spread in magnificent power, the long neck arching as it stretched into the wind. A brilliant azure-blue background framed the bird's crisp white feathers, the clear tones glowing.

He couldn't drag his eyes away. It was the most beautiful thing he had ever seen.

The little sticker beneath said "Tundra Swan," which was a bit confusing — here in England they were called Bewick's Swans. He'd seen a flock once while grouse hunting up near the Scottish border, but never as far south as his farm in Hertfordshire.

"Why are we in Putney again?" Fanta complained, lapsing into her native south London accent. "There's a restaurant just opened in Notting Hill I hear is ever so nice."

Mick adjusted the necktie that had a death grip on his jugular. "Sir Frank wants us patronizing the local establishments while the club's temporary training facility is here, and this just got a Michelin star."

"But there's nobody here, nobody famous at any rate," she muttered with contempt, tossing back her mane of glossy black ringlets. "I mean, what's the point of being here if we're not going to be seen?"

Mick ignored the question and, giving in to temptation, yanked the blasted tie off and unfastened the top button of his starched shirt, almost popping it off in the process. At six-foot-two and over fourteen stone, he was one of the largest players in the Premier League, and finding shirts that fit his thick, muscled frame, especially around the neck and shoulders, was a right bugger. He supposed he could have his shirts custom-made like most of his teammates, but the tedium of the fittings and fussing over fabrics was like to drive you barking mad. He preferred sweaters that fit well and let a guy move.

A young man in thick-framed glasses arrived to take their order, and while Fanta dithered, Mick's attention returned to the paintings. Hanging next to the Tundra Swan was a study of two Canada geese on the shore of a lake, a male gander and female goose. They mated for life, he remembered learning on a hunting trip abroad, raising their goslings together as a family.

"What are you smiling about, Mick?" Fanta asked. "Come on and order."

With an effort, Mick forced his attention back to Chez Bertrand's menu. Half of it was in French, touting poncy confits and reductions, whatever the hell they were. That afternoon's match against Hull City had been grueling and he was bloody well starved, so he pointed to the first thing on the list, not caring what it was. His aunt Sue served more at her dainty teas than these posh places did. Thank God there was a decent pizza place not too far from his house in Fulham that delivered.

Fanta fidgeted with her pastel-colored drink and craned her neck to look at the other patrons. "That's Darius over there. Who's the girl he's with?"

Mick glanced to where his best friend and Kingsbury Town Football Club team captain was sitting a few tables away. "It's his cousin. She's visiting from Essex. Should we invite them over?" he asked, knowing it would annoy her.

Panic flared in Fanta's eyes, then was squelched. "You're so funny," she cooed, her self-control reestablished, "that's what I love about you. You know I'd rather be alone with you. Is there anything you want to talk about?"

Her eyes, he noted, had a keen and desperate look about them. The tabloids had been hinting that an engagement was expected at any moment, and he didn't have to be a genius to figure out where they had gotten that tip.

It wasn't that he was opposed to marriage, quite the opposite, but he knew for a fact he had not yet met the woman he would marry. Who she was and how he was going to find her was a mystery, but he trusted his instincts. He'd know her when he met her. A man didn't need a fancy education when he could trust his gut.

Like when Dad had taken him to see Moorsgate. Even though the farm had been a rundown disaster, he'd known right away it was the property he wanted. After a cursory walk around the grounds and a ten-minute chat with the estate agent, he'd written a check for several million pounds and never regretted it.

He spent every moment he could out there, when he wasn't with the team, of course, and that had caused some hard feelings with Fanta. She'd pestered him to take her out to his "estate," and he'd tried to warn her that it was just a neglected farm, but she wasn't to be dissuaded. The reality became clear when the Range Rover had gotten bogged down in the swampy lane and he'd had to call the local farm lad, Roger, to come pull them out with the tractor. Her disillusion had grown further when she saw the mansion was just a derelict stone farmhouse covered in vines. Then a harmless grey squirrel had crossed their path and she'd run screaming back to the car, her high heels leaving staccato footprints in the muddy path. After that, she'd refused to go back until he "had that mess cleaned up and a proper house built."

They'd been dating some six months now, since they'd met on the weeknight television game show she hosted, *Willy Nilly*. Francine Mertz, as Fanta used to be known, had started out as one of a dozen beautiful girls in skimpy attire the show was known for. With admirable speed, she worked her way up the ranks to individual camera shots, which in turn led to playful banter with the contestants and a small endorsement contract with deodorant company.

Her big break had come when the lead presenter, Cashmere Cassidy, became embroiled in a notorious and well-publicized affair with a married cricket player. The worldwide media coverage had been scorching, and the lanky blonde had manipulated it like a master even after the cricket player dumped her for a Brazilian swimsuit model. *Willy Nilly* ratings had soared, and within a month, she had made the big leap into American television. She was now the co-host of a daily chat show from Hollywood.

Fanta had paid close attention, and when she had been tapped to replace Cashmere, she'd had a plan. Mick had been her first celebrity contestant, and she had introduced herself before the taping began, directing the full force of her personality at him with a blatant suggestion that he visit her dressing room, where they could get to know each other better.

Mick Carr was not a man to pass up an offer like that. Filming lasted two days with frequent dressing room breaks, and when he'd won the top prize, the picture of her kissing him full on the lips was splashed across every tabloid in Great Britain. The *Daily Mail* had captioned it **Fanta and the Footballer**.

They had been an item from that time on. She fit in well with the other wives and girlfriends, or WAG's, as they were nicknamed, and in no time the couple was a tabloid favorite. The girl had a genius for exposure. She also had a penchant for drama, and that was proving expensive, like when Mick would find himself on the outs with her and was expected to buy his way back in. This happened often, as he was well known to have a wandering eye, so visits to Malbrey Jewellers were becoming a grudging habit.

Although, truth be told, Mick's eye wasn't wandering, just bored.

Since there was no chance that Fanta was going to be the future Mrs. Mick Carr, he'd better move the conversation onto safer subjects.

"Have you heard anything more about presenting on *London Now*?"

Fanta rolled her eyes and adjusted the dress's neckline to better display her enhanced cleavage. "As if I haven't been waiting! Elliott is supposed to get them to commit tomorrow and let me know. Might be looking for another agent if he doesn't make this happen. I can't be a presenter on *Willy Nilly* forever. I've got bigger plans."

An attractive blonde with a beguiling smile approached the table. "Mick, sorry to interrupt, but can I have your autograph?"

"My pleasure," he obliged, although he disliked being interrupted during meals out. However, it was part of the job. Fans thought they owned you on the football pitch and off, so he took the paper she handed him and palmed the scrap that had been secreted underneath, which no doubt contained her phone number. Save that bit for later.

"You can make it out to Jillian." She smiled, leaning closer. "And good luck against Spain next week in the Friendly. I'll be cheering for you and England."

Mick signed while Fanta gave the woman a cold, appraising look that chased her off. "Elliot said you made a hash of the press conference for the Friendly. Said they quoted you saying Barcelona was the capital of Spain, not Madrid."

Mick flushed, remembering the searing humiliation when everyone had broken into laughter at his gaffe. Worse still, he had sat there, mystified, until the England manager leaned over and clued him in, which only made everyone laugh harder. It had taken a superhuman effort to quell the directionless anger that engulfed him, and he sat in silence for the rest of the press conference, terrified to open his mouth.

"It was a mistake, okay?"

"You came across looking stupid. Again," she added. "You need a PR agent."

"Dad's my agent," he shot back.

"Your father is a gamekeeper, Mick. You need a public relations agent," she explained as if he was thick, "somebody to coach you before your interviews so that you'll come off better. More educated like. Elliot says he can take you on."

"I am not hiring a PR flack, damn it!" Mick's fist slammed into the table, making the woman at the next table jump. With an effort, he lowered his voice. "Leave that to pansies like Auchincloss."

"Hugo Auchincloss pays Tom Belleville-Howe to keep him out of the papers, not get him in," Fanta informed him, "and when I get on American telly, that's what I'm going to do. Makes it look like you're special."

"Whoever he's got has his work cut out for him," Mick sneered. "The smug prick got his first yellow card this afternoon and it's going to be all over the papers tomorrow."

"Is it because of that girl he was involved with?" Fanta asked in hushed tones. "The one whose fiancé dumped her for that supermodel? Elliot says there's going to be more coming out about that."

Mick shifted in his seat. "She's a nice girl. They should leave her alone."

"It's a love triangle, Mick." Fanta sighed. "And I bet she played them both along, and that's why Hugo got the yellow card, 'cause he's in love with her and all, but she betrayed him."

"Hugo doesn't love anyone but himself."

"Well, he had better be back under control by Birmingham City next week or you lot are sunk," Fanta cautioned. "And Delia says it had better be a win because it was only a draw today against Hull, and Kingsbury Town ain't getting to Europe racking those up."

"*Isn't* getting to Europe," Mick corrected, swallowing his irritation at her constant criticism with a sip of wine. What he wouldn't give for a pint.

"And don't think they won't have noticed you need work marking your man. Why, if I was Birmingham City, I'd set up a play where you're drawn…"

As Fanta droned on, his gaze drifted farther down the wall to a painting of quail eggs nestled in straw. They were lovely. Achingly perfect, each speckled egg different, showing the wide variety of patterns and colors he was so familiar with. Soon, maybe by next summer, he'd be raising quails at Moorsgate, along with ring-neck pheasants and grouse. Then Dad'd get some competition for who had the best shoot in southern England.

"Here's your grilled eel with eggplant and mustard oil, Madame, and your sautéed Scottish lobster with truffled chicken quenelles, sir," the server announced as he set the plates before them. Mick looked at his plate with contempt; there wasn't enough there to feed a bloody cat. He snorted in disgust and asked for a lager.

"And something else—" he read the server's name tag "—Raul."

"Yes, sir."

"These paintings on the wall. Of the waterfowl. Where do they come from?"

"They're by an artist at the Lady Warwick College of Arts and Design down the road. Ella, she's the wife of the owner here, she teaches there and sometimes puts up students' works for sale."

"They're for sale?" That cheered Mick up. "Who painted them?"

"Marie-Claire Wentworth, we call her MC. We're both students there. She's also my housemate."

"Bird lover, is she?"

"Obsessed," Raul agreed. "If you're interested in seeing more, there's a student show Tuesday and MC is exhibiting. Or you can come by tomorrow afternoon; we're setting up then. There might be more there you like."

Fanta made a show of clanging her flatware, signaling that the attention needed to return to her. "Are we going to start collecting art, darling?"

Raul glanced between the two. "You can talk with Ella, she's here tonight. I'm sure she could tell you more."

———◆◇◆———

"If I moved in with you, you wouldn't have to drive so far," Fanta observed as he drove her home to the unfashionable suburb of Lewisham. Her income from *Willy Nilly* was a pittance, and Mick knew she itched for the exclusiveness of his stark, modern townhouse in Fulham, which was gated and had several famous residents besides himself. The place was nice, he supposed, the security was good, and it was convenient to the club's headquarters in Hendon. It was also one of the few places in London where he could get a garage large enough for both the brand-new Aston Martin sports car and his old Range Rover, neither of which he could bear to be parted from.

But despite Fanta's alternating bouts of pleading and petulance, he refused to even discuss them living together. "There's no room for your car," he replied, rubbing his left knee, which had started to throb. That bastard Hull City striker had deliberately tackled him and knew just which leg to go for.

"Then why don't you get rid of that old Range Rover? It's a wreck and it stinks of dog," Fanta grumbled, then perked up as a new idea occurred to her. "Or I could give up the lease on my car and drive this."

Mick laughed out loud at the ridiculousness of her suggestion and was rewarded with cold silence for the rest of the trip.

"Do you want to come up?" Fanta asked, her manner indifferent as he pulled into a loading zone behind her building. "I've taped some of Cashmere's shows from America. We could watch them."

Leaving the engine running, he went round to open her car door and gave her a quick peck on the cheek. "No thanks, love, early morning tomorrow."

Fanta stood in the street, gap-jawed. "Aren't you at least going to walk me to the door?"

"What, and get a ticket? I'll call you tomorrow," Mick promised. Ignoring her dismayed pout, he got back in the car and sped away.

Mick drove back to Chez Bertrand, cutting ten minutes off the trip by racing the Aston Martin down side streets and narrow alleys. He met with Ella and the transaction took place, then the server, Raul, helped him carry the three paintings to his car. When he arrived home, he hung them in a line on the blank living room wall, and then sat on the leather sofa opposite to admire them, liking them even better in his home than he had at the restaurant.

The paintings were full of life and freedom, and as he studied them, he felt a pleasant sense of contentment come over him. The stress of the match and the mortification of the press conference, it all faded away. He knew these birds, knew their world, and the knowledge that there was someone else out there who could appreciate them the way he did was oddly comforting.

He needed to see more.

Chapter Two

MARIE-CLAIRE WENTWORTH dashed through the gates of the Lady Warwick College of Arts and Design in Putney on Monday morning with less than five minutes to spare before her meeting with Professor Dixon. It was unusual for her to be late—she prided herself in her punctuality, but this morning had dawned with rare sunshine, and the opportunity to get in a few hours of sketching at the London Wetlands was too good to pass up. Indeed, the effort had paid off. She'd been able to work for almost two hours before the drizzle had set in, even glimpsing an elusive long-billed jack snipe.

The small car park, formerly the stable yard for the mansion that housed the school, was packed with moving vans unloading equipment loaned from local galleries for the student show the next night. She threaded her way through the bedlam, the March wind whipping her long, chestnut-brown hair into a tangled mess.

The mansion's two-story mews had been converted into the school's studios—sculpting and photography were on the first floor and painting on the second, the aroma of sweet essence of turpentine and lime plaster mixing with the faint scent of old manure. She'd grown up in the farmland of the Eastern Shore of Maryland so this didn't bother her in the least, and the natural light in the second-floor painting studios was quite decent when the sun shined.

Inside the studio, she sprinted up the stairs, passing a pudgy, near-sighted male student on the way.

"I say, MC, there's a film at the Strand tonight and I was wondering if—"

"Sorry, Stephen, I've told Neve I'd help her in the photo lab. Thanks anyway," she called over her shoulder, tossing her leather field bag on her workbench and taming her hair into a ponytail. She left her thick, hand-knit sweater on to keep out the pervasive chill; when the stables had been renovated, no one had bothered adding insulation to the walls. It was rumored the heating system had been installed by Queen Victoria herself.

A girl with startling blue, short-cropped hair ducked around the corner. "Quick, she's coming!"

"Thanks, Sandra." Marie-Claire said a quick prayer and waited.

"It's not bad." Professor Dixon studied the watercolor of a mottled brown woodcock for what seemed like an eternity, then repositioned it to catch a bit more of the weak light filtering through the windows. "I suppose it's the best of the group. But it's labored. Reflected light is fleeting and has to be captured in the moment, not worked up from sketches and studies. Do you have any other examples?"

Marie-Claire shook her head and hugged her sweater tighter around herself, tempted to point out there wasn't much light of any kind to be had in London at that time of year. The woodcock had been a rare find near the Thames embankment, and she had only been able to fill a few pages in her sketchbook before he had flitted away.

The professor inspected the rest of the paintings lined up on her worktable. "These are all very good, MC, but you could have painted them the day you arrived from America. That's why we gave you the reflected light assignment for the Critique. You need to develop more trust in yourself as an artist. It's time to let go of the mechanics and depend on your eye. Paint what is in front of you, not what you saw two weeks ago."

Professor Dixon said it with such nonchalance, like it was the easiest thing in the world.

"I'm trying, but it seems like the harder I try, the worse the results are. It's almost impossible."

"It's very challenging," Professor Dixon agreed, "but that's the idea. You're not supposed to be doing the same work. The Critique is supposed to challenge you as an artist, to grow in ways you never imagined. If you can't, then the Lady Warwick is not the right place for you."

"This is the right place for me, I know it is," Marie-Claire responded with heartfelt conviction, "and I can do this. Just tell me how to fix it and I will."

"This isn't about technique, it's about letting the art come from inside of you. It has to be spontaneous and flow naturally. You need to paint with your heart and not your head, MC, or you'll never pass the Critique," Professor Dixon said bluntly. "Leave your comfort zone and follow your heart."

Marie-Claire stared at her with no comprehension whatsoever.

"Let me give you an example." Professor Dixon gestured to her worktable, where the pencils and brushes were grouped in jars, rolls of tape neatly stacked, kneaded erasers and sponges in baskets, sketches pinned on the wall, and unfinished boards arranged by height between the table legs. "You are a very methodical and disciplined painter. You identify a subject, create dozens of detailed sketches and value charts, work up the studies until you decide on a composition, and then do variations until you get one you're satisfied with."

Marie-Claire nodded; that was true.

The professor turned to a beautiful painting Marie-Claire had just finished. "How long did it take you to finish this Brecon Buff goose?"

"Four months, but—"

"Exactly my point. Now look at Sandra's workspace." Professor Dixon pointed to the table next to hers that was piled high with scavenged scraps of everything imaginable, dirty brushes, and stacks of half-finished projects. "Even though she's mixed media, her work is much looser and spontaneous."

"Are you saying I need to develop habits like that?"

"Heaven's no, Sandra spends half her time just trying to find things. And while her pieces might have a vibrant immediacy that yours are missing, your work is technically superior. It will be a lot easier for you to gain that spontaneity than it will be for Sandra to slow down and understand composition, rhythm, and proportion."

"What about Stephen?" Marie-Claire asked, nodding to an almost empty table across the room. Two brushes stood in a plastic cup next to a blank sheet of watercolor paper, and a forlorn roll of tape hung on a single peg.

The professor's lips pressed into a thin line while she considered the question of Stephen Ashe. "I honestly can't say what his style is. He seems to be in a category of his own."

Recovering her composure, she continued in a matter-of-fact tone, "MC, you didn't come to the Lady Warwick because you want to be a good painter. You're here because you want to be a great painter. That means it's time for you to break free of the rigid structure you impose on yourself. Leave your comfort zone and follow your heart. Focus on the present and let the future take care of itself."

"You make it sound so easy," Marie-Claire grumbled, tucking back a lock of hair that had escaped the ponytail behind her ear.

"Embracing spontaneity will feel like the most unnatural thing in the world, but it will help you learn to trust your instinct, which is what all great painters do. You won't be sorry. *Carpe diem!*"

———◇———

After Professor Dixon left, Marie-Claire tidied her work area, but then left two pencils and an unfinished sketch on the otherwise immaculate surface. It was a start.

A lecture on contemporary urban art was due to start in ten minutes in the main school, so she shouldered her bag and walked down the stairs, chewing over the professor's comments with vexation.

"Oi, MC, you've got an admirer," Raul called across the first-floor sculpting studio.

Moving through the maze of large pieces that were being prepared for the show, Marie-Claire made her way to where he was loading a metal sculpture onto a cart. "I do?"

"You sold three paintings last night at Chez Bertrand."

Her mood improved a great deal with this news. "All three?"

"All three."

Marie-Claire whistled. "Holy cow. Who bought them?"

"Some rich footballer. He was at the restaurant with his tarty girlfriend and he couldn't take his eyes off of them."

Marie-Claire added up the prices Ella had encouraged her to set and felt almost faint. "What's a footballer?"

"Football player, love. Oh. You lot call them 'soccer' players," Raul clarified, draping a shipping blanket around the sculpture. "He's one of the Premier League players. They're the top level, astronomical salaries and huge egos. Bigger than life, especially him."

All of this meant nothing to Marie-Claire. "What's his name?"

"I don't know, I follow cricket. But he looked familiar, really familiar—I think he's on a cereal box. Here, hold this."

"And he bought my paintings," Marie-Claire mused as she held a roll of tape while Raul secured the wraps. This was her first big sale.

"Ella has the check. She had to go down to Brighton today, but she said she'd see you at the show and give it to you then."

"You know what this means?" She grinned.

"Rent?"

"Rent."

———— ◇ ————

Fans and critics alike acknowledged that Kingsbury Town Football Club was a textbook example of how money, talent, and desire could make a lot of things happen in a short amount of time.

Fourteen years ago, it had been a small football club in a working-class suburb of west London whose players labored at the Kingsbury Cement Factory. In good years, they played in the Football Association Second Division, and in others, dropped to the Conference circuit, but the loyal fans filled the ramshackle stands twice a week, regardless.

No fan was more devout than Frank Poleski. His grandfather had joined the club after arriving in England as a penniless immigrant from Poland after the Great War and had learned English from the other players. In addition to being a prize forward, Frank's father was a tireless worker who had been promoted to general manager before he was thirty and then married the owner's daughter. Their children had grown up at the football pitch next to the factory, dreaming of First Division glory.

By the time Frank inherited the prosperous business, he had a plan. It took him twenty years and a keen eye on emerging global markets to grow Kingsbury Cement into a worldwide enterprise, but he succeeded and made himself a fortune in the process. On the day the *Times Of London* declared that Sir Frank—as he was now known—was a billionaire, his lawyers wrote a generous offer for the club which was accepted at once. The current team was retired with generous settlements, then Sir Frank set about turning Kingsbury Town into the most respected and feared football club in Europe.

Included in the sale were the pitch and some outbuildings, but most important, the three vacant lots adjacent to it. A week after the sale, everything had been razed to the ground and a concrete temple to the art of football, Townsend Lane Stadium, was begun. As far as European stadiums went, it was of average size, but had every feature to ensure the fans' comfort and safety. At the same time, a nearby warehouse was converted into the club offices and a spartan practice facility—while he was willing to spend lavish amounts on his team and stadium, Sir Frank was also a businessman and didn't see the point in making everyone too comfortable. There was work to be done.

As construction progressed on the stadium, Sir Frank began shopping for a staff and players. He had rather unorthodox ideas about who he wanted, and first on the list was Giles Roberts, an eccentric Welshman who had been sacked as manager from almost every club in the Premier League. Giles listened with deep suspicion as Sir Frank explained that if he signed on with Kingsbury Town, he would be given a blank check to assemble a team and a long time to form them into a Premier class club. It was important, Sir Frank stressed, that the players be young, hardworking, and willing to have some patience as the club moved up through the ranks. If they were, they would be amply rewarded.

It took almost a week, but Giles became convinced that while Sir Frank might be a mental case, he was an earnest bugger and had the money to back up his daft ambitions. They shook hands on a contract, the details of which were known only to them, and the new manager set about his job with gusto and a penchant for secrecy.

Mick was sixteen years old and playing in the academy for Chelsea when he received a call suggesting a tryout with an unnamed club, and after talking it over with his father, decided it was worth a shot. He'd not stopped growing and his weight was worrying Chelsea, which made any career in the Premier League doubtful, regardless of his uncanny knack for reading an offense.

They drove to a deserted pitch next to a cement factory in Brent, where Giles put him through a cursory workout watched by a lone figure from the sidelines. Afterwards, they were introduced to Sir Frank, and half an hour later they shook hands on a deal that was later formalized to everyone's satisfaction at the Kingsbury Industries world headquarters in London. Mick was one of the first players signed and had been with the team ever since. His signing bonus had bought the Range Rover.

Darius Rutledge, another defender who had already been cut from two clubs, was added a week later and in short order, the two gelled in the center back row. A few midfielders were tried but none seemed right until an underweight wing named Hugo Auchincloss arrived, fresh out of Eton. He was cocksure and arrogant, but blindingly fast with a genius for creating opportunities for the other players. An assortment of other questionable choices filled out the roster and the club was set.

Dismissed as a hodge-podge of misfits, the team's first two years were a disaster, and Mick prayed for a transfer. Then Giles's brilliance began to reveal itself and their individual strengths blended into a powerful unit.

There were no stars on the team and they worked like bloody plow horses, but they won League Two, then blazed through League One. In short order, they got close enough to the top of the Championship League to win promotion to the Premier League and several cups to boot. Now, movement up the Premier League tables was coming in manageable fits and starts. If their luck held, a possible fifth-place finish and European Championship entry were in tantalizing view.

As the club became more successful, Mick noticed that life began to move much faster. The money got better, the women more beautiful, and the trouble much easier to find. He reveled in his newfound celebrity status and admitted things got out of control for a while. The drugs were off-limits, but nothing else was, much to the delight of the tabloid press and its avid readers, as Mick learned.

The paparazzi relished documenting the players' high spirits, but seemed at a loss as to how to cover Hugo Auchincloss. Hugo had proven himself a ruthless and cold-blooded technical specialist on the pitch, and his status as one of the few public school graduates to play professional football made him an interesting oddity on an already eccentric team. His connections to the aristocracy and complete disdain for publicity only enhanced his mystique.

Off the pitch, he treated football like a day job and seemed oblivious to the rest of the world. He was cordial when the need arose and showed up for required club events when duty required, but never willing socialized with anyone. It was even rumored he still lived at home with his mother.

He did have a girlfriend, though, a posh bird with long legs who smoked French cigarettes and seemed to enjoy the fast life. As a rule, teammates' girlfriends were off-limits, and in all honesty, Mick had been dead drunk and didn't remember any of it, but there had been a photographer lurking in the hotel hallway who had gotten a shot of her leaving his Manchester hotel room at three o'clock the morning after a match.

There had been a right blow up in the tabloids, and horrified, he'd gone to Auchincloss to apologize, but the bastard had just looked down on him with those cold grey eyes like he was some scum stuck on the bottom of his custom-made shoes.

Since then, they barely spoke on the pitch, never off, and the son of a bitch never missed an opportunity to make Mick look stupid.

———————◆◆◆———————

To ready the team for the final push to the top of the Premier League, Giles had grudgingly made some necessary changes in the roster. Pozny Gorlinski, a likeable midfielder from Poland who didn't speak a word of English, had been brought in to replace a midfielder whose ACL had given out, and one of Giles's scouts had found a brilliant forward named Samuel Nkomo from Zimbabwe playing in a church league in Costa Rica, of all places. Lars Van Der Beek was still their mainstay forward, but the man was almost crippled, and Mick knew they were looking for his replacement.

Sir Frank had also agreed to build a new training facility in Hendon, but to save money, decided to raze the old building and construct the new one in its place. In the meantime, the club was quartered in a crumbling post-war edifice slated for demolition, St Augustine Catholic School in Wimbledon. The players, many of whom were Essex natives, regarded anywhere south of the Thames as uncharted territory and had launched strenuous objections. But, as much as the school was a slum, the pitch was a jewel and the high walls that ensured the team's privacy trumped all protests.

Mick disliked it intensely. Schools always made him nervous, and this hole was worse than most. Everything had been built for little kids, making his already outsized frame feel like that bloke Gulliver from the story his aunt Sue had read him when he had been a lad laid up in bed with the flu. But they were only stuck there for a year, and the new facility was looking to be world-class. He just hoped to God they set the showerheads higher than five feet.

—◆○◆—

Mondays were a day off, but Giles hadn't been happy with their performance against Hull and ordered them in. Indeed, it had been a brutal month so far; they had lost the sixth round of the FA Cup ten days before, then lost the makeup match against Blackpool on Friday, and then had drawn against Hull yesterday. Fanta was right, they weren't going to qualify for the European Cup this way, and his gut told him things were going to get worse before they got better.

Mercifully, Giles was more interested in getting them all back on the same page than in introducing another one of his harebrained strategies, so they spent the morning in drills and skill work before filing back inside to watch game film of Birmingham City, their opponents on the coming Saturday.

In one of the old classrooms, Jason Edu and Pozny made a funny show of trying to fold themselves into the little desks with the chairs attached, while Mick stretched out on a low bookshelf, keeping his left leg elevated as Duncan, the team physiotherapist, had instructed. He'd also suggested Mick lay off driving the Aston Martin because it crunched him up, a notion Mick dismissed out of hand. True, the car was proving a bit more of a trial than he had imagined, but everyone expected footballers to have flash cars. It was almost part of the job description.

Sheila, the club's customer service manager, bustled about handing out fan mail while Giles called the rabble to order and nodded to an assistant to dim the lights. As the video began, Mick flipped through an assortment of earnest notes from young players, then assessed a flowery envelope containing a half-dozen photographs of a scantily clad beauty before passing them on to Fernando.

Relaxing back on his elbows, Mick focused on the film. Birmingham City had an older and wiser lineup with several big players much like himself. Matches against them were more physical, which he always relished, and while their accuracy was average, their conversion rate was huge — if you let them take chances, they ran with them. Their biggest talent, however, was their ability to find any weakness an opponent had and exploit it. So what holes did Birmingham City see in Kingsbury Town?

As Giles was asking this very question, Mick noticed Hugo Auchincloss slip into the room, looking like hell. He'd shown up late for practice, and Giles had banished him to run laps, which always suited him; as much as Mick hated the bastard, he had to admit there was almost none faster.

Mick watched him in the dim light. Judging by the dark circles under his eyes, Fanta's prediction was right, the tabloids were having a field day with him and the girl he was hopelessly in love with. This cheered Mick up to no end, although it was a shame the girl was being dragged through the mud as well.

He'd met her, Julie something-or-other her name was, a few weeks before at an after-match party and had been rather charmed. She was pretty in a bookish sort of way, like those librarian-types that would turn into a tiger once you got the hair down and glasses off.

He'd chatted her up, and it turned out she was a crop specialist like the kind Dad brought out to consult on the fields, and even better, she knew all about the type of apple trees he'd found growing at Moorsgate. His interest in her as a potential bed partner flew out the window, and they had been in deep discussion about pruning techniques when Auchincloss appeared, incensed because he'd thought Mick was making a play for her.

Never one to pass on an opportunity, Mick had accepted her invitation to visit the gardens she ran at a cooking school up on Hampstead Heath, in part to annoy Auchincloss, but also to learn more about his abandoned orchard. Soon, he'd realized he'd made a mammoth mistake—she was a sweet girl, but when it came to her gardens, her enthusiasm knew no bounds and good Lord, she would not shut up. And half of it was in Latin to boot.

She had droned on for what seemed like hours until a nice lady had come to rescue him. He'd stood for some pictures with the students and then fled in relief. A few days later, she called to apologize that she would not be able to visit Moorsgate to see his orchard herself, but offered up a local arborist who she thought would do a good job. It was obvious Auchincloss was behind that, but Mick had been relieved; he didn't know how much more he could have taken.

Now something had happened between them and some other bird, and the tabloids had gotten their noses in it, and Hugo was suffering.

Mick chuckled. He'd never be so stupid as to let a woman get to him like that.

Chapter Three

AFTER AN HOUR they were dismissed, and Mick showered, shaved, and changed into dark grey wool trousers, a soft cashmere sweater, and the black leather jacket he preferred for town. He headed out to the derelict car park where the paparazzi loitered, waiting for Auchincloss to appear.

"He'll be out in a few minutes, lads," Mick called helpfully, and let them get a few shots of him in the Aston Martin before driving off. Under normal circumstances, he would have been more protective of his teammates, but he was willing to make an exception in Hugo's case.

It was only a short distance from St Augustine to the artsy suburb of Putney. The car park behind the school was crammed with vans, so he parked on the street and climbed the mansion's wide marble steps, pausing at the imposing front doors. A thick brass plaque announced "The Lady Warwick College of Arts and Design."

An erratic tick began to twitch beneath his eye. His memories of school were of embarrassment and awkwardness that typically ended with him using his fists and Dad being called to sort things out. This would be the first time he had walked into a real school since he had walked out of the last one at age fourteen with no hopes of graduating. Not that anyone had missed him; he'd spent precious little time there before that.

The familiar, sickening pressure started to build in his chest, and Mick forced himself to take a deep breath and concentrate on his success. Thanks to Sir Frank, he was making serious cash and hadn't needed an education, just a talent for figuring out what the opposing offense was going to do almost before they knew it themselves. Hell, between him and Darius, they hadn't let a headed ball in goal since September, and that one had only slipped past because the sun had gotten in their eyes. It was almost a league record.

There was nothing on the other side of these doors he couldn't handle. Summoning the nerve, he shoved them open and strode in with his head held high...and crashed into a tower of empty cardboard boxes. Scrambling frantically, he righted them as best he could. The foyer was like a construction zone, with crates and trash strewn this way and that amid the din of hammers and screaming saws. A guy pushing a wheeled cart full of metal scrap yelled, "Coming through," and Mick jumped out of his way, almost toppling a table stacked high with cartons of lightbulbs.

Mick steadied the fragile glass and then looked around. Activity seemed to be centered in a large reception room off to the right, so with cautious movements he picked his way towards it and peered in. People, he supposed students by their age and rather wild dress, darted in and amongst portable walls that broke the large space into smaller areas, adjusting lights and running long lengths of cables.

Venturing further into the chaos, Mick looked for any sign of the beautiful watercolors, but instead was dismayed to see only…well, junk. Weird and ugly creations made with stuff he put in the rubbish bin were balanced on large plywood display benches or stacked right on the floor. In the middle of the room, a girl was arranging painted boots under a collection of socks dangling from the ceiling.

Turning a corner, he came to a dead halt at the sight of a grouping of nude photographs—he was no prude, but even he was shocked. Next to them, a dozen television screens all displayed a silent video of a woman smashing little cakes with a brick. Farther down, a girl with short blue hair was hanging a huge painting he could have done with a can of house paint and his big toe.

"Marie-Claire Wentworth?" he inquired with a sinking feeling.

"Marie-Claire?" The girl repeated. "Oh! You mean MC. Last room, at the back."

Mick made his way unnoticed through the maze of clutter, wondering what the hell he was going to find in the last room, but once there he breathed a sigh of relief. The small gallery was a veritable sea of tranquility compared to the rest of the place.

This was a proper room that at one point must have been an annex to the large reception area. Its walls were painted grey with nice trim work, and aside from a wide, plywood display platform, it was almost empty except for a girl who stood on a ladder with her back to him, trying to adjust a spotlight in the ceiling.

Three watercolor paintings were hung on the wall behind her, all as beautiful as the ones he now owned. Two were smaller studies, about the size of the quail eggs, and the largest was another Tundra Swan in flight, very similar to his but with a paler background. The detail and intimacy were emotional, rooting him to the spot.

Another five paintings were leaning against the wall, waiting to be hung. From the ladder, the girl groped in her back pocket for a screwdriver while she attempted to hold the light in place, jamming her knee under a ladder rung for more support. As she lifted her arms higher, her t-shirt pulled up to reveal a glimpse of smooth back and gentle curve of hip where the low waistband of her jeans shifted.

Mick's attention immediately switched from the paintings to her, and with a connoisseur's eye, he noted how her body twisted gracefully as she struggled with the light that refused to remain in place. Her thick hair was pulled back in a glossy ponytail that hung down her back, the lustrous tendrils swaying to and fro in an unconsciously seductive rhythm. It was a normal color, too, like caramel poured over shiny copper pennies.

A pleasurable tension began to coil in his body as he admired the view. It wasn't hard to imagine what she would look like out of those jeans, that delectable bottom clothed in nothing but knickers, her skin warm and smooth under his caressing hands...

Aware she wasn't alone, the girl glanced over her shoulder and gave him an appraising look. "Have you come to mount me?"

For the first time in a long time, perhaps his entire life, Mick Carr blushed. "Sorry?" he stammered, rooted to the spot.

"Have you come to mount me?" the girl repeated. "Because if you have, I'm almost finished, but Sandra in the main room might need a hand. She's got big canvases."

Mick released his breath. Her voice was soft, the accent flat, perhaps American. Nice. She continued to look at him and he realized he couldn't just stand there and gawk at her all day. "I can help you with these," he managed to get out.

"There's just five more but I can't get this floodlight to work. I think the pivot pin is bad, but I'm sure you're better with these than I am." She descended the ladder and handed him the hammer and screwdriver.

She was pretty. Very pretty, he corrected himself as she got closer, in that unique, fresh-faced way American girls had. She was shorter than he was by at least half a foot, coming to his shoulder, and he found himself staring down into her green eyes, riveted by their twinkling depths. There was a sprinkling of freckles across her cheeks and nose that made her age uncertain; she could pass for a teenager but had the curves of a woman. Generally speaking, not his type, but he couldn't deny the reaction he was having to her.

She glanced back up at the floodlight and bit her lower lip, and he amended that to strong reaction.

Forcing himself to concentrate on the job at hand, he shucked his jacket and then took the tools and climbed up the ladder. "Just needs a bit more muscle," he surmised, and spent a few moments tapping the pin with the hammer until it held. "Good to go. Are the rest of the lights set?"

"Yes, they should be. We just need to mount the rest of my work. Do you need gloves or did you bring your own?" She picked up a pair of white cotton gloves from the display platform. He remembered seeing the people in the other rooms wearing them, to protect the art, he supposed.

When he shook his head no, she left the room and returned with a pair that stretched uncomfortably over his large hands.

After flexing them once or twice, he pointed to the blank wall in front of them. "Which one goes here?"

"The covey of Chukars. They're the—"

"I know what a Chukar is," he interrupted, liking the look of surprise on her face.

"You do? Which one is it?"

He pointed to the five paintings leaning against the wall. "First on the left. Next to the Red-breasted Merganser."

This time she didn't even try to hide her astonishment. He picked up the painting and examined it. "This one's a drake. Most commonly found in the Atlantic Flyway in the Chesapeake Bay. He's a diving duck, a bit different from the Common Merganser at the end of the row. You've done a nice job with the crest."

"Thank you. I'm impressed. There aren't too many people around here that know waterfowl, especially American waterfowl."

"Dad's a gamekeeper in Hertfordshire. We've gone to America twice, to hunt. Amazing time. You're American."

She peeled off the glove and held her hand out in that friendly way Americans had. "I'm Marie-Claire Wentworth, my friends call me MC. I'm from Maryland."

Taking his own glove off, as well, he engulfed her much smaller hand in his, feeling a pleasant jolt as he pressed the softness of her skin. Her smile was genuine, and her scent, intoxicating. It was fresh and warm and reminded him of a meadow in the summertime.

"Michael Carr." Christ, what was the matter with his voice? He cleared his throat and tried again. "Michael Carr. People call me Mick."

He waited for the recognition but none came.

Outstanding.

The expression on her face turned quizzical and he realized he was holding her hand captive.

"Pleased to meet you." She extracted her fingers from his grasp. "Do you like bird paintings? I do a lot of them. Waterfowl mostly."

With an effort, he shifted his attention back to the paintings. "I like these."

"Thank you. I think I'm the only artist in London doing this sort of thing at the moment, but you probably see more than I do."

"They're a sight better than that muck out there." Mick jerked his head back towards the main gallery.

"We all have our own styles," she gently reproved, then pointed to the first painting on the wall. "This is a pair of Shelducks. They roost together closely. And here's a Coot, they're very popular where I'm from."

"Maryland," Mick repeated, noting the small birthmark at the nape of her neck, behind her right ear.

"On the Chesapeake Bay," she nodded, "it's a major migratory path from Florida to Canada. We're always seeing something new each hunting season."

Mick felt almost lightheaded. "You hunt?"

"My brother and father run a waterfowl hunting business on the Bay. I help out, but I'm mostly interested in painting the native waterfowl."

The urge to take her somewhere private and learn everything about her was overwhelming, and Mick struggled for some control of himself. "Are you here for university, then?" There, that sounded normal.

"Graduate school, Master of Fine Arts. I graduated last year from Chestertown College." She smiled and turned back to the paintings, oblivious to his internal struggle. "This one is a Red-legged Partridge. I hadn't seen them until I came here, but they're very similar to Chukars."

Mick followed her as she described each picture, his mind churning.

"This one I finished last week. It's a Snipe. I've only just learned about them. I got to see one on a game estate in January."

He picked the painting up and scrutinized it, anything to stop staring at her. "Are you doing these from photographs?"

"No, I've been taking the train into the countryside on weekends to sketch. I've been to Saxham in Suffolk and Lymesford, which is in Devonshire. That's been my favorite, but the train tickets are expensive, so I have to limit the trips."

"Devonshire, that would be the Docton estate."

"Yes, do you know it? Gosh, it was beautiful. Very steep, the birds were going high. Must be an amazing shoot."

"It's one of the best in the country."

"You've done it?"

"Many times." He heard himself bragging and cursed his tongue.

"Here, I've done a sketch, look and see." She rummaged in a beat-up leather kit bag and pulled out a tall, narrow piece of thick paper showing the hillside painted in quick strokes and the pheasants flying straight up, directly over the treetops. With just a few swipes of the paintbrush, she had captured the exhilaration of the moment. He wanted to buy it on the spot.

They stood together looking at the sketch, her nearness making his body feel like it was vibrating at a soundless pitch.

His fingers itched to reach out to see if her hair was as soft as it looked; with an iron will, he clapped a lock on those desires and dug his hands into his pockets. Because he knew he couldn't trust himself with just her hair. All of her looked so tempting.

Behind them, a door opened and the rattle of a cart announced the tea lady. "Hello, do you have any scones today?" Marie-Claire called to her, then turned to Mick. "Would you like a scone? These are really good."

He reached for his wallet, but she brushed him aside and dug into her own pocket, handing over the coins and taking the teas and scones. "My treat, I'm flush. I sold three paintings last night at Chez Bertrand."

Mick moved the wide display platform to the center of the room and motioned for her to have a seat, and sat next to her. "Congratulations," he said, taking the tea and scone she offered.

"Thank you, I made a killing. Ella, she's the owner's wife and a teacher here, she made me triple the asking prices before they were hung," Marie-Claire chatted on. "Raul, my housemate who works there, said some very rich sports star and his tarty girlfriend bought them. Probably going to hang them over his bar in one of those flashy mansions they live in."

A coughing fit consumed Mick for several moments. Marie-Claire thumped his back in concern.

"Maybe the guy just likes birds," he wheezed when he could catch his breath.

"Lucky for me, now I can pay my framing bill," Marie-Claire conceded as she munched on a scone. "I thought Ella was crazy, but she said the people that can afford Bertrand's prices have more money than brains to begin with. The food really is good, though—what little they give you of it…"

Mick's next coughing fit lasted just a bit longer than the first.

"Are you sure you're all right?"

"Yes, fine," he was finally able to answer, then wiped away a tear of laughter and took a deep breath. "Let's get the rest of these mounted."

Marie-Claire cleaned the glass in the picture frames while Mick finished hanging them. He took the opportunity to savor the glimpses of her breasts that were revealed as she bent over her work; they were round and natural, he noted, and most definitely real.

"How are you here?" he asked, dragging his eyes away from the enticing display.

"A professor at my college suggested I apply. It was a huge surprise when I found out I was accepted. The Lady Warwick is very selective, and if you don't work to the level they expect, you're shown the door quickly."

Mick nodded, already well into plans to show her to the door of his bedroom. "When did you start?"

"It will be a year in June. Although I almost wasn't going to come."

"What made you change your mind?"

A flicker of sadness crossed her face, so quick he might have imagined it. "A few things happened all at once. Then I came into a small inheritance, and that helped decide it."

"It's expensive then?"

Marie-Claire grimaced. "Outrageous. But I'm frugal, and I've got good housemates. We make it through."

"How long will you be here?" He knew he was interrogating her, but her voice was soft and melodious, and he wanted her to keep talking so he could hear more of it.

"I've got two more terms, if I pass the Critique next month."

An earlier check of her left hand had revealed no rings that would indicate another man had laid claim to her, but best to be sure. "What will you do after you graduate? Get married?"

"Heaven's no." She snorted, making it clear the idea was ridiculous. "Starve professionally, I suppose."

Mick shook his head. "You won't starve. You're very good."

"I let the future take care of itself," she declared with grim determination. "There's never any telling with me. I'm very unpredictable."

Drawing the ladder against the wall, she took a sign with her name on it and climbed up to fix it above the paintings. "Is it level?"

Dear God, she was biting her lower lip again. All Mick could do was nod from below.

"Oi! MC!" A man wearing loud plaid trousers and a silly hat interrupted, swaggering into the room as bold as brass. "Get a move on, love, I need that ladder."

Mick's eyes narrowed as he put himself between Marie-Claire and the feckless boy. "She's not done with it, mate," Mick informed him, his voice doing nothing to cloak the menace behind it.

"I'll just be a minute, Dave," Marie-Claire called down.

Dave glanced between them and reassessed his need of the ladder. "Yeah, no problems," he replied, then high-tailed it out of there.

"There's just one ladder, and we do have to share," Marie-Claire chided.

"He was rude," Mick grunted, watching with satisfaction as the man fled.

Marie-Claire climbed down the ladder and checked her watch. "I've got a studio class that starts in ten minutes, thanks for helping me mount. It was a pleasure to meet you."

She shook his hand again, this time withdrawing hers fast, then grabbed a thick sweater and her bag. "Ummm, Michael," she hesitated by the door, "the school show starts tomorrow night at seven. It doesn't cost anything to get in, and they always have really good hors d'oeuvres and drinks."

She paused for a moment, and gave him a quirky half-smile. "You should come."

"His name is Michael. He likes birds," Marie-Claire told Neve as she swished a photograph in a tray of developing solution with plastic tongs, the darkroom's red light casting an eerie glow over them.

"Oh yes?" Neve glanced up from the tray next to her, her voice a lilting blend of Jamaican and British accents. "How'd you meet him?"

"He's one of the guys the gallery sent over to help mount the show. Although he must have been new—he didn't know much."

"Keep the paper moving in the bath, like this." Neve demonstrated the technique. "Is he cute?"

"Handsome." Marie-Claire sighed, moving the paper to the next bath with care. "Big and burly. Very serious, almost intimidating at first. And strong—he moved the blue display platform like it was made of cardboard."

"Gay?"

"I definitely didn't get that vibe. He's not one of those pale types, you can tell he spends time outside. Very blue eyes, almost cerulean. Nice cologne. I flirted with him a bit."

Neve transferred the last batch of photographs to the water tray and frowned. "I don't remember him. What was he wearing?"

"Dark sweater and pants, leather jacket," Marie-Claire described, remembering how well his clothing had fit his thickly-muscled frame. "Rather expensive, now that I think about it."

"I didn't see him."

"It was late, almost four o'clock. You left at three, right after Stephen."

Neve scowled. "You mean right after I found my favorite lens in Stephen's kit bag."

"Really? What happened?"

"He made some weak excuse that he had just *found* it in the store room. Found my arse, I say. He might just find one of my brothers in an alley on his way home some night," Neve grumbled.

"Is it true what they say about him? That he…you know… has done forgeries?"

"As my Jamaican granny used to say, *If a nuh so, a nearly so*," Neve said in a Caribbean accent. "If it isn't the truth, it's close to the truth. When I was an Art Director at Smith-Wessex, he was dismissed for copying another artist's work and submitting it as his own. The weird thing is, he's good. But he's greedy."

"He gives me the creeps."

"Me, too. Hope they toss him out at the Critique. Here, let's start hanging these up to dry. I love developing film, it's so old-school." As Neve passed her the wet paper, Marie-Claire clipped them on a line over the sink. "And speaking of the Critique, what did Professor Dixon say when you met with her this morning?"

Marie-Claire made a face. "She said my work is boring and static. I'm supposed to stop doing preliminary drawings and endless studies and just trust my instincts. 'Paint with your heart and not your head,'" she quoted, doing a fair imitation of the professor.

"You do need to loosen up," Neve concurred.

"I didn't come three thousand miles for advice I could get on a greeting card." Marie-Claire sighed with exasperation. "And how am I supposed to be spontaneous and impulsive when all I do is eat, sleep, and go to school? I have no other life outside of this."

"That's the whole point, see? They give you a challenge you think you'll never be able to do, they tell you what they want to see, and then you've got till the Critique to make it happen. It's that way with everyone."

"What did you have to do?"

"Stop photographing everything like it was going in an advertisement. They even locked my tripod in the closet. I thought I was going to die before it all came together. And lucky for me it did—three in Raul and my class were cut."

Marie-Claire considered her words. "Do you think I'm at risk of not passing?"

"I'm not sure, some very talented people have been shown the door," Neve mused, then draped a reassuring arm around her shoulders. "But buck up, we're not going to let that happen. If they want a bold and reckless drama queen like

Sandra, then that's what we'll make you into. And the whole world is going to know it."

Marie-Claire laughed at the absurdity of the idea. "I asked Michael to the show tomorrow night," she said. "That was daring of me."

"It's a start. Are you ready to test the waters again?"

The reference to her ex-boyfriend put a damper on Marie-Claire's mood, and she pondered the question as they emptied the developing baths. Immersing herself in hard work at the Lady Warwick had left no time to dwell on her heartbreak, and after a year, the hurt had faded to a dull ache. It had also given her some important perspective. No man was worth going through that pain again.

"I'm over Eric and he's certainly over me. They got married six months ago. And if I'm supposed to work on being rash and impulsive, maybe a bit of a romance will help that along."

"Can't argue with that. Do you think you should wear the dress?"

"Maybe I should." Both girls were the same size and between them, they had one good cocktail dress they took turns wearing to events. "And maybe with my sale money I'll splurge on a new pair of heels."

"We have to make rent first, girlie," Neve admonished.

"Right. Absolutely."

Chapter Four

THE DINING HALL at St Augustine School had been outfitted as the club's strength training room, and Tuesday morning, the dull clank of weight-lifting machines echoed off the cement-block walls. Only half the equipment had arrived from Hendon, so Mick had to wait while Hugo sweated through the last reps of his bench press set.

"Stick to the ladies tees, Hugo," he mocked, sliding the pin on the weight stack several notches lower with a stealthy movement.

"Would those be the ladies tees in Madrid," Hugo grunted, straining under the additional burden, "or the ones in Barcelona?"

The precise barb hit home and Mick flushed red with impotent anger. Bloody bastard always knew which buttons to push. "I don't know, Hugo, how about I pay your girlfriend another visit and ask her? The *Daily Mail* might find out and put her on the cover again. That'd be her third day in a row, wouldn't it?"

The weight bar crashed down, and in an instant Hugo had sprung from the bench and rounded on him, bloodlust igniting his icy grey eyes. "I warned you away from her, Carr."

The room fell silent for a tense moment as the two players squared off, years of pent-up hostility boiling to the surface.

"What are you going to do, Hugo, throw a dictionary at me?" Mick taunted.

Seeing the fracas erupt, Pozny bolted from a nearby treadmill and inserted himself between them, smiling at Mick while babbling something in French to Hugo. Whatever it was, Hugo ignored it and shoved him out of the way, and then with lightning swiftness grabbed Mick by his t-shirt collar and yanked hard.

"I'm going to beat you to a bloody pulp like I should have done years ago," he hissed, twisting the fabric tighter around Mick's jugular with primitive fury.

He's as tall as I am, Mick realized with shocked disbelief. He was caught off guard but the surprise was fleeting. In a second, Mick regained his balance and grasped the midfielder's wrists in a vise-like grip, ready to break his hold and anything else that happened to get in the way. This was the way he liked to solve problems, and he relished the opportunity to put the bastard in his place. But his determination was thwarted when a meaty arm wrapped around his neck and jerked him backwards.

"Mick!" Darius barked in his ear, tightening his grip until Mick dropped his hold on Hugo's wrists.

Pozny restrained Hugo, and after a struggle they were able to get the men far enough away from each other that the danger of them doing real harm was avoided for the time being.

"Hugo, they're ready for you in the physio room, best get a move on," Darius directed, still keeping a firm hold on a struggling Mick.

"Make sure they give you a nice buff on your pedicure," Mick spat.

Hugo shook free of Pozny. "Fuck off, Carr. England's next Friendly is with Estonia, better give yourself plenty time to hit the books."

"Public school pansy," Mick muttered. Hugo never missed a chance to let everyone know he had been at Eton.

With a murderous look, Darius released him and pointed at the now-vacant bench press machine. "Get busy."

Straightening his shirt with bad humor, Mick did as he was told. Lying on the bench, he struggled to get control of the adrenaline that raged through his body, his fists aching to bring that bastard down to size. Just one solid blow would do it, one direct hit to wipe the smirk off that smug, aristocratic mouth. Best be patient, he consoled himself. He'd get his shot.

Taking a deep breath, he clenched his muscles and pressed the bar, focusing his concentration on his technique. Measured breath in, exhale on lift, pause, inhale while controlling the drop, count, repeat. The tall stack of weights glided up and down, the movements smooth and steady, the familiar rhythm helping to reestablish some semblance of self-control.

Pausing after the first set of repetitions, he waited for his breathing to steady and his heart rate to recover.

He wasn't going to the student show tonight.

Sliding the pin lower in the weight stack, he braced to press another set. One, two, three…

He had things to do. He was a very busy professional athlete. He had sponsorships, endorsement deals, contracts. There were places to go, people who wanted to see him, and an art show was just not part of the plan.

Seven, eight, nine…

It wasn't that he hadn't wrestled with the decision. The hour he'd spent with Marie-Claire had left him in a peculiar state, almost as if his blood had turned into fizzy water. Very hot fizzy water.

There was something fresh about her that was provocative and unsettling. No doubt part of it was her being an American, they never seemed too concerned about what everyone else thought. And even though she had already been to college, she didn't talk like those snooty people who had their noses in books all day. She talked sensibly about important things like hunting and birds. For some reason that excited him almost beyond bearing.

Fifteen, sixteen...

He'd driven away from her school, surprised he'd never noticed that Putney was a beautiful part of London. The shops, the rows of housing, it was all jolly nice. And the show sounded like a good bit of fun, why not go?

Nineteen, twenty, twenty-one...

But at home, the doubt had crept in. As normal as she had seemed, there was no doubt that Marie-Claire was a serious artist, and the Lady Warwick was a proper school. In fact, it was a college for people who'd been to college once already, almost as if they'd felt shortchanged the first time through. Mick had no idea such a thing existed, but it was clear he had as much business being there as a fish had riding a bicycle.

The show could be a disaster. Posh toffs would be standing around sipping wine and talking about artsy-fartsy things in loud voices. What if someone asked him a question? It would be obvious as soon as he opened his mouth he didn't know a paintbrush from a toothbrush, although judging by the look of some of the dross on display, a lot of the students didn't, either.

Pain began screaming through his muscles and he realized he had pressed far more repetitions than he had intended. He lay for a moment, spent and gasping for breath, letting his exhausted arms dangle at his sides.

She obviously had no idea who he was. Footballers were almost unknown in America, and club tours in the States were mundane, a relief from life here at home where he couldn't pet the neighbor's dog without it showing up in some tabloid. It was refreshing to meet someone who took him at face value and didn't want anything from him. Hell, he thought with a smile, she even thought he was a working-class stiff. And damned if she hadn't flirted with him a little.

However, if he showed up at her school, it would only be a matter of time—minutes, he'd reckon—before someone recognized him and started making a fuss. Then she would become aware of his...notoriety. Something told him she wouldn't be impressed.

Feeling recovered, he increased the weight to its maximum limit for the last set of lifts and centered his mind on the challenge. The bar moved sluggishly, then inched higher with more certainty until it reached the top. He paused, triumphant, panting hard. He was thirty years old, in peak physical condition, had a dream job, a flashy car, and women throwing themselves at him. He had no intention of making a fool of himself. Going to that show would be a daft idea.

Even if she had invited him.

Without warning, the bar wobbled and Mick fought to control its rapid descent. The loud crash it made when it slammed down left his ears ringing.

Bolting off the bench, he began pacing the mats, chewing over the situation with vexation. He'd no idea where she lived.

She had left before he could ask for her mobile number. All he knew was that she would be at the show this evening.

Bugger it, there was no choice.

Chapter Five

FROM THE DOOR of the Lady Warwick College of Arts and Design, Mick scanned the sophisticated crowd. Figuring artsy types liked to dress in all black, he had followed suit and worn his favorite black cashmere sweater, tailored, black wool trousers, and black loafers, and carried his black leather jacket. The gathering looked like a festive funeral, but he fit right in.

They'd done a good job of cleaning up the mess the day before, Mick noted, as servers circulated around the room offering trays of hors d'oeuvres and drinks under the sparkling crystal chandelier. The place had been transformed.

His plan was straightforward—he'd make his way back to Marie-Claire's room as fast as he could, keeping to the edges of the main room and avoiding the displays where groups of people would be collected. With any luck, he'd be able to slip by undetected.

But luck was not with him. A passing server offered him a drink, then sputtered in recognition, "Hey, you're—"

Mick nodded then turned on his heel and headed towards the gallery rooms, but the going was impossible. Walls that had not been there yesterday created a snaking path through endless displays. Clusters of people blocked his way, forcing him to draw attention to himself to get past them. Overhead lights beat down like the desert sun—couldn't these ruddy buggers open a few windows?

Trickles of sweat beaded on his forehead as people recognized him and he heard a faint buzz build behind him as he made his way towards Marie-Claire's gallery. It seemed to take forever to get there, but he was relieved to find it cooler and less occupied.

He saw her right away. She was wearing a sexy black dress with a short, swishy skirt that showed off miles of leg, her hair loose and cascading down her back like a satin curtain. A black girl was taking her picture in front of the painting of the Shelducks, and Marie-Claire laughed at something she said. She blinked a few times after the camera flashed, and then focused on him and smiled, a welcome that made him feel distinctly funny inside. Mick felt his own lips begin to pull in goofy directions.

As he crossed the room, the girl with the camera turned to see what Marie-Claire was looking at. "Oh, my God. That's Mick Carr!"

Blast it, there was nothing to do but shake the girl's hand. "Yes, hello. I'm Mick Carr," he said, then snatched Marie-Claire's hand. "Hello again."

"Do you two know each other?" Marie-Claire asked.

"I told you, he's Mick Carr!" The girl giggled, then clapped her palm over her mouth. "Is this the Michael you were telling me about? Oh! My! God!"

"Yes…" Marie-Claire said, looking to Mick, who was stricken to the spot. "Do a lot of people know you?" she asked, her fine brow wrinkling.

"A few," he admitted, then braced himself.

The rush of pleasure Marie-Claire had felt at Mick's arrival was dampened by the immediate stampede of people that flooded her small section of the gallery, hot on his heels.

Mick moved closer to her and wrapped an arm around her waist to brace her as people clamored around them. "What's going on?" she asked, taken aback by the confusion.

Ella appeared in the throng, her face wreathed in smiles. "MC, this is Mick Carr. He bought your paintings at the restaurant Sunday night."

It took a moment for Ella's words to register. Michael had bought her paintings? How could a gallery worker afford twelve hundred pounds? She looked up at him for an explanation, but he stared straight ahead, his expression grim, and an icy feeling began to spread through her body. He could afford them if he was the wealthy sports star Raul had described. *Rich and famous footballer, having dinner with his tarty girlfriend...* One look at Mick's dour expression confirmed it. Oh, damn.

"We've met," Marie-Claire replied, the blood beginning to pound in her temples. The volume of chatter around them continued to rise and she squeezed her eyes shut, willing the embarrassment to go away.

When she opened them, Mick was peering down at her. People jostled closer and he cursed and turned his back on them, shielding her.

"Your display, it turned out really well." He gestured around the room in a desperate attempt at normal conversation.

She tried to think of something, anything, to say, but was interrupted by the dean, who elbowed his way through the crowd to their side.

"And who do we have here?" he asked in a loud voice, his face a wreath of smiles.

Ella made the introductions and Mick released Marie-Claire to shake hands. The crowd surged closer and she let herself be shuffled towards the back door, then ducked through it and fled.

Neve found her pacing in the bathroom.

"Oh damn. I can't believe it. I made a complete ass of myself."

"I don't see how," her friend countered, "you didn't know who he was."

"He paid over a thousand pounds for my paintings and I insulted him. And his girlfriend." Marie-Claire rubbed her throbbing temples. "Why are there so many people out there?"

"He's really famous. Tomorrow it will be in all the papers he was here."

"Famous for what?"

"Footballing, for one, but there's other things," Neve replied cryptically. "Ella says you're wanted for pictures."

Marie-Claire groaned, but there was nothing to be done for it. She had to face the music. Neve ran cold water on a paper towel and she patted it over her face. Then she squared her shoulders and walked back into the packed gallery.

The dean was escorting Mick around her work and motioned for her to join them. The official photographer arranged them in front of her painting of the swan, with the dean and Mick in the center along with several important donors and faculty, while Marie-Claire was relegated to the edge. The camera flashed for what seemed like ages, the pounding strobe lights feeling like daggers being driven between her eyes.

"What are your impressions of our student show, Mr. Carr?" the dean asked with bombastic aplomb when the photographs were finished.

The room fell silent and from her position, Marie-Claire could see a dull flush start at the base of Mick's neck. His mouth moved for several moments, then he licked his lips and glanced around the walls. "Well," he stammered, "it's quite nice."

The crowd murmured in agreement. "We don't get too many members of your illustrious profession here," the dean continued, a smug smile playing on his lips. "Have you become a fan of contemporary art?"

A faint tick began in Mick's cheek, and she saw a sheen of sweat erupt above his brow. "I'm a fan of Miss Wentworth's art."

"Ah," the dean continued, enjoying the rapt attention of the audience, "and what in particular do you see in MC's reassuringly pre-modern aesthetic?"

Seconds ticked by as Mick's fists clenched and unclenched by his side. He's terrified, Marie-Claire realized with surprise.

"When it comes to her, I like everything I see." He shrugged.

The room rocked with laughter and the dean's grin melted into a sour grimace. With a curt nod to her, Mick fled, his head lowered and broad shoulders hunched as he muscled his way through the crowd. They swept after him and soon the room was almost deserted.

"I think that went well, don't you?" Neve drawled.

"Do you think he's all right?" Marie-Claire asked, perplexed by his behavior.

"I think he's had enough of this place. Right obnoxious of the dean, fawning all over him."

Surely, she had misread the panic she had seen in his eyes, the flare of terror when everyone was looking at him. If he was as famous as Neve and Raul said, he should be used to the attention. What did he have to fear?

"He had to have known he was going to attract all that attention, yet he still came. I think he's quite taken with you," Neve said, a speculative gleam in her dark eyes.

"I'm not interested," Marie-Claire said.

"I thought you were."

"When I thought he was just a regular guy," she retorted. "But why would I want to get involved with a guy like him?"

"It would be an uncharacteristically spontaneous thing for you to do," Neve pointed out.

Marie-Claire glared at her. "Getting involved with some rich sports star is not going to make me a better painter. Besides, I insulted his girlfriend. He probably thinks I'm an idiot."

"When you were hiding in the loo, he gave me his mobile number to pass on to you. You could call him and ask," Neve suggested helpfully.

———⟡———

"Okay, I borrowed these from my aunt's hair salon in Chelsea," Neve announced the next afternoon as she spread an assortment of tabloids and glossy magazines across Marie-Claire's worktable in the studio. "Mick's all over them. You'll see why they call him the Kingsbury Jack-About-Town. He's quite the lad."

With grudging interest, Marie-Claire put her brush down and paged through the overwrought headlines and dramatic photographs. There were pictures of him playing football in front of huge crowds, his concentration fierce. Others showed him off-duty, posing with kids in a hospital. There was even one of him bending down to pet a golden retriever.

Another issue had a racy article showing players taking their shirts off during matches. A prominent picture featured Mick using his shirt to wipe the sweat from his face, revealing a chiseled abdomen and faint trail of hair from his navel to below the waistband of his shorts. His powerful physique stood out from the other players, most of whom looked downright skinny.

"He's a lot bigger than the rest of them," Marie-Claire noted, her throat a little dry. "They look really thin."

"All they do is run all day," Neve concurred, opening another magazine, "but he is a brute. Here he is at Jerry Warren's wedding in January. He's a player for Manchester City."

The article began with a full-page spread of the smiling bride and groom standing on the steps of a castle decorated with ostentatious splendor, surrounded by a legion of bridesmaids and ushers.

"Where was the wedding, Buckingham Palace?" Marie-Claire asked.

"Oh, some place much posher I'm sure."

Guests had been photographed as they arrived, gorgeous women in low cut gowns and lean men in tuxedos, grinning for the cameras. Mick looked handsomest of all in an expertly cut dark suit, a self-assured gleam in his blue eyes. A chic, rail-thin woman clung to his arm, her red lips pulled back in a ferocious smile.

"Who's she?" Marie-Claire asked, feeling an odd twinge.

"That's his girlfriend, Fanta de las Mercedes. She's a presenter on *Willy Nilly*. It's a game show on the telly," Neve elaborated at Marie-Claire's blank stare. "Pretty pointless, but my dad and brothers watch it for the models that do the presenting. They're very sexy. Fanta's one of them."

Marie-Claire studied the picture. The woman looked like a delicate hothouse orchid, expensively coiffed and made up to perfection. No detail had escaped attention. Her long nails had even been painted the same blood-red color as her lipstick. "She's pretty."

"They're always in the papers, but he messes about with lots of women."

That stung. Marie-Claire nodded, catching her lower lip in her teeth. "He is quite the lad."

"That's his reputation all right," Neve agreed, then pointed to a picture of a handsome black man laughing with Mick during a victory ceremony. "That's Darius Rutledge, he's the team captain. He and Mick are best mates. Together they haven't let in a headed goal since September. It's almost a league record."

"Is Kingsbury Town any good?"

"Very good. They've been moving up the Premier League fast, and they might reach the European Cup this year."

Marie-Claire pointed at another tabloid featuring a scowling Kingsbury Town player and a pretty girl under a thundering headline, **JULIE JEZEBEL**.

"Who's he?"

"That's Hugo Auchincloss. He's mixed up in some scandal with a girl and a rum model. People think it's funny because he's quite a snooty toff and hates the publicity. But he's a damn good footballer."

They continued flipping through the tabloids, Marie-Claire awed by the amount of coverage Mick got. An article titled **FOOTBALLER FARMER** accompanied a picture of him on a tractor at a farm in the country. *"Kingsbury's Jack-About-Town, Mick Carr keeps his attention on the ladies, but his real love is his farm, Moorsgate, in Hertfordshire,"* Marie-Claire read aloud. *"Carr bought the farm last year and spends most of his time there. 'I'm out every chance I get, it's coming along well,' he says proudly."*

"Here's more pictures of Fanta." Neve pointed to **FOOTBALLER GIRLFRIENDS OUT ON THE TOWN**, where the scantily clad woman was dancing on a table with a group of girls, her lips drawn back in the same snarling smile.

CARIBBEAN ROMP showed Fanta frolicking in the waves in a minuscule bikini while Mick sat on the beach, a mobile phone to his ear. **FOOTBALLERS AND THEIR WHEELS** featured Mick driving a brand-new Aston Martin sports car. "He paid a hundred thousand pounds for a car?" Marie-Claire gasped when she read the caption.

"He probably makes that in a month. They're paid huge sums." Neve chuckled. "Here's today's *Sun*, page eleven. Poor you, cropped out of the picture."

Under the headline **FOOTBALLER SURPRISE VISIT** was a photograph of Mick and the dean standing by her painting. Marie-Claire was relieved to see she had indeed been cropped out.

"Kingsbury Town FC's Mick Carr made a surprise appearance at the Lady Warwick College of Arts and Design last night at their annual student show," Neve read. *"Sources report Carr was there to view the watercolors by student Marie Bentworth, an up-and-coming artist who he's collecting."*

"It's Wentworth!" Marie-Claire protested.

"Pffft, they never get it right."

Chapter Six

MICK SAT HUNCHED in a hotel chair Saturday morning, dreading the match against Birmingham City. Darius glanced up from where he sat on the bed doing card tricks, idling away the time before they left for the stadium. "You're quiet."

Mick's grunt was noncommittal. It wasn't unusual to feel some tension before a big game and it affected all the players in different ways. Some shook from nerves, others joked and played around, and Mick knew that when he got keyed up, he talked a lot. Brian, the goalkeeper, took a nap.

But today was different. First off, Sir Frank had insisted the team stay the night at this hotel in Hendon and take a motor coach to their own stadium, as if they were the visiting team. All because Hugo-bloody-Auchincloss's expensive fixer couldn't hush up the scandal he had gotten himself involved in, and it had blown out of everyone's control.

The tabloids were having a field day and Birmingham City punters were smelling blood, which made Kingsbury Town security nervous. The Football Association had also weighed in and decreed that both teams were on lockdown until the match.

Under normal circumstances, Mick wouldn't have been too fussed. The spectacle of the high and mighty Hugo Auchincloss being dragged through the mud was worth a bit of inconvenience, but as of late, nothing was as it should be. Practices had been disasters, and not just because of Auchincloss. His own timing had been off, and it had thrown the back four into disarray, which in turn was disrupting the dynamics of the entire team.

Giles had almost cried in frustration, spewing an incoherent mixture of English and Welsh expletives. "Christ, Carr, you get off-sides one more time and I will bench you!" he had exploded at the last practice. "Get your fucking head out of your arse and pay attention!"

The harder he tried, the worse it got. Missed kicks. Unmarked men. Any distraction being amplified a thousand times and breaking his legendary concentration. Nothing had been going right since...well, since the night of the art school show.

There was no one to blame but himself, of course. He had known what was going to happen yet had gone anyway, the lure of seeing Marie-Claire overruling his common sense. "Stupid" didn't begin to describe it, and sure enough, as soon as he opened his mouth, everyone had laughed. Again. Maybe Fanta was right, maybe he did need a minder.

It was small solace that Marie-Claire hadn't laughed, but it was clear she wasn't interested in him. In fact, she had run the other direction. When he had tried to coax her mobile number from her friend, she'd said Marie-Claire didn't have one. Which was utter rubbish. Who in this day and age didn't have a mobile?

That was fine. There was no shortage of women who were willing and eager to have his attentions, no need to chase after the ones who weren't. Why waste his time and effort? He was Mick Carr. Everything got handed to him.

"You're quiet," Darius repeated, "very quiet. Should I call Duncan and have you checked out?"

"You want me to list all the reasons Birmingham City is going to kick our arses this afternoon?" Mick snapped, jumping to his feet and casting about the room.

"No, but you're usually talking my ear off with nerves is all. Fanta coming today?"

"I don't know. I doubt it. I don't think she's talking to me."

Fanta was indeed sulking because he had been in the paper without her.

"An art school show? Whatever did you go to that for?" She had called to complain the next morning.

"Just to look around. You wouldn't have been interested."

"Was it those stupid birds again?"

"Yeah. But it was a bust."

And bust it had been. But why was he feeling guilty? Marie-Claire was the one who had thought he was some worker. He could have corrected her, but what was he supposed to have said? "Pardon me, but I'm your patron." Not likely. He ran his hands through his short-cropped hair in agitation. What would anyone else have done?

"You're pacing," Darius observed.

Mick retorted with a snarled oath, suggesting what Darius could do.

"Well, that would be physically impossible, so I'll sit here and watch you prowl around like a caged lion instead." Darius put the cards down and leaned back against the headboard.

"Mick, we've known each other a long time and I have never seen you as out of sorts as you've been this week. Something's happened, and maybe we should talk about it."

That caught Mick by surprise. "Sorry, did I miss you getting your therapist's license?"

"I'm team captain. It comes with the job."

"Nothing happened. I bought three paintings, what of it? Doesn't mean I'm turning into some toff."

"No, it doesn't." Darius waited a few moments while Mick continued his pacing, then asked with innocence, "Did you find something you wanted at that art school show?"

Mick stood frozen to the spot, his fists curled so hard his nails bit into the palms. With an oath, he took himself off to the shower, stripped naked, and turned the taps to full cold.

The icy blast of water hit his skin like shards of glass. He welcomed the pain and let the shock of the freezing-cold water numb his body and sap some of the heat and confusion from his mind. He turned, letting the frigid water beat against his skin until it was almost numb, then after five minutes he turned off the taps and stood still. A calm certainty settled over him as the water dripped off him in tiny rivulets, easing the confusion until clarity flooded through him. The solution was so obvious. He wondered how he had missed it.

He had to see her again because he had to give her flowers. To apologize for drawing the attention from her and ruining her show.

That was the answer. He smiled for the first time in a week.

———◦○◦———

His concerns for the match turned out to be well-placed. Play was unremarkable until the eightieth minute, when Samuel the forward booted one in low on a rebound and put Kingsbury Town up two-one. Then Birmingham City kicked into gear, and the tempo of the game picked up.

At the eighty-fifth minute, Auchincloss had the ball and was trying to arrange a pass to Lars when he was tackled by a Birmingham City defender, Joss Jenkins, who outweighed him by at least two stone. The referee blew the whistle and awarded an onside kick to Kingsbury Town, and Mick had been jogging back into position when Hugo had become unhinged and punched Jenkins square in the jaw, laying him out like a felled tree.

The entire stadium had sat in stunned silence and then erupted in a mad frenzy, and Mick got a chilling glimpse of how riots started. It took the referees almost five minutes to get control back after they sent Auchincloss off with a red card. After that, the team had worked like mules, defending their lead for the remaining clock. Then both teams were shunted off the pitch through opposite tunnels.

The question still remained of what had happened, but that was for Darius and Giles to sort out. Giles agreed that Mick had played an excellent match and added that whatever he had done to get his head out of his arse, he needed to continue doing on a regular basis.

After a match, it was usual for him to join his teammates for a big dinner and a night of chasing girls at a club, but instead he went home and puttered around for a few hours until he could be sure the dinner rush was finished at Chez Bertrand. He drove over and entered the kitchens through the back door, nodding to the cheering staff that were Kingsbury Town fans.

Bertrand looked up from his place behind the stoves and rushed over. "Yes, Mr. Carr! Good to see you! Would you like a table?"

"No, not tonight, thanks. Actually, I was hoping you could help me with a small problem."

A few minutes later Raul was brought to Mick and the two stood together in a corner. "I need to see Marie-Claire," Mick began.

Raul regarded him with caution. "I don't think MC wants to see you."

"You're probably right," Mick agreed, towering over the smaller man, "I embarrassed her, and that's my fault. I'd like the opportunity to apologize to her."

Mick waited while the waiter fidgeted with his thick-framed glasses. "Maybe you could come and see her at school."

"I'd like to see her tomorrow."

"I don't know if she'll be home."

"That's fine, I'll take the chance. Where do you and she live?"

Raul considered the request. "I shouldn't tell you. She'll be mad at me."

"I'm not very happy with you right now myself, mate," Mick informed him.

Raul weighed the two possible outcomes, and then took a sheet of paper from his apron and scribbled an address on it. "You didn't get this from me."

———◦———

Sunday morning, Marie-Claire awoke at sunrise as usual and tiptoed downstairs to turn on the hot water kettle in the kitchen, taking care not to waken Neve, asleep in the bedroom next to hers, or Raul in his room downstairs.

She left her bed unmade, which was as far as she was willing to go in pursuing a wild and unbound lifestyle.

The debacle with Mick had proven she was an abject failure at being impulsive. The story of how she'd mistaken him for a gallery worker had spread like wildfire around the school, and now other students were calling her a WAG, which Neve informed her was the acronym for the glamourous footballer 'Wives and Girlfriends' she'd seen in the tabloids.

The attention had blown over, but Mick lingered in her thoughts. They had only spent an hour together, but there had been a feeling of easy camaraderie, like they had known each other a long time. It wasn't just his good looks. He had been low-key and easy to talk with, and he did seem interested in her paintings.

The entire episode had left her in an uncharacteristic funk. His check still sat in the kitchen drawer. Of course, it had to go to the bank soon, but she was reluctant to let go of the only memento she had of the gentle spark that seemed to have lit between them.

She had more pressing matters to attend to than mooning over him, she reminded herself as she went back upstairs and began brushing her teeth. Mick seemed to light plenty of sparks all over London, and she was just one on a long list. The Critique was in nineteen days and it was time to buckle down and put all her energies into painting an example of reflected light that would knock everyone's socks off. She could become one of Mick's legions of fans *after* she passed. She couldn't afford expensive keepsakes like his check, so first thing Monday morning, it was going to the bank.

A bit of blue sky promised good painting weather, so today she'd take her field kit to the Thames and hope for something spontaneous and immediate to happen.

Hearing a loud knock at the front door, she rinsed her mouth and pulled a thin robe over her nightie, then hurried down the stairs. At the bottom, she rounded the turn into the kitchen and ground to a halt. Standing in the kitchen doorway was Mick, and next to him, a very guilty-looking Raul.

"Company, MC," Raul blurted out and then fled.

"Good morning," Mick said from the doorway, his piercing blue eyes trained on her. He was dressed in a button-down shirt, twill pants, and a tan field coat that fit his large frame well. In fact, he seemed to fill the room.

Pulling the thin robe around herself, Marie-Claire nodded then glanced away, her mouth dry and her pulse beating a wild staccato.

"I'm sorry to come unannounced, but I wanted to see you." From behind his back, Mick drew an enormous bouquet and presented it to her. "These are for you. To apologize. For causing such a ruckus at your show."

The colors of the fresh flowers radiated in the drab kitchen, hot pink roses mixed with yellow lilies and glossy dark greens tucked in amongst sapphire-blue irises. The bouquet was gorgeous, and she could only stare in astonishment, her mouth forming a silent "O."

She took a step forward, but caught herself. "You didn't need to do that."

"Please. With my apologies." He continued to hold the bouquet out to her, seeming to will her to take it.

With a great deal of misgiving, Marie-Claire took it from him, burying her nose in the fragrant blooms. "They're lovely, thank you."

"You're welcome."

An awkward silence stretched between them as they stood in the spartan kitchen. "Would you like a cup of tea?"

"Yes, thanks." He took a seat at the table and watched her as she moved about the kitchen, putting the flowers in a vase and pouring hot water from the electric kettle into two cups.

Her hands shook as she set the sugar and milk on the table, the tea sloshing close to the rim as she placed it before him.

"I could make some toast..." she offered.

"No, this is fine. Thank you."

She perched on a stool across from him and clutched her mug. "Mick, I want to apologize—"

"Marie-Claire, I'm sorry—" he began at the same time.

"No, me first," she implored. "I insulted you. At school, before the show. You spent all that money on my paintings and I said you were an idiot." She blew her cheeks out in exasperation, remembering how she had nattered on. "I can't tell you how sorry I am for saying those things. It was very wrong of me. I had no idea who you were. And I called your girlfriend a tart," she added, wincing at the memory. "I apologize for that."

Mick seemed more amused than anything. "Who did you think I was?"

"I thought you were from the gallery down the street. They send some of their staff over to help us mount shows. I thought you were one of them."

"Raul told me at the restaurant you had more paintings, and I wanted to see them. That's why I was there."

A small smile curved her lips. "I'm flattered."

"You should be. Your paintings are the first art I've ever bought in my life."

"Really?"

"Really." He took a sip of tea and leaned back in the chair, making it creak dangerously. "I've never thought about paintings before. They've always looked like, I don't know, wallpaper, I guess. But I was having dinner and couldn't take my eyes off them, the Tundra Swan especially."

"But they cost too much. I overpriced them."

"I can afford them," he assured her. "And they're worth it."

Good heavens, when he smiled, his eyes were Prussian blue. With more resolve than she felt, she slipped off the stool and went to a cabinet drawer, took out his check, and put it on the table between them. "I want you to take this."

"I'm bloody well not giving you the paintings back," Mick protested, his expression turning thunderous.

"You can keep them. I still don't understand who you are, but considering the way people reacted when you walked in the room, I made a really big mistake and maybe this is a good way of correcting it."

"You're serious." He stared at her as she pushed the check towards him. "How are you going to pay your framing bill?"

"I have no idea, but that's none of your concern."

He dragged his hand across his scalp in astonishment. "Damn it, you just can't give them to me," he swore as she started to tear up his check, then with an oath, reached across the table and clapped his hands over her own.

"If you tear up this check," he told her, prying the paper out of her grip, "I will just write you another one. Or I will give your housemates the cash to pay the rent. I will not take your paintings, which are now my paintings, by the way, without paying for them."

Their eyes met in silent challenge as his big hands held hers immobile. They were strong and callused, capable of crushing anything he held, yet his grip felt almost tender, like a caress. The intimacy of it was startling in a confoundingly pleasant sort of way.

With reluctance, Marie-Claire surrendered and Mick took the check and moved it to the side. She knew she needed to say something, anything, to return the situation to normalcy. "Neve showed me your pictures in the magazines," she said, shoveling spoonfuls of sugar into her tea. "She said you're a celebrity."

"I'm a footballer," he corrected, "the rest goes with the job."

"You must be used to it."

"You never really get used to it. I haven't always been famous, like I told you, I grew up on an estate and my dad is head gamekeeper."

"Do you ever miss your privacy?" Marie-Claire couldn't resist asking.

"I like it when I go to America and no one knows me. I feel like a regular person there."

"You seemed like a regular person. Certainly had me fooled, anyway."

Taking a sip of her tea, she almost gagged on the sweetness. "It was nice of you to come over and talk with me," she began, standing to clear the table. "I appreciate it, but you didn't have to. I think the school is really happy for the publicity, so it's all worked out."

Mick stood as well, and Marie-Claire couldn't help but wonder if he was deliberately crowding her at the sink. "No, it hasn't, actually," he said. "When we met Monday, if I had asked you to go to the country with me, would you have said yes?"

She realized he had herded her into the corner cupboards. He was near enough for her to catch his scent, an enticing combination of soap and subtle spice and warm male. "Probably," she admitted after a moment, "but I thought you were an ordinary person like me, who I had something in common with."

"We do have something in common. We have several things in common."

"You have a girlfriend," she reminded him, and then amended, "or several girlfriends."

"I'm not asking you on a date," he countered, "I'm asking if you'd like to go see a game estate."

That gave her pause. Seconds ticked by as her longing for the countryside fought a brutal battle with her common sense. "You don't have to do that."

"Are you saying no?"

His obvious amazement that a woman was denying him only strengthened her resolve. "I'm saying, no, thank you."

"And I'm saying, go to your room, get dressed, get your kit, and be down here in five minutes. I'm not known for my patience."

"But I really don't think…" she began to protest, but he grasped her shoulders and ushered her towards the stairs.

"Do as you're told, lass. Carpet diem."

His words stopped her in her tracks. "What did you say?"

"Carpet diem. You know, seize the day, take your chance, strike while the iron's hot. Giles, he's our manager, he says it all the time. Must be some old Welsh saying, he's got a million of them. Now, get a move on."

Chapter Seven

UPSTAIRS, MARIE-CLAIRE pulled a comb through her hair and tamed the unruly length into a ponytail, and then dressed in khaki pants, a buttoned-down shirt and field boots, standard attire for a game estate. She reappeared in the kitchen in almost five minutes to the second, clasping her thick sweater and a leather bag that contained her painting field kit.

Mick glanced up from checking his mobile, his thick eyebrows raised in cool surprise. "That was fast."

"You said five minutes."

"So I did." He grinned and followed her to the front door.

A gleaming silver Aston Martin was parked in the street and Marie-Claire recognized it from Neve's magazine. She balked when Mick held open the passenger door for her—the sports car's value was dizzying. What if she got it dirty or hurt it somehow? She'd never be able to repay the damage.

With a gentle shove, Mick maneuvered her into the passenger seat and made sure she was buckled in. Tucking her bag into the small space behind their seats, he folded himself into the driver's seat and turned the key in the ignition. The engine sprang to life with a throaty growl of power that seemed to fill the street.

Traffic on the motorway was light as they headed west. Marie-Claire sat in the luxurious leather seat, conscious that no matter how she arranged her legs, there didn't seem to be anywhere for her right knee to go except by his left hand, resting on the gear shift.

At close range, she could see that his faded canvas trousers were the same her father and brother favored, and his rugged field coat was of excellent quality. None of it was new; the jacket was well broken-in and his boots were almost as old and scuffed as her own. No magazine country squire here.

They exited the freeway and began winding through the countryside.

"Where are we going?" she asked, enjoying the new scenery.

"Hempland." Mick downshifted as the road narrowed. "Have you heard of it?"

"Of course, Hempland is one of the most famous shoots in southern England. You're a member?"

There was a pause as he considered his answer. "I've got a family membership, so to speak."

She was unsure how to interpret his cryptic reply. "Is it still a private estate?"

"It used to be, but they sold the big house off long ago and the rest is run as a private club. There's a full staff and it's the best in this part of the country. For now."

"You should have told me we were going to Hempland. I would have brought my tweed jacket," she reproved, knowing that a club of such renown would expect the guests to dress in traditional attire.

"It's not the season, so no one will be shooting."

As they entered the next roundabout, she gasped in panic when a large truck seemed to come barreling towards them, but Mick turned into his own lane and the truck sailed past on the other side of the road.

"Are you okay? Am I driving too fast?" he asked, giving her knee a reassuring squeeze.

She let her breath out. "Sorry. I'm still not used to everything being on the wrong side."

"I'm the same way in America," Mick admitted, moving his hand back to shift again. The spot where he had touched her radiated warmth, and Marie-Claire had to force herself to visualize the pictures of Mick and his girlfriends that Neve had shown her from the tabloids to dampen the pleasant thrill his touch had ignited.

"That bloke, at your school, the one that was leading me around," Mick began, "was he the headmaster?"

"That was the dean, yes. Dr. Hewitt."

Mick's grip on the steering wheel tightened. "Right little wanker, isn't he? What did he mean when he asked me about your cosmetics? Does he think you should be wearing more makeup like those other students?"

"My aesthetics, my 'reassuringly pre-modern aesthetics,'" Marie-Claire quoted. "What he meant was my safe and boring style. He's a big fan of contemporary art because he likes mingling with the rich people who buy it, and thinks I should be doing that instead of traditional watercolors."

Mick recoiled in distaste. "What, you mean like that rubbish in the other rooms?"

"That's the work of some very talented artists," Marie-Claire said as they stopped for a traffic light. "But yes, some of it appears to be rubbish. And I did try — in fact, I took an oils class last semester. It backfired, though. I had just finished priming a canvas entirely in red; you know, just a background coat that you do before you start the proper painting. But when he saw it on my easel, he said it was the best thing I had ever done. Then he insisted I be given top marks and even had it hung in the main gallery for three weeks. It was a huge joke and he eventually found out. He's still a bit sore at me."

Mick laughed out loud while trying to stretch his leg in the cramped space. "You certainly put him in his place."

Marie-Claire smiled. "Not as well as you did."

Mick glanced at her. "How's that?"

"It was quite a put-down when you told him you liked everything about me. A lot of the people want the Lady Warwick to remain a traditional fine arts college, and they thought what you said was brilliant."

The light changed and the traffic in front of them began to move, but Mick sat immobile, like he was unable to comprehend her words. "They weren't laughing at me?"

His voice was so quiet that Marie-Claire was almost unsure she had heard it. "No, not at all. They were laughing because it was so clever."

"They thought I was clever?" he repeated with unconcealed astonishment.

"Yes, very. You're a hero."

A horn tooted behind them, jolting Mick back to attention, and the sports car leapt forward. As they drove, he seemed to be ruminating over her words, and Marie-Claire realized that he had thought people had been laughing at him instead of with him. The idea seemed preposterous; the crowd was much too well-bred to do anything like that, especially to a celebrity and fellow collector. But his relief was palpable.

They turned down an unmarked lane that ran along broad fields of planted sorghum and maize. A large barn had been converted into a handsome clubhouse, with a small sign that said *Hempland* posted in front of it. At the end of the drive was a large, stone farmhouse bordered by well-tended flower beds, a barn built of the same stone, and several smaller stone buildings arranged around a graveled central yard where Mick parked.

At the sound of the car, a pair of Springer Spaniels burst out of the barn and galloped towards them in a frenzy of barking and tail wagging. Mick got out and fussed over them both and then helped Marie-Claire out.

"This is Liza." Mick thumped the first dog as she leapt at him, her tongue lolling. She barked louder in ecstasy as Marie-Claire scratched her ears while the younger dog vied for Mick's attention. "And this is my dog, Lacey, she's one of Liza's pups."

This brought Marie-Claire up short. "Your dog?" she asked in confusion as Lacey switched her attention to Marie-Claire, almost knocking her backwards.

Mick steadied her. "Yes, this is my dad's place."

So, Mick had been raised on one of the best-regarded shoots in England, and his father was head gamekeeper. This was a bit of news, but Marie-Claire kept her expression nonchalant. "It's very nice."

A handsome, older version of Mick dressed in work coveralls and a flat cap strode towards them from the barns and shook Mick's hand. "Good to see you, son."

"Dad, I'd like you to meet Marie-Claire Wentworth. Marie-Claire, my father, Gordon."

The man regarded her as they shook hands and Marie-Claire saw where Mick got his piercing blue eyes.

"Marie-Claire is a bird fancier, game birds," Mick added.

"Is that right? Well, you've come to the right place. Would you like a tour?"

Marie-Claire nodded. "I'd love one."

"Rain's turned everything to muck, so let's get you a pair of Wellies. You couldn't have fit your own in that toy." Gordon nodded towards the Aston Martin. "Something the matter with the Range Rover, son?"

Mick scowled and ducked his head. "No. Just thought this would be nicer for a Sunday outing."

His father raised an eyebrow but let that pass. "She can borrow Sue's Wellies, then. She's in Alderwick this morning for church and then a meeting of her garden club, but will be back by lunch."

"Thought those things went all day," Mick said.

"They do. But when you called to say you were bringing out a friend, she changed her plans."

Inside the farmhouse was an immaculate, slate-tiled mudroom. Mick showed her the boot selection and Marie-Claire sat on the long bench and pulled on a pair.

"Who's Sue?"

"Sue, she's Dad's sister. She came and looked after us after Mum died. She never married and has stayed on, and she runs the kitchens at the lodge we passed on the way in. Coffee and full breakfast, elevenses, a proper luncheon, and then tea. The members do like their food. Sometimes it's so good a few will nap in the afternoon instead of doing the afternoon drives," Mick said with evident disapproval.

"Do you really have a hatchery?"

"Shed, nursery, outside runs, the works. Dad does almost everything here."

Back in the courtyard, Gordon was waiting in a four-wheel drive, all-terrain vehicle and motioned for Marie-Claire to join him on the bench seat. Mick was about to slide in next to her when Liza jumped into the spot, and Gordon pointed to a tall pallet of feed bags by the barn.

"Spillers delivered yesterday, son, hoppers need to be topped off. There's a good lad." He grinned as they sped away, leaving Mick standing with his hands on his hips.

Behind the barn was an impressive collection of buildings, teeming with activity. "We're coming to the end of poulting season now and it's been the usual madhouse. Mick's been able to get out when he can, which is a help."

Gordon began the tour at the long rows of outdoor pens, which were covered in thick netting. "These outside runs give us a hard, well-feathered poult, and we've been getting some good-sized, strong fliers."

"The pens are immaculate," Marie-Claire noted.

"Only way to keep disease away," Gordon replied with obvious pride.

Inside the enclosures, mature pheasants strode, the males resplendent in vibrant hues of crimson and gold, the hens a duller shade of brown. "Are those Chinese Ringnecks?"

"Aye, and a Norfolk cross in those pens down there." Gordon pointed to several runs that were filled with young hatchlings. "Then those beyond are the partridges."

They drove around the vast estate on well-maintained farm lanes as Gordon pointed out the shooting drives that crisscrossed the rolling fields. Marie-Claire opened and closed the gates they encountered as they navigated the trimmed thickets interspersed with patches of forest. The area had abundant native fowl, and within an hour they had seen Rock Pipits, Blue-wing Teals, and a Caspian Tern, who Gordon commented had wandered over from Holland for a bit of lunch.

"Mick said your family have a waterfowl business on the Chesapeake Bay," Gordon said as they stopped to tamp out some mole holes.

Marie-Claire wondered what else Mick had told his family about her. "Yes, on the Eastern Shore of Maryland, across the Chesapeake Bay from Washington, DC."

"That's some excellent hunting."

"It's gotten so busy my brother Chase has taken over running the hunting business, and Dad runs the farms."

Gordon chuckled. "That's a pretty good arrangement."

Mick was finishing loading feed into the hoppers when his father returned Marie-Claire to the barns. Working in the direct sun had gotten hot, and he'd stripped down to a black t-shirt that stretched across his well-defined muscles.

"Enjoy yourself?" he asked, helping her out of the all-terrain vehicle while balancing two bags on his broad shoulder.

"It was wonderful, Gordon showed me everything."

"Dad, the boys are waiting for that wagonload of straw for the roosting pens."

"I can take it," Marie-Claire said.

The two men exchanged a glance, and Gordon shrugged and pointed to the loaded wagon in the farmyard. "There you are, lass. Follow the lane around the bend, you'll see the first group of sheds on the left beyond the trees. There's two lads down there to unload the wagon, and then you can bring it back."

Marie-Claire swung up onto the tractor, started it, and with a series of smooth movements, backed the wagon around the yard, whistled for the dogs to follow, and set off down the lane.

Mick and his father watched the wagon disappear around the bend, the dogs trotting behind. "Son," Gordon said with a wry grin, "if you're not planning on marrying her, I think I might."

Chapter Eight

MICK MET MARIE-CLAIRE in the farmyard an hour later when she returned with the empty wagon. "Wait—" he stayed her with a hand on her arm after she jumped down "—you've got straw in your hair."

She stood as he pulled pieces out of her ponytail, his fingers sliding through the satiny strands. "I helped unload," she explained, feeling the need to say something, anything, to break the intimacy of the moment.

"I see," he said, continuing his work with singular focus. "Dad's going to have to put you on the payroll."

"He doesn't have to pay me, it's wonderful just being here. Is there another load to go down?"

"I didn't bring you out here to work." He pulled out the last golden wisp and dropped the lock. "Would you like some drawing time? I can take you around to wherever you'd like to go."

"Your dad said you were going to help him sort eggs. I've never seen a hatchery before. May I watch?"

Mick fetched her bag from the car and showed her the way through the ground floor of the barn. The nursery was several rooms, all spotlessly clean, and before entering they left their boots outside and slipped on sterile slippers and thin paper coveralls.

A rack of eggs had been brought out of the incubator and laid on a wide table, lit from overhead by rows of incandescent lights. Mick cleared a space at the counter and pulled up a stool for her, then rolled up his sleeves and joined his father at the table.

Marie-Claire began to sketch the scene with a soft pencil, capturing damp chicks poking their beaks out of chipped eggs, some almost emerged. Feeling adventurous, she rummaged in her bag until she found a large scrap of watercolor paper and taped it to the back of her sketchbook. Then she opened her tin field kit that held ten pans of watercolor blocks in the basic colors and set it next to her.

Taking a bottle of water from her bag, she poured a measure into a cup she always carried and selected a soft brush with a round tip. Swishing the brush a few times in the water, she dabbed it over the well of Crimson Lake in her field kit, and put brush to paper. Satisfied that the paint was drying quickly in the heated room, Marie-Claire began to work, capturing the warmth of the light that reflected onto Mick's handsome face as bent over the trays, his expression softened with concentration. Cadmium Orange Medium provided the glow of the light reflecting on his skin and French Ultramarine Blue served for the shadows cast by the overhead light.

The paint flowed off her brush easily while Mick worked in silence, sometimes making a brief comment to his father who would reply in a monosyllable. Even though he was a man of considerable size and strength, Mick handled the fragile eggs nimbly, cradling them in his large hands. Marie-Claire remembered the feel of her own hands in his that morning, and while there was no mistaking their strength, there was also a feeling of strength and security when his fingers had folded around hers.

Sitting in the quiet room, Marie-Claire was struck by the contrast between the Mick she was with now and the one in Neve's magazines. The humble hatchery was far removed from the high-voltage drama of his other life, where he seemed to revel in the excesses of wealth and fame. Here, his smile didn't look forced, and he came across as genuinely sincere instead of inaccessible. A shiver pricked her spine; she'd known another who had moved between separate worlds with ease, and the memory stirred caution.

An hour passed and soon a woman's voice called from the yard, announcing lunch.

"Good timing," Gordon said as they finished the last tray. Mick washed his hands at the sink and came over to Marie-Claire, and she showed him the painting with modest pride.

"That's me," he said, sounding surprised. "What, you did that just now?"

Marie-Claire nodded, pleased with her work. "And I did quite a few other sketches. When I get back to school, I might work all of them up into a proper painting."

Mick flipped through her sketchbook. "But these are only parts of pictures. Do you want to borrow my mobile and take a photograph?"

She shook her head emphatically. "No, it's not the same. Photographs never capture what's in the shadows, and sometimes what's in there is the most interesting part."

Mick frowned. "You made that shadow purple."

"Because it is. Purple and Cerulean Blue and a bit of Burnt Umber." She dabbed her brush in the colors and demonstrated.

"See? Shadows are a lot more than black."

"Well, I'll be blowed."

An older woman met them at the door of the farmhouse kitchen. "You must be Marie-Claire. I'm Sue. It's a pleasure." She shook her hand and, without taking her attention from Marie-Claire, called over her shoulder, "And Michael Edward Carr, if you set one foot in my clean kitchen with those dirty boots, you are still not too big to get a smack. And what's that fancy car of yours doing here?"

Mick halted in mid-stride and returned to the mudroom.

"Are you up for some soup and bread?" Sue asked as she bustled about the kitchen. "Although I could have done a proper lunch if I had gotten a bit more notice." She shot a meaningful look at Mick, who ducked his head and grinned as he joined them.

"That sounds lovely," Marie-Claire assured her. The kitchen table was set for four with a vase of fresh lilacs in the middle, filling the kitchen with a sweet fragrance. Marie-Claire bent over and inhaled. "Your flowers are beautiful."

"Just cut them this morning. Lilacs are my favorite," Sue said, ladling the soup into bowls. Mick joined them and turned on the small television on the counter. "Michael! With company!"

"But it's Watford versus Everton," Gordon protested.

"No, it's okay, I don't mind," Marie-Claire said.

"Well, then, you men can watch it in the sitting room and leave us be." Sue shooed them out with their bowls and hunks of bread, and the two women sat down at the table. Marie-Claire tucked hungrily into the lunch, realizing she hadn't had any breakfast.

"Our Michael says you're a painter," Sue began, passing the salt.

"Yes, watercolors. I'm at school at the Lady Warwick in Putney," Marie-Claire said between spoonfuls of soup.

"Short course?"

"No, full Master of Fine Arts."

"So, you've already graduated from university."

Marie-Claire buttered a thick slab of bread. "Yes, Chestertown College, in Maryland."

"Is that near where you grew up?"

"Yes, it's about twenty minutes from my parents' house."

"Bit of an adventure coming here, I'd wager."

"A good adventure, so far."

Mick reappeared, ostensibly to fetch more bread. "All right, then?"

"Yes, fine," she assured him as a wave of gentle pleasure washed over her. A reflexive pang of caution ordered her to ignore it. This wasn't a date.

Sue was delightful company and they spent the rest of the meal in pleasant conversation about her gardens. Dessert was a beautiful strawberry tart that Sue produced from a box and set on the table.

"Do you like strawberries, then?" she asked.

"Yes, I do."

"I got the baker to open special this morning, before church," Sue said. "It's Michael's favorite. I thought we'd celebrate, seeing as you're the first girl he's ever brought round."

Again, Marie-Claire tried to steel her heart from trilling in delight, but it ignored her.

They were finishing slices of the tart with cups of strong tea when Mick brought the plates in from the sitting room. "Right, Sue, MI-5 called, they need your report on Marie-Claire," he quipped, giving the older woman a fond kiss on the top of her head.

"Cheeky lad."

"Dad's organizing some clay pigeons. Would you like to shoot?" Mick asked Marie-Claire. "Or if you'd rather paint some more, I can line up—"

"I'd love to shoot." Marie-Claire cut him off before he went to any more trouble. "But I'll help with the dishes first."

"Heavens no!" Sue scolded. "Go out and shoot, today is a beautiful day. I'll have this done in a jiffy."

Mick devoured a huge slice of tart in three bites, and then held Marie-Claire's chair for her and led the way through the house, ducking under low lintels as they made their way to a narrow room off the foyer. A row of glass-front cabinets stretched along one wall, containing an impressive selection of shotguns. The opposite wall displayed what seemed like hundreds of football trophies, medals, and ribbons, jam-packed together on narrow shelves.

"Are these all yours?" Marie-Claire asked in awe.

Mick grinned with pride. "Yeah, I got most of these when I played for our local team, Dunforth. We were league champions for years. The big stuff near the end, that's when Kingsbury Town won the Football League Two, and then League One, and then two years ago we were runner-up in the Championship division. We got promoted to Premier after that. Dad says he's saving that spot by the door for when we win the FA Cup."

"I think he's going to need a bigger house."

"I hope so." Mick unlocked a large cabinet and motioned to the long line of shotguns. "Would you prefer a pump action?"

It was a subtle test. "I can do either single or pump," she said, examining the selection, "but I prefer a tight choke for clays."

He nodded and pulled a twelve-gauge Holland & Holland over-under off the rack and handed the gun to her. "Give that a try."

She took the gun and worked the action, rolling it in her hands and checking the bore. At the sound, Lacey began to whine, her stubby tail wagging in anticipation.

"Sorry, girl, just clays today," Mick apologized and the dog slunk off and flung herself in the corner with a disapproving grunt. He chose a Beretta Silver Pigeon side-by-side for himself and locked the cabinet and then held the front door for her.

"How did you become a football player?" Marie-Claire asked as they followed a graveled field lane towards the trap shoot ground. "It's so beautiful here, I don't think I would have been tempted to leave."

"It is heaven, isn't it? But when I was a lad all I wanted to do was play football. A scout for Chelsea Football Club saw me play for Dunforth and offered me a place in their academy. That's the developing team for young players. I thought I'd died and gone to heaven, but once I was there I kept growing, and I knew they weren't happy about that."

"That seems unfair. You couldn't help it."

"They're very particular about what they want, and they've got their choice of hundreds of lads. But I got lucky. Giles, he's our manager, gave me a tryout with Kingsbury Town, and Sir

Frank signed me on the spot. That was fourteen years ago, and I've been with the club ever since."

"Is that unusual? To be with a team for so long?"

"Too true. But Sir Frank, he says cement takes a long time to cure, a lot longer than people think. And he's right. Nowadays clubs change things up constantly and there's no time to let things gel. Giles says the same thing. People used to think he was barking mad and they aren't half wrong, but now everyone sees the bugger is brilliant. Our lineup has changed very little over the years. We're zooming to the top, and I think it's just because we know each other so well. Darius Rutledge and me, we're the two center backs, we're practically an old married couple."

The shoot was in a clearing at the top of a hill that backed onto a thick wood. A platform with five shooting stations stood at the crest, and a few yards below, two trap bunkers housed machines that would fling the clay disks, or pigeons, on the command of the shooter.

While Mick helped the men unload guns from the all-terrain vehicle, a teenage boy greeted her and showed her to the platform. "You're Mick's girl, right?" Before Marie-Claire could say anything, he shook her hand and rushed on, "I'm Roger, pleased to meet you. Gordon thought you might like the first stand."

Soon everyone was ready, and Roger ducked into the trap bunker down the hill.

Gordon handed her ear protection and stepped back. "Ladies first."

Marie-Claire loaded a round and took a position at the stand, and on her call, the first clay was released. The round projectile flew high and to the right, and with a precise action she swung the gun to her shoulder, tracked the target, and shot. The clay fractured and she frowned, rolled the action, and ejected the cartridge.

"Winged it. There's a breeze. May I try another?"

"Of course."

She adjusted the choke, reloaded, and let the next one go farther before she shot. The clay exploded, a dead hit. There was a chorus of soft whistles behind her.

"Nicely done," Gordon said.

It was Mick's turn next. He took the station next to her and fired, hitting the target, as well. She nodded appreciatively.

Each of the men took a warm-up shot or two, and then the serious shooting began. Roger seemed to take great delight in sending the clays in wild directions for the men, sparking grumbled curses and good-natured threats when they missed. Mick, though, was used to Roger's antics. He was a quick shot with a good eye and hit all of his with neat precision.

But for Marie-Claire, Roger sent the clays at a predictable forty-five-degree angle and always to the right. She shattered them easily and grew bored, but as a guest, it was not her place to ask for more of a challenge.

Mick nodded to his father.

"Now, Roger," Gordon called down after three rounds, "we're mixing up the line but you're not to look."

After that, the clays flew wild for all. This was much more to Marie-Claire's liking and she enjoyed herself. Mick shot after her each time, matching her hit for hit until, after two rotations through the stations, Gordon signaled a break.

"That's some very good shooting, lass," Gordon complimented her. "You haven't missed yet."

Neither had Mick, and her competitive nature was aroused. "I don't suppose your machines can do simultaneous pairs?" she asked with an innocent smile.

A chorus of loud whistles and hearty guffaws greeted her question, and a broad smile broke out on Gordon's face. "Of course, they can. Who's up for pairs, then?"

Mick was the only one who volunteered and Marie-Claire saw money change hands behind their backs. Gordon went into the second trap bunker and adjusted the clay launcher to trigger from the machine in the first bunker. After a few test fires, Marie-Claire saw she would have, on average, two seconds between her first shot and the second.

When Gordon and Roger signaled they were ready, Marie-Claire loaded two shells in her gun. On her call, two clays flew, one high and one low. She tracked them for several seconds and picked them off to the applause of the spectators.

Mick hit his, as well, two high ones that crossed, which earned him applause. Marie-Claire nodded in compliment. In the next round, she got "loopers" and Mick got two lows, both of which they hit clean. She hadn't shot in almost a year but felt the familiar adrenaline flow, helping her focus and steady her breathing.

Gordon and Roger began sending challenging combinations. She shot clean and Mick kept pace, cursing under his breath but always making the hit. After five rounds, the muscles of her shoulder began to ache in protest, yet she realized Mick could go all day. It was time to finish him off.

"It's a Trumpeter Swan, not a Tundra Swan," she said as she turned her back to the range while she reloaded her gun.

"Pardon?"

"My painting that you bought," she continued, "it's a Trumpeter Swan. Pull!"

Mick watched in concern as the clays flew. "Yes?"

She nodded. "It's an easy mistake to make. You can really only tell them apart by their call."

Then with a saucy smile, she spun around and swung the gun to her shoulder, tracked the targets and shot twice, shattering both in the distance.

"She got them both!" someone yelped.

Mick's face broke into a huge smile and he bowed before her as the men applauded. "No way am I beating that," Mick said, taking her hand in his for the second time that day and kissing it in homage. "I surrender."

It was a gallant gesture, and she curtsied and turned away before everyone saw the warm flush cross her face.

"You took so long on that last shot, we thought you'd gone back for tea," Gordon said as he climbed out of the trap bunker. "You've done this before."

"A bit, but it's been a while. It was fun, excellent gun."

"Right, lads, time for the afternoon feed," Gordon called to the men.

"Do you need a hand?" she asked.

"No, lass, you've done more than your share today. Go in the house and relax. We'll be along in a bit."

———◦◦◦———

Back in the house, Sue had left a note on the kitchen table saying she was sorry but she had to go back to Alderwick to serve tea at a poetry reading, and that Marie-Claire was welcome to visit anytime she liked. When Gordon and Mick came in, all the guns had been cleaned and returned to the cabinet, Marie-Claire was sitting on the settee, sketching, and Lacey was asleep in her basket by the fire.

"What are you drawing?" Mick asked.

She flipped her sketchbook closed and stood. "Just working on some of the sketches I did this morning."

"It's about time we got going."

As they said their goodbyes, Marie-Claire hugged Gordon.

"I like Americans," he winked at Mick over her head.

Chapter Nine

A BEAUTIFUL SUNSET filled the sky as they drove away from Hempland.

"Did you enjoy today?" Mick asked when they reached the main road.

"I did," Marie-Claire answered. And she had. In fact, the day was one of the best she'd had since she'd come to England.

Her answer seemed to please Mick. "How about some supper then? A friend of mine runs a pub. The food's good and it's quiet."

She guessed that meant people didn't bother him there. "Is it expensive?" She reached for her bag to check her wallet. "I didn't bring a lot of money with me."

Mick's expression grew dark. "You're not to pay."

"I thought you said this wasn't a date."

Keeping one hand on the steering wheel, Mick reached over and took the bag from her lap and tucked it in the space behind the seats. "You're to be my guest," he announced, and then cut her off when she began to argue. "No discussion."

Irritated by his high-handedness, Marie-Claire focused her attention on the passing countryside. He was obviously used to getting his own way around women, and with his good looks and self-confidence, probably didn't meet much resistance. The flocks of women he attracted were evidence enough of that.

In the next village, Mick parked in front of a charming whitewashed pub. A brief skirmish ensued on the narrow sidewalk when she reached for her bag, and he blocked her.

"I need my comb," she explained with exasperation and Mick had to relent, albeit with reluctance.

Inside the pub, Mick shook hands with a group at the bar while Marie-Claire excused herself to use the ladies room. Standing before the mirror, she shook her hair loose from the ponytail, and fished the comb from her bag and ran it through a few times, catching a few more sprigs of straw. A fresh smattering of freckles dappled her nose and cheeks, making her look about as opposite from the sophisticated women Mick was photographed with as could be imagined.

"Very glamorous," she muttered.

Mick was waiting for her in a small dining room behind the bar. He held a cushioned leather chair for her and then took his own. Next to them, a fire crackled in the grate, making the room feel cozy and intimate. A feisty girl named Tara handed them menus and cracked jokes with Mick while appraising Marie-Claire.

"Oi, Mick, is this the new one—"

"Now, Tara, how about two pints," Mick cut her off and then glanced at Marie-Claire. "Beer okay with you?"

It sounded like another test. "Unless you've got lager."

Tara snorted and swaggered away, grinning.

Mick read the menu with interest while Marie-Claire stared at hers, uncertain what to order and very uncomfortable spending his money.

"What looks good?" he asked, not glancing up.

She scanned the list until she found the least expensive thing on it. "The soup."

"But we had that for lunch." He read down the list and scowled, and yanked the menu from her hands. Tara reappeared and stood ready with her pad.

"Two gamekeeper's pies, love, and a loaf of bread if it's fresh," Mick said.

Tara winked at her. "Hope you're not on a diet."

"What's a gamekeeper's pie?"

"You'll see."

The bartender delivered their beers, and Mick introduced him as Fred, who was also the pub's owner and a friend of Mick's since boyhood. Like Tara, Fred didn't bother to disguise his curiosity about Marie-Claire, but Mick diverted the conversation away from her and towards the news of the local football club. The men bandied teams and players' names about so fast, Marie-Claire felt her head begin to swim.

Soon, Fred's attention returned to her, and he began to regale her with stories of his and Mick's youthful misadventures. They were quite the hell-raisers, and some of the stories were very funny, such as when he and Mick had let sheep loose in the local school.

"There were three of them," Fred confided with a mischievous twinkle in his eye, "and we painted a one, two, and four on them before we snuck them in. The administration spent an entire day looking for number three."

Mick glared at his friend while Marie-Claire laughed so hard her sides hurt.

"I think you're needed at the bar, Fred," Mick advised and Fred excused himself, but not before taking the opportunity to give her a lusty kiss on the cheek. Mick, she noted, frowned.

Soon golden pies were placed before them, accompanied by a fragrant loaf of bread and a crock of butter. The gamekeeper's pie was indeed delicious, filled with venison in a rich, red-wine sauce and topped with a steaming mashed potato crust that tasted of parsnips, as well. They both ate hungrily.

"You were quite a hellion when you were younger," Marie-Claire said between mouthfuls. "You remind me a lot of my brother, Chase. When he graduated, the principal told him they were changing the locks on the school doors."

"I never graduated," Mick said, not looking up from his plate. "I quit when I was fifteen. Actually, it was more like fourteen. I was supposed to go back and take some tests but I never did."

Marie-Claire was taken aback by the defensive tone of his voice. "You've done pretty well for yourself."

He looked up at her, his eyes hard. "People think I'm an uneducated hooligan."

Marie-Claire considered this for several moments. School was obviously a sore subject. "You might not have graduated, but you're not uneducated."

"What's the capital of Estonia?"

The question took her by surprise. "The capital of Estonia?" she repeated, racking her brain. "Tallinn?"

He nodded. "That's right. See, you knew it right off the top of your head. I had to look it up."

"That's ridiculous. Not knowing the capital of a country doesn't mean you're not educated."

"Where did you learn it?"

He had her there. "*Ethnography of Post-Soviet Cultures,* senior year of college."

"There you are, then." He returned his attention to his plate and they ate in silence, the fire crackling in the grate next to them.

"Maybe if Mum had lived it would have been different," Mick continued, "and I might have stayed in school."

Marie-Claire listened as Mick struggled for words.

"But Dad didn't know any better, and he had his hands full with Hempland. I spent more time on the pitch than I did in school, so I was one less thug for them to deal with. I wasn't missed."

With his size, it wasn't hard to imagine him being cast as a thug. "Did you get into a lot of trouble?"

"I had a lot of anger, mostly over Mum dying, now that I think back on it. Then I got on Kingsbury Town, we started winning, the money started pouring in, and I lost control for a while." He paused, his blue eyes fixed on hers. "There were a few lost years, and I did some things I'm not proud of. I deserve the reputation I have."

Marie-Claire nodded but couldn't help think that his reputation was at complete odds with the man she had spent the day with. "Lots of people go a little wild when they're young."

"I've been in jail."

Marie-Claire paused, her fork halfway to her mouth. "Excuse me?"

"Jail," he repeated, "for assault."

This conversation was getting odder by the moment. "Oh yes? What happened?"

"There was a fight, although I didn't throw the first punch." He waited to see her reaction, and seemed to relax when she took a sip of the warm beer and continued to eat her dinner. "It was in a pub in the East End. A lot of guys want to prove how tough they are, going up against a footballer, and I was younger and didn't mind a brawl. The police showed up and hauled me off, but the charges were dropped after his mates confessed he had planned it all along. It was a right mess and took forever to get sorted."

She listened. It was obviously important to him that she know this.

"Dad got me straightened out, though. He's the one that found Moorsgate, that's my farm. He knew the owners were looking to sell, and he took me out to see it. I fell in love with the place straight off, even though it was run-down and needed a lot of work. I knew right away it was what I wanted and I've never looked back. I spend almost all my time out there bringing everything up to snuff, making Moorsgate a proper game estate. It's given me a purpose and kept me out of trouble."

It was impossible not to smile at Mick's obvious pride in his farm. "I thought football took up most of your time."

"Not really, and that was my problem. We practice most mornings, and there's game days and the travel, but for the most part we've got too much time on our hands. And too much money. Honestly, it ruins people."

"You don't seem ruined."

"That's 'cause I've a life outside of the club. Blokes on the team, they're mostly all like me. Working class, uneducated, too much money and too much time on their hands. And that makes for trouble. Drugs, drinking, the wrong kind of women, all the things that seem glamourous and exciting when you're a lad trying out for a Premier League club. Then when you've got success, you've not got the education to handle it."

"How long will you play football? Is it something you can do for a long time?"

"Nah. I've had a long career already, longer than most, and I figure I've got three years left with Kingsbury Town, five tops, and after that I'm done. Then I'm going to give Hempland a run for its money." Mick scraped his plate and mopped up the rest of the gravy with a hunk of the bread. "You don't seem too fazed by what I've told you."

Marie-Claire ate her last bit of pie with careful nonchalance. "My dad never graduated from high school, either. His father died young and he was needed on the farms. He was too busy to get into any trouble, but my uncles admit they picked up his slack. And my brother Chase has a temper, as well, so you'd find yourself quite at home around my family."

It seemed like a huge weight had been lifted from Mick's shoulders and the conversation moved on to lighter topics. Tara proposed a plum duff for dessert and Mick concurred, but Marie-Claire begged off. They said their goodbyes and walked back to the car, Mick's hand resting at the small of her back. Outside, a full moon hung over the village rooftops, adding to the romantic mood.

Marie-Claire sighed, sated. "That was so good, I swear that was more food than I've eaten in a month."

"Don't you get enough to eat?" Mick asked as he held the car door for her.

She slipped into the satiny leather seats and laughed. "People expect artists to be starving and think you're not talented if you're not."

Mick's eyes coursed over her. "You're very talented, and I'm not letting you starve."

Sunday evening traffic on the motorway back to London was heavy, and she wasn't bothered in the least that her knees were just an inch or two from where his left hand rested on the gear shift. In fact, the proximity was very pleasant. Mick turned on the radio and they listened to a few minutes of the final scores for the weekend's football matches. When the sports chat broadcasters launched into a discourse on the English national team's upcoming Friendly with Spain, Mick flicked the radio off with a sharp gesture.

"Actually, we make out okay for food," Marie-Claire continued. "Bertrand lets Raul bring home extras from the restaurant, and we scrounge from the school, and after receptions there's always lots left over."

Mick nodded, his attention focused on the road.

From her seat next to him, Marie-Claire noted his hands gripping the steering wheel. They were large and strong and had held the shotgun easily, yet had been warm when he had taken her hand and kissed it.

There was no question that she had never been out with such a handsome man. And also no question that it had been a long time since she'd been with any man, let alone someone like Mick. Someone who enjoyed the outdoors as much as she did, who was down-to-earth and fun. He was, she warmly acknowledged, quite a package.

Was this what impetuous felt like?

"There's a big lecture tomorrow night at school, by a famous nature photographer," Marie-Claire said. "You might enjoy it. His work is very good."

Time clicked by on the dashboard clock without Mick saying a word.

"It starts at eight," she added.

"Tomorrow I go to Barcelona."

"Barcelona. That's wonderful, you must be so excited."

There was no answer, although Mick's lips seemed to press together.

"You're excited to go, aren't you?"

"No." It took him so long to answer Marie-Claire thought he hadn't heard her.

"Have you ever been?" she asked.

"Yes."

Of course, he'd been to Barcelona; he must have traveled all over the world.

"At least a dozen times," he added.

"Is it very beautiful?"

"I have no idea. I've only ever seen the hotel and the stadium."

"Surely you get to go out a bit, walk around?"

He shrugged, indifferent. "We'd be mobbed. I'm recognized everywhere I go, as you found out."

That was a sharp reminder of his celebrity status. Straightening in her seat, she folded her hands in her lap and tucked her legs in the opposite direction. "Yes, of course. How do you spend your time?"

"Mostly we find a bar and hunker down, usually at the hotel. We take a coach to practice, and then back to the hotel, and then to the match, and then back to the plane, and then home."

"But Barcelona has so much art, so much beauty..." She couldn't help herself; how could someone go to one of the most beautiful cities in the world and not want to see it?

"I'm there to work. Not gad about like a tourist."

Marie-Claire sat motionless in her seat, knowing she had been put in her place.

Traffic continued to crawl, and Mick stared at the road before them. A thick lump formed in her throat, and she swallowed with difficulty. Needing something, anything, to do, Marie-Claire pulled the sketchbook from her bag and began drawing elaborate doodles, pretending it was consuming all her attention.

Better to have the spell broken quickly, she reasoned. A small jolt now was better than a painful crash later. Mick was a devastatingly charming and handsome man, and she had allowed herself to get swept away by how much fun she'd had with him and how special the day had seemed. This probably happened to him a lot, and no doubt he had learned to put people in their place.

The reality was that he was not a regular guy. He was a wealthy sports star who lived in a world vastly different from her own. He'd felt bad about the art show, and had taken her to the country for the day and treated her to a nice dinner by way of an apology. Anything else she might have thought was brewing was just a figment of her overactive imagination.

Now the day was over and maybe there was a beautiful woman waiting for him in London, which was why he was impatient to get back. Which was fine.

Marie-Claire snapped her sketchbook shut when they reached Putney. "You can drop me off at the Lady Warwick."

Mick glanced at her. "But it's nine o'clock at night. Isn't it closed?"

"The studio never closes. We all have key cards."

Her answer only seemed to increase his irritation. "How late will you work?"

"Awhile. I've taken the day off, so I have to make up for it."

"How do you get home?"

"I walk," she answered, thinking the answer was rather obvious.

"What, in the middle of the night? That's not the smartest thing in the world, is it?"

"It's just three blocks." And that wasn't any concern of his.

He seemed to want to argue this further, but instead snapped his mouth shut and downshifted the car with a sharp jerk.

At the Lady Warwick, he insisted on parking in the small inner lot and walking her to the studio door, and then towered over her while she sorted through her bag for her key card. The tension in his body was palpable.

"Look here, why don't you have a mobile?" he asked.

"No need. Plus, it's expensive, and everyone I know is here at school, so I see them every day. I have a card to call home, and the school lets me use their phones for that."

He frowned and twice started to say something, but then seemed to think better of it.

Her key card had wedged itself between the pages of her sketchbook, and she fished it out with relief. So, this was the end. She'd never see Mick again, that was a given, and the knowledge made her feel a little reckless.

Leave your comfort zone and follow your heart, Professor Dixon had commanded.

"Thank you for the day, it was lovely," she murmured, and stood on tiptoe to brush her lips against his cheek, the slight stubble of his beard warm beneath her lips.

Mick stood immobile, his eyes wide with surprise.

Marie-Claire stepped back. She didn't know what she expected his reaction to be, but it certainly wasn't flummoxed. Mumbling good night, she swiped her key card in the sensor and slipped into the building, taking the stairs two at a time till she arrived at the small window at the top of the landing.

Peering out, she saw Mick below, still standing on the stoop and staring at the door, transfixed. After a moment, he pulled up the collar of his jacket and walked away.

Chapter Ten

ON THURSDAY MORNING, the team ambled through the cavernous corridors of St Augustine on the way back to the locker rooms. Practice had been good, Mick decided. The new plays were progressing well, and the entire team seemed to be humming like a well-oiled machine again, which was a right relief after the train wreck they'd been the week before.

Auchincloss had gotten his suspension reduced to one game, and Lars was sound again after another stint in physio rehab. The Friendly against Spain had also gone well. Mick had gotten almost twenty minutes of play and blocked a sneaky rebound shot on goal. The match had ended in a 1-1 draw, but he had felt focused and back to normal.

Quite a bit better than normal, truth be told. Last night when the plane had landed, the urge to see Marie-Claire had been powerful, and he had felt cursed that he couldn't ring her up and at least hear her voice. He wanted to tell her about Barcelona, tell her that he had gotten out and walked around the city, and she was right, it was beautiful. There was a messy-looking church with tall, spiky spires, and colorful hillside terraces that overlooked the Mediterranean. He'd walked the winding avenues amidst lovers linked arm in arm, oblivious to everything but each other, and saw couples sitting in charming courtyards drinking wine, talking and laughing as the sun set over the sea. He knew by instinct she would have loved it.

But did she want to see him again? That was the question. She had seemed to enjoy their day in the country, but then again, she was a polite girl, and you could never really tell with those types. The question of whether or not she was already seeing someone still nagged at him, although he was certain she would have mentioned it if she could have used it as an excuse not to go with him Sunday. Raul was protective of her, but in more of a brotherly way. There hadn't been any territorial issues when Mick had made his interest clear.

The other problem was the effect she had on his blasted mouth. He hadn't planned on telling her about his mother. In fact, he had never spoken about her to anyone, aside from Dad, of course. Somehow, everything had just come spilling out like he was on some chat show on the telly. The remarkable thing was, he had felt good telling her. And she hadn't flinched when he'd told her about his problems with the law. In fact, she had seemed rather unimpressed.

Then he'd ruined it all by getting worked up about Barcelona, and all for nothing. The Barcas, it turned out, were chuffed at his mistaking their city for the capital, and had serenaded him with a happy little ditty the Spanish players translated. Still, to Marie-Claire he'd come off as being Mister Worldly and spouting off that he was jetting around European cities on a regular basis. Which he was, but still, you didn't need to remind someone who was struggling to make her own rent of the fact. She had been silent the rest of the trip back, and no wonder, he couldn't stand a braggart either.

But she had kissed him goodnight. The fleeting feel of her soft lips against his cheek had detonated an explosive tangle of emotions inside him, like his head and his heart and his groin were all wired to the same high-amp circuit. The old Mick would have snatched her against him and kissed her soundly, but all he'd been able to do was stand there, rooted to the spot like an imbecile.

The bugger of it was, he had no idea how to begin pursuing her. For starters, she wasn't throwing herself at him, which was a novelty in itself. Since he had been a lad, girls had hung around the pitch, friendly and available. Not that he had much cared—football was all that mattered. If she had been like the rest, he would have played it cool, waited a bit before calling her, and then dazzled her with some flash and cash before reeling her in. Instead, he'd almost had to throw her into his car for a day in the country, and then fight to buy her a simple pub supper.

Now he was panting after her like a stag in rut, and there was every chance he'd make an even bigger idiot of himself than he already had. She was new and dangerous territory, and maybe it was best if he cooled things a bit until he could get himself under control. Give it a week, maybe two, and then see if she fancied meeting up for a drink. That would have to be the plan, Mick decided with regret.

"Oi, Mick, you've got mail," Sheila called from the temporary reception desk that had been set up in a windowed office off the lobby.

"Ta, Sheila, send them a photo with a nice note."

"I think you'll want this one. It looks special."

He walked over to her desk. "What you've got there, love? More knickers from the maths teacher in Blackpool?"

"Noooo…" she said, and pulled a card out from her desk drawer and presented it to him. "It looks different from the others. More special-like."

He opened the square envelope and pulled the card out. It was a small piece of thick paper with a watercolor sketch of Lacey curled in her basket before the fire, the black and white Spaniel's nose tucked towards her stubby tail as she slept. Beneath, a neat hand had written, "Thank you, it was wonderful. Marie-Claire."

The breath stuck in his throat. He couldn't take his eyes off the paper in his hand.

"So, I was right," Sheila clucked. "Thought it looked special."

"It was sent here?"

"Arrived today, love. The office drove the mailbag down from Hendon this morning. So, who's this Marie-Claire?"

The seemingly innocent inquiry was a douse of cold water, and he adopted an indifferent attitude. Everyone knew that Sheila had many good contacts among the paparazzi and was the frequent source of the best gossip about the team. "Oh, she's the grandmother of a kid I took out for some shooting at Dad's," he lied, "dabbles in a bit of art. Nice of her." He pocketed the note and gave Sheila a big kiss on the cheek. "Now how about sharing some of those naked pictures girls are sending to Fernando?"

Sheila squealed in mock protest. "Oh, my word, I never!"

Mick sauntered down the empty hall, and once he rounded the corner, ducked into an empty classroom, shutting the door behind him. Pulling the card out again, he stared at the lovely picture, the brushstrokes evoking so much. Simple, beautiful, it captured Lacey perfectly. He ran his hand through his hair in distraction, feeling like his insides were being run through a velvet meat grinder.

A fist banged on the door. "Oi, Carr, get a move on, team meeting."

———◦———

The grocer down the street from her house had a wide assortment of soccer—no, *football*, Marie-Claire corrected herself—magazines displayed just inside the door of the store. Mick was featured on the cover of one, running hard, his concentration fierce.

Turning into an aisle, she came face-to-face with his picture on a cereal box, just like Raul had said, and farther down was a sports drink display featuring a life-size, cardboard cutout of Mick holding a bottle and smiling. Good heavens, he was everywhere.

Aside from trips to the market, Marie-Claire had resigned herself to the fact that she wouldn't be seeing him again. Mick Carr had made the situation very clear—he was a busy man, he had things to do and places to go, and a bevy of women waiting for him when he got there. His press coverage vouched for that.

She needed to accept that their trip to the country was the last time she'd see him. He was a decent guy and it had been a nice thing to do, nothing more. Things were settled between them, and that was going to be that.

———◦———

Later that night, Mick drove towards the Dorchester Hotel, the London streets wet and glistening with rain.

"Does the hotel have a covered entry?" Fanta fussed from the Aston Martin's passenger seat.

"I'm sure Sir Frank will have thought of that. It's his wife's birthday party, after all. He must have asked over four hundred guests."

"They'll have the press inside then."

"I imagine." She never called them paparazzi, Mick observed, always "the press."

"In Hollywood, it's always outside because the weather's nicer and it hardly ever rains. Room for lots more press. Cashmere told me so."

Mick tugged at the collar of his starched shirt, trying to loosen the relentless grasp the black bow tie had on his jugular. "Who?"

"Cashmere!" Fanta reminded him. "Cashmere Cassidy, my friend who's on American telly."

"Oh, right, sorry." The line of cars waiting for the valet parking was at least ten long. Ten expensive cars, Mick noted, drumming his fingers on the steering wheel as they sat.

"Are those your real nails?" he asked.

Fanta examined her perfect manicure. "'Course not."

"How do you manage? I mean, with the washing up and the like?"

She looked at him, her expression blank. "Washing up? I don't wash dishes."

The rain began to pound in earnest. "Jesus, if I return this dress with wet spots, *Bon Temp Roulez* will never let me borrow anything again," Fanta muttered under her breath, brushing imaginary lint off the clingy, red-sequined sheath.

The minutes ticked by. Her mobile phone broke the silence, chirping to announce a text message. "Oh, look at this, Mick!

Elliott has gotten us an invite to the opening of the new Nicole Kidman film next Friday."

"Next Friday? Can't. I'll be at Moorsgate. They're digging the foundations for the nursery pens."

"But it's bloody Nicole Kidman! Don't you want to meet her?"

"Only if she knows how to operate a backhoe."

Fanta fumed in silence. "Maybe I'll ask Jean-Georges."

"Suit yourself."

His indifferent tone made her nervous. A different tack was needed, so she twisted towards him and slid a stealthy hand out to caress his muscled thigh.

"Okay, you big lug, you win," she crooned, moving her hand up his leg. "I've missed you the last few days. It seems like ages since we've had any time together."

He shifted into a low gear and inched the car forward. "Watch your heels on the leather."

"I could stay at your place tonight, I don't have to be at work till ten. We could sleep in."

"I've got early practice," he said, moving her hand back to her own lap.

Undaunted, she slid her hand under his tuxedo coat and caressed his torso. "Why so grumpy tonight?" she pouted.

Realizing he had the steering wheel in a choke hold, Mick forced himself to relax. "Look, Fanta, we need to talk," he began, but paused as her hand continued to move up his chest. "Wait, don't—"

But she had pulled Marie-Claire's card out of his breast pocket before he could stop her. "What's this?"

"No, Fanta." He tried to grab the envelope from her, but she twisted away and turned in her seat to examine it. Damn.

"It's a picture of that dog of yours, isn't it?" she asked, examining the card. "And who the hell is Marie-Claire?"

He swore under his breath. "Just a friend."

"Wait. Wasn't that the name of that artist you bought the paintings from last weekend?" Fanta de las Mercedes did not get where she was in life without having some smarts.

"Yes." Why the hell had he brought it with him? "It's just a thank you card."

"What was 'wonderful?'" Fanta demanded to know.

"I took her out to Dad's for some shooting."

"She shoots guns? Like you and your dad?" Fanta's face screwed up in curiosity as she considered this new information. "Is she a lesbian?"

Relief flooded through Mick and he choked back a laugh. "I don't know."

"Is she pretty?"

"No." She's beautiful, Mick thought. No, better than beautiful.

This satisfied Fanta and she tossed the card onto the dashboard without a second thought. Cameras greet them at the door, and Fanta worked the red carpet, posing as cameras flashed and photographers called out to them.

"Mick, stand a little closer to Fanta!"

"What's the matter, Mick, she got a cold or something?"

Fanta's trademark smile developed a brittle quality. "Put your arm around me," she muttered like a ventriloquist and Mick was forced to oblige, but dropped the contact as soon as they stepped into the hotel.

⸻◦◆◦⸻

"A pint," Mick signaled the barman some hours later.

Darius joined him at the bar. "Make that two, on Mr. Carr's tab. Say, mate, Fanta and Jean-Georges seem to be enjoying each other's company."

Mick glanced at the dance floor where Fanta was entwined with the French midfielder. Darius was right, Fanta was throwing herself at him and the ever-willing Jean-Georges was not turning her down. He didn't feel jealous, didn't feel anything at all. Fanta was a nice girl, they'd had some fun together, but she wasn't what he wanted. What he wanted was on the other side of London in a dicey part of Putney and it was time he ended things with Fanta. But best to do that someplace private.

"Mick, time to dance." Fanta materialized by his side, sweaty from the dancing and disheveled from the champagne. Grabbing his hand, she dragged him onto the dance floor.

"You haven't been paying any attention to me." She sulked, grinding against him as the music blared.

"Sorry."

"You've been practicing too hard, haven't you? Jean-Georges says so."

"Actually, yes, I am tired," Mick admitted. When the song ended, he took her by the elbow and led her to the empty marbled hallway outside the ballroom. "I think we should say our thank-you's and leave."

"Why? I am having a good time!" She stomped her foot, impassioned. "Why do you always want to leave when I am having a good time?"

"Because we need to talk."

"Bah. Talk, talk, talk. All you want to talk about is those filthy birds and dogs. It's all you care about. You don't care about me."

This was not the first time he had heard this rant. "Okay, stay then. I'm leaving."

"What?" she screeched, grabbing his arm and yanking him back, her nails biting into the jacket fabric. "Are you walking out on me?"

He disengaged her fingers. "Look, Fanta, it's been fun, but it's over. We've both gotten what we want out of this relationship, and now it's time to move on. Let's part as friends."

Fanta's expression went blank, and Mick had a brief moment of wild hope that she was going to be reasonable and everything would work out well.

Which was immediately squelched when Jean-Georges appeared around the corner and slouched against the doorway. "Is everythin' okay?"

It was, Mick realized, like watching the final seconds tick down on a time bomb. Filling her lungs to capacity, Fanta pointed a jeweled finger at Mick. "He is mad with jealousy!"

Her shrill voice echoed through the cavernous hallway so loudly he was sure everyone in the party could hear. It was the hallmark of her tantrums.

"No, I'm not," Mick said.

Jean-Georges snorted. "You think I am stealing your woman, Mick?"

Mick walked over and clapped him on the shoulder. "You're welcome to her, mate."

It was late, almost one o'clock in the morning, when Mick drove back across the Thames and parked outside Marie-Claire's house. The narrow street was deserted and her house was dark. He wondered which window was her bedroom and considered throwing pebbles, and then decided against it. Instead, he sat in his car, staring at the portrait of Lacey until a sense of peace settled around him. Finally, reluctantly, he drove home.

Chapter Eleven

BY THE END of the week, the inspiration from the trip to Hempland had faded and Marie-Claire was back to square one. A labored attempt at a Crested Wren sat drying on her worktable next to a Bobwhite study that was just plain sloppy. She tossed the paintbrush across the worktable in disgust.

The afternoon light was almost gone and if she wanted to get some dinner before Life Drawing class at the Art League, she'd have to get a move on. She washed her brushes and cleaned her palette for a fresh start tomorrow, and then packed up her leather kit bag and pulled on her thick sweater. Outside on the sidewalk, she paused to wrap her scarf higher around her neck against the cold wind, and then swung her bag over her shoulder and set off for home.

"I'm not stalking you," Mick said, appearing by her side as if by magic.

Her heart began hammering in delight, knowing he'd been waiting outside for who knew how long. Waiting for her. She ducked her head and kept walking.

"You don't have a mobile so I couldn't ring you to ask to see you," he continued, falling into step beside her.

"No, I don't." Letting her hair fall forward to veil her face, she cast a sideways glance at him. He was wearing dark twill trousers, a black sweater that emphasized his large physique, and the leather jacket he'd worn to the student show. He was fresh-shaven and heartbreakingly handsome.

"That's a problem," he continued.

A throng of schoolchildren flooded the sidewalk and they had to press against each other to pass, the contact rattling Marie-Claire's senses. "For whom?"

"For me. Because I can't call to ask you if you'd like to have dinner with me."

Her pulse leapt, but her common sense took immediate command of the situation. "That is a problem," she said with what she hoped sounded like polite regret. "I could have saved you a trip. Thanks, but I have class tonight."

"I'll have you back in time for that," he countered, matching her stride.

When they reached the end of the block, she turned to look him straight in the eye. "You have a girlfriend."

He nodded in recognition of her rebuff. "All right then, I want to discuss business over dinner."

"What business?"

"I want you to paint a picture of Liza. A proper portrait, like the one of Lacey on the card you sent me, only a bigger one. I'd like to give it to Dad for his birthday."

Marie-Claire paused, disconcerted. "How large? What setting?"

Mick shook his head. "No, lass, over dinner. I'm starving."

"Nothing expensive."

"Whatever you want."

"I have to be at the Art League in Wandsworth by seven," she added.

"I know the area. You will be."

"There's a really good Italian place about halfway to the Art League."

"We'll go wherever you want," he repeated.

There was a line of customers at the restaurant when they arrived and Marie-Claire glanced at her watch. "It's going to be a wait, this place is very popular."

Mick surveyed the situation and then grasped her elbow and waded in, his heavy shoulders separating the crowd as he maneuvered them to the front of the line.

The busy maître d' looked up from a long list of reservations. "You wait at back of the line," he snapped in a thick Italian accent.

"What, do you think I play for Tottenham?" Mick asked with mock indignity.

The man scrutinized Mick, and then a huge smile broke out on his face and things changed quickly. Rapid orders were barked in Italian and moments later Mick was standing for pictures with the owners, keeping a firm hand around Marie-Claire's waist when she tried to move out of the photograph. More pictures followed with the staff, and with sly winks, they were escorted to a secluded table near the back of the restaurant.

"That's a good trick," Marie-Claire said after the waiter finished making a show of lighting the candle on their table.

"Fame comes in handy at times," Mick agreed, perusing the menu.

Did he know his left leg had trapped hers against the table's pedestal leg?

"Thank you for the card. It's beautiful," Mick said after they had given their order. "You also left one on the table for Sue, of her lilacs. That was a very nice gesture."

"It was a very nice day," Marie-Claire said, trying to arrange her legs so that they didn't brush against his. Avoiding them was impossible, they were too big. "I'm surprised you got it so fast. I just sent it to the club's address on their website."

"They bring the mail down to Wimbledon almost every day from Hendon."

"Why is your training facility in Wimbledon? I don't know much about the area, but isn't Kingsbury Town much farther west?"

"Northwest by about twenty miles. Sir Frank is having our Hendon training facility redone, huge renovations, it's going to be brilliant when it's ready next year. So, he found this old school, St Augustine, in Wimbledon, right on the high street and across from the Underground station. The place is a sty, but the pitch is lovely."

Marie-Claire gave in to the pleasant pressure of his calf against hers. "That's close to Ella and Bertrand's restaurant. Is that why you were there?"

He smiled. "Getting to know the neighborhood, so to speak. Good bit of luck, that."

The waiter brought a bottle of Chianti and poured them each a glass, and Mick raised his in a toast. "To luck."

"So, the painting of Liza," Marie-Claire began. "When is your dad's birthday?"

"November," Mick admitted and then had the good grace to look ashamed. "I wanted to give you lots of time. Would you like to hear about Barcelona?"

⚜

An hour and a half later, Marie-Claire was laughing so hard at a story Mick was telling her she could barely put her hand over her glass when he reached to pour in the rest of the bottle of Chianti. "No more. I still have Life Drawing tonight."

"What's that?" he asked, mopping up the last bit of tomato sauce with a slice of garlic bread. His appetite was astonishing. Not only had he finished her dinner when she couldn't, but also his own, two baskets of garlic bread and an enormous salad.

"It's a drawing class where we do nude studies. It's my favorite class of the week."

Mick perked up at the word "nude." "Why is it at the Art League and not your school?"

"It's easier for them to get the models. Their studio has better heat. They get a different model each week and we come down."

"Nudes? Like girls in the buff and all?" He wagged his thick brows with evident interest.

"And men," Marie-Claire added with mild indignation. "Old, young, the more types the better, actually. I just hope the model shows up tonight."

"What happens when they don't?"

"We take turns."

His eyes traveled over her. "Oh yes? That would be a class worth signing up for."

"I haven't had my turn yet." She dabbed her lips primly with the napkin.

Mick signaled for the check and paid it, and helped Marie-Claire pull on her bulky sweater. "This is quite a bit of wooly," he said, pulling her hair out from the collar and smoothing the long tresses down her back.

"My mother knitted it for my father years ago. He used to wear it when we'd go fishing out on the Chesapeake Bay. It's warm and helps keep me from being too homesick."

Outside, the streets were brightly lit and Mick fell into step next to her. A bus rolled by with a huge advertisement for Premier League Football plastered to the side and his face featured prominently. He glared at the jumbo-sized version of himself and pushed his hands into his pockets.

"What's it like then, seeing your face everywhere?" she couldn't help but ask.

"Bloody nuisance," he muttered.

"You've got your own cereal box."

"That's really good cereal. I can get you a couple of cases, if you like."

Marie-Claire laughed. "Thanks. I'll share them at school."

"I never knew how much time students had to spend at school," Mick said as they crossed a pedestrian plaza. "You spend as much time at school as I spend with the team. I thought college was a lot of carrying on and partying."

"For some it is, but they don't last long, especially in fine arts. Eventually, you have to produce something. A lot of something. Sometimes I think they should just put cots in the corner of the studio, it would save a lot on rent and walking back and forth."

"But it's worth it, right? I mean, you're doing really well."

"Not as well as I'd like. My professor says my paintings are too detailed, too rigid."

Mick snorted. "That's bollocks. You're brilliant."

"No, it's true. I analyze things too much. Everyone else can just paint spontaneously, but I have to do studies, and then value charts and sketches...sometimes it's weeks before I start a painting, let alone finish it."

"So, they're saying you overthink things. You don't trust your instincts."

She nodded. "I'm working hard at loosening up, at being spontaneous and taking risks, but the more I try, the worse the results are. I only need one example for the Critique but it's killing me."

The shops they passed were shuttered for the night, and with a quick movement, Mick pulled her into a dark entrance, trapping her against the wall with a hand on either side of her.

"You're taking a risk, being here with me," he informed her, his face close to hers.

Her pulse jumped. "I am?"

He nodded, his eyes holding hers while his body pressed against her with intent pressure. "All alone at night, with a dangerous bloke like me. There's no telling what I might do."

Her gaze dropped to his lips and her breath felt hot in her chest. "Should I run away?"

"That would certainly be the smart thing to do," he agreed, his blue eyes dancing with wicked delight, "but maybe you should follow your instincts."

He was giving her every opportunity to pull away. While her mind was screaming that he was a playboy and that's what she should do, her body demanded she pull his lips down to hers. So that's what she did.

The feel of his lips on hers was devastating, and without a doubt, Marie-Claire had never been kissed like that before in her life. His mouth plundered hers in deep sweeps, his arms gathering her against him in an iron-like grip. There was no tentative searching, no delicate kisses, it was total possession that was exhilarating in the honest desire it conveyed.

She kissed him back, reveling in the feel of the sinewy strength of his arms, the heat of his lips on hers. He peppered her face with hard kisses before reclaiming her lips with an intensity that turned her core to molten fire.

She heard herself moan as the kiss became deeper, the velvet of their tongues sliding in delicious friction. Time seemed suspended as they explored each other in the dark alcove, their fervent enjoyment of each other making the outside world seem far away.

One hand buried in her hair while the other dropped to her hip, molding her against his hard body. "You're loosening up nicely," he murmured with obvious satisfaction, pressing his lips across her brow and then tracing a line to the delicate flesh of her ear.

"I'm quite liking this danger business," she said, small explosions detonating along her spine when he tenderly bit the lobe. "I should have followed my instincts ages ago."

His lips dropped to claim the sensitive column of her throat, making her blood feel like molten lava. Dear Lord, did this man do anything by half measures?

Nearby a church bell chimed seven times. Mick swore and held her close, smoothing her hair. His body felt like a citadel of strength, so solid, so warm, Marie-Claire never wanted to leave.

She pulled away with regret. "I have to get to class."

"Wait." He released her with reluctance, and reached in his jacket pocket and pulled out a small box. "I saw this in Barcelona and thought you might like it."

Curious, she took the box and opened it. Inside was a tiny bird nest made of thin silver strands, with three tiny speckled porcelain eggs tucked in the middle. The delicate nest was strung on a simple black satin cord and was exquisite.

"Do you like it?" he asked.

"It's beautiful." The tiny nest was exquisite and obviously cost a great deal. Her heart sank. It was one thing to indulge in the desire she felt for him, but quite another to accept an expensive gift that might have strings attached.

"There was a little shop in a square, I saw it in the window. I don't speak any Spanish so there was a bit of a go-round, but I got it in the end," he said, his pride evident.

"I can't take it." She pressed the necklace back into his hand. At his look of consternation, she took a deep breath and exhaled. "I really enjoy being with you—"

"I am a hell of a guy," he agreed.

"But you're also seeing someone."

"We've broken it off. Yesterday, as a matter of fact."

"I'm sorry."

"I'm not. I should have ended it ages ago, but just couldn't be bothered. But it was the right thing to do, because there's someone I'd like to see more of." His blue eyes locked on hers. "A lot more."

He seemed so earnest, so intent, but he must have said the same thing to a dozen girls.

"You think I'm chasing every skirt in London, don't you?" he asked, seeming to read her mind.

"You have quite a reputation."

"Had a reputation," he corrected, "and well deserved, I might add. You're probably thinking you're one of many and will be history by next Friday, and normally that would be the case. But it's different with you."

Marie-Claire fixed him with a skeptical eye. "Does that line work a lot?"

"Job's boots, woman," he swore in frustration. "You missed your calling, do you know that? Any Premier team would love to have you on their defense."

He pressed her back against the wall, his eyes searching hers. "If I was one of those blokes at your school, I could probably say all sorts of fancy things that would make you go weak at the knees. But all I can tell you is this—when you're concentrating, you bite your lower lip. You shatter clay pigeons like you have a laser bead on them. You can paint the most beautiful birds in the world. And—" he drew his finger along the fine line of her jaw "—and, I want to get to know you better."

Was this the spontaneous leap Professor Dixon was talking about?

Marie-Claire weighed her options. He was a handsome rogue with an earthy, male appeal that drew her like a moth to a flame. When they were together she felt relaxed and confident, and after spending just one day with him, her painting had improved noticeably.

She forced herself to consider the downside. The relationship could also end badly, but how bad was bad? Eric's cheating had been a shock, but her eyes were wide open as far as Mick was concerned. And she was desperate. The Critique was in fifteen days, and if she wanted to stay at the Lady Warwick, he might be her only chance.

"You're hard to say no to."

He grinned with satisfaction. "That's the idea."

"I wouldn't expect this to be exclusive."

Rubbing his knuckles down her cheek, he chuckled. "Marie-Claire, you don't have to worry about that—"

"For either of us."

At her words, the smile disappeared from his face and he snatched her against him, hard, kissing her with an intensity that blotted all reason from her mind. Pulling away, he lifted her hair, looping the necklace around her throat and hooking the clasp at the back, and buried his face in the nape of her neck.

"I have to get to class," she gasped, her voice rough.

The profanity Mick muttered was muffled by the thick wool of her sweater collar. Marie-Claire smiled.

They walked the rest of the way to the Art League, Mick's arm around her shoulder keeping her close against him. "What time will you be done?" he asked when they reached the ornate front doors. "I'll swing by and pick you up."

"We all walk back together," she apologized.

That news was met with a frown. "Can I see you tomorrow, then? Dinner?"

A shiver of happiness passed through her and she smiled. "I'd like that."

As they stood in the gentle glow of the streetlamp, he drew her against him and framed her face with his hands, as though he were drinking in the vision of her. Then he kissed her again, this time with devastating gentleness, savoring the moment.

From an unmarked van parked across the street, a shutter clicked eighty-two times and the photographer grunted with satisfaction. "Money shot."

Chapter Twelve

MICK SAT IN a whirlpool bath that had been set up in St Augustine's dungeon-like kitchens, willing the vicious throbbing in his knee to go away.

The morning's scrimmage had been going well until Samuel slipped on the wet turf and plowed into Mick with terrific force, knocking him to his bad knee and sending bolts of pain in a million different directions.

The poor guy had been horrified and insisted on helping Mick off the field and into the team physio's office, the entire time babbling apologies in a tortured mixture of English and whatever the hell they spoke in Zimbabwe. Duncan had done a cursory exam and found no real damage, and then sent him into the baths. Samuel had checked in on him for what seemed like every five minutes until Mick had ordered him to leave; it had been an accident and Samuel was one of the most decent blokes he had ever played with.

His blasted knee throbbed like the devil so he tried centering his thoughts elsewhere, on something pleasant, on Marie-Claire.

He could still taste her on his lips, so soft, so tender beneath his. All of her was soft and warm. And the way she had fit in his arms, like she had been made for him. She had kissed him back passionately with no hint of fake coyness, her desire matching his own. Being with her was everything he had fantasized about and more—Jesus, just thinking about her made him hard, even in this frigid bath.

He couldn't believe the way he had talked at dinner. He had never talked to a woman so easily before, had never felt so comfortable. He'd told her about Barcelona and she had known the church he'd seen, said it was the called the *Sagrada Família* and had wanted to hear all about it. Seemed it was designed by some painter named Gaudí. He was dead and they kept building it. Evidently, the bloke thought it would take hundreds of years to build, but it was almost finished.

He must have talked for over an hour, and she had listened, even laughing at the funny things he told her. Amazing.

She had liked the necklace, he could tell. He'd seen it in the window of a tiny shop just off the harbor, and he'd known she had to have it. The price was very reasonable, which was disappointing; he'd rather have paid a hundredfold. But the jeweler had assured him the necklace was an original, or at least that's what Mick thought he was trying to get across, so it was a bit of solace that she had the only one.

Getting her to take the damn thing had been a bit more of an effort than he'd supposed, but something had convinced her and he wasn't going to waste time trying to figure out what it was. The important thing was that she had accepted the necklace, along with his obvious interest, and then sealed the deal with a kiss. That was all he needed.

And not exclusive for either of them? That was a laugh—he'd sort out anyone that got near her.

The therapeutic water jets continued to blast his leg, lessening the aches. Time to make plans.

He wanted her at tomorrow's match against Queens Park Rangers. The logistics would be a challenge; the stadium was out at Shepherd's Bush, and he didn't want her struggling with public transport. Phillip Trent was with the club on an internship from some fancy city school, but was in reality the player's step-and-fetch lad. He'd give him the task of getting her there.

After the match, he'd introduce her around at the postgame meet and greet and then whisk her off to dinner at Le Cheval Rouge, a swank little restaurant that just happened to be down the road from his house. Phillip could tell her to bring along a frock to change into, and maybe she'd choose that sexy black number she'd worn to the student show.

A warning flag rose in his mind—Le Cheval Rouge was posh, and he remembered her aversion to spending his money. Best call ahead and make sure she got a menu with no prices.

From there it would be a logical progression to go back to his place, and he relaxed back in the bath and closed his eyes, his lips curving with pleasure as he considered the possibilities the night might hold. He made a mental note to put a bottle of champagne in the fridge.

"See you've been busy, mate." Darius slapped the *Mirror* across the back of his head, and dropped it on the table next to him, opened to page six.

Mick scowled and picked up the tabloid newspaper. A grainy photograph taken with a high-powered lens had been given the prime spot on a page cluttered with celebrity gossip, and even though it had been taken from a distance, it clearly showed him kissing Marie-Claire under the lamppost on the steps of the Art League. A dead hit. The caption below read:

"**Kingsbury's Jack-About-Town Mick Carr was caught kissing a young lovely in Wandsworth last night—wonder if Fanta de las Mercedes knows?**"

Mick paled. "Oh, fuck me. Can't I ever catch a break?"

———————◇———————

Marie-Claire sat at her worktable in the crowded studio the next morning, humming a tune as she swirled a brush in Alizarin Crimson and flicked it over a sheet of scrap paper, long brushstrokes forming lazy hearts. She fingered the silver bird nest around her neck for what seemed like the hundredth time that morning, the memory of Mick warming her against the pervasive chill of the building.

Neve appeared at her shoulder and slid the *Mirror* under her elbow, pointing to a page.

Her paintbrush clattered to the floor. "That's me!" Marie-Claire gasped in shock when she saw the grainy photograph. A few people glanced over as she bent to retrieve her brush, and she lowered her voice to a violent whisper. "Someone was taking our picture?"

Neve grinned. "Guess so."

Marie-Claire looked around, then refolded the paper and shoved it back to Neve. "Has anyone else seen it?"

"Just Raul, and he won't tell. All the same, you want to be careful. Mick's dating Fanta de las Mercedes, and you don't want to mess with her."

"He said they broke up," Marie-Claire declared.

Neve raised her eyebrows in cool disbelief.

"Well, he did," Marie-Claire repeated, and pressed her lips together when several students turned to stare.

———————◄○►———————

From that point on, it was impossible to concentrate on anything. Classes ran until one o'clock and as soon as the students were dismissed, she tucked the necklace in its box and shrugged on her sweater. Neve lent her a wide-brimmed hat that she tucked her hair under, and then she slipped out a side exit and darted down the street towards the Underground entrance, wary of any more photographers that might be lurking.

After getting off at Wimbledon, St Augustine School was easy to find. The dilapidated building was like a fortress, surrounded by a tall brick wall that ran the length of the road. At the end, a weed-filled car park was filled with expensive cars. There were no guards, just a half-dozen seedy-looking men with cameras loitering outside the gated main entrance.

A stealthy walk around the block showed that the only other way in was a vestibule near the front doors that at one time must have been a trade entrance. It was, however, in full view of the photographers, so she took up a spot across the street behind a parked van and waited.

Minutes ticked by and nothing happened. Marie-Claire was beginning to lose hope of getting in undetected when one of the players emerged, a thin, well-dressed man with pale blond hair who got into a black Jaguar. The paparazzi sprang to life, their cameras focused on him as he revved the car's engine viciously, and then unleashed it and drove through the lot at a fearsome speed, unconcerned for the photographers who stood in his path. They continued to snap, headless of the driver's bloodlust and only jumping out of his way at the last second.

In the midst of the scene, Marie-Claire darted across the road and through the small gate, running until she reached the school's front doors.

A matronly woman behind a counter looked up as she burst into the lobby. "Can I help you, luv?"

It took her a moment to regain her breath. "Yes, I have something for Mick Carr. May I leave it here?"

Sheila's internal antennae began to twitch. Beautiful girl. Student from the look of her, but a bit older. The accent—American or Canadian, she could never tell the difference. A bit confused and out of place, obviously not one of them stalking fans. "Course you can, love. Why don't you come over here."

Sheila held the office door open for her. "Come on through, you're not going to rob the place, are ya? Care for a cup of tea?" she continued in her best mothering voice. "I was just making one myself. You can join me." Not taking no for an answer, she patted a chair and began to prepare two cups.

Marie-Claire sat and accepted the tea with trepidation.

"My name's Sheila, I'm the Customer Service manager here at the club."

"MC." At Sheila's encouraging look, she grudgingly elaborated, "Marie-Claire."

Bingo. Grandmother my arse, Mick Carr. Hair about the right length for the girl in the photo in the *Mirror* this morning. Holiday was going to be Costa del Sol this year, thanks to this girl. "Pleased to meet you. First time here? Well, welcome to Kingsbury Town Football Club. That's soccer to you Canadians."

Marie-Claire took a sip of the hot tea. "American, actually."

"Oh, well, you, too. Very confusing, I always say. What with your football, as well. Sometimes we get Americans expecting to see that instead. It's funny when they want their money back!" She erupted in girlish peals of laughter. "So, what brings you to London?"

Marie-Claire squirmed in her seat. "School."

Sheila nodded and sat in attentive silence, stirring her tea. Marie-Claire eventually added, "Art school. In Putney."

That detail brought a huge smile to the woman's face. "Would that be the Lady Warwick?"

"You know it?"

"Know of it, don't know much about art myself. George's niece, that would be my second husband's brother's girl, our Deirdre, she went there. Took awfully nice pictures, she did. Is that where you met Mick?"

The woman's studied nonchalance put Marie-Claire on guard. Taking a hasty final swallow of tea, she set the necklace box on the desk and stood to leave. "Actually, he left this at the school and I wanted to return it to him."

"I can see that he gets it, love, but they're just finishing up —"

"I have to go. Thanks for the tea."

Sheila wasn't about to let this fish off the hook so fast. Reaching for the phone, she blocked Marie-Claire's path and punched a button. "It's Sheila. Tell Mick he has a visitor at the desk and he's to come now." She listened for a moment and her brow darkened. "And I say, if you want your fan club letters answered without girls' parents calling the police, you'll do as I say!" Hanging the phone up with a look of smug satisfaction, she winked. "He won't be a moment."

Marie-Claire didn't want to see Mick, but couldn't think of an excuse to leave fast enough. She sank back into the chair, her throat dry, and a moment later a door swung open. Mick came through, dressed in shorts and a sweaty t-shirt that stretched across his wide biceps, and paused, obviously surprised to see her.

He glanced at Sheila and then back to her. "Hullo."

Sheila bustled over. "Oh, there you are, Mick. The conference room is free if you'd like to use it for a quick visit." She held the door for Marie-Claire and motioned them through, and then watched as they walked down the corridor.

Mick led the way to a windowless cinder-block room filled with an enormous mahogany conference table surrounded by thickly upholstered chairs. When he shut the door, the effect was claustrophobic.

"I guess you've seen the *Mirror*," he began. "Don't worry about it, that pap, he just got lucky. They don't know who you are."

Mick's casual take on the situation astounded her. "My face is on every newsstand in Great Britain."

"Actually, it's my face and your back," Mick pointed out reasonably. "Does anyone else know it's you?"

"Neve. And Raul."

"Is that all?"

"I think so."

Mick smiled with considerable nonchalance. "Good. So, they have a picture of me kissing a pretty girl in Wandsworth. They've been covering me for years and they know there's no news there. Tomorrow it will be Jean-Georges and some woman with an angry husband."

"That's not the point. It's creepy that someone was taking our picture."

"You'll get used to it."

She stared at him in slack-jawed astonishment. "I could never get used to that!" With a huge effort, she reined in her temper. "They mention your girlfriend, Fanta."

This time Mick's temper flared. "I told you, she's not my girlfriend anymore. I ended it."

"Shouldn't you have, I don't know, put out a press release or something?"

Mick stepped back, affronted. "Don't be ridiculous. This is my private life."

"Well, your private life isn't very private, is it? But mine is and I'd like to keep it that way." Rifling through her pockets, she withdrew the little box and with a shaking hand, laid it on the table. "I came to give this back to you."

Drawing himself up to his full height, he towered over her, his blue eyes holding hers. "This is all going to blow over, Marie-Claire."

She shook her head. "No, I don't want any part of this. Maybe you can patch things up with Fanta because I'm not interested in seeing you. I'm not going to be the other woman again."

She tried to brush past him, but he blocked her path. "Marie-Claire, listen to me for just two minutes." Seeing her mutinous expression, he added, "Please."

She crossed her arms and waited.

"I broke up with Fanta on Wednesday, the day I got your painting of Lacey," he began. "There was no hardship. It had been over between us for a long time, and there wasn't much to begin with. From the second I met you, I knew you were what I wanted."

Only the visualization of the tabloid picture could extinguish the gentle swish of delight that coiled through her body at his words.

"I wish I was an ordinary bloke and that we could get to know each other the proper way," he continued, "in private. Unfortunately, that's not the way it is. Things are a bit out of order, but there's nothing to be done for it. You're who you are, I'm who I am, and there's no changing that."

His quiet voice and the rational tone of his words began to unwind the intense mortification she was feeling.

He reached out to trace the line of her jaw with his thumb. "Now. I like your company and I think you like mine. I want to see more of you, and I have no problem keeping a low profile —it would be a bit of a relief, actually. And this will all blow over, something else always comes up, someone new. As long as you're not the type to look for the publicity, they'll get bored quickly. Although how anyone could get bored of you, I have no idea."

Her skin tingled where he touched, yet she forced her expression to remain dubious.

"All I'm asking for is a chance," he said.

"I'm here to go to school," she said firmly.

"I know that. I respect that. I won't get in the way."

"I don't like being in the papers."

"You won't be. All of that stuff is set up. Most of the time the photographers are tipped off where to be and when to be there. It's all publicity, for those that want it. For those that don't, well, they get ignored because it's too much work. You don't want the publicity, I don't want it, so they'll find someone else who does."

Seamlessly, his arms wrapped around her and he gathered her against him. "I will keep you safe." His lips grazed her brow, making her body feel heavy with desire. "Will you at least give me a chance?"

It was impossible to think with his body pressed against hers like this. She felt her willpower dissolving as he kissed her brow, his warm breath fanning her face as his lips traced a path to her ear. Exquisite explosions detonated down her spine when he caught the lobe of her ear in his teeth, making her pitch weakly back against the thick table.

His mouth took hers, the friction of their tongues like rough velvet. Her arms wrapped around his neck and she returned his kiss, hungry for more of him. Impatiently his hands explored the edge of her thick sweater until he found the warm skin of her back, the touch of his roughened hands electric.

He broke the kiss, his breathing rough. "Answer me, Marie-Claire."

Outside in the corridor came the sound of loud male voices speaking in a mishmash of languages, punctuated by the unmistakable thumps of a football ricocheting off the cinderblock walls.

Mick pulled back, grinning. "Give me a sec to lock the door."

Marie-Claire steadied herself against the solid mahogany table. "I have to get back to the studio."

The voices got louder and he sighed, but acquiesced. "We're done for the day, I'll drive you back."

"But there are lots of people in the car park with cameras, we can't go out there together."

"They're called paparazzi, they're celebrity photographers. I'll get Jason to drive my car around the back, there's a loading dock there, and you can duck down. Wait here a moment while I get changed?"

"Okay."

He pressed a kiss on her forehead. "That's my girl."

<hr/>

"Hang on a minute, it's started to rain." Mick halted in the dank stairwell and draped his field coat around her shoulders, smoothing her long hair down her back in one caressing motion.

"I think your hair is the softest thing I've ever felt," he murmured, taking the opportunity to brush his lips against the sensitive curve of her ear.

A delightful shiver passed through her as he wrapped his arm around her shoulder and opened the exit door for her, the rush of cool air feeling pleasant on her face.

Then Mick cursed and the world exploded in a flash of strobe lights.

Chapter Thirteen

"MARIE-CLAIRE! MC!" Voices screamed over rapid camera clicks. "That's your name, right? How long have you been dating Mick? Aren't you afraid of Fanta?"

Cameras jammed through the gaps in the fence just feet away, rough bodies jostling each other as the paparazzi continued to scream her name.

A young player hopped out of the Aston Martin and ran towards them. "Jesus, Mick, they're all over the place!"

She threw her hands over her face, having no idea where to turn.

Mick cursed again and tightened his arm around her, dragging her towards his car while more flashes exploded, yelling to be heard over the fracas. "Keep your head down."

"MC! Marie-Claire! Over here! Mick! What does Fanta say? How long have you been seeing each other?"

Using his body to block the view of her, Mick yanked open the passenger side door and shoved her into the seat. He jumped into the driver seat and spun the car in a tight circle, the tires screaming. The Aston Martin shot across the parking lot and entered the road at top speed, their pursuers racing behind on motor scooters and in compact cars.

It was like the world had gone insane. Mick drove fast through the urban side streets, the chasing cars tailing his every turn.

Marie-Claire twisted in her seat to see how many were following them. "Those paparazzi, how do they know my name?"

Mick glanced in the rearview mirror. "They got tipped off. Probably Sheila."

Marie-Claire groaned and sank in her seat. "That woman at the desk?"

"She's got connections with all of them. The club looks the other way because it generates buzz. They welcome it."

"I don't."

"Neither do I, but there's not much we can do about it at this point. I'm sorry."

"Take me home."

"Can't do that, not yet. Do you want them to find out where you live?"

"No!"

"Then just sit tight."

The Aston Martin made its own rules of the road, and Marie-Claire held onto her seat for dear life as other motorists gave way. Mick was an expert driver and seemed to enjoy weaving through traffic, at one point taking a cutoff across a pedestrian plaza filled with farm market stalls. A group of schoolboys cheered as the sports car raced past them and turned the wrong way up a one-way alley.

Mick maneuvered the car nimbly back onto the main road. Seeing a broad stretch ahead, he accelerated to top speed and glanced in the rearview mirror with a triumphant grin. "Looks like we lost them."

The grin vanished when Marie-Claire pointed towards two motorcycles approaching from a side street, each with a photographer riding pillion and training a long lens at them. Muttering obscenities, Mick downshifted and made so many illegal turns, Marie-Claire lost count.

After they crossed the Thames, Mick picked up his mobile phone. "It's Carr, I'm being tailed. We should be there in two minutes."

They sped through the affluent shopping districts of west London, veering down hidden alleys and through barely passable narrow lanes. Mick seemed unfazed by the fact that at any moment they could become trapped by a truck making a delivery, and then what would happen? They'd be cornered like prey.

The paparazzi got close several times but never reached the car, and after a dizzying series of turns, Mick swung sharply into a driveway flanked by open gates. The gates slid shut behind them and the line of trailing motorcycles skidded to a halt, the photographers jumping off and pressing against the high gate, the furious snapping never stopping.

They emerged into a hidden cul-de-sac of modern terraced homes designed like huge, stacked boxes of glass and steel. Balconies jutted out at random angles and shiny, corrugated metal roofs sloped in sinuous lines, while some walls seemed to be made entirely of glass. Mick pushed a button on the dashboard and a garage door opened near the end of a row, revealing a white Range Rover with muddy paw prints on the rear door. The Aston Martin fit in behind and the garage door rolled closed.

"Here we are then, safe and sound." Mick turned to her with a maddening grin, like he did this every day.

Marie-Claire was still trying to catch her breath. "Your house?"

"Yeah, let's go in."

Mick led the way up the steps to the main living area. The floor was a polished stone that Marie-Claire had seen in high-end galleries, and the living room was dominated by an entertainment center with an enormous wide-screen television. A mirrored bar had been fabricated to look like a continuous sheet of steel, and the pale walls were bare except for her paintings that hung opposite a long leather sofa. Slab stone stairs running to the second floor were fenced with what looked like piano wire railing. The entire effect was sterile and expensive.

She stepped towards a tall window at the end of the room. "You can look out, no one can see in," Mick said. "It's got some sort of filter on the glass."

"No one followed us?"

"No. There's full security. It's why I live here."

Looking outside, Marie-Claire saw the houses had been designed around a small park, where a woman jogged with a baby stroller and dog on a leash, followed by a young boy on a tricycle, peddling to keep up. The charming scene was a jarring contrast to the bedlam they had left outside the gates.

"How long will those people be out there?" Marie-Claire asked.

Mick joined her at the window. "I'm not sure. An hour, maybe two. Depends on what else they have going on."

"I have to get back to school."

"In a bit. We need to let them lose interest, and then we'll make a plan. Right now, I'm famished, come on, I'll make us some tea. You'll feel better after you've had a cup."

The kitchen was down another set of steps and fitted out with the latest stainless steel appliances and yards of granite counters. Unable to resist, Marie-Claire ran her hand over the polished surface, her fingers leaving a faint smudge. A beautiful antique kitchen table and chairs looked conspicuously out of place in the modern setting.

Mick turned on the teakettle and set about putting bread in the toaster and cutting thick slices of cherry cake. "So, what do you think?" he asked, motioning around the room.

Marie-Claire groped for words. "It's very impressive. You have good taste."

"Not my taste at all—guy I bought it from included the furniture in the sale. 'Cept that table, and the chairs, they were Mum's. Sue wanted something larger, so Dad let me take them."

He handed down plates from a tall cupboard and Marie-Claire set the table, admiring the old walnut finish aged to a deep brown patina. The scuffs and scrapes only added character to the beautiful piece.

After seating her, Mick poured the tea, and then without asking, dumped two heaping spoonfuls of sugar in both cups and stirred. The combination of sweetness and strong tea was bracing, and he was right, after a few minutes she did feel better.

He loaded her plate with buttered toast, a hunk of cold chicken, and a slice of cake, and then began to devour his own.

"You're not eating." He took a piece of the cherry cake and held it to her lips. "Come on, be a good girl. It's Sue's specialty."

She let him coax her into taking a few bites and then pushed the plate away. "I should get back to school now."

"In a bit. First, I'd like to hear about this ex-boyfriend of yours."

His statement took Marie-Claire by surprise. "How do you know I have an ex-boyfriend?"

"Back at St Augustine, you said you weren't going to be the other woman again," Mick said as he helped himself to another slice of cake. "That would mean you used to have a boyfriend, I'm guessing in America, and that he was two-timing you. It's still pretty raw, so you probably broke it off right before you came over here, and that's why you overreacted when the *Mirror* printed that photograph today."

"I didn't overreact," she said, surprised by Mick's perceptiveness.

"No, you're right. It was an intrusion of your privacy, and I'm very sorry it happened." Mick apologized, contrite. "What was his name?"

Seeing he wasn't going to be diverted, she took a sip of tea. "Eric. He's a lawyer, in Washington, DC."

Mick nodded. "High-powered and all that?"

"He's a partner at one of the biggest tax law firms in the country."

"How did you two meet?"

"He and some of the other partners would drive over from Washington to hunt with Dad and Chase."

"When was this?"

"Two years ago." She took another sip, the hot liquid soothing the dryness in her throat. "It was the end of my junior year at college and I'd help Dad and Chase on weekends when they had a lot of clients. This particular group of lawyers came hunting several times, and then Eric started coming over by himself, and when Dad or Chase was busy, I'd take him out.

Pretty soon, it was clear he was coming just to see me. He put all the moves on me and I fell hard."

As she spoke, she realized talking about Eric didn't hurt as much as it used to. The pain was still there, but was duller. "It got serious pretty quickly. Eric came over almost every weekend," she continued. "I had a small apartment in Chestertown, right off campus, so we spent most of our time there. He kept a sailboat in the Chester River, and sometimes we'd sail on the Bay."

As she spoke, Mick took the napkin she was kneading with her fingers and covered her hand with his own. "I thought we were madly in love. But there started to be problems."

"Like what kind of problems?"

"He could come off as arrogant, and my parents and Chase didn't like him. My friends didn't either, and he didn't like them. I started to feel very isolated and my work began to suffer.

"I only saw him on weekends, and in the beginning that was okay. Then I started to wonder why he didn't invite me to visit him in Washington. When I asked, he said he hated the city and wanted to be with me in Chestertown, but I began to feel like I was only seeing half of him."

"And the other half was seeing another woman."

Marie-Claire nodded. "I was the bit on the side."

"Bastard," Mick muttered.

"She was a lawyer, as well, an associate at his firm. She traveled a lot, so he had time on his hands."

"How did you find out?"

"A lawyer from another firm hunted with Chase and clued him in."

Mick's jaw hardened. "I hope your brother beat the hell out of him."

"I wouldn't let him. I confronted Eric myself and he didn't deny it. He said they were engaged and were getting married as soon as she made partner, but he saw no reason why we should break it off. It was all working fine for him." Marie-Claire winced at the memory. "He's very arrogant."

"So, you sent him packing."

"Yes. My teachers at Chestertown had encouraged me to apply to the Lady Warwick for graduate school, but everyone knew how competitive it is and that they hardly ever accept Americans. I thought I'd be getting married so it wouldn't matter if I was turned down, but the day after I found out about Eric, the letter arrived offering me a place. England was far away, the Lady Warwick was a new beginning, so I took my inheritance and was on the plane the next week. That was last June."

"Did he follow you here?"

"No. They were married last November, actually."

A broad grin spread across Mick's face. "If I ever meet him I'd shake his hand."

She looked at him in disbelief. "Whatever for?"

"Because he's a fool." Mick pulled her triumphantly into his lap, his strong hands rubbing the tension out of her neck and shoulders. "And I'm not. He might have lots of expensive education, but he's still a fool. I, on the other hand, left school when I was fourteen but I know something good when I see it. He was an idiot for letting you go."

"I didn't want to be found," Marie-Claire said, resting her head on his shoulder. "He was the first guy I was ever serious with, and I felt stupid and embarrassed and just wanted to lick my wounds in peace. My family knows where I am, but to everyone else I went to Europe for art school."

He brought her hand to his lips and kissed her palm, and then her wrist. "And you're happy here because this is where you belong. You know that, don't you?"

"I was happy until those photographers showed up," she answered as he pushed the sleeve of her sweater back to press more kisses up the sensitive skin of her arm. "But what happens if they find out where I live? We'd never get a moment's peace."

"That's not a problem, because you're moving in here with me," Mick said, as if the answer were obvious. "I can keep you safe here. And there's a guest bedroom upstairs," he added when she began to protest, "with its own bath, and there's some shops around the corner, we'll call over and they can send some outfits for you, and an apothecary, we'll get you whatever you need."

She could only stutter in amazement. "H-how would I get back and forth to school?"

"You can take the Aston Martin, I'll drive the Range Rover."

The idea of being responsible for the expensive sports car made her stomach lurch. "No. I like where I live. It's close to school and I know my way around. I'd be lost here."

"What if I sold up and got a flat in Wandsworth?"

He asked the question so intently Marie-Claire got the distinct feeling he would do exactly that. "No. Mick, I'm here to go to school, not be your girlfriend."

"You can do both," he assured her.

"I don't think so. Not if it means our picture is going to be in every newspaper in the country."

"I told you, this is all going to blow over—"

"No, Mick, it's not. You think all this is normal but it's not. Normal is waiting in line at a restaurant, it's sitting in traffic and not driving on the sidewalk, and it is most definitely not being chased by photographers who could get lots of money for your picture and seem willing to do anything to get it."

He began to take issue with what she was saying, but she cut him off. "And under other circumstances it wouldn't be a problem, it might even be fun. But I can't take the risk. It's going to take everything I have to pass the Critique."

Marie-Claire could see her words were sinking in and that Mick didn't like them.

"Why is this Critique so bloody important?" he asked in exasperation.

"If I pass the Critique I can stay."

"And what happens if you don't? Do you have to repeat the year?" he asked sarcastically.

"No. If I don't pass, I'm done."

Something in the tone of her answer made him pause. "What do you mean, done?"

"They say thank you and show me the door. I go home."

"Home, you mean to your house in Putney?"

She shook her head. "No, home to Maryland. America."

"What, immediately?"

"Yes, you get shown the door that afternoon. And if I'm not a student, my visa is revoked, so I'd have to leave, or else."

Mick paled. "Or else?"

"Or else be deported."

"Bloody hell." Mick stared at her, horrified, and then stood abruptly, almost spilling her to the floor. "Can't you go to another school?"

Marie-Claire blinked, trying to adjust to his changing mood. "No, not really. It would take me at least until September to get into another program, even if I wanted to. But there's no other school I'd want to go to."

Mick paced the kitchen in furious concentration, his expression hard. "When is this Critique then?"

"In eleven days."

"And it's all or nothing?"

"Yes."

"Right, then, time to go." He pulled her to her feet briskly. "Come on, lass, get a move on, time to get you back to work."

"What about the photographers outside?"

He ignored her and pulled his mobile out of his pocket and pressed buttons, giving her a smart whack on her bottom to get her moving along. "Darius. It's Mick. Yes, I know it was quite a flap. Help us out."

Chapter Fourteen

HALF AN HOUR later, Mick crammed himself into the backseat of Darius's BMW Roadster. "You could have brought that SUV of yours, mate."

He pulled Marie-Claire down on top of him and Darius spread a tartan rug over them and then got behind the wheel and sped out the gates, keeping a close eye on his rearview mirror. "Okay, they didn't seem too interested."

"How many were there?" Mick asked as they unfolded themselves.

"About five or six that I saw. But let's drive around a little, make sure they don't have friends."

Darius drove a circuitous path around London, crossing the Thames three times before arriving in Putney just after dark.

"Is that your house in the middle of the road?" Darius asked as he drove past the intersection of the cross streets. "I see at least three snappers out front, maybe four."

Mick pointed down the road. "There's an alley around back, take the next left."

Mick's knowledge of her neighborhood surprised Marie-Claire.

Darius parked two blocks away and they made their way down the alley, taking care to keep to the shadows. The garden gate was locked, so Darius boosted Mick over the brick wall first, and then Mick caught Marie-Claire when she scrambled over, followed by Darius.

At the back door, Marie-Claire tapped the glass. "It's MC, let us in."

Neve opened the door. "Are you okay? Those photographers in the street, they didn't see you, did they? And how did they find out where you live?" As the men followed Marie-Claire into the kitchen, she looked Darius up and down with amazement. "And who are you?"

Marie-Claire brushed leaves and dirt from her sweater. "Cup of tea first."

Raul joined them, and introductions were made as Neve set the kettle to boil.

"The paparazzi got tipped off that Marie-Claire and I are dating. They're going to cause a fuss for a bit," Mick said.

"We aren't dating," Marie-Claire corrected.

Mick ignored her. "I want Marie-Claire to move in with me until this blows over, but she wants to stay here."

Neve's lips pressed together as she poured the tea. "This is her home. She should stay here. But it's hell an powdahouse out there."

Darius's lips twitched. "Come again?"

"All hell is breaking loose," Marie-Claire translated.

"You're going to feel like you're living in a fishbowl for a while. You'll have no privacy," Mick said. "It would be better if she was with me."

"We have curtains," Raul pointed out and Mick scowled at him.

Darius clapped his hands together and leaned forward. "Here's the deal, then. They can't photograph you in private places, or even semi-private, like doorsteps. But the street, sidewalks, everywhere else, is open season."

"So, it's just the walk back and forth to school?" Neve asked.

"Yes, but they're notorious for getting physical and starting situations just to get you to react. It could be a rough walk, especially for a tender morsel like you," Darius added with a wink at Neve.

Marie-Claire swore her housemate blushed.

Neve smiled. "I think we can handle this."

<hr />

Darius left first through the back gate to get his car, while Mick hung back in the dark garden with Marie-Claire. The night air had a chill and he pulled her against him, the warmth of his body flooding hers. Their lips found each other's and she realized she could never, ever tire of kissing this man. Yet she had to give him up, and the feeling of infinite sadness was almost unbearable.

"I can't see you again," she whispered, her arms wrapped around him.

"'Course not." He nuzzled her neck while his hands slipped under her sweater to caress the curve of her hip. "You've got to concentrate on your schoolwork."

She pulled his lips back to her own. "That's right."

His undisguised need for her almost crushed her resolve as their tongues tangled and slid, their dance growing deeper and stronger. He pulled her hips against him and she could feel the thrill of his arousal. Her fingers dug into the muscles of his arms, letting him mold her pliable body to his one last time.

His mobile phone chirped twice, stilling them.

"Is that Darius?" she asked.

Keeping one arm around her, he fumbled in his pocket and checked the device. "Yes, he says it's clear."

She kept her arms wrapped around him, wanting to remember everything about him—the warm, woodsy scent of him, the feel of his strong body, the way his arms felt around her. "So, it's goodbye."

He disentangled himself from her and kissed her forehead. "Right, yes, goodbye. Good luck with your work."

And then he walked out the garden gate without a backward glance.

Raul and Marie-Claire were eating breakfast the next morning when Neve came into the kitchen and deposited a stack of tabloids on the table.

"What's up?" Raul asked.

Neve held up the top one with a flourish. "Trouble and plenty of it."

FANTA ON A RANT-A! The tabloid cover screamed in huge letters over an enormous close-up picture of Fanta snarling at the camera. Marie-Claire's stomach lurched.

"Fanta de las Mercedes knows a problem when she sees one!" Raul began to read. *"And our exclusive picture of her boyfriend kissing a lovely lass in Wandsworth has her baring her fangs. 'She better back off! Mick is my man! We are in love and I will fight for him! We've been together now for almost a year and our love is strong,' declared the hot-blooded*

presenter for Willy Nilly. Mick is, of course, Kingsbury Town defender Mick Carr, a well-known Jack-About-Town, and the beauty in question is American student MC Wentworth, who is studying at the Lady Warwick Art School, Putney."

"At least they got your name right," Neve said as Marie-Claire buried her head in her hands.

"But does Fanta know more than she's letting on about this Wandsworth cutie?" Raul continued reading. *"'I might know something, I might not, but all I'll say is that I don't blame a girl for wanting to try a real man on for size, especially if it's not her regular cup of tea. But if she's going to experiment with guys, she should look elsewhere.' Better watch out, MC, Fanta's got her claws out!"*

"Why does she think you're a lesbian?" Raul asked when he had finished reading.

"I have no idea," Marie-Claire answered, miserable. "Where did these all come from?"

"That mob on the street threw them over the gate—the stoop is littered with them," Neve said.

Raul sorted through the stack of tabloids, assessing each article. "Aside from Fanta giving slightly different variations on her moaning, they didn't say much more about you, other than you're at the Lady Warwick and that you're from Maryland."

"Everything I told that woman at the club," Marie-Claire said. "Why is Fanta doing this? I broke it off with Mick."

Neve flipped through the pages, making scathing remarks. "Attention whore. My aunt does the hair of one of the girls on *Willy Nilly* and she said Fanta wants to get on American telly, just like the last presenter. If that's her plan, then she's going to turn this into a right stink. There'll be no stopping her."

Marie-Claire pushed her chair out and stood. "This is ridiculous. I'll just go out there right now and tell them that Mick and I aren't together and that Fanta is welcome to him. That will stop everything."

Both housemates jumped to their feet and blocked her path to the hallway. "You'll do no such thing, Marie-Claire Wentworth," Neve said. "That will only make the situation worse, and it's just what they want."

Marie-Claire dropped back into her chair. "I guess you're right. Do you think she really wants him back?"

Neve snorted. "I think what she wants is lots of publicity."

"Maybe we should oblige her," Raul said, a sly smile playing on his lips.

The loitering photographers jumped to life as the three left the house, Marie-Claire dressed in jeans and her bulky sweater with Neve's wide-brimmed hat jammed down to her brows. It was the most innocuous outfit they could pull together.

Raul held the front gate for the girls to pass through, pausing to stuff the notes that had been wedged in the wrought iron gate stiles into his pocket. "Phone numbers," he said amidst the clamor. "They want you to call them for an exclusive."

Once on the sidewalk, the paparazzi descended on them like a swarm of pushy bees, jostling for shots while screaming questions. How long had Mick been cheating on Fanta with her? Was she going to his match this afternoon against Queens Park Rangers? Were they engaged? Was she pregnant?

Marie-Claire hurried along with her eyes downcast. When they reached the Lady Warwick, they saw the gates had been shut and the lone security guard, who liked to nap in the warmth of the mansion, was waiting anxiously to let them in. The gates slammed closed behind them, but not before a woman sidled up to Raul and thrust an envelope in his hand.

Inside the studio, Raul opened the letter and read the contents.

"What's that say?" Marie-Claire asked.

"It's one of the tabloids, they want to pay you five thousand pounds for your story."

At the next worktable, Stephen Ashe's head snapped up.

"Throw it away, Raul," Marie-Claire said as a student, Margaret, hurried across the room.

"MC, dean wants to see you."

Chapter Fifteen

BY AFTERNOON, THE passel at the school's gate made going out for lunch with the rest of the students impossible. Instead, Marie-Claire stood at the window and watched her classmates entertain themselves by posing for pictures and answering every question about Marie-Claire with the most ridiculous answers they could think of. She envied them the ability to treat the situation as a huge joke.

To add insult to injury, the day was beautiful and she might have gotten quite a bit done if she had been able to go to the reservoir or the river. But they were public spaces and she'd be hounded incessantly, so instead, she was reduced to working from a snapshot of a Mallard in flight.

"That was jolly good fun," Neve said after lunch. "We told them you came to England by stowing away on a cargo ship and that your great-grandfather invented toothpaste. Here, we brought you back a sandwich. Did you talk with the dean?"

"I did," Marie-Claire said, pushing the sandwich aside, her appetite nonexistent. "I told him that I had been seeing Mick but I've broken it off. He let me know he wasn't thrilled that the press was causing such a ruckus and reminded me that the Lady Warwick is a serious academic institution and was not interested in publicity. And that he resented having to come in on a Saturday. "

"Ha," Neve scoffed, "he was the first to run up when Mick came to the student show."

"I know. But I got the warning loud and clear."

"They look bored," Margaret announced later that afternoon as she looked down from the studio window at the crowd milling on the sidewalk below. "They've been standing out there all ruddy day, don't they have anything better to do?"

"They'll be following me home soon," Marie-Claire said, gathering her brushes. "I'm getting nothing done here."

"We should wait until dark," Neve cautioned, "the pictures won't turn out as well."

Yvette, a second-year costume design student, snapped her fingers. "I've got an idea. Sandra's about the same size as MC, let's disguise her and send her out in the opposite direction."

"You mean like a decoy?" Marie-Claire asked.

"Exactly."

The idea was approved and the two girls exchanged outfits. A brunette wig was found to cover Sandra's spiky blue hair, and Marie-Claire had to admit that from a distance, the disguise was convincing. Neve's hat was the finishing touch.

The ruse worked to perfection. Sandra, flanked by Raul, Neve, and a dozen other students who insisted on joining the fun, disappeared down the street surrounded by photographers. Marie-Claire slipped out a side door undetected.

Taking a roundabout way through side streets and narrow lanes, she reached her garden gate undetected. At the back door, a gift bag hung from the doorknob with a wrapped box inside, along with a card with a note written in a strong, slanted hand.

Call me when you get this.

Inside the box was a high-tech mobile phone, which, when powered on, displayed an image of Mick kicking a football. This made her smile, and after a few more buttons were pressed, a directory appeared. His number was the only one programmed in.

He picked up on the first ring. "You got it, good."

"One of your endorsement deals?"

"I wish. Lars has them. I had to fork over good money for this one."

"This isn't the same number you gave Neve at the student show," Marie-Claire observed.

"Ah. No. This is to my private mobile."

"Where does the other number go?"

There was a brief pause. "A party line, so to speak. One that's been disconnected. Try it, you'll see."

"I believe you. But I can't take this—"

"It's for your safety," he advised. "You're to keep it with you always. Those paps can get very rough. Call me anytime and I will come get you."

"One of them offered me five thousand pounds for my story today." She waited while he swore. "How could they possibly offer me so much? Why would anyone care what I have to say?"

"It's chicken feed to them. And I'm sorry about Fanta, the stupid cow just wants the publicity. The best thing to do is just ignore it. How are you coping? Did you get home all right?"

"No problem at all. The second-years dressed Sandra up as me and are leading the photographers on a wild goose chase around Putney."

"She's that girl with the blue hair, right?"

"They found a wig."

"That's brilliant," Mick approved, "but what about that painting you have to finish? This ruckus isn't disturbing you, is it?"

"Everything is going well," Marie-Claire lied. "You had a match today, how did that go?"

"Queens Park Rangers beat us like a drum. They knew we'd be weak at left midfield with Auchincloss out on his suspension. We're just getting ready to leave and the coach will have us back at St Augustine by seven. How about I come by with some supper?"

"Mick, no. If they see you they'll mob the house again."

"They won't see me—"

"Mick, I meant what I said last night. I can't see you. I'm going to work here tonight and can't be disturbed."

Mick made a distinct attempt at negotiation. "You agreed," she reminded him.

There was a long sigh from the other end, but Marie-Claire had the impression it was not of surrender. "Right, good night, then. Sleep well."

Mick drove home from St Augustine, tempted to ignore Marie-Claire's warning and go see her anyway, but Marie-Claire was right, she needed to concentrate on her painting. She was being a very good sport about all the fuss, and it would blow over in a few days anyway, no need to stir the pot. He'd seen to it that Sheila was banished back to Hendon, not that it made any difference now, and there wasn't anything more he could do. He'd just bloody well have to have some patience.

At home, he changed into a t-shirt and shorts and lay on the sofa with his left leg elevated on the pillows and an ice pack on the knee. After a check of the sports channels, he turned off the telly and contemplated her paintings hanging on the wall. The geese, the mated pair, had become his favorite. The drake was the larger, a bit taller than the hen, his neck bent protectively over her. He drifted off to sleep with a smile on his face.

A loud knock at the door jolted him awake. This was unusual; with the security at the gate, unexpected visitors were rare. He opened the door with caution.

"Hello, Mick." Fanta stood on the stoop wearing red high heels and a trench coat belted at her waist, a cunning smile playing on her red-painted lips.

"Fanta. Bit late, isn't it?"

"I tried to call your mobile but you've had it disconnected."

Mick remained unmoved. "How did you get past the guard? I didn't leave word."

"I told him I was going to pay you a surprise visit," she smirked, and slipped past him into the foyer, opening her trench coat to display her thin body clad in a black lace bra, panties, garter, and stockings.

Mick glanced around the neighborhood and slammed his door shut. "Cover up," he barked in disgust.

"Why? You've always liked this before," she said, her voice a low purr.

"Not anymore."

She switched gears to a pout. "Mickey, I miss you."

"Fanta, it wasn't working."

"It was, Mick, it was!" She gripped his arm. "We were in all the papers!"

He snorted in disgust and turned away from her.

"Mick, I need the exposure," Fanta pleaded. "Cashmere Cassidy said she's got something for me in Hollywood. I just need to generate some buzz to get their attention."

"Find someone else. What about Jean-Georges?"

"He's nice and all, but he can't risk it. His divorce isn't final and he has to be really careful. We could just be seen together, that's all I want. You can keep your bit on the side, I won't fuss."

He looked at her with pity. "Get it through your head, Fanta, I don't want you."

Seeing Mick was unmoved, Fanta dropped the coquette facade and went to his bar, splashed an inch of vodka in a glass, and downed the drink in one gulp. "She's that artist, isn't she? The lesbian."

"She's not a lesbian, and you're to leave her alone. She doesn't want the publicity."

"What do you mean, she doesn't want the publicity?" Fanta asked, bewildered.

"I mean, she has a life. A real life, and talent. She doesn't need the attention. She's going to make it on her own by working hard and letting people judge her work for themselves."

Fanta stared at him with no comprehension. "Whatever for?"

"Just drop it, Fanta. I'm not interested, she's not interested. Now get out."

Cinching the coat back around her, she set her jaw and stomped to the door. "You're being stupid, Mick. It could be really easy. Why won't you go along?"

"Because I don't have to. Give it up, Fanta."

"But I need the exposure, Mick."

"Fine, go get it elsewhere. And leave Marie-Claire out of it, or you'll be sorry."

"You're going to regret those words, Mick Carr," she fumed, and then spun on her heel and slammed the door behind her, rattling every window in the house.

———————•◇•———————

"That was a hoot!" Neve crowed when she and Raul arrived home later that evening.

"Sandra was brilliant," Raul agreed. "The paparazzi followed us to all the galleries and shops we thought could use some publicity."

"But we drew the line at the sex shop below Gibson's Tavern, had to keep it classy," Neve added.

"Oh, thank you very much for that," Marie-Claire said.

"Those obnoxious photographers didn't have a clue until Sandra's wig snagged on a doorframe and came off," Raul said. "It's a shame, we could have done that again."

"There's not going to be an 'again.' This will all blow over fast once they realize I'm not seeing Mick."

Neve and Raul traded dubious looks. "'Course it will."

Chapter Sixteen

MICK DROVE BACK from Moorsgate Sunday night, tired and irritated. The cement truck for the footings had gotten bogged down in the lane Friday and created a huge mess, and now he'd have to have gravel brought in as a temporary fill if he wanted any more heavy equipment back there before summer. Dad had pointed this all out in January, of course, and had been correct. Which rankled him more.

Then there was Fanta, who was keeping up the media blitz with another tabloid cover. **KEEP AWAY FROM MY MAN!** featured more pictures of her and Mick at premieres and parties and a rehashing of her supposed love for him. The *Daily Mail* recounted in gleeful detail Mick's history of feminine conquests, scattered with pictures of tawdry-looking women he didn't even remember. There was Delia, of course, but she'd been hanging around forever, and some of her chums. They had been plentiful and interchangeable and he wished he had never set eyes on any of them.

Had Marie-Claire seen the papers? He checked his mobile again—nothing. He'd texted her twice already today but had gotten no reply. Traffic inched along and he drummed his fingers in increasing irritation. Marie-Claire wouldn't pay that crap any mind, she was a smart girl and would know she was worth a hundred of those tarts. But for Christ's sake, how many more pictures were they going to unearth?

It was eight o'clock by the time he arrived in Putney and parked some blocks away from Marie-Claire's house. Still dressed in his country clothes, he pulled down the crown of his wool cap and hunched up his jacket collar, and set off at an easy pace designed to not attract attention. Luck was with him. Not only was it raining, but a dense fog provided excellent cover as he crisscrossed the roads, ducked down her alley, and hopped over the back wall.

The bottom floor of her house was dark but there was a light on upstairs. He'd just have to risk that it was her bedroom. He tossed a small stone against the window, but there was no response. A larger one hit harder, but still—nothing. In frustration, he flicked the next one with a bit more effort and cringed when it ricocheted off the glass.

The window flew up and Marie-Claire leaned out, peering into the gloom. The light from the room behind her revealed she was wrapped in a towel, her damp hair hanging around her shoulders in a glorious, tangled mess.

"Marie-Claire!" he half yelled, half whispered, to the entrancing figure above him.

"Mick? What are you doing?"

"I did text," Mick replied in hushed tones, "and I didn't think you'd want me coming to the front door."

"Your car isn't around here, is it?"

"No, I parked blocks away."

"Wait a moment."

The window slammed shut and a moment later she appeared at the back door, wrapped in that thin, pink dressing gown she'd worn the first day he'd come to her house. She ran into his arms and he clasped her against him.

"You're lucky Neve isn't here, she keeps a cricket bat in her closet," she murmured against his chest.

"Another reason I can't stand cricket," he said, his eyes casting over her. "How are you?"

"Fine. I just got out of the bath."

He scrutinized her a bit closer, noticing a faint darkness under her eyes. "It's not been too rough on you, has it? How is getting back and forth to school?"

"It's going better. Raul and Margaret have been calling in tips to the tabloids that they've seen me in other parts of the city and about half the paparazzi leave to chase them down."

Mick nodded approval. "And your painting, that's going okay?"

"I've been very busy."

Over her shoulder, Mick caught a glimpse of a stack of tabloids on the kitchen table. "You're not reading that trash, are you?"

He felt her stiffen in his embrace. "They toss copies over the gate."

"It's all a load of rubbish, what they're printing. I told you I have a bit of a past, but that's what it is, past."

She wouldn't look him in the eye. "It's none of my business."

"It is."

"Mick, we're not together."

"'Course we're not," he murmured, dropping his nose to nuzzle her ear, inhaling her wonderful scent, the warmth of her skin radiating through the thin wrapper. "If we were together, I wouldn't be able to stop thinking about you."

She made a sound like a quiet gasp, and the effect on him was electric. His mouth found hers hungrily, and he tried to control himself, honest he did, but Jesus, the way she moved, fitting herself against him, she was enough to drive a man insane.

"I broke it off with you," she insisted, her hands running unchecked over the expanse of his muscles.

How could any woman be so soft? He reveled in the pleasurable feel of her supple body, letting his lips explore lower. "You're giving it a jolly good try, I'll give you full marks for that."

His hand cupped a full breast and felt the crest tighten through the thin fabric. It responded to the brush of his thumb over the tip, setting every nerve in his body alight. The pleasure he could give her was unbounded. All he needed was a chance.

A garage door opened across the alley and bright lights illuminated the gloom. "You should go," she said, pushing him away. "If someone sees you here it will be mayhem."

"Are you sure you don't need anything? I could comb your hair, tuck you in..." he offered, refusing to let her go.

"Please." The desperate look in her eyes nearly unmanned him. "Goodbye, Mick."

Ah, hell. With a tremendous act of willpower and against his better judgment, he released her. "Good night, then."

"Don't come again."

"I won't," he assured her.

The next night he brought pizza.

"How did you get over the garden wall with a pizza?" Marie-Claire asked in astonishment when she opened the back door.

"Wasn't the easiest thing in the world," Mick admitted, handing her the box and giving her a hearty kiss. This time she was dressed in her jeans and a t-shirt, her hair tamed back into the usual ponytail. "How are you? The *Observer* said there had been a problem at the studio, that something got spilled all over your work."

Marie-Claire nodded as she set out plates and napkins on the table. "I'm not sure how it happened. There were workmen replacing a broken windowpane in the skylight and somehow rainwater spilled on my worktable. We were in class at the time and no one saw what happened."

"Did you lose much stuff?"

"Not really." In fact, the painting she had done of Mick at Hempland had been destroyed along with two other promising pieces. "I was more surprised that the tabloids found out."

"It was bound to happen. They offer a lot of money for tips."

"I know," she sighed, "but the fact that they found out means someone from inside the Lady Warwick is telling them. I'm disappointed."

"Come on, you'll feel better after you eat something."

They were just finishing the pizza when a commotion from the street announced Neve was home. "What rot!" she complained from the front hall. "Those note papers are cluttering the front garden terribly, I must have picked up a dozen. And the neighbors are peeved. Mr. Hughes from number sixty-three just gave me an earful about them blowing into his rose bushes. Oh, hello, Mick. Good to see you. Glad you're here, you can see the pictures."

"What pictures?" Marie-Claire asked.

"You at Royal Ascot races, for starters." Neve grinned and opened her kit bag. She laid before them a large photograph of the Queen talking with a dapper man in a crowd of well-dressed people.

They looked at it closely and then at Neve.

"See, there you are, in the yellow dress right behind the Queen. Pretty good, huh?"

A closer examination showed that the photograph had been digitally altered to put Marie-Claire's head on another girl's body. Mick whistled between his teeth. "Well, I'll be blowed. Who did this?"

"Us second-year photography students. It was jolly good fun," Neve said, and laid out more pictures. "Here you are outside Number 10 Downing Street when the new cabinet ministers were announced, and at the White House, and at last year's French Open."

All the pictures had indeed been skillfully edited to include Marie-Claire somewhere in the crowd. "What's the picture with all the military?" Mick asked.

"That was at the Royal Naval exercises in Portsmouth last week."

Marie-Claire studied it. "Which one am I?"

"There, piloting the helicopter."

"Neve!"

"Okay, maybe we did go a bit overboard on that one," she conceded with an unabashed grin.

"What are you going to do with them?" Mick asked.

"We're passing them to some of the tabloids, see if they do their homework."

"That's dishonest," Marie-Claire scolded.

"Don't spoil the fun. We're not taking any money for them."

"You need to be careful," Mick warned. "Fanta doesn't have a sense of humor."

"Well, someone has to teach that nasty witch a lesson. Besides, it's art."

———————◦———————

Marie-Claire waited at home the next night, torn between wanting to see Mick and knowing that the risk of him being seen far outweighed her desires. The half-dozen or so photographers that had set up residence in the street were bad enough. If they even got a whiff that she and Mick were together, the situation would be mayhem.

The day's tabloids were scattered on the kitchen table. They contained the doctored pictures Neve and her classmates had created, which indeed looked realistic. The one of Royal Ascot made the cover of the *Mirror*, which gave everyone immense satisfaction. Marie-Claire had enjoyed the ruse, as well, until the story inside revealed more pictures of Mick's other girlfriends.

"You need to put these away and get to work," Neve admonished, folding the papers up and tossing them in the rubbish. "We'll take care of this. You keep painting pictures of the pretty birdies."

The mobile phone trilled and Marie-Claire fumbled to answer it.

"Someone must have seen me, they have your alley staked out now," Mick said.

"It's okay. We shouldn't be seeing each other anyway."

"Dammit, Marie-Claire, I want to see you. Can I go to your school? Is there a back way in?"

"No!" Her eyes widened in horror. "We can't do that. The dean isn't very happy with me. He's had to lay on extra security, and the staff is getting annoyed."

"My car is just around the corner. Pack a bag and sneak out," he urged.

There it was. An easy solution and probably a smart one. She'd be safe, and everyone could go back to living in peace. Moving in with Mick would be no hardship, but the attention wouldn't go away. In fact, the hysteria would double when Fanta found out and used the information to create more frenzy. Mick would no doubt move heaven and earth to help her get to school, but the chaos would be too distracting for her to create the final piece she needed for the Critique. And then she'd have to leave.

She'd be damned if she went out that way.

She could live with failure as long as the failure was her own. If the professors at the Lady Warwick evaluated her work and decided she didn't have what they were looking for, so be it. They were professional artists in their own right and their critical evaluation was what she'd signed up for.

But Marie-Claire wasn't about to let a publicity-hungry ex-girlfriend and a few people with cameras—all right, perhaps the entire British tabloid industry—dictate her future. There were just nine days until the Critique, and she could be tough. And if she was lucky, perhaps something else would divert the attention of the people camped outside her door, as Mick had predicted.

It was time to live in the moment and focus on creating her last piece. She might go down in miserable flames, but not because she didn't try her hardest.

"I'm sorry," she whispered, and hung up.

Chapter Seventeen

FANTA SUICIDE WATCH!

Friday's *Observer* had been left in clear sight on the bench by Mick's locker at St Augustine. Mick balled it up in his fist with a scorching oath, and threw the tabloid in the rubbish bin. Suicide, his ass.

The locker room was deserted, the other players either still in the gym or out on the track, running laps. Mick wrapped an ice pack on his bad knee and swallowed two aspirin, and then flopped on the bench and elevated his leg on a nearby side chair.

He hadn't seen Marie-Claire in four days—since Monday evening, to be exact. He'd driven over every night since, but the paparazzi had stationed kids as sentinels as far as four blocks away who were on the lookout for the Range Rover as well as the Aston Martin. Wednesday night, he had even borrowed Darius's SUV, but that had stood out just as much in her run-down neighborhood.

He checked his mobile again but knew there would be no message. She'd turned hers off, which was the right thing to do, of course, since she had to concentrate on her work. And there was nothing for him to do except leave her to it and have faith that she'd be able to paint whatever the hell it was they wanted to see.

Still, he ached for just one message. Instead, the mobile just sat in his hand, mute and blinking, and he fought the urge to throw the damn thing through the grimy window.

"I see you're keeping the paps busy, lad, they're five deep out there," Brian the goalkeeper said, ambling into the locker room. "They even snapped a few pictures of me this morning. That'll make the grannies happy."

Mick winced. "Wish they were still making Auchincloss's life hell instead of mine."

"No chance of that. He's on cloud nine now that he and Julie are together," Brian said, grinning. "I swear he's a new man. Have you met her? She's a love."

"Too nice for the likes of him." Mick grudgingly agreed with Brian, though—the left wing had gone through a miraculous transformation.

"Your new girl is giving Fanta quite a run for her money," Brian continued, stripping off his thick gloves. "Bloody brilliant what her friends are doing. Connie's been following it and says they're making Fanta look a right chump."

Mick nodded but was uneasy. Brian was right, the students were doing a straight-up job of making Fanta and the tabloids look like fools. The high-quality doctored pictures of Marie-Claire had run for two consecutive days before they were exposed as fakes by the students themselves, who declared they had pulled off the ruse in the name of art. Then they had switched to dressing up as Fanta and posting embarrassing candid pictures on social networking sites. Yesterday's was a blurry image taken outside a prominent plastic surgeon's office.

It was all very funny, and as Brian said, everyone was getting a good laugh out of it, but he was worried. Fanta was being made to look a fool and he knew she wouldn't take that well. They were making the paparazzi look like idiots, as well, and he knew from experience they could get very rough.

"Marie-Claire's not at all used to any of this," Mick said. "And she has an important examination next week, could decide if she stays or has to go. This all couldn't have come at a worse time."

"What, she has to do her schoolwork with that lot breathing down her neck?" Brian asked.

"They've got her staked out. I want her to move in with me but she won't, she wants to stay near her school."

Brian raised his eyebrows. "I thought you liked your space."

"I'm just trying to be sensible."

Brian nodded. "So, she's a sitting duck. Poor thing. Say, what are you doing on our day off tomorrow? If you want to go to the Cup, Grimsby sent me two tickets just to make sure there were no hard feelings."

"Sporting of him," Mick said sarcastically, remembering how the Liverpool striker had feigned an injury to get around Darius, and then tapped the ball into the net while Brian was in the other corner. It had been the winning goal, knocking Kingsbury Town out of the FA Cup race. "But no thanks. You're not going to use them?"

"I told Connie I'd take the boys up to Tinsbury for her granddad's birthday. Annual trip. She said she could manage, but I worry about her tiring with the next one due soon." Brian and Connie had been childhood sweethearts, had married right out of school and were very much in love. They had two small boys and another baby on the way.

"When is she due?"

"Still another two months, but you'd never know the way she just soldiers on. She's an amazing girl. God help me if I had been stuck with one of that lot," Brian jerked his head toward the collection of seductive fan photographs Fernando kept pinned to his locker wall.

Mick, who had taken his own collection down and tossed them in the rubbish the week before, silently concurred.

———————•◦○◦•———————

"It seems like they're double the number today," Marie-Claire complained as they squeezed through the school gates Saturday morning, the rude photographers pushing at them. "Fanta's not really threatening to commit suicide, is she?"

"'Course not. How could she, when there're pictures of her all over the internet purchasing toilet paper and diet pills at the chemist's yesterday afternoon?" Neve asked innocently.

Once in the studio, Marie-Claire sank onto her stool and surveyed her worktable. An assortment of bird photographs was taped to the wall and botched paintings lay in uncharacteristic disorder across her table, some half-finished, some barely started.

Nothing was working. Paper that could be counted on to hold a glaze instead just soaked up water, ridges were forming on stretched paper, expensive pigments were drying too light and leaving gritty sediment.

She was pushing herself to exhaustion, and her body ached from spending hours hunched over her work. Days and nights blurred, and what little sleep she got was punctuated by nebulous nightmares. Mick would text several times a day, and she would read them and then steel herself not to respond.

She had to remain focused on the work at hand. There were only seven days left until the Critique, and any distraction would be fatal. Mick didn't seem to mind and continued sending encouraging messages, convinced that a miracle would occur and she would paint a masterpiece that would allow her to stay. Somehow, that made everything worse.

A nauseating wave of panic rose in her throat and she squeezed her eyes shut, her breathing coming in hard gasps. From behind, Neve put a compassionate hand on her shoulder.

"Take some deep breaths. There, that's good, and another, and another. Sandra, love, how about a cup of tea over here?"

Sandra returned with a cup and Marie-Claire drank while Neve produced a box of tissues. "Blow your nose," she ordered, and then lined up the work in progress on her worktable. "Let's have a look at what you've got."

Together, the three of them surveyed the paintings before them. "Tell me the rest of your portfolio doesn't look like this," Sandra said.

"No, I've had the rest finished and ready for ages."

"Your theme is strong," Neve said. "Maybe you can get by without it."

"I can't risk it. How do you do it, Sandra?"

"Well, I jolly well don't have my man's ex-girlfriend throwing a fit and half the British tabloid press camped out on my doorstep. And I'm pulling my hair out trying to do 'a proper finished work with a series of studies that displays mastery of rhythm and composition' like you."

"Maybe you should do each other's," Stephen Ashe suggested from his worktable.

They ignored Stephen's remark. "You need a break. Come with us to the Muybridge museum in Kingston today," Neve suggested. "They've got a mini-coach taking us down. There will be room."

"Everyone is going," Sandra concurred.

Marie-Claire rubbed her aching temples. "What I need is to be outside and around the birds. These photographs are impossible to work with. There should be at least three hours of sunlight today and if I can get to the London Wetlands, I might get lucky."

"But how will you get there?" Sandra asked.

Neve smiled. "I've got an idea."

———————◦◦◦———————

The small bus glided to a halt at the London Wetlands entrance and Marie-Claire jumped out and waved goodbye to her friends. She dashed through the gates and found the place almost deserted, with only a few hearty souls walking the grounds on the blustery day. Dark clouds stacked on the horizon, but the abundant waterfowl were active in the open water.

There were, by her estimation, at least two hours before the forecasted rain would arrive, plenty of time to get a good study started. Circling the lagoon scouting for an interesting subject, she spotted a Tufted Duck drake patrolling the shoreline and found a low spot to observe him from. There was every chance he'd stay in the area and be joined by more friends.

Sitting on the ground, she pulled her painting field kit from her bag and removed a block of watercolor paper from its protective canvas wrapping. The expensive block was large and unwieldy, and in fact, she had never taken one into the field before. However, since her professors were looking for a finished painting done on the spot, she had no choice. It was either the block or paper already stretched on a heavy board.

A thin wash of Cerulean Blue sky dried well and she continued to paint in the background. The drake swam off to investigate a clump of submerged weeds, so she sat and waited for another subject to appear, her mind wandering, as usual, to Mick. He'd like the Wetlands.

A wild splashing made her jump and she spun around to see a Cormorant struggling with a large eel in the middle of the marsh. The two thrashed for almost a minute until the sleek, black water duck pointed his bill to the sky and swallowed the eel whole, bobbing his head in satisfaction when he was done. He swam to the shore and perched on a low log, spreading his glossy wings to dry.

Marie-Claire knew he could stay in that pose for a while, long enough for her to capture his elegant poise. Saints be praised, he was facing the sun, and if she moved down the path just a bit, she'd have an unobstructed view of him. She was scrambling to her feet and collecting her paper and paints when a sharp glint of light across the lagoon stopped her.

Two men hurried along the path, each holding a camera with a long lens. They were dressed in the same garish jackets and baseball caps favored by the paparazzi camped outside the house, and Marie-Claire knew right away they were hunting her. At a turn in the path, they stopped and focused their cameras across the marsh, the sun reflecting off the lenses again.

There was no time to think. They'd be upon her in a minute if she didn't do something. The loop they were on had several splits, and if she was very fast, she could elude them long enough to get back to the entrance gate and flee to the road.

That hope was dashed when the men split up, one taking a path to the right and the other to the left, trapping her between them. There was no cover anywhere nearby except a tall stand of reeds at the end of a wooden bridge that might hide her for a few seconds. She ran to it, peering through the stalks as the men worked their way toward her.

A Tufted Duck hen cackled from its nest under the wooden bridge, a long span that lay about two feet above the water. The bridge was wide enough for a car to drive over and might conceal her. The water was frigid but there was no choice.

Stuffing the block of paper in the protective canvas bag, she then wrapped the straps of her kit bag around it and without hesitating, stepped into the marsh. She gasped as the icy water rushed into her boots, and with slow steps she waded deeper until the water reached above her knees and then to her waist. Gritting her teeth against the numbing cold, she hoisted the kit bag on her head and ducked under the bridge. She was hidden.

Crouching under the supports, Marie-Claire reminded herself that she and Chase had done this hundreds of times at home, and luckily the marsh bottom wasn't covered in sticky mud. She could feel submerged roots and debris ready to tangle her feet and wished for the pleasant sand she was used to in the Chesapeake Bay. At the opposite end of the bridge, the Tufted Drake hen stood in ruffled warning over her nest, and then relaxed when Marie-Claire moved to a shadowed spot. The hen clucked reprovingly several times before tucking herself back over her eggs, keeping a beady eye on her.

Seconds later, heavy footfalls thundered across the slats overhead. They passed and then returned, and she heard a man breathing hard. Marie-Claire cursed the fact she couldn't see anything from under the bridge except the far reaches of the swamp in front and behind her.

Minutes passed, and the other man arrived from the opposite direction, also out of breath. They met up directly above her.

"Bloody 'ell, that text said she was here," one cursed in a cockney accent so thick, Marie-Claire could barely make out his words.

"She's here. And if she's around, he's around. He's never too far from her."

There was the crinkle of cellophane and the strike of a match, and an empty cigarette box landed in the water inches from her. Keeping one hand on the bag on her head, she reached out and snatched the trash as it floated past her.

"D'ya think she slipped out?"

"Dunno, but that tipster's been right every other time, costing me a bloody fortune. Let's give it a minute."

"Where's Carr? He at the FA Cup?"

"Naw, they none of 'em go after they've been knocked out."

"What's Auchincloss doin'? Maybe we could get some snaps of him."

One man spat over the bridge in disgust, luckily in the other direction. "They're at some pub in Finchley, bold as brass. He's as happy as a clam and doesn't care who sees them, pictures are worthless now. There hasn't been a snap of these two together in a week, first one will be worth a mint."

The other man sighed. "I don't get why we're tailing her. Carr'll tire of her in a month. He always does."

"Not this one. There's something different about her."

"Well, I'll give you that. The rest of 'em knew the working end of a hairbrush."

Marie-Claire glared up through the slats.

"But what I don't get is," he continued, "she's smart and Carr is as thick as a brick. What's she see in 'im?"

The other man laughed lewdly. "She doesn't get a stud like him in her bed every day. That night I got that first picture, in Wandsworth, she was all over him. Thought she was like to tear 'is clothes off."

A flush of Mallards chose that moment to land nearby with a loud splash, covering Marie-Claire's indignant gasp.

The two men stood on the bridge smoking leisurely until large raindrops began to speckle the cold water in thick plops. "Oh, that's just lovely, in'nt it, more rain. Come on, there's one of those gazebos we can watch the front gate from."

She waited several minutes until she was sure they had left, and then, shielded by the tall grass, sloshed out of the water to the shore and put the bag down, shaking out her aching arms.

Mick's mobile phone was in her kit bag and she fumbled for it, her fingers numb. He'd said it was for emergencies, and if this wasn't one she didn't know what was. He answered on the first ring.

"It's MC," she said, struggling to keep her teeth from chattering.

"Where are you?" Mick snapped.

At the sound of his voice, relief flooded through her. "I'm at the London Wetlands. I, I…" She struggled to get some control of herself. Falling to pieces now wouldn't do her any good. "I was trying to paint when a pair of paparazzi came in."

"Are you all right?" Mick demanded.

"I'm okay. I'm hiding."

"I'm in the car now, I will come get you. Stay put."

"No. They'll see you. There's a line of houses to the west, big ones, and I'm going to try and make for them."

"How will you do that? Is there a path?"

"I'm going to take a shortcut."

"What, across the bloody marsh?" he shouted. "You're daft! The water must be freezing, and—"

She cut him off. "Mick, just meet me there."

Chapter Eighteen

HOISTING HER BAG back on her head, Marie-Claire gritted her teeth and stepped back into the knee-deep murky water, her shoes filling with a sickening squelch. By now, the dark storm clouds had joined together, producing a raw drizzle driven by a cold wind.

Glancing back, she saw the men in the gazebo hunched over the railing, still smoking and talking. From their lookout, they could see across the wetlands, but the reeds were tall enough to conceal her. Her clothing should blend in, and with luck the dull light would be all the camouflage she would need to escape.

She moved at a slow pace, any sudden movements could tangle her feet and send her stumbling into the freezing water. As she followed the edge of the protective marsh grass, she peered through the dense clumps and saw her luck was holding. They were focusing on the entrance and paths and keeping their backs to the water.

The drizzle turned into a miserable, steady rain. The kit bag and paper block on her head offered scant protection, and the drops ran down the inside of the sweater sleeves as she struggled to keep the load balanced on her head. The thick leather bag would protect her painting supplies, but the canvas wrapping around the expensive paper wouldn't keep the rain out forever. She pushed faster through the now thigh-deep water, groping for invisible footholds while trying to avoid underwater thickets. A nest of Common Terns lay hidden until she was almost upon them, and once flushed, they flew away with loud squawks. She froze and glanced back to the distant bank to see if they had drawn the attention of the men there.

But the men had disappeared.

Craning her neck, she scanned the shoreline, her teeth chattering uncontrollably. The park looked deserted but she couldn't take that chance and instead plunged on, pushing herself to move faster. Her legs began to move like they were made of frozen lead, and she stumbled once, putting her free hand out to break her fall and soaking her chest and arm in the process.

Gradually, the far shore grew nearer and she could see the backyards of the large houses, their lights glowing warmly in the gloom. Mick appeared, sprinting through a well-manicured lawn until he reached the water's edge. At the sight of him, her strength failed and she ground to a halt, her tears mixing with the rainwater.

He saw her and plunged in, splashing towards her.

"Marie-Claire, I'm coming," he called, and then he was there, snatching her against him, peppering her face with hot kisses.

"My bag," she said, her voice a croak, and he snatched the sodden load off her head. Her arms fell to her side, numb.

He bent to lift her into his arms but she struggled. "No, the b-bottom is too—too unstable," she protested, so he wrapped an arm around her waist and half-carried, half-dragged her to the shore. Once they were on firm footing, he carried her to the road where the Aston Martin was parked.

"I can't get in your c-car, I'm s-soaked."

"Bugger the car, get in!" he ordered. Once inside, Mick turned the dashboard controls until blasts of hot air poured from the vents and held Marie-Claire's numb hands over them, making her flex them until the feeling began to return in painful pinpricks. Then he stripped off her drenched sweater, the water pooling on the floor at her feet.

He managed to get her boots off, as well, and then drove out of the neighborhood, fast. "Tell me what happened," he demanded, checking the rearview mirror.

"Everyone was going to Kingston today, so they snuck me out in the mini-coach and dropped me off at the Wetlands." She paused to wipe her running nose on a handkerchief Mick produced. "I was painting, and those photographers came in and started looking for me. There was no way I could get past them, so I hid under a bridge."

"What happened then?"

"When the rain started they went to the gazebo and, and," she paused to sneeze, "and then I called you and struck out across the marshes."

"Do you think they saw you at all?"

She shook her head, water droplets falling around her. "No. And when I was very far away, I looked back and they had gone. But, Mick, when I was under the bridge I could hear them talking. They said they had gotten a text saying I was there."

His expression darkened. "Did someone see you there? Recognize you?"

She shook her head. "No, there was almost no one there. I don't know who would have told them."

"Someone tipped them off," Mick said, weaving through the traffic.

"But who?"

"Someone on that mini-coach from your school."

"No," Marie-Claire denied, "they're all my friends. They would never do that."

Mick's lips pressed together. "I wouldn't be too sure, the paps are offering lots of money."

Soon they were back in Fulham and turning down the street to Mick's enclave. Before they reached the gates, Marie-Claire ducked down to hide but Mick stopped her. "No, wait, there's no one out here."

The guard confirmed that the paparazzi had been there but vanished an hour ago.

"Do you think Fanta called them off?"

"Not likely. Something else must have happened."

Once inside his garage, he carried her straight up the stairs to the second floor and through his bedroom to an enormous bathroom. Depositing her on a teak bench, he went to the glassed shower stall and began turning nobs and levers until water seemed to spring from a dozen places in the tiled wall. The chamber filled with steam while he pulled her to her feet and began stripping her naked, the sodden clothing making puddles on the floor.

"Mick, wait." She tried to still his efficient hands but was interrupted by another sneezing fit.

"Do you think I'm going to molest you after what you've just been through?" he demanded, holding a clump of tissues to her nose. "Blow. Now in you go."

When he opened the shower door, a blessed rush of steam poured out, and delicious hot water sluiced from every direction. She stepped in and felt her skin buffeted with warmth.

"Soap's over there," he said, "and the main temperature control is here, see?"

She nodded, tired and awed by the luxury.

"You're sure you don't need a hand?" Mick asked, reluctant to leave. "I could wash your hair, scrub your back, make sure you don't drown…"

A fit of giggles convulsed her. "Drown in a shower?"

"It's the number one cause of accidental deaths in this area of Fulham," he quoted knowledgeably, reaching out to fondle a lock of her wet hair. "I'm just thinking of your safety."

"I'm all right, thanks."

The endless supply of hot water was an unheard-of luxury. Marie-Claire relished it, washing her hair with a small bottle of hotel shampoo Mick had dug out of his travel kit. As the cold and damp ebbed, her limbs began to feel like they weighed a hundred pounds each.

Her eyes grew heavy, and as she leaned against the tiled wall, she closed them for a moment until a brisk tap on the shower door woke her.

"Figured you were falling asleep in here." He reached in to turn the water off and engulfed her in the soft folds of his thick bathrobe. Sitting on the bench, he pulled her onto his lap and dried her hair with another thick towel.

"I'm so tired," she yawned, patient under his careful ministrations, "but I have to call Neve and tell her I'm okay."

"Taken care of, I sent Darius over to tell her," he said, drying each lock of hair.

"Tell him I'm sorry for the fuss," she murmured, resting her head on his broad shoulder.

"He didn't seem fussed at all. When was the last time you ate?"

That question took a bit of thought. "Thursday."

Her answer was met with a frown.

"I couldn't go out with everyone, there was too much attention," she explained, "but Sandra's mother sent over a cake for her birthday, and I had a slice of that."

Marie-Claire put a finger to his lips to silence the string of curses that exploded from them. "It wasn't a problem, I really haven't had any appetite."

Mick wasn't going to be put off. "Get much sleep?"

"Some." She avoided those perceptive blue eyes and tried to change the subject. "Neve said you didn't have a match today because there was an FA Cup semi-final. Who won?"

"I have no idea."

He picked her up and carried her into his bedroom, which was dominated by an enormous bed. Thick pillows were stacked beneath a tufted-leather headboard, and a down-filled duvet seemed to float like a cloud over the top.

Mick found a t-shirt emblazoned with the Kingsbury Town Football Club crest in a drawer and pulled it over her head, then drew back the sheets and tucked her beneath the covers. He kissed her forehead, and the last thing she heard before she fell asleep was him barking orders on his mobile in the hallway outside the door.

Chapter Nineteen

IT SEEMED LIKE only moments later Mick was nudging her awake. Groggy, she opened her eyes and saw a loaded tray on the bedside table with tantalizing aromas rising from it.

"Wake up, love, time for dinner," Mick announced.

Propping pillows behind her against the padded headboard, he helped her sit up and slipped a satin cord around her neck. She smiled, fingering the small silver nest. "My bird's nest."

"Right where it belongs," he nodded, plumping more pillows behind her.

She leaned over to glance at the tray. "That looks wonderful."

"It is wonderful, and you may have some in a moment. But first—" he produced a thermometer from his pocket "—open up."

"But I'm not sick—"

Mick ignored her protest and stuck the plastic stick in her mouth.

"You stood in freezing cold water for God knows how long, you'll be lucky not to catch your death of pneumonia," he chastised, crossing his arms over his chest while she glared at him.

A minute later the digital beeper chimed. "Spot on," he announced with satisfaction.

"See?"

"What I see is a girl who's on bed rest for the next twenty-four hours," he said as he lifted the huge tray onto her lap.

It was filled with a steaming plate of beef bourguignon, a basket of rolls with a dish of creamy butter, and a glass of water. Marie-Claire's stomach growled as he tucked a napkin on her lap. "You didn't have to do this, I could have gotten something. I just needed a nap."

"Yes, I know, you've got it all under control," he agreed as he held a forkful of tender beef to her lips.

It tasted like the best thing she had ever eaten in her life and her appetite roared back with a vengeance. "Do I have to share?" she asked.

He buttered a flaky roll for her. "No, I've had mine. Have some of the mash and green beans, they're excellent."

Indeed, they were. "Where did all this food come from?" she asked between mouthfuls.

"I convinced the restaurant down the street, Le Cheval Rouge, to deliver."

"*Le cheval rouge*, the red horse."

Mick blotted a dot of sauce from her lip with the crisp linen napkin. "You speak French?"

"Fluently. My mother's mother was French. She married my grandfather in France during the war and moved to America with him. I'm named after her."

"Did you know her?"

"Oh yes, they lived right down the road from us. We had to speak French with her at all times, and I usually speak it with my mother."

When the plates were empty, Mick produced a bowl of shiny red strawberries. "*Fraise* is the one word of French I know. I heard you tell Sue you liked strawberries, so I had them send these."

"They are my favorite," Marie-Claire said, biting into a sweet berry. "They remind me of home. On one of our farms, there's a big strawberry patch near the road, and they should be ripening in early June."

Mick selected a berry for himself. "How many farms does your family have?"

"There are six all together, spread around Kent County. There were eight, but my grandmother sold two and left the proceeds as an inheritance for Chase and me."

"That's the money you used to come here?"

"Yes."

It didn't take long until she felt full, and then she had never felt so tired in her life.

"Sleep now," he said, taking the tray from her lap and kissing her forehead.

She was asleep before he got to the door.

<hr>

The ship rose before her in the dark, a foreboding behemoth surrounded by black, oily water. Fog swirled around her feet, and everything was cold, so cold. Marie-Claire struggled against the invisible hands that were pushing her towards it, trying to explain that she didn't want to get on the ship, she didn't want to leave.

"Marie-Claire! Marie-Claire!" photographers called as their cameras flashed. The hands kept pushing while she fought against them.

At the base of the gangplank stood Fanta dressed in a long, sequined gown, her bony arm extended in a macabre gesture towards the waiting ship. She grinned hideously.

"I don't want to leave, don't make me leave," Marie-Claire implored but the hands gripped her arms more tightly, shaking her.

"Marie-Claire," Mick's voice urged, "wake up, love. Come on, wake up."

Her eyes flew open, and she sat bolt upright, her heart pounding. A single lamp illuminated the bedroom and she saw she wasn't on a dock—she was in Mick's bedroom and she was safe. She slumped against him in infinite relief.

Sitting on the bed next to her, he pulled her into his lap and held her, his strong arms cradling her against him.

"I don't want to go home, I don't want to leave," she sobbed.

"It's just a dream," he crooned, stroking her hair. "You were having a bad dream."

"There was a ship and they kept pushing me to get on it. It was going to sail."

"You're not going anywhere, love," he murmured against her hair.

She could hear Mick's heart beating beneath her ear, solid and reassuring, and the tremors slowed. He must have been asleep and heard her cry out, she realized, since he was dressed only in a pair of shorts. His chest beneath her cheek was bare, and his skin was warm and pungent with his male scent.

"I kept telling them I didn't want to get on but they kept pushing," she croaked.

"They'll have to go through me first. Have you been having this dream a lot lately?"

She nodded, miserable. "Every time I go to sleep, the same dream. It's awful."

"It's the stress," he announced, pulling the covers back to her hips. "Let's have a look at you."

Rolling her onto her stomach, he pushed the t-shirt up until the full expanse of her back was revealed. Kneeling over her, he began to massage the muscles, his calloused hands cupping and drawing the skin in long, patient strokes.

Pain shot through almost every place he pressed. "That hurts," she panted as he explored the tense spots at the base of her neck.

"I'm not surprised. Good Lord, you're one huge knot. Feel that?" She answered with a sharp yelp. "That's your trapezius muscles. They make your shoulders move. You've been sitting hunched over, I can tell."

Marie-Claire nodded into the pillow, gritting her teeth as he continued to prod. "The oil painters get to stand, but we have to work at tables."

Sweeping her hair to the side, he started at the base of her neck and probed his way across her back, ignoring her sharp intakes of breath as he pressed and stroked. At some points, his fingers felt like they were trying to dig straight to her bones, making her body spasm uncontrollably.

He moved to straddle her buttocks to give himself better leverage, encasing her between his muscular legs. Then, using his weight, he pressed down on her spine before moving to flex her arms in painful positions.

"You're pretty good at this," she panted, her muscles screaming.

"We have a masseuse at the club, Rufus, and I get a rubdown at least once a week," Mick told her as he worked down her spine. "Bastard has fists like Dorset hams, but he's a genius."

Marie-Claire giggled, then almost cried out when he hit a knot in her lower back, her hands clasping fistfuls of sheet.

Mick worked with single-minded determination, and by small measures, her muscles began to relax. Soon, she was whimpering with unabashed pleasure as his hands roamed over her skin in broad sweeps, the skin now pliant under his fingers.

"Oh yes, right there," she writhed, arching her back in pleasure, her bottom wriggling between his muscular thighs.

"That's better, isn't it?" Mick asked, his voice rough.

"It's wonderful," she moaned into the downy pillow. Better than wonderful. The sensation of his rough hands on her skin, so powerful yet so tender, was devastating. He paused when he reached the satiny line of her panty, if only he would—

With an abrupt movement, he tugged her t-shirt back down in place and pulled the duvet over her. "That should do the trick."

Why was he stopping? Reluctantly, she rolled over. "Thank you, that was amazing."

"Not a problem. Now it's time for to you to get your sleep," he replied, reaching to turn off the bedside lamp.

"No, don't turn the light off."

"Are you afraid the nightmares will come back?"

She bit her lip and nodded, embarrassed.

He seemed to be holding his breath. "Do you want me to stay with you?"

She nodded again, and reluctantly he climbed onto the bed next to her, stretching his long body on top of the feather duvet.

"You can get under the covers with me," she offered.

"You need your sleep," he answered and pulled her into his arms. Curling close against him, she inhaled his warm scent and fell asleep right away, listening to the steady drumbeat of his heart against her ear.

———◦○◦———

Weak light filled the windows the next morning when Marie-Claire woke, her back nestled against Mick's front and his body draped around hers. Sometime during the night, the down comforter had worked its way to their feet, and now their bare flesh was intimately intertwined. She snuggled deeper against him and felt his arousal against her bottom, bold and intent.

As he stirred awake, one hand began to rub languorous circles on her stomach and she heard the rhythm of his breathing change. A contented sigh escaped her lips as he began to explore further, his hand traveling to caress her hip and then sliding to cup a tender breast.

Thrills shot through her as he claimed the sensitive mound, and she felt his excitement as the soft flesh filled his hand. His thumb brushed over the tip, making it tighten with excitement while his lips descended on her neck, plundering with hungry desire.

Rising on one arm, he rolled her beneath him.

"Good morning," she murmured, rubbing the back of her hand over the bristle of his cheek.

"I'm pretty much a bear in the mornings," he said, his voice gravelly with sleep.

"Nice." She smiled and pulled his lips down to hers.

She kissed him, loving the feel of his weight on her. Their lips feasted on each other without preamble, tongues twining boldly.

Now it was her turn to explore him, and she stroked the smooth skin of his back and luxuriated in the feel of the sleek sinews and muscles as they bunched and rippled. He was like a Greek statue transformed into flesh and hot blood—a magnificent, aroused male.

Pulling back, he removed her t-shirt, and grasped her wrists in each hand and held them captive at her sides while his mouth claimed a breast. His tongue blazed across it, followed by his lips, tugging and kissing until he reached the pink-crested tip.

The primitive possession drove her mad. He teased the sensitive peak until she writhed beneath him, his hands holding her captive while his mouth pleasured her at his leisure. She moaned in ecstasy as he lavished attention to each breast in kind, sensations exploding deep within her. He seemed to enjoy toying with her arousal, building it to growing peaks.

Drawing her arms over her head, he lay on her, pressing the full length of his arousal against her. She shivered with pleasure, adjusting her legs to nestle him between them, urging him closer against her. With a deep groan, he settled himself in the welcoming cradle, intent and very ready, only the thin fabric of his shorts and the wisp of her panties separating them.

Hooking one finger in her panties, he began to draw them lower and Marie-Claire felt her breath catch in her chest. An unbearable pressure built up, and rolling her head away from him, she sneezed.

Mick jerked back, horrified. "You're sick."

"No, I'm not, I just sneezed," she assured him, trying to draw him back down to her. "Really, I'm fine."

He ignored her and clapped his hand on her forehead. "You're hot. And you're breathing heavily."

"Of course, I am! I was in the middle of being ravished. I'm not sick."

Refusing to listen to reason, Mick went to the bathroom and returned with the thermometer, which he wedged in her mouth. Propped against the pillows with the duvet drawn to her chin, Marie-Claire fumed, glowering at him as he pulled on a pair of jeans and a polo shirt.

It was easier to breathe without his enormous weight pressing down on her, but that was about the only benefit, Marie-Claire thought. The thermometer showed her temperature was normal but nonetheless, Mick insisted she take two aspirin.

"Now it's time for breakfast," Mick announced.

"But I'm not hungry," Marie-Claire began to get out of bed but Mick hoisted her back on it.

"You're to stay in bed until I say."

Their standoff was interrupted by the ringing of the phone next to the bed. "Send them on back," Mick said and hung up. "That was the gatehouse, it's Darius and Neve."

"I want to see her."

"I'll bring her up."

She clasped his hand. "Mick, I'm fine, really. And I promise that if you let me come down to the kitchen, I'll eat all my breakfast."

It was obvious Mick wasn't used to having his orders negotiated. "All right," he gave in. "I sent your clothing out to the laundry last night, they're sending it back with Darius."

"Do you keep extra toothbrushes for your overnight guests?"

"I've never had an overnight guest before." He grinned and she felt pleased. "But I do have an extra toothbrush, and it's yours."

When she emerged from the bathroom, her clothing from yesterday was laid on the bed along with a bag Neve had packed. She changed into fresh jeans and a shirt and went to join everyone downstairs.

In the kitchen, Mick was busy at the stove, and Neve and Darius were sitting at the table with cups of tea. Neve hugged her with relief while Darius held a chair for her.

"Thanks for packing a bag, sorry for the fuss," Marie-Claire said, taking the offered seat.

"No fuss," Neve said, "just glad you're all right. Did you really have to wade across the wetlands? Poor you, I'm surprised you haven't caught your death of cold."

Marie-Claire ignored Mick's loud snort from the stove. "I'm fine, I've been wading in water all my life."

"How did they know you were there?" Darius asked, helping himself to a slice of toast from a stack on the table.

"When I was hiding under the bridge, the two paparazzi said someone from the Lady Warwick has been texting them tips. And they've been paying them."

"But who would do that?" Neve asked, appalled.

"Maybe the coach driver?" Darius suggested.

The girls considered the idea. "If he did, he was sneaky about it," Neve said. "It was another hour on the road after we left the Wetlands."

"One of your schoolmates, then?" Mick asked.

"If it is, I pity them," Darius said with a grin. "When I got to the Lady Warwick, Neve was ready to give all the paps a right bollocking in front of the school when I told her what happened. And I'm sure if I understood Jamaican Patois it would have been ten times worse."

The two smiled at each other for a moment, seeming to share a joke between them.

Mick set a heaping plate filled with eggs, sausages, beans, and ham before Marie-Claire. "And there's the toast and jam," he added.

"Mick, I'll never be able to eat all that," she said, noticing that the plates he set in front of everyone else were only half as full.

"But you'll give it a good try," he insisted.

"Come to think of it—" Neve said, tucking into her own plate "—there weren't any paparazzi outside the school when we returned from Kingston, nor in front of the house this morning."

"I've been wondering the same thing myself, so I texted a reporter who's friendly," Darius remarked, checking his mobile. "Ah, here we go. He says there's a rumor one of the royals is getting engaged. There's a bit of luck."

This news was met with a hearty whoop from Mick and Neve. Marie-Claire stared at them in confusion.

"That explains why the pap's disappeared yesterday. It means they'll all be covering them," Mick explained, exchanging a high five with his best friend, "and we are officially old news."

<hr>

"You need a day off," Mick announced after Neve and Darius left.

"Might as well take the next week off, for all the good trying to work at the studio will do me," Marie-Claire admitted.

"I thought things were going well with that last painting you needed to do."

Marie-Claire found her bag and rifled through it, pulling out a dozen paintings and spreading them on the table. Mick looked them over, the furrow between his brow deepening as he cast one aside after another.

"They don't look like much," he concluded, "certainly nothing like your others. It's like they're cartoons, like you painted them in a spotlight or something."

"I've had to work with models from the prop room and rigged lighting."

"This one, though, it's not too bad," he pointed to a blurry grey bird. "That's a House Wren, isn't it?"

"Chipping Sparrow."

"Then that one there, that's definitely a Bullfinch."

"Scottish Crossbill."

Mick swore and pulled his mobile phone from his pocket. "This is all Fanta's doing and I've bloody well had enough of it. I'm going to call a reporter I know who will print the truth about that scheming bitch—"

"Mick, no," Marie-Claire reached out to still his arm. "It's not Fanta. I mean, yes, it might be better if that distraction wasn't there, but I can't blame her. It may be that I don't have the talent to do this."

"That's rubbish and you know it. You're brilliant with talent to spare. But you haven't been eating, nor sleeping, to say nothing of being properly ravished by me on a regular basis. I'm surprised you can write your own name."

"Are you suggesting we go back upstairs?" she asked hopefully.

"Cheeky minx!" he admonished with mock censure. "Some fresh air is what you need. The weather is supposed to clear in a bit. How about we go for a drive? I thought you'd like to see Moorsgate."

Chapter Twenty

THE MOOD IN the car was somber. Mick was right—now that she had a full stomach and a good night's sleep, her head was much clearer and the reality of her situation was obvious. She had tried everything to create the example of reflected light Professor Dixon was looking for, but had failed, and with the Critique just five days away, the odds of a thunderbolt of inspiration striking were slim to none. Her situation was hopeless, along with any chance of a future with Mick.

Her boots had dried overnight, but the cleaners had required another twenty-four hours to finish her bulky sweater and would deliver it the next day. Mick had lent her his buff-colored, canvas field coat and found a dark, oilskin mackintosh for himself, and they packed an umbrella and a thermos of hot tea for the trip. She'd added her field kit and the block of paper, almost as an afterthought.

Mick drove the Range Rover, which accommodated his large frame much better than the Aston Martin. As Darius had said, the road outside Mick's gate was deserted and they left Fulham undetected. Grey clouds produced a steady drizzle as they drove northwest, the dull city sprawl soon replaced by pleasant countryside. His left hand rested on her knee as he drove, the weight warm and reassuring. The roads looked familiar and Mick said they were heading in the general direction of Hempland. After they passed Fred's pub, the road narrowed until, at some points, it seemed only a bit wider than the Range Rover. Marie-Claire had no idea what they would do if they met oncoming traffic.

Mick turned into a rutted lane that was almost undetectable through a break in a dense hedgerow and apologized as he negotiated the rain-filled potholes. "I didn't want to redo the road until we had all the heavy machinery out."

The rough lane wound through overgrown woods before emerging in a meadow. Mick parked and helped her out, holding the umbrella over her as they walked to the edge of the grassy field. A panoramic view of Hertfordshire unrolled at their feet.

Marie-Claire couldn't help but gasp. Even rain-soaked, it was beautiful, with hundreds of cultivated fields spread before them like a carpet of colors and textures. To the east, a verdant forest covered the sides of two hills divided by a brisk flowing stream, and in the distance a bell rang in a steepled church.

"This is the first thing I saw when Dad brought me out here, this view," Mick said, draping an arm around her shoulders. "Thank God the rest of the place measured up, I was ready to write the check without going a step further."

As the rain settled into fat droplets, the sun flared like a beacon through the dark clouds, lining them with brilliant silver light. Bright beams highlighted vivid patches of landscape below, and a breeze kicked up, making the earth smell fresh and alive. Marie-Claire breathed in exuberant lungfuls of the sweet air.

Mick shook out the umbrella and used it to point out the distant boundaries of his property. "I bought this parcel and that copse over there two years ago, and then in January I bought that property at the bottom, where those two streams come together. The lot came with an apple orchard—I thought they were eating apples, but it turns out they're cider apples. The whole thing is overgrown, but an expert is coming out to see if there's anything worth saving. If it is, we might find ourselves in the cider-making business."

Marie-Claire looked up at him. "We?"

A curious mixture of emotions passed over Mick's face. "I mean me," he stammered, "and maybe Dad, if he's up for it."

"How close is Hempland to here?"

"About ten miles east as the crow flies, over that hill."

They stood enjoying the view until Mick gave her a clap on the bottom and directed her to a path that led deeper into the property. "Come on, lass, time to see the rest of the kingdom."

Like a schoolboy with a prize, Mick showed her everything and watched to see her reaction.

"That went in last month." He pointed to a long run of chestnut fencing. "It's supposed to keep the deer out but they seem to be enjoying the exercise of jumping over it."

"Many foxes?"

"Not this year, but I'm sure we'll, I mean, I'll be seeing them eventually. I've been working with the National Wildlife Trust. They suggested I put out a few native birds to see how they get on, and they've been flourishing."

The going got rougher the farther they went in, and Marie-Claire could see the extent of the property's neglect. The farm had obviously been prosperous at one time, but now the stone walls were crumbling and the dense underbrush threatened to consume everything. Mick had his work cut out for him.

At the end of the tract was a large clearing with a new barn in the middle. The building was stone and similar to the one at Hempland, with gleaming copper gutters, a slate roof, and hand-hewn wooden doors. Beyond were six new pheasant pens and two sheds with foundations poured for more.

"I tried to save the old barn, but the drainage was muck and it collapsed, almost buried a dozer. It worked out for the best. They were able to clear the entire area and correct the drainage, so now it's dry and everything has a good foundation. There's still the nursery left to be built, and two more sheds, and then I'll be in business."

Through the tangled thicket, Marie-Claire caught a glimpse of whitewashed walls and windows. "There's a house in there," she said, peering closer.

"It's the original house. One of the neighbors said parts go back to the sixteen hundreds. Wait, what are you doing? Marie-Claire, come back here," he yelled, but she had already scrambled over a stone wall and into the underbrush to have a better look.

"I bet those walls are a foot thick," she said over her shoulder.

"Careful," Mick called, following closely through the dense brush.

Brambles tore at her hair and coat, but she pushed forward until the beautiful stone house revealed itself, dignified behind the overgrown facade. Up close it was larger than it first appeared, a full two stories with a third tucked under the roof. The farmhouse was substantial, the front door centered between pairs of tall windows whose glass was mostly intact.

The wooden portico over the entrance had collapsed and blocked the way in, much to Marie-Claire's vexation, but as they circled around, she saw a much older wing, squat in style and with a different stonework. At the far end, a Dutch door stood ajar.

"I bet that entire wing is the kitchen. Look at the size of the chimney, it's enormous." She made her way through the overgrown brambles as Mick struggled to keep up. "Let's go in."

"It's not safe," Mick cautioned, but she had already pushed the door open and stepped inside.

It had been a kitchen a long time ago, but was empty now except for a massive stone hearth and debris blown through the broken windows. The dull, limewashed walls were crumbled in some spots, but remarkably sound around most of the room.

"No one's lived here for a long time, have they?"

Mick glanced around as he pulled brambles from his coat. "At least thirty years from what they told me, probably closer to fifty. Watch out, the floors are gone in some spots."

A wide hallway led to the main part of the house. The roof there was solid and the interior remarkably well-preserved. Marie-Claire explored, delighted with the detailed woodwork and well-proportioned rooms. Mick followed close behind her.

The two front reception rooms had marble fireplaces, and bits of detailed plasterwork still clung to the ceilings. "It's fantastic," she said quietly, not sure why she was whispering, but the old place had an inherent grace that seemed to deserve their respect.

"This must have been the dining room, and those are hand-painted murals on the wall." She looked closely at the birds painted on a faded blue background. "Look, Mick, these are all local species. There's a Yellowhammer, and a Waxwing, and that's a Goldeneye. This took someone ages."

He grunted, unimpressed, but she took his hand and drew him closer, showing him the details. "I think it's gouache," she murmured, tracing a light finger over the detailed painting, "a form of watercolors but with more pigment. I can't believe someone did the entire wall."

In the foyer, a central staircase beckoned and she started up.

"No, don't go up," Mick caught her arm. "Everything's wobbly."

"It feels fine, see?" She pulled on the balustrade to show the wood was solid.

"I've never been up there, it's dangerous," Mick insisted.

"Dangerous for you, but I weigh half what you do."

"Marie-Claire—" he protested, but she slipped out of his reach and skipped up the steps, and he stood worrying at the bottom as she wandered through the rooms above.

"It's wonderful," she called down in delight. "There's five big bedrooms, an old bath, and stairs to the attic. And there's trunks and furniture and everything. The roof's leaked and there's some damage, but the floors are good."

"Come back down right now," he said sternly.

"In a minute. There's another set of steps towards the back. I think they lead down to the kitchen. I'm going to try them."

These steps were much less stable and creaked dangerously as she descended. She measured her step, not wanting to cause a cave-in of rotten timber. Mick met her at the bottom, lifted her by the waist, and set her down before him.

"It's like Aladdin's cave up there, you should see it!" she exclaimed in delight as he wiped a smudge of dirt from her cheek.

"No need. I'm having it all torn down."

Marie-Claire was dumbstruck. "Knocked down…but there's nothing wrong with it. It must be hundreds of years old, but the walls are solid and I bet the foundation is fine."

"It's just an old pile of stones and plaster as far as I'm concerned. I'm having plans drawn up for a much bigger place."

She swallowed hard, her throat tightening. "Of course. You'd need something much grander."

"No," he snapped. "No, I don't need a *glam* house."

"Don't be defensive. I saw the pictures in the magazines. You'd want one of those big modern mansions, like the others, with acres of rooms and enormous windows."

"I'm not being defensive!" he yelled. "I just don't want to live in a drafty pile of stones where I hit my head on every doorjamb. Had enough of that growing up."

She swallowed hard. "That's reasonable. But the ceilings are high and the walls could be insulated. It just seems a waste."

"Yes, well, it's my waste to make."

She nodded, looking around the walls one last time. "You're right, you can do whatever you want with it. It's just hard to figure you out sometimes. I keep forgetting you're two different people."

They stood motionless in the silent house, her words seeming to confound him. "Why do you think I'm two different people?" he asked.

She shrugged. "You're a country man and a city man. You have two different cars, two different homes, two different careers. I'm not sure, but I think you have two different sets of clothing." And two different tastes in women, she added to herself. "It gets confusing sometimes."

She turned and left through the door they had entered, not wanting to stay another minute in the beautiful but doomed house. For some reason, she felt a kinship with it—both their fates intertwined, both teetering on someone else's whim.

<hr />

Outside, she followed a path that wound down the hill, her shoulders hunched and hands shoved deep in the pockets of Mick's field coat. She paused at the bottom where a footbridge crossed the wide stream, and leaned over the rail to watch a squadron of ducks paddle in the water. The sun was making a more determined attempt to break through the clouds, its weak rays dappling the water with glistening light.

Mick joined her at the rail and together they watched the ducks in brooding silence. Two Mallard hens sunned themselves on the rocky shoreline while three drakes patrolled the shallows, their occasional squabbling over perceived intrusions into their territory breaking the tranquil silence.

"I know I'm two different people," he began. "Believe me, it confuses me, too. Growing up out here, I thought success was living in London, having the poshest car, going to the hottest clubs, getting any girl that caught my eye."

Marie-Claire frowned, not happy to discuss that topic.

"The drugs never appealed to me, thank God, mostly because I'm too cheap," Mick continued. "A bloke at a party once had a pile of cocaine and offered me a try. I asked how much it cost and he told me. It was the same that Dad charges for a day's shoot. I decided then and there I wasn't going to put a bloody brace of partridge up my nose."

It was hard not to smile at that. More strands of golden sunlight began to flood the little valley, illuminating the lush ferns that lined the stream.

"The fast life was fun, for a while. But then I started to see that the people I was hanging out with were fakes. And even worse, lazy. And boring."

"The vacations looked like fun," Marie-Claire said.

"If you're talking about the trip to Barbados I got roped into over the holidays, it rained every day except one. Plus, I was in the middle of negotiations to buy that two-hundred-acre wood over there, and I spent most of the time on the phone. Those bills alone cost me a fortune. Also missed out on some excellent quail hunting," he added with disgust. "But I'll be retiring soon and that part of my life will be over."

As he spoke, the Mallard hens decided to join the drakes in the water, waddling out to swim in lazy circles beneath the bridge. "Retire? But you're only thirty."

"My body feels like it's twice that. The left knee's had two surgeries, and I'm in physio after every practice. My speed hasn't dropped yet, but if I add on more matches playing for England, it's only going to accelerate the decline. No, I've got it all planned out—when Giles gives me the nod, I'm done. Then I'll work here."

"You're going to commute back and forth from London?"

Mick shook his head vehemently. "Hell, no. I'm not raising my family in the city."

"You plan on living here full time?" she asked, trying to imagine one of the women he'd been photographed with plucking a pheasant or sloshing down the lane in Wellies to pick up the post. She moved to the other side of the bridge, pretending to look at a pair of drakes who were drying their feathers in the warming sun, so he wouldn't see her amusement.

"Of course. My kids aren't going to a posh school," he said dismissively, following her. "They'll go to a good country school and stay there. Guys in the club, they're sending their kids to those fee schools. I've never seen a bunch of youngsters so screwed up. I don't want that for my kids. They're going to get good educations, go to university, make something productive of their lives." He paused and added, "Like you."

The ducks quacked conversationally to each other, their orange feet bright beneath the shallow, sparkling water.

He stepped closer and reached out to sweep aside a stray lock of hair that had fallen across her face. "I've never met anyone like you before," he said, gazing at her intently, "and now I might lose you, and I can't bear it."

She stood motionless, watching the scene below.

Mick brought her hand to his lips, grazing the knuckles. "Marie-Claire, I know we've only known each other a few weeks, but it's like I've known you my entire life."

The pressure of his hand around hers gently increased. "We're good together, Marie-Claire, you and me. We're... right. I've never felt this way about anyone before, so certain."

Marie-Claire continued to stare into the water, mesmerized by the blue-grey rocks speckled with glints of gold.

"I know I've made things really hard for you the last few weeks, and I'm sorry, but it wouldn't always be that way. You saw the way the paparazzi vanished yesterday, they've completely lost interest in us."

He took a deep breath and released it slowly. "There's still the problem of your school and that test. About your student visa. But I think I have a solution to your problem, so you wouldn't have to leave."

Silence stretched between them as sunlight filled the little valley. A minute passed, and then two.

"Do you understand what I'm trying to say?" Mick prodded.

A drake waddled onto a rock in the middle of the stream almost directly below Marie-Claire, the now-constant sunlight illuminating the iridescent, green plumage of his head. Unconsciously, her right hand began to furl and unfurl around an invisible brush. She saw the image exactly, fully formed.

Perfect.

"Marie-Claire?" A hint of irritation crept into Mick's voice.

"Mick," she said, her focus locked on the ducks below them, "I need my field kit."

"What? Marie-Claire, if you could spare a bit of your attention here, love, I'm trying to—"

"And my block of paper."

"No. You need to relax and rest."

"Mick, I really need my field kit," she repeated, not taking her eyes off the ducks. "Right now."

Mick followed her gaze down to the water. "All right. I'll be right back."

———◦———

The water continued to lap against the rocks as the ducks toddled in and out of the stream. Marie-Claire sat on the deck of the bridge, dangling her legs over the edge, almost in a trance. When Mick returned, she took the watercolor block and began sketching the scene in rapid pencil strokes. Squeezing fresh blobs of Winsor Orange and Prussian Blue onto the palette and then wetting a medium round brush, she set to work.

The background she painted dried fast in the direct sunlight. Satisfied, she began painting the ducks in vivid colors, working from lights to darks with deft strokes of the paintbrush. The duck's webbed feet, visible through the clear water, were painted in Winsor Orange straight from the tube, and she let speckles of white paper show through the thin blue wash, sunlight reflecting off the water onto their downy stomachs.

Mick sat next to her, watching as her brush flicked across the paper, laying a broad line here or the thinnest detail there. She let parts of the paper dry and worked on others, and as the sun climbed higher in the sky, the finished painting began to take shape.

From a distance, the hum of a motor scooter grew louder and a teenage boy drove down the path and parked next to them.

"Mick! Oi, Mick!" The teenager called, ambling towards them.

"Robbie, good to see you." Mick stood and shook his hand. "Marie-Claire, this is Robbie, Roger's younger brother."

Robbie doffed his cap. "Heard that was quite some shooting last weekend at Gordon's. Roger said he never saw anything like it nor is he likely to again."

Marie-Claire glanced up from her watercolor and smiled. "I just got lucky."

"That's a pretty picture you're painting there," Robbie said, looking at the work keenly. "You got them drakes spot on, even with the funny colors and all." He turned back to Mick. "I watched the game against Queens Park Rangers last week, you were awesome. Bloody shame Fernando let that one get by him on the assist. Pozny did okay subbing in for Hugo but you guys really need him back."

Mick snorted. "He talked his way out of the two-game suspension, he'll be back for West Ham."

"Kingsbury Town will drop to ninth, but that's not too bad, is it? West Brom lost, as well."

Mick took exception to that. "West Brom had their arses handed to them. We just lost by one."

"I play for the Alesford Wanderers here in town, and I'm going to try out for a big club soon," Robbie told Marie-Claire.

"After you graduate," Mick added.

"Oh yeah, after I graduate." Reaching into his backpack, Robbie pulled out a paper bag wrapped in string and handed the package to Mick. "Mum made these apple pasties and thought you'd like some. Are we on for Tuesday with the arborist then?"

"Aye," Mick said, "he'll be here at half-past one. Can you meet him in case I'm late? Take him down to the orchard. You know where he should start."

"Done deal, mate," the boy said, and waved goodbye and sped off the way he had come.

"Robbie's a good lad, but he's got his head in the clouds, thinking he wants to be a professional footballer. This is where he should be." Mick settled back down next to her on the bridge and eagerly opened the package, removing a large golden pastry with an intricate fluted edge. "Ah, one of Mrs. Gosney's famous pasties. Be a good girl and have a bite."

Marie-Claire took a mouthful and returned to her painting, interrupting the brushstrokes only when Mick would make her eat another bite.

Soon the painting was finished and she propped the block against a railing post. Mick helped her to her feet so she could admire her work from farther away, and with a huge sigh of relief, she threw her arms around him, happier than she had ever dreamed.

"I did it, I trusted myself to paint what I saw. And, look, it's beautiful."

"It is. You're brilliant."

She kissed him with all the joy she felt and he responded, as inflamed with happiness as she.

Pulling away, she began rinsing her brushes and repacking her kit bag. "We need to get back, Mick, right now. You have to drop me off at the studio, I need to get this taped on a board, and I might be able to do another one from memory tonight—"

Mick barred her way off the bridge. "No. No studio until tomorrow. And you're moving in with me, at least until the Critique."

"Mick, it will be okay. The photographers are gone, and so it will be easy to get back and forth." Seeing his scowl, she kissed him again. "Mick, really, this is what they want to see," she whispered, her lips against his. "I know it. Everything's going to be okay."

Chapter Twenty-One

FRIDAY AFTERNOON ARRIVED like a death sentence. Mick Carr simultaneously wanted the Critique to never come and yet wanted to get it over with as soon as possible. As if that wasn't enough to drive a man barking mad.

His pulse raced uncontrollably as he paced the front steps of the Lady Warwick College of Arts and Design, waiting for his fate to be sealed. It had been exactly five days since he had reluctantly left Marie-Claire at her studio after they returned from Moorsgate, innumerable hours waiting in dread for the outcome of this bloody Critique and an eternity since he had held her and felt peace.

At least Marie-Claire was happy. He'd convinced her that if she wouldn't move in with him, she had to let him be in charge of her meals. She'd grudgingly relented and Chez Bertrand had been delivering a basket to the studio every evening at six o'clock. Marie-Claire would dutifully call to report what she'd eaten, and he suspected she was sharing, but he could tell by the tone of her voice that she was happy and sleeping well. What with the press off hounding the royal family and Fanta nowhere to be seen nor heard, she said life was almost idyllic.

Actually, she was sounding entirely too cheerful and confident, which in his opinion was needlessly tempting fate. Didn't she know anything could happen?

The bells of a nearby church tolled six times and he muttered a scorching oath. Six o'clock, hadn't she said the Critique would be over by now? How much time did they need to decide someone's fate?

But this, this was a living hell. He hated schools, and this just reinforced his gut feeling. What business did they have saying she'd have to go home? She was a brilliant painter, anyone could see that. Who were they to decide if she was good enough for them? They weren't good enough for her. Very little was good enough for her in his opinion. Except himself, and he was all that she needed.

Positive thinking was key here, he reminded himself. First off, he would whisk her away from this damnable place and get her alone. There was a bottle of champagne cooling in his refrigerator, and he'd reserved a table for the entire night at Le Cheval Rouge, all in anticipation of good news. Then for the match tomorrow, she was set up to be in the club's skybox with the rest of the girls, with an all access pass and instructions that her glass was never to be empty. It was time she took her official place as his girlfriend.

This was how everything would play out. He refused to even consider another outcome.

Street lamps flickered to life and pedestrians, bundled against the evening chill, walked past as if everything was perfectly normal. Then there she was, at the top of the stairs, wearing a short black skirt and tall boots and wrapped in his field coat, her long hair streaming in the wind. Around her neck, she wore the silver bird nest looped on its black satin cord.

Mick's world ground to a halt as she descended the stairs, her expression inscrutable.

"Sorry I'm late." She stopped on the step above him, her gaze focused on something in the distance. "I stopped to call my parents with the news."

"What news?" he asked, the words burning his parched throat.

Seconds ticked by and pressure filled him like a steam kettle, horrible and nauseating. He reached out to grasp her hands like a drowning man. Then she smiled brilliantly, her eyes dancing with mischief. "I'm in."

The air burst from his chest in a roar and his knees went wobbly, like they did when he took a hard hit on the pitch. It took him a moment to recover, and then he snatched her against him, lifting her off her feet and spinning her around.

"Wench," he murmured hoarsely and kissed her soundly, not caring that they were on the steps of the school, not caring that there could be a hundred cameras trained on them, not caring about anything except the fact that she was staying.

Marie-Claire kissed him back with joyful abandon, her arms wrapped around his neck, molding against the length of his body. "They loved everything, especially the ducks from Moorsgate," she managed to tell him as he peppered her with rough kisses. "I got off the easiest of all of us."

He buried his face in the mounds of her soft hair. "Don't make me ever go through that again."

"It will all be a lot less stress from here on. There's still a lot of work, but once you've passed the Critique, the workload is a lot easier. Raul and Neve both say the first year is hell, and the rest is bliss by comparison."

"It had better be."

She rubbed her hand over the rough stubble of his unshaven cheek and kissed his furrowed brow. "I wouldn't have passed today without you, I know that," she whispered. "If I hadn't met you, I wouldn't have been able to break free and just trust myself to paint what I saw. You helped me do that. I don't know how, but you did."

"You're too smart, is your problem," he told her solemnly, "and you needed a thick-headed oaf like me to balance out all your brilliance." Then he kissed her again, drinking in her soft lips.

Knowing he needed to get her alone, and soon, he grasped her hand and began to lead her down the steps to where his car was parked. "Come on, I've got plans for tonight—"

The doors of the school burst open and dozens of students flooded down the steps, engulfing them in a happy throng. They hugged Marie-Claire, hugged him, and hugged each other in a wave of mass euphoria.

"Who else passed?" Marie-Claire asked amid the clatter.

"Everyone passed. It's a first!" The girl with the blue hair, Sandra, shouted.

"Everyone? Even Stephen?"

"Everyone. Now it's time for the party!"

The cheerful mob moved down the street, taking them with it. "You're having a party?" Mick asked Marie-Claire, cursing his luck.

She smiled contritely and took his hand in hers as they walked. "Yes, the second-years throw a party for the first-years, it's a school tradition. Neve and Raul are back at the house. I imagine it's already started. It might get a little wild, everyone needs to let their hair down."

He'd enjoyed enough victory parties to know she deserved this one, so he went along with the crowd, contenting himself with having Marie-Claire at his side and hoping that maybe they could duck out after an hour or two.

The music grew louder as they approached her front door, where partygoers crowded the small stoop and narrow entrance hall.

Raul met them in the hallway, holding a bottle of cheap champagne and plastic glasses. "Well?"

Marie-Claire waved her hands in victory. "The reflected light put me over the top, they loved it."

"Wouldn't have expected differently." Raul grinned and leaned forward to give her a hug, but switched to an awkward peck on the cheek when he saw Mick's foreboding expression over her shoulder. "Comments?"

"Excellent control, strong sense of proportion, understands relationship between light and color. Needs to balance composition against line quality. Drawing needs work."

"They always throw that last bit in," Raul said, and handed glasses around and sloshed in the champagne.

He raised his glass. "To MC Wentworth, the hardest working watercolorist in England. Even if she is a Yank."

Shouts of "hear, hear" rang out as they all clinked glasses and drank the bubbly, sweet drink. Shrugging off her coat, Marie-Claire took Mick's hand and pulled him into the throng. "Come on," she yelled over the din, "I'll introduce you around."

Everyone was in a happy mood, and Mick began to enjoy himself as they passed from group to group. The older and slightly more respectable-looking people turned out to be professors at the school, and to Mick's relief there was no repeat of the debacle at the student show. In fact, no one seemed particularly awed by his presence, and he and Marie-Claire circulated easily in the eclectic crowd, the attention on her where it belonged.

The party spilled into the back garden where tiki torches blazed and lilting Caribbean music blared on portable speakers. Neve waved to them from across the garden and ran to hug Marie-Claire. "I never had a doubt. And I see someone else is happy you passed." She winked at Mick.

Without warning, a strong hand grabbed Mick's arm from behind and twisted it in a vise grip against his back. "Oi! Who let muck like you in?" a man's angry voice shouted in his ear.

Mick stiffened, and with a swift movement, hooked Darius's leg and dropped him to the ground.

"Didn't they teach you how to fight in Essex?" He bent over his friend, who lay grinning at his feet. "Spend all your time on the tennis courts, my son?"

Darius laughed as Mick gave him a hand up. "Too busy chasing after the girls," Darius conceded and gave Marie-Claire an affectionate peck on the cheek. "Congratulations, MC, I guess we'll be able to live with the brute now."

As the girls chatted, Mick glanced at Darius. "What are you doing here?" he asked over the loud music.

Darius cast a sidelong, appreciative glance at Neve. "I got invited. And I'm beginning to see where you've developed your taste for the arts, decided I might try it. Now go get a beer, and get me another, as well."

A makeshift bar had been set up in a corner of the garden. Mick took two beers from a cooler and then stood and watched

Marie-Claire as she talked with Neve and Darius.

A burly man wearing a t-shirt that read "Fear No Art" took a beer, as well, popped the cap and with a nod to Mick, offered a toast. "Here's to the first-years." After draining the bottle, he belched appreciatively and followed the direction of Mick's gaze.

"Like what you see?" he asked.

"Yes, I do."

"You've good taste. American. Quite charming, the original 'farmer's daughter,' like from a movie. Rather talented but miles to go. Great tits," the man said, continuing his leisurely assessment as Mick's fingers began to clench into fists, "but you don't stand a chance."

"Oh? Why not?"

"She's seeing some Premier League footballer, heard he's as big as a house and ugly if anyone gets near her. She's completely smitten, won't give the rest of us lads the time of day. We're hoping he screws up soon, you know, gets caught by the *Daily Mail* with his pants down with someone else. Then you're welcome to queue up."

"Would he be that stupid?" Mick asked, relaxing his grip.

"Footballers?" the large man replied with a snort. "Come on, lad, they think with their dicks."

Ridiculous happiness flooded through Mick. First, because everyone knew she was taken, and second, because he knew he would never be tempted to screw up the way the man was suggesting.

Crossing back across the garden, he took her hand in his. "Come on, let's dance."

A tiny area had been cleared as a dance floor and was filled with people grinding and bumping to the pulsing Caribbean rhythms. He held her easily as they danced, together then apart, and then pressed together again, their bodies brushing sensuously against each other.

After a half-dozen songs, Marie-Claire begged for a break. Neve refilled her plastic champagne glass from a bottle that was being passed around and she drained the contents thirstily.

"Easy there, love, don't let it go to your head," Neve teased. "You might not be able to find your way back from Olympic Stadium."

"Olympic Stadium?" Mick asked in surprise. "When did you go there?"

Marie-Claire shot a disapproving look at her housemate. "Wednesday."

"You mean you came to the match Wednesday night against West Ham?"

"Technically speaking, yes," she admitted.

"What happened?" Mick persisted.

"You're not going to be too impressed."

"Try me."

"I couldn't find it."

"You couldn't find what?" Darius asked.

"She couldn't find the stadium," Neve provided helpfully. "Even though it's as big as an airport."

Marie-Claire nodded sheepishly. "I wasn't planning on going, but I was feeling adventurous. Neve wrote out the Underground directions for me and said it would probably take about fifty minutes. The game was supposed to start at eight o'clock, so I left the house at six-thirty, but the stations were so busy I got confused."

"How many times did you have to switch?" Darius asked.

"Four times, but the lines are on different levels, see? Then when I finally arrived there was only ten minutes left in the game and the lady at the window wouldn't sell me a ticket."

Mick swore colorfully. "What did you do then?"

"There was an older man who was listening to the game on a radio outside the end zone. I stood with him and listened while Kingsbury Town scored a goal and won the game. He said you'd had a good game, you're a solid player and always get the job done. After that I went home."

"How long did that take?"

"Oh, that went much faster, I was able to take the buses. But I accidentally got out at Stockwell and ended up walking the rest of the way."

"You walked from Stockwell to Wandsworth?" Mick exploded at the thought of her walking around south London alone at night.

"It wasn't bad and I needed the exercise. I walked up the Strand and saw some swans in the Thames. And I found out Shifton's not a very good neighborhood."

"Jesus." He stopped her and put his hands on either side of her face. "Tomorrow I will make sure—"

He was interrupted by a very drunk Stephen Ashe, who swung an arm around Marie-Claire's shoulder with a familiarity that made Mick see red. "Hey, MC," he slurred, "tuition is due next week, would you mind running naked down the street so I can take pictures to sell?"

Darius and Mick were on their feet in an instant, towering over the pudgy artist who grinned at them blearily.

"Stephen, don't be such an ass!" Neve scolded while other students scrambled to pull him away.

"Who was that git?" Mick asked, his narrowed eyes following Stephen's retreating path.

"Stephen Ashe," Neve said. "First year along with Marie-Claire. He's had too much to drink."

"I'd like a word with him."

"No!" both Marie-Claire and Neve yelped at the same time. Grabbing Mick by a tense bicep, Marie-Claire pulled him towards the house. "Come on," she implored when he seemed reluctant to give ground, "let's go inside."

He glanced at Darius, who subtly nodded his head and followed her into the house. Rock music blared inside the crowded kitchen and another glass of champagne was thrust in Marie-Claire's hand. She drained it in one gulp, and then to Mick's surprise, scrambled up on to the table and began to dance, whipping her hair back and forth with wild abandon to the cheers of the partygoers. But the table was as unsteady as her balance, and Mick only just managed to pluck her off and into his arms before she would have crashed to the floor.

Marie-Claire laughed, her face flushed from exertion. "That's a lot harder than it looks. Come on, let's go someplace quieter."

They navigated their way up the steps to the second floor and stopped at a door. Marie-Claire knocked, and after a pause, a couple emerged, adjusting their clothing.

"I guess you go to parties much wilder than this," Marie-Claire said, pulling him into the tiny room and slamming the door closed behind them.

"Not by much."

She giggled. "Maybe I better lock it."

As she rattled the doorknob, Mick took a look around. The closet-sized room was obviously her bedroom, the dull light from the alley illuminating a wooden chair, dresser, and single bed. A newspaper clipping about him was taped to the inside of a wall mirror, the only ornamentation in the room.

Lying on her side on the narrow bed, she patted the empty spot next to her. "Come and join me?"

Outside, a man bellowed something in Russian and a woman laughed.

Marie-Claire rose to her knees before him, brushing her chest against his hips seductively and drew him down to the bed with her. The metal frame creaked under his weight.

"All the way," she whispered, nudging him to lay back.

Reluctantly, he stretched out, feeling the springs dip into the center as she lay on top of him, wriggling to mold herself against the full length of his body.

"I missed you all week," she murmured, biting the sensitive lobe of his ear.

Sensations detonated deep within his body as his hands found the warmth of her silky skin under her blouse. "I missed you, too."

She kissed him eagerly, her lips tasting of sweet champagne. He kissed her tenderly and she responded feverishly, their tongues twining and sliding in sensuous strokes.

"You're so strong, nothing feels as good as you do," she whispered, rising to pull free of her blouse.

"Easy, Marie-Claire," he murmured, "we don't need to make up for any lost time."

She drew his hands to cup her breasts through the sheer bra, arching her back to fill them with tender flesh. "I meant what I said. I want to take chances! I want to seize the day! Or-r—" she paused to hiccup "—the night."

He eyed her warily. "Has the champagne gone to your head?"

"No." At his skeptical look, she reconsidered. "Well, maybe just a little, but I know what I want. I want you."

Her lips reclaimed his and she seemed to have no inhibitions. "Marie-Claire," he groaned, "easy, slower…"

She ignored him and doubled her ardor. Her hands worked to unbuckle his belt and slipped lower to caress him, a satisfied sigh escaping her lips as she encircled the full measure of his desire.

A loud knock at the door interrupted them. "MC, where are your extension cords?"

"There's one in Neve's room," she called while she pulled his sweater off and tossed it to the floor, where it joined her blouse. With passionate kisses, she feasted on the skin of his chest like a barbarian princess, her hair streaming over him as her lips traveled lower towards his navel, and then lower still.

With a sudden movement, he jerked back and rolled to sit up, breaking the searing heat that connected their bodies.

"We're going to stop now," he ground out, reaching to pull his sweater back on.

Marie-Claire lay still, her breathing labored. "Why?"

"Because I still can, and very soon that will not be the case."

"I'm okay with that."

"No. Not like this."

She looked around her bedroom, perplexed. "Not like what? I thought this is the way it is with you. Spur of the moment, no commitments, just enjoyment."

"Usually, yes. But it's different with you."

She sat back and drew her legs up to her chest, confused by his rejection. "Why is it different with me?"

"Because everything is different with you."

"You're not making much sense. You're Mick Carr, Kingsbury Jack-About-Town, and I'm throwing myself at you."

"I don't want that with you."

She sat in stunned confusion. "You don't want me?"

"Yes. I mean no." He stood abruptly and began to pace the claustrophobic room. "I mean, not in that way."

He didn't want their first time to be a quickie romp in her broom-closet of a bedroom with a party carrying on around them. He didn't want other people around, other distractions; he wanted her alone, so he could show her he could be a tender and considerate lover.

Mick looked at her sitting on the bed, heartbreakingly beautiful, and tried to sort out the tangled mess of his emotions. "I want you more than I have ever wanted anything, or anyone, in my life. I know none of this is making any sense. I'm sorry. I wish I understood myself."

Bending over he kissed her forehead. "Now I think I'll go take a dip in the Thames. I'll see you tomorrow after the game."

Chapter Twenty-Two

"MICK LEFT EARLY," Neve observed the next morning as they cleaned up the kitchen. "Darius said he's usually the last one to leave a party."

"Yes, well, he obviously had better things to do," Marie-Claire replied tersely as she sorted bottles into recycling bins. "Darius left early, as well."

"They have a match this afternoon. He said he needed some rest."

Raul returned from taking the garbage out. "There's a chap in the foyer. I found him on the street, he says he's here for you, MC."

Neve followed Marie-Claire to investigate. A clean-cut young man wearing a suit and tie stood in the small hall, jingling a set of car keys.

"My name is Phillip Trent, and I am from the Kingsbury Town Football Club," he explained. "I am here to escort you to the match this afternoon."

Marie-Claire looked at Neve in confusion. "I'm not going to the match this afternoon."

"Mick Carr said I am to escort you, and Miss Clark if she'd like to accompany you, to the match this afternoon at one o'clock. So, if you would be so good as to get your coats—"

"I said I'm not going to the match," she repeated.

"Look, miss." Phillip winked. "Mick said you might balk. But he gave me liberty to tell you that I am, like yourself, attending college and the fifty-quid tip he's going to give me for delivering the both of you to the grounds this afternoon will go a long way towards fees."

"Is that true?"

"The London School of Economics isn't free, miss."

"We'll just get changed and be right down," Neve said and ushered Marie-Claire up the staircase.

"Neve, this is not a good idea," Marie-Claire told her once they had reached the top.

"'Course it is! The lads are treating us to a match. It will be a hoot."

"No, really, it's not."

Neve paused. "Why? Did something happen between you and Mick last night?"

Marie-Claire hesitated, uncomfortable to divulge how things ended between them. "I don't know. I mean, I thought things were going great. We came up here to my bedroom, and then things weren't so great."

"How so?"

Marie-Claire bit her lip, uncertain how to describe what happened. "All of a sudden, he just stopped."

"Stopped? You mean in the middle of—"

"It didn't get that far, but far enough."

"Did he say why he stopped?"

Marie-Claire looped a lock of hair behind her ear. "It turns out he's not interested in me."

"Is that what he said?" Neve asked. "That he wasn't interested in you?"

"Not exactly. He said he didn't want that with me."

"Did he say why?"

"He said it was because it was different with me."

Neve's eyes widened. "Really."

"But that doesn't make any sense, Neve. How am I different? I know I'm not as glamorous as his other girlfriends, but I thought that didn't matter to him. And I was trying to be more like them, you know—wild and adventurous—but when I did, he ran out. I don't know what's going on, and I have no idea why he sent someone to take us to the match today."

Neve considered this information as Phillip's voice called up the stairs. "If you ladies wouldn't mind putting a light under it, this isn't the best neighborhood and the SUV belongs to the club."

Turning Marie-Claire by the shoulders, Neve nudged her into her bedroom. "I don't understand what Mick is thinking any more than you do, but I think you should give him the benefit of the doubt. Put on a cute outfit and let's go. It'll be fun, you'll see."

Marie-Claire looked at her jeans and light sweater. "What's the matter with what I'm wearing?"

"Well, go brush your hair at least," Neve scolded.

Reluctantly, Marie-Claire changed into a fresh white blouse and neat tan trousers, looped the bird's nest around her neck, and brushed her hair while Neve changed into a bright pair of pants and embroidered jacket. Back downstairs, Phillip helped her into Mick's field coat and held the front door for them.

Outside, Marie-Claire pulled more slips of paper from the gate and stuffed them into the pockets of Mick's coat before they blew around and littered the neighborhood.

"Why do the paparazzi keep leaving their numbers?" Marie-Claire asked in dismay as she got into the backseat of the luxurious black and yellow SUV.

"I suppose it's better than having them stationed out here," Neve answered, "although I bet that royal wouldn't agree."

"Been peaceful around here with all the royal wedding rumors?" Phillip asked as he pulled into traffic.

"Quiet as a tomb," Neve said.

"I see it all the time," Phillip boasted, "one week you're the hottest thing since sliced bread, and then the next they're on to someone new. You'd have to start a riot to get any attention now."

"That's a great idea," Marie-Claire said. "I'll have to remember that."

———◆◇◆———

Traffic in Hendon slowed to a crawl as people dressed in yellow and black thronged towards the imposing stadium. Once in the car park, Phillip drove through a gate marked No Admittance and pulled up to a uniformed guard manning an unmarked door.

"This gentleman will show you up. Enjoy the game, ladies," Phillip announced and sped off.

The guard greeted them by name, ushered them into an elevator, and pressed the top button. The girls looked at each other with wide eyes, their lips pressed together in silent mirth.

Seconds later, the elevator opened to reveal a huge luxury box with a sweeping view of the pitch. Groups of women dressed in the latest designer creations stood chatting in idle clusters around the room. They reminded Marie-Claire of mannequins in store windows, carefully posed with flashing jewelry and thick layers of makeup. She'd never seen so many different shades of blonde hair in her life, all perfectly coiffed into elegant styles.

"Would you look at them," Neve whistled under her breath. "I'm glad we changed."

"Oh yeah, that makes all the difference," Marie-Claire snapped, smoothing her hair behind her ear.

An attractive hostess checked their names against a clipboard and took their coats, and then hung laminated "All Access" passes around their necks while a waiter appeared offering a tray of champagne glasses filled to the rims.

Marie-Claire declined, but Neve giggled and took a glass. "Don't mind if I do. I'm going for the full experience." Closing her eyes, she sipped and smiled. "That's the good stuff, that is," she sighed and looked across the room, her jaw falling open. "Cor, would you look at all that food."

A buffet had been arranged along one wall, loaded with elaborate trays of cheeses, fruit, crudités, sandwiches, and miniature sweets, all of it crowned by an ice sculpture of a player kicking a ball. The effect was lavish but the food was untouched by the rest of the guests. Marie-Claire ignored the demanding growl of her stomach.

They walked to the rows of plush seats lined up before the windows and saw the pitch below, a neat green carpet that looked smaller than Marie-Claire would have supposed. Outside the windows, spectators filled the rows of black and yellow stadium seats. The noise should have been much louder, but the sounds from the other side were muffled by thick glass that ran the length of the room.

Neve pointed out Kingsbury Town's side of the pitch and then Fulham's, and launched into a long discussion about the relative merits of both teams. Having three brothers, Neve possessed remarkable knowledge.

"You must be the famous MC Wentworth," a voice interrupted from behind them.

They turned around and were confronted by two women, both wearing tight pantsuits that clung to their almost unnatural curves.

Without waiting, Marie-Claire reached out and shook their hands. "Hello, yes, I'm MC." Their fingers were limp and unresisting in her grasp.

The one in green appraised her with unconcealed curiosity. "I'm Dee, I'm with Pablo. This is Kami, she's with Samuel."

"Pleased to meet you. This is my friend Neve Clark. She's with…me."

Neve balked, but after a sharp prod from Marie-Claire, shook hands, as well. "Charmed."

Kami's eyes narrowed. "Wot's that mess o' wire yuv got 'round ya neeck?"

Her northern English accent was so thick Marie-Claire needed a moment to understand what she was asking. "Oh, it's a bird nest, see?"

Dee leaned in closer and squinted. "Mick give it to you?"

Marie-Claire smiled. "Yes."

Dee snorted, unimpressed. "He can afford much better than that, love, believe me. Or maybe he figures he can get off cheap with you."

Marie-Claire bristled at the woman's rudeness. A stinging retort was forming on her lips when the women's attention pivoted to a stunning redhead who emerged from the elevator.

"Delia!" they called in unison.

The room seemed to come alive as the stunning redhead strode across it. Even in the gilded crowd, she stood out in a shimmering blouse that was almost transparent, a skin-tight leather miniskirt, and four-inch high heels that drove her height to over six feet. Her eyes, Marie-Claire noted, were glittery like a hawk's as she scanned the crowd while waggling her fingers in greeting at some groups and blowing air kisses to others. Her focus locked on Marie-Claire and she adjusted her course towards them.

Kami and Dee greeted her like a queen, but Delia never took her attention off Marie-Claire and Neve. "Introduce me to our new friends, girls," Delia said in a throaty Irish accent.

"This is MC Wentworth and..." Kami looked vaguely at Neve. "...and her friend."

"Neve," Marie-Claire filled in, shaking Delia's hand. "Pleased to meet you."

Neve stood at her shoulder, saying nothing.

"So, you're the little painter that's given our Fanta a run for her money." Delia's silky accent belied her words.

"We were just admiring her necklace," Dee trilled. "It's a bird's nest."

Delia stepped closer to run a finger along the smooth ribbon, her lacquered nail tracing a thin line across Marie-Claire's neck. The gesture was innocent, but felt like a stiletto knife was being held to her throat.

"You've obviously escaped your cage, darling. Whom do we call to report we've found you?"

"I guess Mick," Neve answered.

Delia took a step back and sized the black woman up. "Well, that won't be too difficult. Every girl in this room has his number in their mobile."

"As well as the fleet's when it's in, I'd wager," Neve shot back.

"I bet you're one of those students that's sending those fake pictures to the press," Delia surmised. "You must think it's quite clever."

"We know it's quite clever," Neve corrected her.

"You're making Fanta look like an idiot."

"She doesn't need our help."

Delia's eyes flared. "Might be interesting to see how you lot like it—"

"You must be MC," a cheerful woman said, inserting herself into the group and shaking hands. "I'm Connie Bathurst, Brian's wife. He's the Keeper, would step in front of a speeding train if you don't watch him. So glad you could make it to a game, Mick's been hoping you would. They just brought out some smoked salmon, shall we get some?"

Marie-Claire had never been happier to meet a friendly face in her life and let Connie maneuver them towards the buffet and away from the seething trio.

"First time at a football match?" Connie asked, taking a glass of juice from a passing waiter. "You'll enjoy it. The team is doing well this year. Ninth place in the league standings, and with a push they'll finish sixth or seventh. They won't make the European Cup, which is a disappointment, but it will be nice to have Brian around the house this summer with another baby arriving." She patted her round stomach happily.

Marie-Claire liked her immediately. "How many do you have?"

"This will be our third. Another boy, Lord help us."

Connie insisted the girls sample the treats at the table, making them laugh with her envy of their slim waistlines. After their plates were full, she led them to a sitting area and chatted while they ate.

"You want to watch that crew, they're nothing but trouble." Connie nodded to where Delia, Kami, and Dee stood. "They're Fanta's chums, and I know she's been stirring the pot, as well. But our Mick is a good lad, and he deserves someone like you. Hang in there."

People continued to fill the room as the muffled roars of the crowd could be heard through the thick glass.

"Come on, they're about to start," Neve said.

The spectator seats in the skybox were all taken, so they stood at the railing behind them. "That's Fulham, coming out now, they're in the black and red," Neve pointed out. "And here comes Kingsbury Town."

Marie-Claire spotted Mick as the team walked out the tunnel and onto the pitch, towering over his shorter and much thinner teammates. Her heart leapt at the sight of him.

Both teams lined up facing the skybox for the playing of "God Save the Queen," and Marie-Claire smiled as Mick sang along. A few indistinct announcements were made and after the handshake, the players broke apart to warm up.

After a few minutes of ball tossing and short passes, everyone took their places and the roar of the crowd began to swell. Neve gave her a program from a table and pointed out the team's lineup. "Kingsbury Town plays a traditional four-four-two formation, and Mick's a defender so that means he's in the back row. See, there's Fernando Garcia-Lopez, and then Darius, then Mick, and Jason Edu on the outside."

"Who are the rest?"

"The midfielders are Hugo Auchincloss, Pozny Gorlinski, Jean-Georges Mayotte, and Lars Van Der Beek. Wait, no, he's out again. That's Dylan Rhea in for him, it's going to be a rough day. Those two in front, that's Samuel Nkomo and Marco Cantamessa. They're the strikers."

"Are they the only ones who can score?"

"No, anyone can score and anyone does. Their manager, Giles Roberts, he's so barmy nobody'd be surprised if he had Connie's husband boot in a long one."

The game began and Kingsbury Town's offense was instantly active, pushing the ball towards Fulham's goal. Marie-Claire watched, fascinated, as the ball was kicked back to Kingsbury Town and the defense went to work, blocking a Fulham midfielder. Mick's focus was complete, and she saw him making quick motions to his teammates seconds before something happened.

The play was fast and furious, and Mick had a neat tackle and cross pass to Darius, who booted the ball far up the field. The crowd cheered and started singing a song, the words to which Marie-Claire couldn't work out.

Ten minutes into play, a Fulham player went down and people in red and black raced from the sidelines to tend to him. Kingsbury Town took the opportunity to regroup, and while everyone in the box began chatting, Delia appeared at Marie-Claire's side and slipped an arm through hers, drawing her away to a quiet spot.

"I thought we might have a chat," Delia began, accepting a glass of red wine from a passing waiter. "Here, have a glass, you haven't had anything to drink since you got here."

Marie-Claire declined, feeling a need to keep her wits about her.

"We've started out on the wrong foot, and I apologize," Delia said. "But I wanted you to know I've seen your press, and I feel sorry for you. Truly."

Marie-Claire studied Delia's features, which remained motionless even though she seemed to be trying to express emotion. "Thanks."

"It's an art, you know. Handling the press, getting the coverage you want. And at this level—" Delia gestured toward the players on the field "—all the attention is on them and you. The guys know there's no room for mistakes. One slip-up and they'll turn on you. You're done."

Marie-Claire shrugged. "Mick says it will pass and to just ignore it."

Delia laughed. "He would say that, but let's face it, he'll say anything to get into a girl's knickers."

"Will he."

Delia rolled her eyes. "MC, I've seen it before. Mick talks up a good story, but all he really cares about is himself and that ratty farm he's got going in the middle of nowhere. He's out for a good time and when that good time is done, he moves on. He's quite the lad."

Anger began to burn in the pit of Marie-Claire's stomach. "Fanta must be a saint to put up with that."

"She is. And I'm not just saying that because she's my best friend. She's a smart girl, and she's patient. They've been together for ages now, and she's been through it more than once, let me tell you. But they were very happy, you know, and Mick was starting to settle down. There was even talk of them getting engaged."

"Why didn't they? It seems like they had every opportunity."

Delia brushed that aside. "They're both incredibly busy people. Fanta's schedule is booked. She's wanted everywhere. It's the world we live in, all of us here. I don't think you'd understand."

Marie-Claire stared at her stonily. "I guess not."

Delia recognized her line of attack was not working and switched gears. "MC, you seem like a really sweet girl. Very, ummm…" She looked her up and down appraisingly. "… natural. Yes. *Very* natural. But you're an American, dear, and fans don't like footballer girlfriends to be foreign. Especially Americans. They like nice girls from the UK for their lads."

"Which box are the nice girls watching from?" Marie-Claire asked curiously.

"What I'm trying to say," Delia bit out, her temper on a tight rein, "is that you don't belong here. Mick's had his fun with you, and Fanta is ready to take him back. Now. And you need to let that happen."

"I've tried, repeatedly. Mick won't let me go."

"Try harder."

"I think I'll keep him around," she countered.

"Right now you think Mick is so honest, so noble," Delia said, dropping all pretense of concern. "What would you say if I told you he's come on to most of the women in this room, even me?"

Marie-Claire stared Delia straight in the eye. "I'd say I'm not surprised. He told me he was raised in the country, so I figured he knew his way around a barn full of sows."

Delia's eyes ignited with anger, and with a furious snap of her wrist, she threw the contents of her wine glass over Marie-Claire. People who had been watching them covertly gasped in shock as the red liquid splattered across her blouse and pants, soaking the fabric before running in rivulets to the carpet.

In an instant, Neve was at Marie-Claire's side, grabbing her arm. "Come on, we're out of here." She marched them to the door and let it slam shut behind them.

Chapter Twenty-Three

THE HALLWAY WAS lined with anonymous doors and the girls paused, unsure which direction to go.

"This way," Neve directed and together they ran to a stairwell at the end of the corridor. Marie-Claire's heart pounded as they sprinted down endless flights before emerging onto the main concourse.

"What'd she say to you?" Neve asked when they could catch their breath.

"She was telling me to drop Mick so he'd take Fanta back."

Neve swore colorfully. "What'd you tell her?"

"I declined." Marie-Claire managed to grin and then realized that her splattered clothing was drawing curious stares from the crowd. "Let's find a ladies room, I need to get cleaned up."

In the cavernous restroom, the girls worked to blot the stains from her white blouse and light-colored trousers as best they could, hearing intermittent groans or roars from the distant crowd. The bright pink splotches refused to lift and they soon had to admit defeat.

Marie-Claire threw a paper towel in the bin. "It's no use, come on, let's leave. I don't belong here."

"We're not going anywhere," Neve declared. "That lot of nasties is not going to scare us off. You have as much right to be here as anyone, and besides, Mick wants you here. So, we might as well find some seats and enjoy the game."

Marie-Claire fished in her pockets and pulled out a few pound notes and three coins. "I only brought five pounds."

Neve searched her own pockets. "I've got seven, but I'm sure seats are much more than that."

They stood for a moment in indecision, until Neve grabbed the pass that hung around Marie-Claire's neck. "I know, why don't we see if these will get us seats?"

Without waiting for an answer, Neve took her hand and set out on the concourse.

"We'd like closer seats," she told a uniformed usher. "Do you know if there's anything available?"

The usher inspected the passes and had them follow him through a tunnel into the stadium, where he pointed to a pair of seats several rows up from the pitch at about midfield. "You can have those two, they belong to the club. I don't think they're being used today."

The girls took their seats in the noisy crowd. Kingsbury Town and Fulham were tied with one goal apiece with six minutes left before halftime. Kingsbury Town clearly had their hands full as Fulham kept the ball in Kingsbury Town's half of the field. This kept Mick in almost constant motion as he sprinted to the ball and blocked, several times giving the ball a powerful boot up the field. Marie-Claire felt pleasant goose pimples spread over her as she watched him play.

Soon the referee blew the whistle for halftime, and the players trudged off the field, Mick and Darius in close conversation with several of their teammates.

"Better be planning how they're going to stuff Radjovik," the lady next to Marie-Claire grumbled, then looked her over head to toe. "What you got all over you, then?"

"Someone spilled some wine on me," Marie-Claire explained.

The woman chortled. "Looks like you took a bath in it."

Neve went and got a meat pie that they split, and then play resumed. Fulham took possession of the ball and seemed to be shooting it between themselves for several minutes until one of the Kingsbury Town strikers snagged it, and with a high kick, booted it into the Fulham net. As the crowd cheered, Marie-Claire couldn't take her eyes off Mick. Was she imagining things, or was he favoring his right leg?

"Isn't it funny," Neve mused as the play clock ticked, "those two men with the cameras have walked past three times already, looking in the stands. They haven't once looked at the pitch."

"You're paranoid," Marie-Claire said, watching the play, "too many paparazzi outside your window."

"I don't know. It just seems strange."

The teams fought on until Kingsbury Town scored a third goal. The crowd's cheers were drowned out, however, by the referee's whistle calling an offside penalty against Kingsbury Town and the goal was disallowed. A last-minute burst from Fulham came too late to matter, and the game ended in a 2-1 win for Kingsbury Town.

"Should have been 3-1," the woman next to her muttered, "teach those lads to watch their fouls."

The home crowd began to file out sourly even though their team had won, while the players lined up on the field to shake hands.

"I wonder how we get home from here?" Marie-Claire began to say, when a man at the rail below them pointed towards her, a zoom lens camera in his hand.

"There she is!"

He and another photographer began pushing against the tide of exiting spectators, using their shoulders to bully their way forward and not caring who they knocked over in their fight to get a shot of Marie-Claire.

Marie-Claire and Neve watched in horror as a beefy young man stepped in front of a blonde girl, bent over, and charged the two paparazzi like a raging bull. He knocked them so hard they flew in separate directions, one falling on a woman and the other tumbling over seats and landing on a man. Unfazed, they were back on their feet in an instant, shoving towards Marie-Claire and throwing elbows at anyone in their way.

One man refused to yield and was rewarded with a sharp elbow to his midsection. He folded over and collapsed on the woman behind him, who screamed and fell against Neve, knocking her to the ground.

Bedlam exploded around them. The fallen man scrambled to his feet and swung a meaty punch at the second photographer, but he ducked and the blow landed squarely on another man behind him, knocking him into a young couple and sending them backwards over their seats. Marie-Claire grabbed Neve and helped her up, and they clung to each other, looking for a way out.

Fists were flying everywhere as the photographers fought their way closer, stopping to snap off a picture, and then pushing and shoving whoever got in their way. Neve screamed as a man was thrown to the ground between them, and as she bent to help him up, another man was knocked on top of her.

Marie-Claire tried to reach her, but a burly fan wrapped a thick arm around her and began dragging her backwards. "Neve!" she screamed, her arms flailing as she tried to break free.

———◦———

On the field, the players were trudging back to the locker room when the screams from the stands halted them in their tracks. Yellow-jacketed security was swooping down on the fracas around the midfield line, highlighted by intermittent bright strobe flashes. The team watched, stunned, as over two dozen spectators threw punches and the melee seemed to spread like an epidemic.

Mick scanned the crowd uneasily, an odd feeling in the pit of his stomach. Surely Marie-Claire was up in the team's skybox where Phillip had escorted her; he'd given Mick the thumbs-up as the team had gone on the field. He glanced up to the skyboxes but saw nothing except the reflection off the glass, and then heard a scream that sounded like "Neve!"

What the hell? That was Marie-Claire's voice! Sprinting to the wall, he hauled himself up and over the railing, with Darius and Hugo Auchincloss following close behind.

Security had already begun to surround the area and Mick searched the scene in desperation, now hearing Marie-Claire's screams clearly. Two men with cameras seemed to be at the center of the battle, and it appeared the crowd was enjoying their assault on the photographers, who were frantically trying to fight, yet get more shots at the same time.

Through a gap in the brawl, Mick saw Marie-Claire in the clutch of a huge bear of a man, fighting him desperately.

Seeing red, he lunged into the battle and fought his way to where she was.

"Let her go!" he bellowed, grabbing the goon by the back of his collar and pulling him down from behind.

The man released Marie-Claire but she immediately dove back into the fight. "Sodding oaf, I was pulling her out!" the man protested.

Mick lunged after her, throwing brawlers out of the way. Flashes continued to go off around them until he landed a heartfelt punch across a photographer's smug face. He caught up to her as she knelt where Neve had fallen between the seats.

Darius appeared, his expression horrified.

"We've got to get them out of here," Mick yelled as he scooped Marie-Claire up in his arms. Darius lifted Neve and together they pushed their way through the crowd as police sirens began to wail in the distance.

Once in the main concourse, a guard motioned them towards a room where they were able to lay the girls on the ground.

"Are you okay?" Mick demanded, crouching over Marie-Claire.

She fought to catch her breath, tears spilling from her eyes. "I don't know. My chest hurts, he was holding me so tightly."

"That bloke landed on me," Neve gasped as Darius checked her over. "He knocked the breath out of me."

Darius paled visibly. "Dear God, there's blood in your hair. Mick, get the team medics."

———————⋅◦⋅———————

Two hours later, the diagnosis was that Neve had suffered a concussion and moderate cut behind her ear, and Marie-Claire had just missed a cracked rib. Both girls were battered and blood-smeared, with ugly bruises starting to form on Marie-Claire's arms and chest. Mick and Darius had been banished from the examining room against their loud protests, and after the medics had finished, the police told them they needed to give their statements.

The narrow corridors under the stadium were a beehive of activity, and Marie-Claire was shown to a tiny office with a hard, wooden chair and a metal desk. It was freezing cold and her shirt was torn, and a policewoman draped a blanket over her shoulders and left her alone.

There were no windows in the room. A console telephone sat on the desk, but the connecting cable had been removed. She sat immobile for what seemed like ages, hearing muffled voices through the thick door. Once she thought she heard Mick's voice and her heart jumped, but minutes ticked by and nothing happened.

Finally, an austere man with thinning grey hair entered the room and introduced himself as Detective Chief Inspector Parker. He was accompanied by a policewoman, who set up a recording device on the desk and motioned for Marie-Claire to take a seat on one side. The detective and policewoman sat down on the other, their faces carefully composed.

The detective started by asking Marie-Claire to state her name, address, and occupation. She complied and the policewoman played back the recording and nodded. No one seemed to be in any hurry whatsoever.

"You're a United States citizen, I've been told?" he asked when she finished.

"Yes."

"May I see your passport?"

"I, I didn't bring it with me," Marie-Claire fumbled, taken off guard by his request.

"I see." His brow furrowed and he wrote for a moment in his notepad. "Would you please tell me your recollection of today's events?"

It was a struggle to pull her thoughts together. She attempted to recall, but everything was still so shocking that the words came out in a senseless jumble. The man made careful notes as she spoke, his face inscrutable, encouraging her to continue when she apologized for being so disjointed. When she finished, she sat, her tongue numb.

"Why were you sitting in the stands, Miss? Hadn't arrangements been made for you to watch the game from the club skybox?" the detective inquired pleasantly, as if he was asking her what she'd had for breakfast.

She squirmed in her chair. "Yes, but…it was hard to see. We decided to try and find seats in the stands."

They were interrupted by a knock at the door. The inspector excused himself and stepped out while the policewoman stopped the recording and sat back, staring at her stonily. When the inspector returned, Marie-Claire saw that while his outward appearance remained unruffled, his demeanor had changed considerably. And he was carrying Mick's coat.

He nodded to the policewoman to restart the interview and laid the coat on the desk between them. "The paparazzi are saying they were called and told that you had left the skybox and were sitting in the open. They say they were given the exact section and seats."

Marie-Claire eyed the coat. "There were a lot of people sitting around us. Maybe someone recognized me and called them."

"They are saying you called them."

The statement was so ridiculous she couldn't help but laugh. "I didn't call anyone."

He consulted his notepad. "At 1:22 p.m. today, they received a call from a mobile phone registered to Mick Carr, which he admits he purchased for you and that you have temporary use of. The caller suggested they come and photograph you sitting in the stands watching Carr play, and a fee was agreed on."

"I didn't call anyone," she repeated.

The inspector handed the policewoman a pair of synthetic gloves and asked her to empty the coat pockets. "Do you recognize these items?" the inspector asked when everything had been laid before them.

"Yes."

"Please identify them."

"There's the mobile Mick gave me," Marie-Claire said, "a tube of lip balm, a tissue, and three scraps of paper I took off our front gate this morning."

The inspector leaned into the recording device. "Let the record show that Miss Wentworth correctly identified the items presented, including a paper with the mobile number that corresponds to the phone of suspect number two."

For a brief moment, the room tilted crazily on its axis and Marie-Claire squeezed the arms of her chair.

Flipping the notebook page, he continued. "Phillip Trent says that as he was transporting you to the stadium this morning, you expressed dismay that the photojournalists outside your door were greatly reduced in number. Quote: 'Then I told Miss Wentworth she'd have to do something dramatic to get their attention back, like start a riot. She said that was a very good idea and thanked me for it.'"

"I didn't mean it!"

"Miss Clark admitted that you and your friends have been playing multiple pranks on the press."

The air in Marie-Claire's lungs began to burn. "They were jokes. Because they were harassing me."

"You and your friends have been playing quite a few jokes. Is it true you've been ringing up these same paparazzi and telling them of different sightings of you across London?"

"I haven't but my friends have, and I appreciate it. I wouldn't be able to walk home if they hadn't. It wasn't like there was any police protection," she added recklessly.

The inspector ignored that. "The photographer's phone number was found in your pocket."

"They leave them on the gate every morning, and we take them off because they litter the neighbor's rose bushes and he gets annoyed. I put them in my pocket this morning and haven't been near a waste bin."

DCI Parker's face remained expressionless. "These two photographers are reputed to be the most aggressive out there and have a record of starting altercations just to create a story. And you claim you have no idea how they knew you were in the stands today."

Her throat was so dry she could barely summon words. "None."

The detective nodded to the policewoman, who powered the mobile phone on. The device came to life with a brief trill, and after a few taps, displayed the number of the last call made.

"Do you agree that the telephone number displayed here matches the number on this scrap of paper?"

It did indeed.

"And that the time and date the number was called correspond to today's date at approximately thirty-three minutes into the match?"

Marie-Claire could only nod.

"Please let the record show that Miss Wentworth replied in the affirmative to both questions," he said and scribbled in his notebook. When he finished, he snapped the little book shut and stood.

"A terrible crime was perpetrated today, Miss Wentworth, and a tragedy only narrowly averted. It is my duty to now place you under—"

A sharp knock at the door interrupted the inspector and a policeman entered the room and handed him a note. DCI Parker read intently before handing the note back to him and turning off his recorder.

"We'll need to keep all of this," he announced. "You are excused, for now, but are advised to notify us if you leave the vicinity of London in the next few days."

Something had happened—what, exactly, Marie-Claire was unsure. But there seemed to be a reprieve of some kind. "Do I need a lawyer?"

His answer was curt. "It might not be a bad idea."

———◦O◦———

The stadium was still swarming with police when Marie-Claire was released. She numbly followed the warren of hallways under the stadium, refusing to ask anyone for help until eventually she ended up in a large foyer with doors to the parking garage. Realizing she had no way of getting home and even less of a chance of finding Mick, she counted the money in her pocket and wondered if the few coins she had was enough to get her a bus going south of the Thames.

Marie-Claire pushed the door open, bracing as the cold night air engulfed her. Across the empty garage, she saw Mick waiting by his Aston Martin. He'd changed into jeans and his leather jacket and stood stiffly, his arms crossed and his expression unreadable. The distance seemed to stretch for miles as she walked towards him, trying to maintain some dignity in her torn and splattered clothing.

"Where's Neve?" she asked, stopping a few feet from him.

He scrutinized her coldly. "They fixed her up here and Darius took her home."

Marie-Claire nodded and rubbed her forehead, which had begun to pound. "Is everyone else okay?"

"Eleven spectators went off to hospital, but no one was seriously injured. No thanks to you."

She winced. "That's harsh."

"It's no worse than you deserve."

"It just happened," she explained, trying to hold back the tears. "The game ended, we stood up to leave, and then those men started taking pictures and everyone started fighting. I don't know how they knew we were there."

"They said you called them."

"That's what the police said."

"They showed me the phone, had me ID it," Mick lashed out savagely. "It's in my name, I pay the bill, and if thirty-two thousand people couldn't swear to my whereabouts when the call was made, they would have arrested me on the spot."

"I'm sorry."

The guys know there's no room for mistakes. One slip-up and they'll turn on you. You're done.

"Is this something you and your friends dreamed up as another joke?" Mick demanded. "Were you missing the attention?"

Marie-Claire searched his face, stunned. "No. God, no."

"Well, you've got it now, my girl, and in spades." Mick was shouting now, his voice echoing off the concrete pillars. "Don't you have any sense? People have been killed at these matches. How could you be so stupid? Even Fanta wouldn't have tried that."

The mention of Fanta's name was the last straw. The injustice of the situation welled up inside her, choking Marie-Claire with the intensity of the unfairness. Hot tears stung her eyes and she wiped them away furiously on her ragged sleeve.

It was useless fighting when the one person she thought would believe her, didn't.

Chapter Twenty-Four

EXHAUSTION FLOODED HER body and she became tired of denying everything, tired of everyone thinking the worst of her. If this was Mick's world, full of intrigue and lies, Delia was right. She didn't belong in it. She turned and walked away.

Mick followed after her. "Where the hell do you think you are going?"

The night was bitterly cold but she didn't feel it. "Home."

"Get in the car."

"I'll take the bus." Her teeth began to chatter but she kept walking.

"Great, and start another riot. Get in the bleedin' car." He took her arm, marched her back to the car and shoved her none too gently into the seat. Revving the engine mercilessly, he sped out of the car park.

Gridlocked traffic frustrated Mick's efforts as soon as they reached the main road. Minutes ticked by as they inched forward, the drumming of Mick's fingers on the steering wheel the only sound in the car. She sat next to him, the hot air pouring from the car vents doing nothing to dispel the icy atmosphere.

Unconsciously, she reached to her neck but her bird's nest was gone. The necklace had probably been torn off in the fighting and was being swept up with the rest of the debris. After all that had happened that day, she felt this blow the hardest.

"Why did you send Phillip to the house this morning?" Marie-Claire asked, a flicker of curiosity stirring the numbness.

"I wanted to surprise you," Mick said, his expression hard. "You said you wanted to see a match and obviously can't navigate past Putney, so I sent Phillip to get you. I know I should have asked you last night, but…"

"But you left in a hurry," Marie-Claire finished for him. He gripped the steering wheel so tightly, his knuckles turned white.

In slow measures, the traffic ahead of them folded into one lane. Marie-Claire barely noticed. Beyond that, the roadway opened up and they were able to accelerate to a normal speed.

"Why didn't you stay in the skybox?" Mick asked, seeming to have more control of himself. "It's the lap of luxury, all the food and drink you could want, and a great view of the pitch. All the other girls, the skybox is all they've wanted."

Marie-Claire pressed her lips together. "They're welcome to it."

"You and Neve were supposed to watch the match from there with the other wives and girlfriends. It's a party," he persisted, "and they're a jolly fun bunch, I know them well."

"So they said."

"Why did you leave?"

Marie-Claire fought back the angry words that jumped to her lips. Accusations were useless; she and Mick were over now and nothing she could say would fix anything. "I don't think we met the dress code."

He glanced over at her. "What's that red stuff on your trousers?"

"Merlot. I think."

Mick's mobile beeped twice, and at a red light, he checked the message. "The Football Association is having an inquest Tuesday," he told her. "If they fine Kingsbury Town, the club will sue you for it."

It was like being hit again. With an effort, she sucked breath back into her chest and licked her dry lips. "How much of a fine?"

"The last spectator that caused a riot went to jail and was fined £10,000. But you should make the tabloids help you pay, they've made a mint off of you today."

The light turned green and she squeezed her eyes shut, feeling sick.

"MC, you should just come clean and confess," Mick tried to reason with her. "If you do, they'll go a little easier on you. Believe me, I know."

It was the first time he had called her by her nickname. "If I plead guilty I'll be deported."

"They'll deport you anyway when they prove you did it. But it might save you having to go to the nick."

"What should I do if I'm innocent?"

The question seemed to stump him. "Pray, I guess."

He drew up in front of her house and photographers mobbed the car, three deep in places. Flash strobes exploded and bizarre faces pressed against the car windows and windshield, all of them yelling.

"Here you go, lass. Your adoring public."

She sat like a statue, the punches of flashing strobes illuminating her pale face. "I did enjoy the game."

Mick got out and fought his way around the car to open her door and pulled her out, blocking the gang that crowded around, shoving and yelling and snapping pictures. She fought back tears as they made their way from the street to the front walk, not able to take a step without a person with a microphone blocking her path. At the door, he pushed her inside and slammed it shut behind her.

She slumped against the doorjamb and let the tears overwhelm her. "Fine," she whispered. "Fine."

It was close to midnight when Neve let herself in through the garden gate. Marie-Claire heard her coming up the path, humming a tune.

"You seem awfully happy for someone who was in the middle of a riot this afternoon," she said, looking up from where she sat at the kitchen table, a sketch pad sitting before her, untouched. "Are you okay?"

Neve grinned. "Not bad, yourself?"

"Sore."

"Me, too." Neve dropped into a chair and sighed. "Darius is ever so nice."

A tired smile tugged at Marie-Claire's lips. "Oh yes?"

"He took me out for a drink to calm my nerves, and we ended up having dinner. I told him everything that happened. He's lovely." Neve examined her housemate more closely. "You look like you could use a drink yourself."

Marie-Claire began to refuse but Neve ignored her and went to the cupboard where they kept their bottle of whiskey. "You know, the riot is on all the news," Neve said over her shoulder as she poured two glasses. "I had to call Mum and tell her we're okay."

"Mick thinks I did it as a publicity stunt," Marie-Claire told her as Neve set the glass before her. "In fact, that's what everyone thinks."

"No. How do they get that?"

"The photographers said someone called them and tipped them off that I was in the stands, and gave them the exact location."

"But that could have been anyone around us."

Marie-Claire downed the contents of the glass in one gulp, gasping as the liquid burned a fiery trail to her stomach. "The photographers said they were called directly," she wheezed, "and when the police checked my mobile, it showed their number."

"How could that happen?"

"I have no idea."

"And Mick believes that dross?"

"Yes. I don't think I'll be seeing him again."

Neve swirled the whiskey in her glass for a few moments then slammed the glass on the table. "Your mobile was in your coat pocket, wasn't it? I mean Mick's coat."

"Yes."

"We left it there when we bolted from the skybox, didn't we."

The truth of Neve's words dawned on her. "Do you think one of them used it to call the photographers?"

"I'd bet a year's tuition on it," Neve snapped. "Come on, we have to go to the police."

Relief flooded her and she jumped to her feet, but then sat down again when she tried to think it through. "And say what? My now ex-boyfriend's ex-girlfriend's best friends plotted to create a riot and are trying to frame me for it?"

"But it's what happened."

"How could we prove it? Everyone seems to have made up their minds."

Especially Mick.

Neve's shoulders sagged. "So, what are you going to do now?"

"I don't know. I thought the police were going to arrest me, and they still might. In the meantime, there's going to be an inquest Tuesday at the Football Association, so I'll go and talk with them. I hope it's not too awful."

"My cousin Jane is a lawyer, let's call her and see what she says," Neve decided. "We'll get through this, just you watch."

Chapter Twenty-Five

RAUL ARRIVED HOME from Chez Bertrand's at midnight with the news that Fanta had been giving television interviews all evening, and that some members of Parliament were demanding a special inquest. Jane was called, and her advice was to sit tight until the police decided to press charges.

"This is a very high-profile case and the authorities are all over it. If they haven't pressed charges against you already, it might be as Neve says, it's best to wait it out. But if they do," she added ominously, "you've got my number."

Her advice was sound, but following it was easier said than done. Marie-Claire lay in bed, unable to sleep, and realized she'd left her sweater at Mick's the weekend before. He'd told her it had come back from the cleaners, and she'd just assumed she would get it the next time she went to his house. Now she might never see it again. Despair flooded her, releasing the floodgate of tears that had been pent up inside her. She cried wretchedly into her pillow until she fell into a troubled sleep.

In the morning, the sidewalk outside the house was jammed with photographers, and Neve said that the bounty for pictures of her had tripled.

The police still had Mick's jacket, so Raul lent her an old coat. With Neve's hat pulled down over her brows, the housemates set off to school, while the neighbors stood on their front stoops and frowned. The paparazzi swarmed around them as they walked, yelling questions and bumping them rudely as they pushed their way down the road.

"MC! Why were you in the stands?"

"Why didn't you call me, love?"

"Eleven people were hospitalized. Do you have a comment?"

"Is Mick back with Fanta?"

Marie-Claire concentrated on the sidewalk before her, desperately trying not to wonder the same thing.

A garishly dressed woman pushed a note into Raul's hand. "The *Sun* wants to pay you ten thousand pounds for an exclusive," he read.

Two lucky photographers got shots of Marie-Claire's horrified expression before she yanked the brim of her hat down and Raul threw the offer in a trash bin.

———◇———

At school, the mood was tense. A heap of the morning's tabloids had been stacked on her worktable, and she saw she'd even made the front page of the more reputable papers.

YANK PRANK? asked the *Daily Mail*.

The *Sun*'s headline was **CALL MADE FROM MC's MOBILE**. *Police sources have informed the Sun that the calls to the two paparazzi charged in the incident were indeed made from MC Wentworth's mobile phone. "It's very serious when these footballer girlfriends use the press to get attention for themselves," Detective Chief Inspector Parker told the Sun.*

"It's all well and good to get your picture taken on the red carpet but to use a football stadium as a venue is unforgivable. The young lady is lucky more people weren't injured."

There were pictures of the Kingsbury Town players on the field as the fight was breaking out, looking up into the stands. Mick had his hand over his eyes and was looking up in horror, and the next photo showed him sprinting over the railing towards the stands.

The *Morning Express* had found a picture of Fanta looking soulfully into Mick's eyes. **BACK TOGETHER?** it mused, with a detailed interview from Fanta. *"Of course, people could have gotten seriously injured,"* Fanta de las Mercedes explained in a telephone interview right after the riot, *"especially my Mick. But he's always the first to wade into a fight no matter who's involved. I think he was just trying to save the Kingsbury Town fans."* Kingsbury Town defender Mick Carr was unavailable to answer questions.

"I see Fanta jumped right on the bandwagon, as usual. They should just give her a daily column," Neve said as she thumbed through the *Observer*.

Marie-Claire's heart twisted in her chest. "Do you think they're going to get back together?"

"I think we're going to do exactly as Jane says and wait this out," Neve declared, grabbing her by the arm. "Come on, we're going to clean the prop room."

That night, the arrival of a police car outside their house set off a firestorm of camera flash strobes. By the time the officer reached their front door, Marie-Claire was sitting in the front room with Neve, her passport in her pocket and her parent's phone number in Maryland written on a pad of paper. She sat while Raul answered the door, trying to be brave, and actually felt relieved that something was going to happen. Even if that something meant she was going to be arrested.

But instead of arresting her, the policeman handed her a bag that contained Mick's jacket, the mobile phone, and the rest of the contents of her pockets. After she had duly signed for the items, he either couldn't, or wouldn't, answer any questions. He left and the three housemates could only stare at each other in bemusement.

Upstairs in her bedroom, Marie-Claire sat on her bed and turned on the mobile phone. The device stirred itself to life with a few trills and bursts of color on the screen and fell silent. There were no notifications of messages or texts, but perhaps the police had erased them? No, all of Mick's messages were still stored in the memory and his was still the only phone number listed in the directory.

She crawled into bed and clasped the phone to her chest like a talisman. The desire to call and tell him what had just happened was overwhelming, and if she pressed the number one and SEND he might pick up and she could hear his voice.

Should she do it?

The spidery cracks in the ceiling overhead were illuminated by the street lamps, and Marie-Claire studied them, trying to divine an answer. If he did pick up, what would she say? Maybe she could ask how Lacey was. Or she could ask if the contractor had arrived to build the first pheasant run at Moorsgate, which was supposed to have happened today. Perhaps he'd like to meet up for a drink after classes tomorrow and tell her about it?

The tiny picture of him on the screen glowed silently, a mute testament to Mick's indifference.

One slip-up and they'll turn on you. You're done.

The clock on the nightstand read almost two o'clock in the morning. How wretched could she be that she was even considering calling him at this hour? And more chilling, what if he wasn't alone? The tabloids were full of speculation that he and Fanta would be getting back together, and she doubted Fanta would have wasted any time making that happen.

The idea brought back the stinging tears. Too distraught to consider any possibilities, she went to her dresser and opened the top drawer, and with almost superhuman strength, turned the phone off and put it inside. Closing the drawer firmly, she returned to bed and fell asleep immediately.

<hr />

Rain pelted her bedroom windows the next morning. She woke slowly, the clock by her bed reading nine o'clock, an almost unheard-of time for her to rise. She'd overslept by three hours, but she felt clearheaded and refreshed.

She brushed her hair and dressed, taking care to avoid the top drawer of her dresser. It was impossible not to look at the piece of furniture while she made her bed, and when it was time to go downstairs, she gave in to its magnetic attraction and opened the drawer and took the mobile out.

While the kettle heated for tea, she reasoned that she'd had a good night's sleep and was ready to face whatever the day might bring. Taking a deep breath, she turned the mobile on and prepared herself for the audible flourish followed by the rejecting silence.

Instead, it gave two short beeps to indicate a message had been left. Her heart leapt with a joy she couldn't believe possible. With clumsy fingers, she pushed buttons until the message that had been recorded an hour before played back.

"Miss Wentworth, this is Inspector Barnes from the Hendon police. I wanted to let you know we will not be pressing charges against you in relation to the riot at Townsend Lane Stadium Sunday. Your involvement in the case is over except as that of a victim, and if you choose to press charges please call me or come down to the station and we'll arrange it."

He left his contact information and hung up. The mobile shook in her tight clasp as she gasped lungfuls of air, relief washing over her in torrential waves. She replayed the message several times, her heartbeat gradually returning to normal.

Press charges against whom? she wondered.

This was very good news, she reminded herself. She wasn't to be arrested and deported, she could stay. That didn't mean she was off the hook with the Football Association, but not being arrested was a step in the right direction.

It took several minutes to tamp down the desire to call Mick and tell him the good news.

———————————◆————————————

At noon, she took the Underground to Soho Square and found the Football Association offices in a corner of the leafy quadrangle.

A receptionist looked up as she entered the foyer. "May I help you?"

"I'm here for the FA inquest on the riot Sunday at Townsend Lane Stadium."

"Your name?"

She ran her tongue over her dry lips. "Marie-Claire Wentworth."

A flicker of interest lit the receptionist's eyes. "Through that door, up the stairs, first conference room on the left."

She took the stairs with measured steps, and then knocked on the conference room door and let herself in. She was taken aback; instead of the austere courtroom she had expected, she was in a bright and modern conference room. A dozen people sat around a large table, including Detective Chief Inspector Parker.

She stood for several moments before a woman noticed her.

"Yes? What can we do for you?"

"I'm here for the inquest."

"This isn't an inquest, but it is a closed meeting."

"I'm supposed to be here. It's about me. I'm Marie-Claire Wentworth."

At her words, the room fell into a hushed silence. Swallowing the lump in her throat, she took a seat at the table and folded her hands before her.

A tall man stood and extended his hand. "Miss Wentworth. May I introduce myself, my name is Richard Lambton, and I am the Chairman of the Football Association."

Marie-Claire stood and shook his hand. "Pleased to meet you, Richard."

"Lord Lambton," a voice behind her said softly.

Lord Lambton then went around the room and introduced the other members of the organization, including the woman who had first spoken to her, Marjorie Dawes, who was in charge of operations and security for the Football Association.

"And you know DCI Parker, I believe," Lord Lambton added dryly and motioned for everyone to take their seats.

"What can we do for you today, Miss Wentworth?"

"I was told..." Marie-Claire began and then paused. "Do you want me to swear on a Bible or something?"

There was a snort of laughter, which was immediately stifled.

"I was told you would be meeting today to decide the punishment for what happened on Sunday," she began again. "I'm responsible, and I want to make sure that the punishment goes to me and not Kingsbury Town or anyone else."

Her words hung in the air while the officials regarded her with cool interest. Lord Lambton exchanged glances with DCI Parker, who opened a small notebook in front of him and began to write.

"And how are you responsible?" the detective asked. "When I interviewed you Sunday you said you had no idea how the riot began."

"That's correct. I don't."

"Then how are you responsible?"

"Because I was there. I didn't know we weren't supposed to leave the skybox," she explained, the words rushing out, "and I didn't know we weren't supposed to watch from the stands without permission, but because I was there the paparazzi found me and hurt some fans, eleven seriously enough to be taken to the hospital, although they were released, and I tried to find out who they were, but the hospital wouldn't tell me, and if you know I'd really like to at least write them all apology notes. I have no idea how the call came from my mobile phone but it's mine and I'm responsible for it. Anyway, I was there and if I wasn't the riot wouldn't have happened so I am to blame and take full responsibility."

The group listened to her rambling declaration in silence.

"Why did you leave the skybox?" the woman in charge of security asked.

"Because someone spilled wine on me."

She flipped through her notepad. "Miss Delia Shannon."

"How did you know?"

"Because it's my job to know," the woman replied curtly. "How did you end up in those particular seats?"

"After we left the box, we tried to buy tickets but hadn't brought enough money. I wasn't quite sure what to do, but we were still wearing the passes we had been handed at the door and an usher let us sit in the club seats."

"What do you remember from the game?"

"It was wonderful. Very exciting. Neve, she's my housemate, I wouldn't let her come today because she had nothing to do with this, she knows a lot about soccer—"

At the surprised look on their faces, she hastily corrected herself. "I mean football. She knows a lot about football, and she explained what was going on. We had a really good time."

"Did anyone talk to you or approach you during the game?"

"No, no one. We just said a few words to the people around us."

"Did you notice anything odd?"

"Neve did. She noticed two men walking in front of our aisle in the second half. She thought they looked familiar. They were the photographers who came at us after the whistle blew."

"At the end of the match?" Marjorie asked.

Marie-Claire nodded. "It had just finished and the teams were shaking hands. I honestly don't remember anything more than saying 'I wonder how we get home from here,' and then a man was thrown back on Neve and the flashes started going off."

"You didn't know how to get home from the stadium?" a man down the table asked skeptically.

"No. Mick, Mr. Carr, had sent a car to pick us up, but I didn't know how we were going to get home. I wasn't sure where we were and what Underground stations were around."

"Surely you had plans to meet him after the game?"

"No. It was all a surprise. I hadn't planned on going to the game at all, I was cleaning my house."

"So, Carr hadn't told you that you were to meet him in the team skybox after the game for the reception?"

"No."

"Had you ever been to a Premier League football match before?" another man asked.

"No."

"And you had no idea where you were?"

"No. Well, somewhere near Hendon and I think that's northwest of London, isn't it? I only know my way around Wandsworth and Putney."

The officials looked at each other, frowning. "I'll say thrown to the wolves," one muttered under his breath.

"Miss Wentworth," Marjorie began, "when you were dropped off at the VIP entrance to the stadium, you became the guest of the Kingsbury Town Football Club. As such, they were responsible for your safety. They were also responsible for the behavior of their other guests, which includes preventing one guest from assaulting another with an alcoholic beverage. They were lax in this responsibility, and it is the duty of this board to decide the disciplinary actions against them."

Marie-Claire nodded. "I understand they'll pass it along to me. So, if you'll just tell me how much money it will be, I can start trying to make arrangements to pay it. I can't pay it all at once, but I can pay a bit at a time." She turned to DCI Parker. "The Hendon police called and said they didn't need anything else from me, but if you are going to press charges against me, let me know where to go and I'll cooperate fully. I brought my passport today if you want to take it." She rummaged in her bag, and with trembling hands laid the small book on the table before her.

DCI Parker seemed to be suppressing something very amusing and his expression twisted almost as if he were in pain. "I think we'll let you go with a warning this time."

"Miss Wentworth, perhaps you're not understanding what we're saying," Marjorie interrupted, her tone sharp. "First of all, Mr. Carr has acknowledged he was at fault for surprising you with the invitation to the game, which, after speaking with Phillip Trent, I would characterize as more of a kidnapping. He also said he assumed you would be comfortable in the skybox and know that the team returns there after a match to socialize with their guests. Secondly, Kingsbury Town Football Club had a responsibility to make sure its guests were comfortable and safe. Thirdly, Miss Delia Shannon is being arraigned on charges of conspiracy to incite a riot in the Crown Court of Ireland on Friday for stealing your mobile and using it to call the two paparazzi, who are friends of hers, and alerting them to your whereabouts."

"Delia called them?" Marie-Claire said in shock.

"Yes. We have security video of her in the coatroom of the skybox going through your coat and using the mobile. We also have security footage of you at the exact same moment eating a meat pasty in the stands as the call was placed. The photographers confessed yesterday that they spoke with her and so did she. The victims, and you may consider yourself one, are free to press charges against all three. I believe all of those that were hospitalized have already retained lawyers and are negotiating with Kingsbury Town as we speak."

"Is everyone all right?" Marie-Claire asked.

"Just some scrapes, but they should be very well compensated."

"And Kingsbury Town?"

The group exchanged glances but no one spoke until Lord Lambton cleared his throat. "I met with Sir Frank this morning and discussed the matter with him. I think you can look forward to a substantial token of his regret in lieu of a fine from us."

"I don't want anything." Nothing but Mick, she added to herself.

"That is between you and Sir Frank, my dear."

It took a moment to digest everything she had been told, and then it felt like an enormous weight had been lifted from her shoulders. "So, everything's okay?"

"For you, yes," Lord Lambton said. "And may I say, on behalf of the Board, that we have never been in the unique position of talking someone out of taking responsibility. You are truly an exceptional young lady."

Marie-Claire stood and shook everyone's hand gratefully and left the building on trembling legs.

***

"I told you!" Neve said triumphantly later that night. "I told you it was one of them from the skybox. I hope they throw the stinking book at her. Did they say why she did it?"

"No, but I think it was to scare me off. And show Mick what a liability I am."

"But you didn't do it. He's got to know."

"He'll know by tomorrow, they're having a press conference at noon to announce it."

"Call him now, tell him." Neve urged.

"And tell him what?" Marie-Claire flopped into a chair. "That he was wrong? He didn't believe me when I told him the first time. Besides, I don't think he's going to care."

"I do. I think he cares. He's been miserable."

"How do you know?"

A half-smile played around Neve's lips. "Darius told me. He called yesterday to see how I was and asked about you. He said there were a lot of rumors flying around about what Delia said to you up there in the box, and that Mick's been a right bastard to everyone."

A fleeting stab of hope tapped her heart and Marie-Claire struggled to dampen it. "I'm glad Darius called you. Something good seems to be coming from this."

Chapter Twenty-Six

TUESDAY AFTERNOON, MICK sat alone at the bar of the Crown and Hart trying very hard to drink Marie-Claire Wentworth the hell off his mind.

So far it wasn't working. Her absence was wearing him raw, and a suspicion was festering in his gut that something was terribly, terribly wrong.

A terse phone call from Giles on Monday morning had informed him that the entire team was under orders to lay low and not speak to anyone until the mess could be sorted. The coaches who ran practice were mum, and Darius was absent and not returning his calls. Finally, Mick had gotten a brief text from him saying Mick wasn't being held responsible, which was a relief of sorts. But for Christ's sake, what was going on?

Practice ended at noon and he'd spent the rest of the day pacing his house like a caged lion, filled with restless rage. The anger was pointless and futile, and impossible to direct at anything or anyone except himself. The news on the television showed Marie-Claire going to school surrounded by her chums, stoic and unsmiling, almost like she was the victim instead of the instigator. She continued to make herself as plain and unremarkable as she could, and he had to admit it was brilliant, she was creating a frenzy. Fanta could learn a lot from her.

Surprising the girls with the VIP treatment had sounded like a good idea when Darius had suggested the plan, and he had been eager to make up for the bollocks he had made of the night before. They were supposed to have been escorted to the skybox and treated like queens, and then they'd meet up with them at the mandatory club party after the match. He'd done the same thing lots of times before, but nothing was ever normal when Marie-Claire was involved.

Mick studied the news on the television in the corner of the bar intently. He hadn't called her or tried to see her, knowing he needed time to cool off and figuring that the police would get to the bottom of things. She wasn't stupid—once she was presented with the evidence, she'd have to confess, and then he would see what he could do to help her. Deportation was a certainty, and in truth, she deserved it. The irony of the situation was not lost on him; just when they thought she was in the clear after passing her Critique, he had made her leaving a reality anyway.

And now nothing was making any sense. Why would a girl who would stand in freezing cold water for over two hours deliberately attract the attention of the very people she was desperate to avoid? Was she angling for the money? He dismissed the idea immediately—she hadn't sold her story, even though she could have made a fortune. Money was not a priority with her.

Had her chums talked her into it? Neve had been with her and was certainly a hothead. Maybe she had put Marie-Claire up to it?

He drained his pint and signaled for another.

Sleep had come in fits and starts, and he'd spent most of the nights staring at his ceiling, replaying the haunting memory of her sitting in his car, stubbornly refusing to admit her guilt.

It had been two days and the police hadn't arrested her, nor had they contacted him again, and he wanted to hit something. Badly. He desperately wanted to see her, needed to see her, and he didn't care if she fought him, yelled at him, hit him, he could deal with anything as long as he was with her. He wanted to shake some sense into her, kiss her, hold her. Why in God's name did he want to beg her to take him back?

He gripped the glass so hard it shattered in his hand.

"Easy there, mate," the barman said, and mopped up the pieces and gave him another.

In the gloom of the pub, an overwhelming urge gripped him to buy all the roses in London and lay them in a path from her doorstep to her school so that she wouldn't have to walk on the cold pavement.

How did she do it? She never raised a finger, but unless he had her warmth and softness at the center of his day, he couldn't function. Maybe he was going mental. She scrambled his feelings so completely, going insane was a distinct possibility. When she wasn't around, he felt restless and out of sorts, but when she was, he felt a simple happiness he never thought possible.

He was on a slow trip through hell and he knew it.

"Whotch ya doin', mate?" Darius slapped him on the back, hard, making the beer he was lifting to his lips slosh perilously close to the rim.

Mick scowled. "Trying to get drunk. Very drunk, if you don't mind."

"I'll keep you company."

"Don't bother."

"Oh look, here's Brian and Jason. Let's get a table."

"Let's not."

"Move your arse, Carr."

They took a booth in the back and ordered a round. "Carr is paying," Brian announced to the barman. "Least you can do, you've been a right bastard. You almost took Nasser's arm off at practice this morning."

"What do you lot want?" Mick grumbled.

"To talk about your girl," Jason said, grinning.

Mick's jaw set firm. "Off-limits."

"She got set up, Mick," Brian announced.

"What do you mean, set up?"

"My Connie saw the entire thing," Brian said. "Just after she and her friend arrived, Dee and Kami started talking to them, and were saying some pretty snotty things."

Darius snorted. "There's a stretch."

"Connie thinks they were probably filling her in on some of your more memorable indiscretions," Brian continued as their pints were set before them.

Mick's stomach began to churn. "Go on."

"Anyways, they let her know just how unwelcome she was. Then Delia went in for the kill, took MC aside and started telling her how she needed to back off, that you and Fanta were the real deal, and she was standing in the way of true love. MC basically told Delia to go screw herself, and Delia threw a glass of red wine on her."

The sick feeling got progressively worse. "Why would Delia do that?"

Brian shrugged. "She and Fanta are best chums. They look out for each other. So, the girls left, and Kami and Dee followed them and saw them get seats in the stands. Then they ran back and reported to Delia, and she stole MC's mobile from the coatroom and called two of her pap friends. Delia told them they'd have to wait till after the game, but after that it was open season. MC never had a chance."

Mick's mouth went dry. "How do you know that?"

"The police watched the security tapes and saw the entire thing, and Delia fessed up yesterday. Also, Julie Randall, Hugo's girl, was in the stands with one of the students from her school, and he's the one that actually threw the first punch because he thought the paps were there to harass her. But he's been let off, as well."

"That hasn't been in the news," Mick sputtered, rage flooding his veins.

Jason laughed. "Ha, Hugo's got his fixer working overtime to keep that quiet."

"Is all this true?" Mick asked Darius.

"It all squares with what Neve told me," Darius agreed. "The police and the FA have it, as well."

"Are they going to acquit Marie-Claire?"

Darius laughed. "Not if she has anything to say about it. The police aren't pressing charges, and from what I've heard she showed up at the FA meeting almost demanding to be fined and arrested. Refused to *not* take responsibility for it. The board said they'd never seen anyone like her. Seemed to be convinced it was all her fault just because she was there." Darius looked at him narrowly. "Or had been convinced."

Mick swore under his breath. "But it's all straight then?"

"They finally got her to admit she had nothing to do with it. Delia's being brought up on charges tomorrow in Belfast, and Sir Frank is being allowed to settle privately with the victims, including the girls. They just announced it at a press conference."

The table was very quiet. Mick rolled his head back and closed his eyes, feeling like a dagger had been thrust between them. "Why didn't she tell me? About Delia throwing the wine on her and everything?"

Darius looked at him in pity. "Would you have believed her?"

No, I probably wouldn't have.

"Hey, Mick, if you've blown it, can I have a go at her?" Jason asked cockily.

Brian and Darius sprang forward and managed to pull Mick off before he could do any real damage to Kingsbury Town's prized outside defender.

Chapter Twenty-Seven

MARGARET STOOD ATOP the ladder in the studio, weaving copper wire through tall wooden poles, making the framework of a monumental sculpture. Marie-Claire stood at the bottom, tasked with keeping the poles straight.

"Oi!" Margaret protested. "MC, pay attention."

"Sorry."

"And pass me that next spool of wire."

Marie-Claire mechanically did as she was told.

Raul came up the studio stairs with an armload full of the afternoon's tabloids and dumped them on a table next to her.

"Raul, get those out of here," she said in disgust.

"No, you should see them," Raul urged, showing her the one on top. "They've gone one hundred and eighty degrees. You're a heroine now."

Margaret climbed down the ladder and picked up the top one. "**MC JUST A REGULAR FAN**. *Despite earlier reports that footballer girlfriend MC Wentworth had incited a riot, investigations have exonerated her,*" she read. "*Closed-circuit security cameras show that she and friend Neve Clark had in fact watched the entire game from the stands. 'She was ever so nice, very friendly. But then again, she's an American, isn't* *she,' reports Mrs. Annie Smith of Number Three, Crescent Downs, Ealing, who sat next to MC and was briefly hospitalized as a result of injuries. 'Very pretty girl. Cheered for Mick whenever he did well on the field. We had no idea she was a footballer girlfriend,' Mrs. Smith added. 'She wasn't all snooty like the lot of them. Mick Carr is a lucky man.'"*

"Well, isn't that nice," Margaret said. "They got the story right for once."

Marie-Claire poked through the tabloids, pleased that they had the story mostly correct. Several had excerpts from the FA press conference the day before, and most ran the same pictures of her either coming to or leaving school. Even she couldn't tell what day they had been taken.

"There's no interview from Fanta in here," she said.

Raul grunted. "I bet her friend Delia ending up in prison has stuffed a wad in her piehole. Do you think Mick has seen these?"

Marie-Claire shrugged. "I'm sure he has, but I think it's clear it doesn't make any difference."

Neve clattered up the studio stairs dragging more poles for Margaret. "There's a reception for Edwina Sandys tonight at the Montfort Gallery," she announced loudly. "We should all go."

"Good idea," Raul seconded. "You too, MC."

"Sure I won't cause a riot?"

Neve looked at her pityingly. "You seriously need to get over yourself."

<hr />

After the reception, the group developed a sudden hunger for pizza and decided to stop on the way home. Marie-Claire protested, saying she wasn't hungry and just wanted to go to bed, but the group overruled her.

"We all have to walk home together, so just sit and have a cup of tea or something," Neve coaxed. "I'm famished."

"But we've already had dinner," Marie-Claire pointed out as everyone squeezed into a circular booth at the back of the busy restaurant. "I'm not really hungry," she protested as she was handed a menu. A shadow fell over the table and everyone went silent.

Mick stood across from her, his body tense and his expression guarded. Even though he was dressed in his expensive city clothes, he looked haggard, and she unconsciously rose to go to him. Sandra put a hand on her shoulder and pressed her back down into her seat.

"Don't leave," he said, "I'm not staying. And don't be mad at them." He nodded to her friends. "I told them I needed to see you and they set it up."

Marie-Claire sat in stunned silence, her pulse racing. Raul stretched to rest his arm on the back of her chair and Mick's eyes glinted dangerously.

"I wanted to apologize about last weekend," he began. "I know what happened, everything that happened, in fact. I know how rude everyone was to you. I know it was Delia that called the paparazzi on your mobile after she threw the wine on you. You were right to leave the skybox and go get seats in the stands. You didn't have anything to do with starting that riot. It's my fault more than anyone's, and I'm sorry for putting you in that situation. Both of you." He nodded stiffly to Neve, as well.

Reaching into his jacket, he pulled out an envelope and laid it on the table before her. "It's from Sir Frank, with his apologies." Mick then handed another envelope to Neve.

Marie-Claire fumbled open the envelope, her fingers thick and clumsy. Inside was a check, which she read curiously and then dropped on the table as if it were on fire. Raul picked it up and whistled through his teeth, and then looked at Neve's. Both checks were passed around the table, eliciting startled comments as they went from hand to hand.

"I can't take that." Marie-Claire shook her head mutinously, refusing to look at the check when it came back around to her.

"Neither can I," Neve agreed, pushing hers back towards Mick as well.

"Why am I not surprised," he mused under his breath. "I told Sir Frank you might not take the money, and his suggestion was that together you decide on a use for it."

The group sat in silence. "The heating system in the studio at school is muck," Raul said, "and those would buy a new one, easy."

Everyone agreed with Raul's suggestion, and Marie-Claire drew herself up. "That's what we'll do then," she said, working to keep her voice as neutral as Mick's. "If Sir Frank would like to buy a new heating system for the studio, we would be grateful."

"I'll let him know." Mick nodded and tucked the checks back in his leather jacket. "It turns out I was wrong about what it's like being with me," he said, speaking just to her, "and that got you injured and in a lot of trouble. I'm very sorry. I hope you'll forgive me." He took one last look at her and then nodded to the rest of the group. "Good night," he said, and then left.

Her heart left with him.

It was impossible to sleep that night. Marie-Claire lay motionless in her bed, still excited from having seen Mick. Being with him was always that way, she realized. Whenever they were together, everyone else just faded into the background.

He had been so close she could have reached across the table and touched him. Probably for the last time. She buried her face in her pillow and moaned quietly.

It was over. He knew she wasn't to blame and he had come to apologize. The people who had been injured were going to be well compensated and seemed very happy, the person responsible had been caught and was going to jail, and the school was getting a new heating system. Fanta might even get a call from Hollywood, Marie-Claire added cheerlessly.

Now was the time to pull herself together and realize that while she didn't have to be happy, she should damn well be satisfied. Soon the press would be on to the next story, and she could fade back into oblivion and get on with her work. Everything was square, everything had worked out for everyone, and there were a lot worse outcomes.

Yet she was more miserable than she ever thought possible, and there didn't seem to be any end to the tears that poured from the well of her soul. She wanted to be with Mick, her body ached for him. He was like a drug that she had unknowingly become addicted to, and the withdrawal was threatening to engulf her.

The mobile he had given her was clasped to her chest as her head spun. She hadn't returned it, reasoning that the police might still want it when Delia's case went to court. The mobile was still a lifeline, of sorts, to him, and if she pressed the number one and SEND, he might pick up and she could hear his voice. Should she call him?

The tabloids had been full of speculation that he and Fanta would be getting back together. If he had wanted her back, wouldn't he have behaved differently at the restaurant? Wouldn't he have found a way to meet with her alone?

Her thoughts ricocheted at lightning speed. Maybe she should make him understand she was just offering to be friends, since Mick hadn't made any secret of the fact that he wasn't interested in her sexually. Or maybe he was. He seemed to be, most of the time, but then sometimes not.

But he had made sure she was with other people when he saw her, and there was probably a reason. And the only reason that made sense was that they were over.

She cried harder.

Chapter Twenty-Eight

GORDON ARRIVED AT Moorsgate Wednesday afternoon as Mick was finishing tying netting over the new pheasant run.

"Do you realize you missed three support poles on the other side?" he observed.

Mick muttered a scorching oath that raised his father's eyebrows. "Best not let Sue hear that language out of your mouth."

"Sorry."

"Bad week, son?" he asked as they surveyed the long length of crooked covering.

"Week from hell."

"I see. Nothing to do with MC, I suppose?"

"I don't want to talk about it, Dad."

"Of course."

With a grunt, Mick turned his back on the disastrous project and began to carry bags of grass seed his father had brought with him into the barn. Gordon helped him and together they stacked bags in silence.

"It wasn't her fault, you know," Mick said after a while, not looking up.

"How's that?"

"The riot. It wasn't her fault. A bunch of the girlfriends ganged up on her in the skybox and drove her off. Then they tipped the paps off that she was in the stands. She was set up."

His father nodded with concern. "Is she all right?"

"As far as I know."

"I see. Mick, best not pile those bags on the floor, get one of those pallets."

"Yes, Dad." Of course, you didn't pile seed on a damp earth floor, any idiot knew that. Mick shook his head as if to clear the cobwebs and forced himself to concentrate.

"I saw her," he said. "I apologized."

"That's always a good thing."

"But I don't know how to put it right." Mick sat down on the sacks and buried his head in his hands. "After the riot, the police showed me her mobile. She tried to tell me she didn't do it, and I didn't believe her. It was all so bloody damning and I was a right bastard."

"And now?"

"Now I'm going insane without her."

Gordon brushed off his hands and sat down on the sack next to him. "I was like that with your mother."

Mick looked up. His father rarely talked about her.

"No other woman, just your mother. It seemed to me that she somehow controlled whether or not the sun came up each morning. She had a boyfriend that I wanted to tear limb from limb at the time, even though he was a mate of mine. I had a bit of a past, like yourself, that she knew all about, and she wanted nothing to do with me."

"What did you do?"

"I wouldn't take no for an answer. I kept after her until I wore her down. She said later she knew I would be faithful to her when I drove all the way to Abergavenny to pick her up from a Christmas concert she had sung in, just to be able to spend the time with her, driving her home. Your grandparents didn't quite approve of me." He winked.

"I don't think it's going to be quite so easy, Dad. There's an army of paparazzi camped on her doorstep waiting for me to show up. It would just cause more trouble."

A smile twitched at the corners of Gordon's lips. "So maybe you have to be a bit more creative."

From across the showroom of Malbrey Jewellers in Mayfair, an assistant made a discreet gesture signaling the arrival of a VIP customer. Robert Paulson, the manager, hastily handed off a necklace he was examining and straightened his tie.

"Mr. Carr, always a pleasure," he greeted the footballer. The staff had strict instructions to drop everything when a Premier League player came in the store, especially when they were on the outs with their girlfriends or wives. As distasteful as the chore was, it always paid to keep up with the scandal sheets.

"Mr. Paulson," Mick nodded stiffly.

"What can we show you today, sir?" Robert asked. Now here was the tricky part—he could be shopping for the new girl, the American who they said had started the riot but then had not. That could be a challenge, as she didn't look the expensive let's-make-up gift type. Fanta de las Mercedes was a much easier sell. The question was, just how much bling Mick Carr thought he had to put up before she'd take him back?

The jeweler waited as Mick glanced around the display cases, noting the dark shadows under the man's eyes. "I need to see the big stuff."

No clue there, but he had never asked to see "the big stuff" for Fanta, she only got little trinkets. "Of course, sir. This way."

Thick, grey carpet muffled their footsteps as they followed a corridor to an elegant room with sophisticated lighting and comfortable seating. This was the high-end merchandise, nothing here under five thousand pounds. The private showroom was usually reserved for their preferred customers like Hugo Auchincloss, who had a long relationship with Malbrey and was notoriously discerning. Just the other day, in fact, he had personally sold the young Mr. Auchincloss a stunning diamond and sapphire necklace that he'd had the foresight to make sure was on display when that esteemed gentleman had come to pick up a rush cufflink repair job. The cleaning woman's granddaughter was at a cooking school on the Heath and had mentioned that Hugo seemed smitten with one of the instructors, whose eyes happened to be blue. Salesmanship was an art, and Robert considered himself a master.

"Perhaps we should start with bracelets?" Robert suggested, pulling out a black velvet tray filled with winking diamonds and emeralds. The American's eyes were green. Sometimes you had to follow your instincts.

Mick looked each piece over carefully. "No."

"Perhaps something more…artistic?" Robert ventured and was rewarded with a ready nod.

They moved to another case filled with magnificent pearl brooches set in geometric settings, cabochon-ruby earrings surrounded by onyx sprays, and diamond and emerald pendants in weird and fantastic settings. Mick studied each intently.

"Do you have anything with birds?" he asked. "Or feathers?"

The closest thing Robert could produce was a spray of diamonds set in the Prince of Wales three-plume design. Again, his recommendation wasn't right and Robert said a silent curse. "How soon does sir need this gift? We can certainly have something made up to your specifications…"

"Saturday."

Like all true businesspeople, Robert knew the value of a sacrifice sale. "She's an artist, right?"

Mick nodded his head eagerly. "Yes."

"So's my wife. She can have the pick of the store, but when I need a special present I go here." He scribbled the name of an art store on the back of his business card. "They're the best in London. Ask to see the Kolinskies. They'll know what you mean."

Chapter Twenty-Nine

BY SATURDAY MORNING, Marie-Claire decided she had moped around long enough, and while a change of scenery wasn't going to mend her broken heart, it might at least distract it. The paparazzi outside the door had dwindled to two or three diehards who had become much more respectful, and they were welcome to trail her however far as she could get from Wandsworth for the day. She was going to enjoy herself if it killed her.

Jamming Neve's hat on her head, she shouldered her kit bag, swung the front door open, and came face-to-face with the same well-dressed young man that had stood on her stoop one week ago to the day.

"Phillip."

"Good morning, Miss Wentworth. I am here to escort you to the game today—"

"No, Phillip," she cut him off, her heart beginning to beat for what felt like the first time in a week. "Thank you, but no. No game today."

Phillip slid his foot in the jamb before she could slam the door in his face. "Miss Wentworth, I wish you would reconsider."

Her pride demanded she put up a fight. "How much is he paying you?"

"For today, a hundred quid for delivering you to the grounds and another fifty for staying nearby to make sure that World War III doesn't break out."

Marie-Claire stood her ground. "Phillip, I have a question for you. In the plaza of the London School of Economics, there is a large sculpture. What is it of?"

The young man didn't miss a beat. "It is of a chess piece, miss, the knight I believe, by the sculptor Edwina Sandys. Stainless steel, but I could be wrong. If you were to balk, I am to inform you that Darius is matching his offer if I also deliver Miss Clark to the grounds with you."

She squeezed her eyes shut and pressed her forehead against the door. Bastards.

"Now, if you would be so good as to collect Miss Clark and get your coats?"

Upstairs, Neve greeted the news with a whoop of joy. "Get something pretty on," she fussed at Marie-Claire, leading her to her room. "That pink skirt, and the green top. It'll be warm enough."

Marie-Claire sat on her bed, clasping her stomach. "I can't go, Neve."

"Of course, you can go. Mick knows you didn't do it, he apologized, and I bet this is his way of getting back with you."

"No, it's better if things just end like this." At her housemate's snort of disbelief, she continued. "Really. Delia was right, I don't belong in that world, and that's the world he lives in. He might say it's just his job but a lot of people take it very, very seriously."

"I think Mick's woken up to that."

"People got hurt, Neve, including you."

"I'll give you that it hasn't been easy since you hooked up with him, but I've never seen you happier."

There was no denying that.

"And like it or not, you probably wouldn't have passed the Critique without him," Neve reminded her. "I think he at least deserves a chance."

Everything Neve had said was true. Reluctantly, Marie-Claire brushed her hair while Neve picked an outfit for her, but she flatly refused to wear any makeup.

"No. I am not going to look like the rest of them."

"Suit yourself," Neve said and went to get changed.

———◦◦◦———

At the stadium, Phillip handed the SUV off to an attendant and escorted them through a series of doors and winding corridors until they emerged at the pitch. The spring sun was bright overhead, and at least a dozen yellow-coated security staff noted their arrival and then resumed their scan of the stands. Phillip ushered them to a box of seats almost on the fifty-meter line.

In the box, Gordon stood to welcome her. "MC, good to see you."

"Gordon!" Marie-Claire exclaimed in surprise and clasped his hand warmly, and introduced Neve.

"Glad to see my son has things a bit more under control this time," Gordon mused as they settled into their seats. Around them, a few people took her picture with their mobiles but she ignored them.

The fans roared as the team ran onto the field, and her pulse quickened. Mick was towards the end, and as the players began their warm-up, she thought she saw him glance in their direction. Darius scanned the seats and smiled when he saw them, or rather Neve, and she in turn smiled brilliantly and gave a small wave back.

Newcastle filed out and "God Save the Queen" was sung. A few announcements were made and the match began. For a long time, both teams seemed to just punt the ball back and forth idly, and Gordon pointed out that Kingsbury Town liked to toy with their opponents at the beginning, feeling out their strengths and weaknesses, while Newcastle was doing the same. There would be the occasional burst of action but then play would settle back into an almost mundane pace.

Presently, the Kingsbury Town fans began singing a song, thousands of them in unison, and Marie-Claire blushed bright red as the words became clear. "Gordon, do these people know there are children present?"

"I think they're singing the loudest," he said. "Parents usually say that football matches are the one place the kiddies don't have to watch their language. Good place for them to let their hair down. Within reason, of course."

As if by a silent command, Kingsbury Town's focus seemed to sharpen and the sluggish pace was thrown off. Mick dropped back and tackled a Newcastle player, winning possession of the ball and booting it across the pitch to the left wing, who then moved so fast he was almost a blur. The ball crossed the pitch between Kingsbury Town players in a frenzy of movement until a striker headed it into the net. The crowd exploded with roars, and Marie-Claire felt jubilation coursing through her body.

That had to stop immediately, she sternly scolded herself.

If she was smart, she'd watch the game, enjoy the afternoon, thank Mick, and then find a bus back to Wandsworth. She hadn't spent the entire week in agony just to go running back to him. She wouldn't be rejecting him out of spite, she reminded herself, self-preservation was just good sense. If the stadium hadn't been wired with security cameras, she might be sitting in a jail right now instead of Delia, and she might not get so lucky next time.

The thought sobered her. Things were wrapped up. They could part as, well, maybe not friends, but at least on amicable terms. That plan was for the best.

She sat stoically, watching the way Mick's face lit up when a teammate made a good play. You still want to be with him, her heart told her in a clear voice. You want to forgive him. Yes, he might have overreacted at first, but his reaction was understandable given the horrible history of riots at English soccer matches. And even when he thought she had started one, he had still offered help.

At the end, Kingsbury Town won 2-0 on a goal booted in by Hugo Auchincloss and the crowd rejoiced with more songs and chants. The players circled the field, waving to the fans, radiating pleased exhaustion, and the stands began to empty out.

"Well, that was fun," she told Gordon, pasting a broad smile on her face and pulling her coat on. "It was lovely to see you. Please tell Sue I said hello—"

"Nay, lass," Gordon interrupted solemnly, "time for the meet and greet upstairs."

Her smile vanished. "I can't go back up there. Gordon, you understand, I don't belong up there. I made a mess of it last time and look what happened."

He nodded. "I see your point, but that bollocks was none of your making. And if you are one-tenth as crazy about my son as he is for you, you should go up there with me."

The breath felt like fire in her lungs. "I do care for him."

"Then do this for him. He can be a great hulking moose at times, but he's a good lad. You're going to have to give him some room to make mistakes. He's been a part of this world for too long and he forgets how the rest of us live. But he's moved heaven and earth to make this a good day for you."

She thought for a moment and then turned to Neve. "You ready to try it again?"

"Absolutely." The girl was radiating happiness.

"Good." Gordon steered them out of the box towards the stairs. "Put a smile on and let them see they haven't gotten to you."

Gordon was grinning from ear to ear as he led the girls into the club skybox. The room was packed with people and the tone was much friendlier than the last time she was there. She supposed a good win could do that. An older gentleman approached them and clapped Gordon on the shoulder. "Good to see you, Gordon! When was the last time you came to a match? It must be years."

"Aye, I prefer watching Mick on the telly from my chair by the fire. But he asked me to escort these two lovely ladies and that tempted me too much. Oswald Poleski, Kingsbury Town Managing Director, may I present Miss Marie-Claire Wentworth and Miss Neve Clark."

The director made a deep bow and kissed their hands gallantly. More old friends of Gordon's joined them, and they chatted until the players entered to a round of applause.

The men strode into the room like rock stars, all dressed in finely tailored suits and flashing devilish smiles. "Cooey, it's like Christmas, isn't it," Neve whispered in her ear.

Mick was toward the back, looking achingly handsome in a tailored, charcoal-black suit and crisp white shirt, with a yellow-and-black striped tie. People swarmed around him and he accepted their congratulations, all the while moving closer until he stood before them.

"Dad," he nodded stiffly, shaking his father's hand.

"Nice game, son. Left it a bit late on the last play."

"The knee's not yet up to snuff. And I'm not getting any younger." He glanced at Marie-Claire. "How are you? Did you enjoy the match? Can I get you a drink?"

Her throat was so dry she could only nod. From a passing server's tray, he took two glasses of champagne and gave one to her and the other to Neve, and then Darius appeared at Neve's shoulder to welcome them. When Marie-Claire turned back, Gordon had vanished and she was left standing alone with Mick.

Figuring the icy liquid might loosen up her throat, she took a large swallow.

"Amazing game," she gasped as the fizzing exploded in her throat. "Congratulations on your win."

Mick yanked a napkin out of the hand of a woman behind them and pressed it into Marie-Claire's.

When her breathing had returned to normal, he said, "I'm glad you came today."

"I didn't have much choice. I'm putting Phillip through college."

Mick had the good grace to at least act ashamed. "He's a good lad."

Silence stretched between them until she couldn't bear it any longer. "Thank you for inviting me today, it was nice to see your dad. I've got a lot of work to start—"

"MC, so good to see you!" Connie appeared and hugged her warmly. "Come with me, there's some people I'd like you to meet." Not waiting for a reply, she took her arm, and with a mothering motion, guided her towards the crowd. Mick followed.

Names flew as Connie made introductions. Wives and girlfriends who had been openly hostile a week ago now presented limp hands to be shaken, and then promptly disappeared. Kami and Dee were nowhere to be seen.

Connie glanced at the retreating vixens and winked at Marie-Claire. "They're afraid they'll be the next Fanta."

They circulated easily, and Marie-Claire found herself enjoying meeting Mick's teammates and their wives. Most had young families and seemed down-to-earth and normal.

"There is someone who'd like to meet you," Mick said, and led her to a quiet corner of the room where a few gentlemen were standing.

"Sir Frank Poleski, Miss Marie-Claire Wentworth," Mick made the introduction.

Marie-Claire hesitated a moment, and then held out her hand to shake the older man's. "Sir."

"Miss Wentworth. Did you enjoy the match today?"

"Yes, very much so. Thank you. And thank you also for the generous donation to the school. We'll enjoy the heat."

"My pleasure. You are aware the estimate came in significantly less than what was offered?"

"No, but that's fine."

"Remarkable girl," he murmured to the club president as she and Mick left.

Mick was called to have his photograph taken with some sponsors, and Marie-Claire begged off to get a glass of water. As she made her way towards the bar, a thin, well-dressed man stepped into her path and flashed a cool smile.

"Hugo Auchincloss, left wing, at your service." He bent and kissed her hand. "May I get you a drink?"

So, this was Hugo Auchincloss. "Actually, I was just going for one."

"I'll walk with you." At the bar, Hugo procured a glass of water for her and a tomato juice for himself, and then led her towards the balcony that overlooked the pitch. "Let's talk here, it's quieter. My ears are ringing."

He raised his glass to her. "*À votre santé.*" To your health.

"*Et à la vôtre,*" And to yours, Marie-Claire replied.

Hugo raised his eyebrows fractionally, and then continued in flawless French, "I'm sorry you got mixed up with that mess at the match last week. I'm glad they got it all sorted. You were very brave going to the Football Association the way you did."

"You heard about that?" she answered easily.

Hugo snorted. "Everyone heard about it, it's all anyone's been talking about. Richard Lambton told my mother it was all they could do to not offer you a seat on the committee."

"Lord Lambton knows your mother?"

"His brother and my father rowed together in the eight-man shell at Cambridge," Hugo answered, as if that explained everything.

"After the riot, you were there in the first aid station with a girl. Is she all right?"

"Actually, that was my girlfriend, Juliet Randall," Hugo said proudly, "and yes, she's fine. In fact, I wanted to pass along our apologies. It was a student of ours, I mean hers, who saw the photographers and punched the one he thought was taking a photograph of Juliet. That's what triggered the riot."

Marie-Claire's eyebrows lifted in surprise. "That hasn't been in the papers."

"Ah, no. And it won't be. We worked it out with the police and security. Matthew was provoked. He's pulling his life together splendidly, and everyone agreed he doesn't need that on his record."

They continued to converse until Mick reappeared at Marie-Claire's elbow, glaring at Hugo.

"I say, Mick," Hugo switched back to English and indolently passed his empty glass to Mick, "our glasses are empty. Go fetch us some refills, there's a good chap."

"And I say fuck off, Hugo," Mick said, his voice like steel.

"You're a bore, Mick," Hugo sighed and kissed Marie-Claire's hand with elaborate bravura. *"Ma chère, au revoir, vous pouvez faire beaucoup mieux que cette chèvre."* Farewell, my dear, you can do much better than this goat.

"What was he nattering on about?" Mick's voice raised delightful hairs on the back of her neck as Hugo departed.

"That you need to watch your corners when you're doing an onside kick."

"You're a terrible liar," he murmured.

Neve swung by, her eyes sparkling. "Mind if Darius takes me home?"

Marie-Claire's smile widened. "Of course not."

"Your sweater is back at my house," Mick said quickly. "I'll run you back there to get it, and then take you home."

Her heart raced but her head refused to give up without a fight. "I don't want you to go out of your way."

"It's not a problem. Will you come?"

She took a deep breath and nodded. "Yes."

Chapter Thirty

THE DRIVE BACK to his house from Hendon was agonizing. It was impossible for Mick to read Marie-Claire. She sat in the passenger seat next to him like a beautiful statue, her expression inscrutable. Dear Lord, let everything work out, and not be too late.

At his house, he skipped the garage and instead parked in the narrow street, and led her up the steps to the front door. She followed, and when he opened the door, he heard the breath catch in her throat. Inside, the candles had been lit and were casting a warm glow around the living room, and on the bar, a bottle of champagne sat icing in a silver bucket next to two stemmed glasses. A delicious smell wafted from the kitchen below. The mood was utterly romantic.

"All this is for me?" she asked, standing stock-still in the doorway.

"Yes."

"You were awfully sure of yourself."

"No, I wasn't. Not at all." Nudging her gently inside, he helped her off with her coat, and picked up a long, white box wrapped with a red ribbon from a narrow side table. "These are for you."

Her hands, he saw, trembled as she unwrapped the box and lifted the lid to reveal two dozen perfect, long stem red roses. "They're gorgeous."

"They're American Beauties. It seemed appropriate."

Marie-Claire gestured around. "How did you arrange all this?"

"Bloke down the row, Todd, he owns a restaurant. I kick the football with his boys. Would you like some champagne?" Mick asked, eager to get her whatever she wanted.

"No, thank you." She shook her head and sat down on the edge of the leather ottoman, holding the box of roses in her lap.

Of course, she doesn't want champagne, you great ox, the girl wants to keep her wits about her.

Taking a seat on the sofa across from her, he ran his hand across his scalp and cleared his throat. "Marie-Claire," he began strongly, and then noticed she was biting her lower lip and his confidence deserted him. "Did you enjoy the game today?"

She nodded. "Yes, very much, thank you."

"Good, good." He blew his cheeks out as his left foot tapped the stone floor in a rapid staccato.

"Neve enjoyed it too," she added.

"Good."

"It was nice to see your dad."

"Yes, he comes down for a match every now and then."

The clock over the bar ticked away the seconds, the sound echoing around the hard surfaces of the room, and the thought occurred to him that he didn't own any carpets.

Marie-Claire glanced at her watch. "Is my sweater—"

"Marie-Claire, you have to know that—" he began at the same time and they both stopped. Then she nodded, her green eyes focused on him expectantly, and he continued.

"You have to know that…" Oh damn, what came next? He'd rehearsed this speech a dozen times and he forced himself to concentrate. "Marie-Claire, I know that you probably never wanted to see me again after the mess I made of last weekend. I can understand that, I was a—"

"What's that smell?" she interrupted, glancing towards the steps to the kitchen.

He paused and sniffed. "Dinner."

"Oh…" Her voice trailed off uncertainly. "I'm sorry, you were saying?"

It took Mick a moment to remember himself, so he took a deep breath and started over from the beginning. "Marie-Claire. I know that you probably never wanted to see me again after last Sunday, and I can understand that, I acted like a complete—"

"What *is* for dinner?"

"I honestly don't know. I left it up to Todd."

A crooked half-smile played on her lips as she stared absently at the floor, as if she had retreated into a memory. After a moment, she seemed to remember he was there and nodded for him to continue.

"I acted like a complete ass."

"You did?"

"Yes."

"When?"

"Last Sunday!" Mick barked, his sorely tested nerves at their end. "At the riot? Hello? I'm trying to apologize here, love, if you could spare me a moment of your attention."

Instead, Marie-Claire stood up and laid the flowers on the coffee table and walked down the steps to the kitchen as if pulled by an invisible string. He followed her and watched as she stood before the wall oven and inhaled with her eyes closed. A small tear slipped down her cheek and he realized she was crying.

"Bloody hell, what's the matter?" he panicked, racing to her side.

"I can't believe what I smell," she whispered brokenly.

With an oath, he grabbed a mitt and yanked the oven door open, taking out a tray with four golden mounds of crab and setting them on the counter before her.

"Crab cakes," she murmured, the tears rolling down her cheeks unchecked, "with Old Bay seasoning." Then the dam burst and she broke down in tears.

He pulled her into his arms and held her as she cried, her body shaking with teary convulsions. "Marie-Claire, tell me what's the matter," he implored, shocked at her reaction.

She couldn't answer and instead only wept harder.

"Sweetheart, if you don't like them I'll get something else, anything else, just don't cry. I can't bear it if you cry," he pleaded, but it was no good. Her anguished tears tore him apart but he could only hold her, his mind racing. He stroked her hair, trying to get her to calm down. "I'm sorry. I'm sorry if it upset you, I'll throw them out. Tell me what's the matter, and I'll make it better."

She sniffled and shook her head forlornly. Reaching for the box of tissues, he gently wiped her tears away and made her blow her nose several times until finally, blessedly, the storm seemed to pass.

"I love crab cakes and Old Bay," she whispered, her head resting against his chest. "My mother makes them. They're my favorite and I haven't had them in so long, and, and," she hiccupped, "and it's making me miss home, and I missed you so much, and you thought I had started the riot, and I hadn't, and I thought I'd never see you again—" She broke down as the tears overwhelmed her again.

Relief flooded through him. He held her tenderly, stroking her hair, keeping her pressed against his chest and murmuring soft words in her ear for what seemed like an eternity. When the emotion seemed spent, he ran cool water on a tea towel and pressed the cloth against her face to wipe away her tears, and then took the tray of crab cakes and led her to the table. Scooping her onto his lap, he held a forkful of crab to her lips. She savored the taste, her eyes closed.

"I haven't tasted anything so good in so long," she murmured, and picked up a morsel with her fingers and fed it to him. "Have you ever had this?"

The creamy tenderness of the crab and the rich spices of the seasoning were remarkable. "No, I haven't. My word, it's delicious."

"They're almost as good as my mother's." She licked her fingers clean and put her hand over his as he lifted the fork to feed her another bite. "No, use your fingers, crab is always better that way."

There was the familiar tightening in his groin as she ate from his fingers, her tongue delicately running over the tips.

"How did you know? How did you know this was my favorite?"

"I didn't," he admitted as he watched her. "I told Todd to make something so good you'd stay, at least until I had a chance to ask for your forgiveness."

"There's nothing to forgive. The riot wasn't your fault."

"It was, I was stupid, I didn't think it through, all I wanted was to have you at the match," he said, the words pouring out of him in a bitter torrent. "I sent Phillip because I didn't want you getting lost again. All of the other girls, all they've wanted is the skybox, and it didn't occur to me what vicious bitches they could be. I set you up, and you could have been hurt badly. But the worst part is, I didn't believe you when you said you didn't do it."

"I don't think I would have believed me," she said. "Delia did a pretty good job convincing me I had no place being there."

Mick's jaw hardened. "What else did she tell you?"

Marie-Claire paused before feeding him another bite. "That you and Fanta were the real deal, you were going to get engaged, and that I should clear out and let that happen."

"That's hogwash," Mick objected, "I never for one second thought about marrying Fanta."

"You mean you're not back with her?"

The very idea appalled him. "Of course not. The only woman I am with is you—that is, if you'll still have me." Taking her head in his hands, he looked her straight in the eye. "I was horrible to you last weekend. I doubted you and I shouldn't have, and I've never been sorrier for anything in my entire life. Will you forgive me?"

"Will you feed me another piece of crab cake?" she asked with an impish smile.

He brought another mound to her lips and she took his fingers in her mouth in a smooth motion, eating the crabmeat off them and sucking each finger clean. Her blouse parted as she reached for more crab, giving him a tantalizing glimpse of the swell of her breasts cupped in almost unbearably innocent, sheer, white lace. Jesus, she was turning this into the most erotic experience he'd ever had.

He knew he wouldn't be able to endure much more of this, and given her ability to shred any restraint he might have, he knew that if he didn't shut this down immediately there was every chance he would find himself ravishing her right there on the kitchen table. With a swift motion, he moved her off his lap like she was a burning coal and stood.

"Damn it, Marie-Claire, how do things get so out of control when you're around?" he swore. "I brought you here because I need to tell you some things and you need to listen."

She sat in the chair, bewildered, as he paced the kitchen.

"I know I've been behaving oddly," he plowed on, "but I've got very good reasons. I have never felt this way before, the way I feel about you. I have never been involved in anything serious. Until now."

He turned to face her, hoping she was able to follow his convoluted thoughts. "Almost every day since I've met you has been either complete heaven or complete hell," he told her, "the heaven being you, the hell being completely of my own making."

A smile broke out on her face. That was good.

"I tried to forget you after the riot. I tried to put you behind me. And it was impossible. I realized that I didn't care if you'd started the riot or not, it didn't matter. And the thought that I had ruined it and driven you from me almost drove me mad. I need you to forgive me for all of it."

She stood and leaned against him, drawing his head down to hers. "I forgive you," she whispered and then kissed him.

He resisted, his body tense, but she ran her tongue between his lips and pressed her body against him, her kiss a hungry feast of him. With a groan he relented, clasping her against his chest with a possessive hunger that blotted out everything else. He kissed her urgently, as if he was afraid she was going to disappear before he could capture her heart and soul the way she had captured his.

His lips moved to devour her neck, wanting to brand every delicate curve and hidden crevice as his. She purred, leaning back against his arm, surrendering to him completely as his fists clenched the folds of her silky blouse.

With a Herculean effort, he drew back and held her at arm's length, breathing hard.

"Why are you pushing me away again?" she asked, hurt and confused. "Is this some kind of game with you?"

"No, I have to stop, this is important." Needing to put her at a safe distance, he wrapped his hands around her waist and lifted her onto the counter. "Now be a good girl and pay attention," he implored.

She attempted to sit primly, with her hands folded in her lap and her ankles crossed.

"I meant what I said, I want you," he began. "Badly. I've been behaving like a rutting buck since the day I met you. For some reason that only God knows, I have no control when you are involved. None, and if you let me start making love to you, you will not be able to stop me."

She smiled and leaned towards him. "Okay, I'm warned."

Dear Lord, she would tempt a saint. "I want you badly," he repeated, "but only for myself. Completely for myself, and I'll not abide others. You said once you didn't expect this to be exclusive. Well, I bloody well do, and that's why I stopped and left so quickly the night of your party. I don't want our first time to be some fling at a party with a hundred people outside the door."

Solemnly, he took her head in his hands. "It's your choice if you come willing to my bed or not, but if you do, you'll not be leaving. Do you understand what I'm saying, Marie-Claire?"

"You want this to be serious."

"Yes."

"You want a commitment."

"Yes. This is all or nothing. But before you make your decision, you need to know some things. I've been with a lot of women."

His words sobered her. "So I've been told."

God, he hated doing this but he plowed on. "You need to know, I have always used protection. Always," he added meaningfully. "I've no children out there, not like a lot of the other footballers. I knew from the beginning I wouldn't be able to spot a gold digger, and who knows where they had been before me."

She thought about that for several moments. "I've only ever been with one man before, and that wasn't very…" she groped for words, "…educational. I'm not sure how I would measure up against your other, ah, partners."

"You're being ridiculous," he snapped in disbelief. "For God's sake woman, you wear a huge wooly sweater and I get so hard I can barely walk! This isn't about experience."

"And I'm not taking contraceptives," she continued. "I stopped when I left home to come here. I knew I didn't want to get involved with anyone, so I came off them."

"You're involved with me," he reminded her.

"Yes, and I don't want to be with anyone else." She fumbled for the words. "But I'm here to go to school and this past week has taught me I have to be happy to do any kind of work. I can't be stressed or sad. I have too much to do."

Taking her hands in his, he made a solemn vow. "I will promise that I will make you very happy. I will make you deliriously happy if you let me. I know you will not put up with any of my crap, and I will not give you any reason to."

"Then I only have one condition."

He swallowed. "What is it?"

"I don't want to talk about the future."

"That's fair enough," he conceded.

"I mean it, Mick. I want to concentrate on what's in front of me, on the here and now, and let the future take care of itself."

"All right," he agreed. "Now you have a decision to make."

"You'd let me walk away?"

He nodded sternly, crossed his arms over his chest and lied through his teeth. "It's your last chance. You'll come to my bed knowing the terms or not at all."

She drew in her breath, and for a hideous moment Mick thought she was going to start crying again. Instead, she exhaled, slid to the edge of the counter and hopped off lightly. Then, without a backward glance, she disappeared up the kitchen stairs.

Mick stood rooted to the spot, panic constricting his throat as he waited, listening for any sound that would indicate where she had gone. Bloody hell, a man just never knew with her. She could drag him through hell just by flicking her finger or twirling her hair.

A minute passed, and then two, and he forced himself to move. Upstairs, the living room was deserted and he blew out the candles as he passed them, seeing no sign of her. Had the front door opened? Had she slipped out? He cast about desperately, and then saw a scrap of fabric hanging over the edge of the stairs leading up to his bedroom.

It was her skirt, lying in a fluffy pink puddle on the third tread from the bottom. A few steps farther up was her blouse, and as he followed her trail, he discovered a sheer, lacy bra. At the doorway to his bedroom were her panties. He swallowed hard and pushed the door open.

Darkness was falling, but there was still enough light that he could see her form outlined on his bed. He paused, drinking in the sight of her as she reclined on her side, naked, her lustrous hair spilling over her shoulders and breasts.

He moved to the side of the bed and she rose to kneel before him, lifting her hands to his chest and tilting her head back, her breasts pressed against his taut stomach like a pagan sacrifice.

"Is this willing enough?" she breathed.

Chapter Thirty-One

MICK REACHED OUT a tentative hand to cup the soft curve of her hip, and in the gentle dusk, she could see the relief in his expression. Had he really thought she would leave?

With nimble fingers, she began to unbutton his shirt, her fingers flying down the front until she could spread it to expose the wide expanse of his chest. Greedily, she caressed the warm flesh of his muscled torso, delighting as his hands moved to tangle in her hair. She tugged the shirttails out of his pants impatiently as he shucked the shirt and threw it on the floor.

There was a jagged scar across his abdomen about three inches long. She ran the tip of her finger over the rough, white line in curiosity, and he shivered at her feathery touch.

Marie-Claire looked at him inquiringly.

"Opponent's spikes," he rasped, "when I was sixteen."

With tantalizing slowness, she traced the line with her tongue, the soft, pink tip flickering over his warm skin, and then traveled lower, letting the fullness of her breasts nestle intimately against his hardness. The waistband of his pants stopped her and she placed her hand on the buckle, idly fondling the smooth metal.

Muttering an oath, he swept her hands away and jerked the belt off, followed by his trousers and briefs. Her eyes widened in surprised delight, her lips forming a silent "O" of astonishment.

Intensely curious, she tugged him down on the bed next to her, rocking back on her heels to study the perfection of his body. With a grin, he propped himself up on one arm and let her inspect the length of him.

"You're magnificent," she breathed, "like a marble statue come to life." She moved higher on him, her hair falling around them like a curtain, and studied his face, lowering her lips to his. He remained still, responding eagerly to her feathery, light kisses and encouraging her to probe deeper.

Taking her hand in his, he pressed warm kisses into the palm and drew her on top of his body. She lay with one leg between his, her flat stomach pressed into his throbbing maleness.

"I thought I had lost you," he told her, his eyes a stormy blue that reflected the torment in his soul. "I couldn't bear it."

"You haven't."

"I wanted to make it right today, I wanted to show you I could do it right."

"You did," she assured him. "It's perfect because you're here. You make it perfect."

"No," he babbled on, "I was such a fool, Marie-Claire, and it drove me insane, not having you with me, needing you, worrying about you."

It was impossible. He was being too gentle, too considerate, treating her like she was a piece of porcelain. That was the last thing she wanted. She needed to feel his rough hands all over her.

"Mick, hush." She pressed her palm against his mouth. Leaning forward, she nipped the lobe of his ear and sucked the tender skin between her lips, enjoying the shockwave her teasing sent down his body. "Now make love to me."

Her words seemed to unleash him. With a swift motion, he was on her, pressing her back into the bed, taking her hands in his and drawing them over her head, forcing her to arch against him as he settled his considerable weight on her.

He lowered his mouth to suckle one breast, his tongue making wet traces around the tip as he drew in the satiny fullness. With a skilled motion, he circled the nipple with his tongue, devoting himself to her pleasure. After an eternity, he moved to the other breast and lavished it with attention until she heard herself moaning aloud like a wild creature.

He caressed her thigh, then slid his hand higher between her legs. Her body immediately tensed and she grabbed his hand before it could move any further.

He paused. "Am I hurting you?"

She bit her lip in vexation. Her romantic experiences with Eric had been woefully abrupt and mostly about Eric satisfying himself. Mick was an expert lover who seemed to know a thousand ways to give her pleasure, and the difference was intimidating.

"No, not at all…it's just that, I've never really done that before," she confessed, "or had that done to me. I mean—"

He stilled her nervous ramblings with his lips. "Marie-Claire, you're so beautiful, I want to know every part of you. But if you don't want me to, I'll stop."

She definitely didn't want that. "No, don't stop, I just don't know what to do."

"You don't have to do anything," he assured her. "It will be wonderful, I promise. You're so beautiful, every inch of you, you're like a drug I can't get enough of. Let me do this, love."

Casting aside any reluctance, she lay back and let him resume his gentle exploration. When his fingers found her core, she gasped as they slid into her, the slippery heat inflaming them both. She arched against him as he explored her in a gentle rhythm, watching her reaction as he expertly massaged that delicate part of her body.

"You were made for love," he groaned, feeling immense satisfaction that he was the first man to show her this kind of pleasure. He increased the rhythm, guiding the sensations that built upon each other, demanding more and more as he drove her towards a shattering climax.

She lay languid in his arms, drawing in lungfuls of air as wondrous pleasure washed over her body.

"I hope I'll always be able to satisfy you so easily," he teased.

When she had calmed a bit, he reclaimed her mouth but with a more urgent desire. Pressing her to her back, he hovered above and settled deeply between her thighs, letting her feel the immediacy of his desire. Her slippery wetness enthralled him and he was just about to plunge forward when she grasped his wrist, staying him.

"Are you going to use protection?"

He jumped out of bed, cursing his lack of foresight in keeping the condoms in the bathroom.

He sprinted back and practically dove on her, and she gasped as the searing heat of his shaft pressed home. She threw her head back and arched against him, her legs wrapping around him, pulling him to her. With a moan, he pressed his urgent maleness into her soft, pliant flesh, already sensitive from his early attentions, and she groaned out loud.

He tried to be careful, to be gentle and considerate, but damn it, she was writhing beneath him like a wild creature and he was powerless to control the wanton cravings she so effortlessly conjured. He drove into her and began a primal motion, feeling like he was drowning in her velvety tightness. Almost instantly, the sensations became too much, and a strangled cry escaped him as he climaxed with an unparalleled release. Pulse after pulse reverberated through his body, and he collapsed on her, every nerve ringing with pleasure and deep satisfaction.

Sated, he drew her close against him. "I hope I'll always be able to satisfy you so easily," she murmured.

He was too spent to give her tart little rump the smart whack she deserved.

They slept in each other's arms, happily exhausted. In the early morning hours, Marie-Claire awoke to the feel of his hands exploring her body and she rolled to her side, spooning against his very large, very insistent erection. His growl of pleasure tickled her ear.

"Do you really think my big wooly sweater is sexy?" she murmured.

"Unbearably," he admitted, sinking his teeth into her shoulder and sending shivers down her spine. "You could wear an arctic parka and I wouldn't be able to stay off you."

Rolling her underneath him, he began a slow and intent seduction, taking his time to build her to a fever pitch of desire. He kissed her in places that made her gasp, in places that made her blush, in secret places that no man had ever tasted and branded them as his own. Finally, he slipped on a condom and slid into her, stretching and filling her almost to the limit. He smoothed the hair back from her face and kissed her eyes, her nose, her lips, just reveling in the joy of her, till she began to urge him to move, begged him to move. But he only continued to kiss her.

Desperately, she arched her hips into him, her long legs pulling him against her and urging him to move. He resisted, letting her arch and slide against him until he lost all control and their desire blotted out everything. She reached the pinnacle first and her body clasped tautly around him, pushing him over the edge as ecstasy poured out of him in wave after wave.

As the storm abated, he tried to roll on his side but she wouldn't let him.

"But I'll crush you."

"I don't care," she whispered, keeping him on top of her.

He lay on his elbows above her, nuzzling her neck, her satiny hair tangled around them. "I can't believe you're here, lying in my bed. It's like a dream come true."

"I'm lucky to be here. If it wasn't for the surveillance cameras, I think it would be me in a prison cell instead of Delia."

"She can rot in there, the scheming bitch," he cursed, his anger flaring unchecked. "You were very brave, going to the FA the way you did."

"They were nice. Hugo Auchincloss told me that it was actually someone he knew who started the riot, the boy who punched the first photographer."

"Aye, I heard that. Don't worry, I'll take care of him," Mick vowed. "Is that what you two were nattering on about?"

"Yes. His French is excellent."

"He likes to show off."

"He wasn't showing off. He can speak fluently, and his accent is perfect." Seeing her defense of his rival was infuriating Mick, she changed the subject. "You know, when I was hiding under that bridge at the Wetlands, I heard those paparazzi talking."

She felt him stiffen. "Oh yes? What rubbish did they spew?"

"They said some things that were true."

"Like what?" he asked suspiciously.

"Like I don't know the working end of a hairbrush." She laughed, and then ignoring his indignant snort, wrapped her arms around his neck and pulled his lips down to hers. "They also said I didn't get a stud like you in my bed every day. They were right about that, too."

As their tongues intertwined, her hands slid down his back, delighting in the feel of his muscles flexing under her fingers.

"Wait, I have something for you." He rolled off her to open a small drawer in the bedside table. From within, he pulled out the bird's nest on its thin, black ribbon.

"My bird's nest."

"They found this in the stands," he told her as he clasped it at the nape of her neck, "and one of the security pictures showed you had been wearing it."

She fingered it in relief, tears welling in her eyes. "I'm so glad. I thought it had been lost."

"Would you like to trade it in for something in emeralds? Sapphires?" He paused and then added, "Or diamonds?"

"Never." She clasped the necklace protectively, her green eyes wide in panic. "It's special, I was devastated when I thought it was lost. I wouldn't trade it for the world."

At her words, a tidal wave of emotion washed over him, more potent than anything he had ever felt in his life. Perfect certainty engulfed his heart, the fierceness of clarity blotting out everything but his need for her.

Without preliminaries, he pressed her back into the pillows in one motion.

"Mick, you can't possibly be ready again so soon—" She groaned in ecstasy under his sudden onslaught.

"Can't I?"

The bed was cold when she woke. Still half asleep, she reached out for the warmth of Mick's body, and found nothing but empty bed. She grumbled and stretched full-length, some muscles a bit sore after the passion he had worked on them. Outside the window, birds sang and a squirrel scampered across several tree limbs. She watched the scene drowsily, hearing noises from the kitchen below.

Rubbing the sleep from her eyes, she threw on his shirt and followed the sounds. Mick stood at the counter, dressed only in jeans that rode low on his hips, whisking eggs in a bowl. She stood in the doorway, admiring the view.

"Good morning. If you had waited a bit longer, you could have had breakfast in bed," he said.

"Your breakfasts could feed small communities. Just eggs is fine for me."

"You're sure? I've done sausage, toast, kippers—"

"Eggs are lovely." She took a slice of toast from a stack on a plate and bit into it. "Where did you learn to cook?"

"Sue taught me, said she could tell I'd be a bachelor for a while and it was a good skill to have."

He pushed the eggs onto two plates, pulled a bottle of champagne from the refrigerator and popped it, filling her glass and one for himself. "To the most beautiful woman in England," he toasted her.

She drank, the effervescent bubbles evaporating in her mouth. "Champagne and scrambled eggs for breakfast? You're spoiling me."

"Get used to it, you're going to need your strength." He grinned, and tucked into the mountain of food on his plate.

They had a leisurely breakfast and she helped him with the dishes. After everything had been dried and put away, he took her hand and led her up the stairs to the living room.

"Sit here." He patted the sofa next to him but instead, she sat in his lap, wiggling suggestively.

"Oi! Enough of that," he scolded with fake shock and gave her a light slap on the rump.

On the end table next to him was a slim black box she hadn't noticed the night before.

"This is for you," he said.

The name of the most exclusive jeweler in London was embossed across the lid. A chill flashed through her, an unpleasant reminder of the women in the skybox loaded with jewelry.

"Mick, I don't want anything from you."

"No, really, you'll like it. I picked it out myself." When she continued to resist, he put the box in her hands. "Why don't you open it and decide."

Reluctantly, she flipped the lid and glanced inside, expecting to see an extravagant piece of jewelry. Instead, there was a paintbrush.

"A Kolinsky wash brush," she exclaimed, removing the brush reverently from the case. "I've always wanted one. How did you know?"

"Chap at the art store told me they're the best in the world."

"These cost a fortune."

"I have to agree with you there. What's so special about it?"

"They're made from the tail hairs of Kolinskies, which are a kind of mink. The very best ones, like this, are all male hair. When they're wet, they're supposed to snap right back, not like my regular brushes. They're rare—I've never even tried one." She twirled the brush experimentally between two fingers, the balance perfect.

He closed her hand around the brush and brought her fingers to his lips. "You deserve it. For putting up with me."

She sighed and stroked his face. "It's a dog's job," she agreed, her accent a perfect imitation of his.

"I imagine."

"People don't know…" She nibbled his ear and felt a jolt of electricity go through him. "There's so much of you. So much skin to taste. It's going to take me weeks—"

She was cut off by him yanking her into his arms and carrying her up the stairs to his bed, where she belonged.

Chapter Thirty-Two

MICK WAITED PATIENTLY for Marie-Claire outside the Art League. Today was Thursday, her Life Model class night, and afterwards they were supposed to go to the opening of a gallery show where two of Sandra's works were being exhibited.

He knew that London was the same city, England was the same country, and Earth the same planet, but somehow everything was better. Everyone seemed happier, the thin April sun seemed brighter, the colors more intense and vibrant. Even St Augustine didn't bother him as much. Everything hummed with a vital energy that only he could hear, all because Marie-Claire was with him.

Overnight, his world had changed from the darkest pit to the happiest heaven he had ever known. They talked every day, he knew when he was going to see her, and he knew that when he did she would be happy to see him. Nothing could be better.

Marie-Claire seemed to adjust well to his constant ardor, which was a good thing because he couldn't seem to help himself when she was around. He had taken it for granted that she would move in with him, but she quickly disabused him of that notion. School came first and that was that, but they fell into a comfortable routine, finding time together between his playing schedule and her schoolwork. He would call her in the morning, they would talk during the day, and he would pick her up after she was done at school and they would be together.

Luckily, she kept sane hours and was up at dawn, the same as him. Mick learned that most of the students were night owls, but Marie-Claire liked mornings. The studio was quietest then, she told him, and she needed the light.

Life was blessedly mundane. Sometimes they would drive to a park and walk, sometimes they would go back to his house and make dinner, and other evenings he would be invited to hang out with the students in the studio.

To his surprise, these were the evenings he preferred best, if he couldn't be alone with her. Her friends were smart and talented and accepted him as if he were one of them. And truth be told, he felt he fit in with them. He had the same intensity about his work, he was talented as well, and they all understood that without discipline all the talent in the world would take you nowhere. The fact that he was a dropout didn't seem to matter. He understood and respected hard work, and that was what counted.

"It's going to be mobbed, they know we're coming," Marie-Claire predicted glumly once she was in the car.

"She's your friend, we should go anyway," he said, navigating the Aston Martin through the narrow streets.

"The school hates us getting this kind of publicity."

"Our showing up doesn't mean her stuff is going to sell any faster."

"You just watch."

As they walked toward the brightly lit gallery, he saw she was right, of course. Photographers hovered at the door and began shooting the instant they approached. Wrapping a protective arm around her, he shouldered his way through the throng. Questions were shouted at them left and right about Fanta, the riot, were they going to get married? Marie-Claire winced, and he grimaced.

The gallery was packed with people and was only a bit more civilized. Everyone seemed to want to meet them, and the overhead spotlights made the space stifling hot. They were soon separated, much to his distaste, and he was trapped by a fawning couple who were rabid Kingsbury Town fans.

After what seemed like an eternity, Raul appeared at his side with a cold beer and Mick had never been happier to see another guy in his life. "Bloody zoo, sorry," Mick said, accepting the bottle.

Raul shrugged. "Don't be. Sandra appreciates your coming, and she's already sold both her works. And as long as we're not too successful, the school won't get fussed."

"Why don't they want that? Isn't that why you're at their school to begin with?"

"The Lady Warwick prides itself on being a serious academic institution, not an art institute," Raul explained. "The dean wants it to be recognized as the training ground of the next generation of important British artists. So, any whiff that a student is commercially successful or wants to go into art for the money is pretty much grounds for dismissal, although they won't come out and say so. We're allowed to sell the odd stuff here and there, like at Chez Bertrand's, because they know we need something to live on. But any more than that is off-limits.

Everyone knows going in. They do have a reputation to uphold."

Sandra and Margaret appeared, and Mick posed with them for a roaming photographer. He then spotted a city-type guy deep in conversation with Marie-Claire and showing entirely too much interest. He abruptly excused himself and returned to her side, sliding his hand possessively along the small of her back and introducing himself to the man, who promptly fled.

"Thank you," she whispered, "he was overbearing. I've never seen an exhibit opening standing room only before."

"You're being a trooper. It's almost over, and Darius and Neve will be arriving soon. We can leave then, don't want to steal their thunder."

A waiter passed with an hors d'oeuvre tray, and Marie-Claire slumped when they saw it was empty.

"Hungry? How about we go and get a bite to eat?"

"I'd like that. They had sandwiches at Life Model class but then the model didn't show up and it was my turn to—"

A stunning blonde stepped into their path and boldly interrupted. "Can I have your autograph, Mick?"

He reluctantly removed his arm from Marie-Claire's waist and took the pen and paper the woman handed him with a sly smile.

"To Deirdre," she leaned in, her voice husky.

Mick scribbled his name and handed the paper back, gathered Marie-Claire close to him and started to walk towards the exit.

A piece of paper fluttered to the ground. Marie-Claire stopped to pick it up and examined it curiously, noting the phone number written on it.

"I think you forgot this." She tried to hand the scrap back to the woman, who blanched guiltily and fled.

She turned to Mick, who flushed red and glanced away. Understanding slowly dawned on her.

"Oh," Marie-Claire fumbled, embarrassed. "I guess this was for you."

She tried to press the paper into his hand, but he threw it on the floor in disgust. Marie-Claire took a step away from him and seemed to have trouble finding her breath. He felt her withdraw and go far away, taking all the warmth and happiness with her and leaving his insides turned to ice. With an oath, he grabbed her elbow and dragged her out the door.

Once they reached the sidewalk, she gently disentangled herself from him and walked in silence, her head down and her hair falling forward to veil her mortification. The Aston Martin was parked two blocks away, and a few photographers dogged their steps for a minute but turned back when Neve and Darius arrived.

"I didn't ask for that," he snapped when they were alone, fighting to keep his emotions in check.

"Didn't ask for what?" Marie-Claire kept walking, the tone of her voice indifferent.

"Her phone number. It's what they do, to hook up with a footballer."

She nodded, concentrating on the sidewalk in front of her. "Clever."

"I can't stop it."

"Of course not."

Her composure grated on him like a raw wound. He hated it when she was like this, patient and reasonable, as if he were an elderly uncle who was a bit doddering. He kept up with her brisk pace, irritation mixing with panic. "I haven't taken any since I met you."

"Any what?"

"Phone numbers. I haven't taken any since I met you."

"Good for you."

She kept her hands jammed in her pockets, and her face, when he could see it, was carefully expressionless. She had retreated to someplace inside herself, doors locked, shop closed, and he could just stand outside and beat on the window till his knuckles bled.

As they approached the parking garage, Marie-Claire made no effort to turn into the entrance but instead kept up her brisk pace. Surely, she didn't intend to walk all the way back to Putney, did she?

Enough was enough. With a swift movement, he moved a step ahead of her and used his body to block her path. "It's time we had a talk."

"Here?" She gestured to the well-lit street.

"Yes, here. I've told you that you and me—us—is very serious to me. But you think I'm still the way I was before, and nothing could be further from the truth. The way I was before is over. I was horny and bored," he explained, "and you, love, are anything but boring, and you're doing a very good job of taking care of every need I have."

A blush rose in her cheeks, and she relaxed a bit.

"Now, it has occurred to me that I demanded a commitment from you, but you never asked for one in return."

She glanced away. "I didn't think you were the type to make commitments."

"I didn't used to be," he agreed, "but that was because I'd never met anyone like you. No one else has ever made me as happy as you do. And believe me, no one else can throw me into miserable hell at a flick of her wrist like you can."

He gently gathered her coat lapels and pulled her against him. "I know I come with a lot of baggage, which is why you need to be sure I have never been more serious about someone in my life. Demand I make a commitment to you. Demand I never look at another woman. Demand I have only you in my heart."

"I can't do that," she whispered.

"Why not? I want you to feel as certain about this as I do." Cradling her face in his hands, he kissed her, his blue eyes intent upon her. "I will worship only you. I will protect only you. I will want only you. And I will give you all the time in the world to get used to all this, as long as you trust me."

A small smile played around her lips. "So, I should have yanked her by her skanky weave and told her to back off of my man?" she said, imitating Neve's accent perfectly.

He laughed, relieved. "I'd have paid good money to see that."

Chapter Thirty-Three

ON THURSDAY, THE team practiced outside in chilling drizzle, the session dragging on for bloody ages before Giles was satisfied and blew the final whistle. By that time, the cold and damp penetrated to the bone, and Mick followed the team down the maze of drab hallways back to the locker rooms, looking forward to a hot shower, even under St Augustine's trickling showerheads.

Miserable weather aside, things had been going well. His knee was holding up tolerably well, and they were on a nice winning streak of four games. Wolverhampton the weekend before had been easier than the 3-2 final score showed. He'd had two assists and Marco had made a brilliant back-heeled goal in the sixty-fourth minute that seemed to take the wind out of their opponents' sails. They spent the rest of the match punting the ball back and forth between themselves.

The weekend had also offered the opportunity to get up to some mischief that should have put Auchincloss in his place, well and good. Mick had been holding a grudge since he'd found out about that bastard's involvement in the riot and his willingness to let Marie-Claire take the fall for what rightfully was his own girl's fault. He also hadn't forgotten the left wing chatting up Marie-Claire at the party after the Fulham match, and when he'd overheard Pozny ask (in such terrible French that even he understood) if Julie was coming up to Wolverhampton, he'd worked out that she was indeed arriving the night before and meeting Hugo at the team hotel.

It had taken a bit of doing and a huge bribe, but he'd managed to arrange for Julie to be given Mick's room number and key when she arrived at the hotel. When the team returned from dinner, she was supposed to have been discovered there instead of in Auchincloss's room, and Mick had made sure there would have been a scene, just like when Auchincloss had found his fiancé in Mick's hotel room several years earlier. Hugo would have had a right meltdown, and Mick had been justifiably proud of his brilliant plan.

But somehow Darius had gotten wind of his machinations and gotten Julie hustled out of his room and out of the hotel with no one the wiser. Hugo remained clueless and Darius had given him an ass-chewing for the ages. But if it had worked, it would have been worth it, and Mick was patient. Other opportunities would present themselves. He could wait.

Marie-Claire had been at the match, though. Connie had offered her a ride up with her and the kids, and the Sunday papers, even the respectable ones, had shown Marie-Claire holding one of the little boys on her lap and helping them cheer. Afterwards, she'd met him back at his house and made them a nice dinner, and then they had made love all evening. Mick sighed at the memory.

Bournemouth this coming weekend was looking winnable. They were on their third manager of the season, and no one seemed to be at the helm. Some good players, but overall no match for Kingsbury Town's skills and Giles's cunning.

Mick smiled to himself. Yes, Bournemouth was winnable—as long as Marie-Claire was there. People were beginning to notice that she had been at every game they had won.

———————◆○◆———————

The poorly lit locker room was silent as Mick entered, and he wondered what had quieted the usual mayhem of clanging doors and player chatter.

The cover of the *Observer* had been taped to his locker door. As he approached he could see it was a charcoal sketch of a reclining woman, her back to the artist, under a thundering headline. Mick blanched—the woman was nude and very familiar.

OOH-LA-LA LOVELY MARIE-CLAIRE! *Now here's an eye-full for you! Lovely footballer girlfriend Marie-Claire Wentworth, normally so shy, posed nude for her Life Drawing Class last week at the Wandsworth Art League. Fellow classmate Stephen Ashe, whose sketch is featured here, recalls, 'Oh, she had no problem stripping when the scheduled model didn't show up.'*

"What the hell?" he thundered, his blood rising to a boil.

Hugo stepped forward. "Ooh-là-là. That's French, Mick, would you like me to translate? It means all of England now knows that your girlfriend has a lovely ass."

Mick balled the paper in his fist and waved it under Hugo's nose. "Are you responsible for this?"

"Wish I was. It would have been money well spent," Hugo spat back. "I told you to stay away from Juliet."

Mick's eyes narrowed. And then all hell broke loose.

———————◆○◆———————

"Mick, stop it!" Marie-Claire demanded twenty minutes later as she blocked his way up the stairs to the studio above. Thank goodness Darius had called to alert them Mick was on his way with bloodlust in his eyes.

"Stephen Ashe, I am coming to beat you to a bloody pulp!" Mick bellowed up the stairs.

"There was no harm done," she tried to reason with him. "Let it go."

"It's not right, what he did. I'll break all his bloody fingers. Then I'll rip his fucking head off!" He shouted to make sure he could be heard in the studio.

He tried to move her out of his way but she flattened herself against the interior door.

"I know it's not right, and I think he's having second thoughts after hearing your reaction. And I've already yelled at him and made him give the money back." She glanced up the stairs to where the other students were hastily shepherding Stephen out of the building through the back door.

"You posed for this?" He shook the cover of the *Observer* in disbelief.

"Yes," she said in exasperation. "Mick, I'm an artist. The human body is beautiful, it's art." She rubbed his arm soothingly. "The model couldn't make it, and I told you, when that happens, we students take turns. It was my turn."

He looked at the cover again, furious. "So why did that bastard go and sell it?"

She shrugged. "The money. He's like the rest of us, not much left over after fees and rent."

"Marie-Claire, I'm not going to stand for it. Get out of the way." Mick put his hands on her waist and tried to move her aside, but she refused to budge.

"Why?" she asked stubbornly. "I thought you said to ignore what these tabloids print because it doesn't matter."

"It does matter!"

"How? The sketch is tasteful and you can't see anything. You see more when girls wear skimpy bikinis on islands."

He snorted indignantly. "It's altogether different."

"How?"

"I don't care what some people wear on a beach. I do care that your body is papered all over the United Kingdom. Aren't you upset?"

"I'm not happy about it, but I'm not upset. It's not great art, but it's still art. More embarrassing for him—he drew my shoulders too narrow. Are my shoulders really that narrow?" She stroked his bulging bicep but steadfastly refused to yield the door. "I won't let you go up there. It's what they want, the newspapers. They're waiting for you to make trouble, and I won't let that happen."

Mick grunted, his focus still on the stairs behind her.

"Look at me." Taking his face in her hands, Marie-Claire could see the fury still gleaming in his eyes. "Mick, you were right. The paparazzi, the reporters, they'll always be there. I'm not going to let it bother me anymore. All that matters is us. We're all that matters."

Pulling his head down to hers, she pressed her lips to his flushed brow and then to his cheeks, kissing him until she felt the tension begin to leave his body. Finally, he wrapped his arms around her and drew her against him, burying his head in her neck and inhaling deeply.

"Do you love me?" he asked in tormented desperation.

"I love you," she breathed in his ear and felt the ripple of seismic shock go down his spine. "I love us."

"I love you, Marie-Claire." He searched her eyes intently and then his mouth engulfed hers in a passionate kiss.

After a moment, she broke away slightly, just far enough to whisper against his lips, "Promise not to beat up Stephen?"

"Promise not to pose nude ever again. I can't stand the thought of other men looking at you."

She considered that for a moment and nodded her head in agreement. "That's fair enough. So, I guess I have to call the *Daily Mail* and decline their offer?"

"What offer?"

"They sent a message." She pulled it out of her pocket and began to read, "Dear Miss Wentworth, We are prepared to offer you £10,000 to pose nude for our publication—"

"Bloody hell," Mick moved to snatch the paper from her hands but she lightly danced out of his reach.

"Oh no." She waved the offer in the air. "I'm going to have this framed and hung on the wall so I can look at it when I'm very old."

"How do you think it's going to go against Bournemouth tomorrow?" Gordon asked Mick as they worked in the apple orchard at Moorsgate the next day.

"Giles heard from a spy that Montoya is cleared to play, so Lars is going to have his hands full. And according to the *Telegraph*, they're favored by a goal, but our good luck charm will be showing up."

"Is there anything to that?" Gordon asked.

"'Course not. Just a pretty good coincidence."

Gordon laughed. "And I guess a good way to stir up a bit of drama and sell more papers."

Mick nodded and regarded the gnarled tree before them. "I want to marry her."

Gordon nodded, a faint smile playing around his lips. "I see."

"What do you think?"

"I don't think you could choose better. When are you going to ask her?"

"I want to do it right away."

"Don't you think you should meet her family first? Speak with her father?"

"Yes." Mick chafed at his father's suggestion. "And she doesn't want to talk about the future until she's done with her courses."

"That sounds reasonable. When is she finished?"

"Next March, almost a year."

"Wait a bit, son. Respect her wishes," Gordon advised, not without pity. "She's worth it."

Of course, Dad was making perfect sense and there wasn't much Mick could do but nod in agreement.

"It won't be easy, but you'll have the rest of your lives together. And Mick—" Gordon patted his shoulder sympathetically "—wait to buy a ring. It will only burn a hole in your pocket."

───────◦───────

It wasn't readily obvious, but the dynamics of the team had shifted. For years, Mick and Darius would claim seats at the back of the team motor coach along with the other bachelors, while the more settled players filled in the middle. Hugo always sat in the first seat behind the driver, reading a book and ignoring everyone.

But Friday night, the coach ride to Bournemouth was different. Darius now sat in the middle with Marco, who had been married for five years, and Mick sat with Brian. Jean-Georges had been tasked with keeping Hugo and Mick as far away from each other as possible, so he sat with Pozny, and together they chatted with Hugo in French at the front.

"I heard Sir Frank sent a car for MC." Brian smiled broadly as the coach sped north.

Mick glanced around nervously. "Pipe down, mate, you want every wife and girlfriend on the warpath?"

This only made Brian's grin widen, but he dropped his voice to a conspiratorial whisper. "Guess he'd have to hire an entire fleet, wouldn't he? All the same, old bugger's more superstitious than I thought."

Mick sank down in his seat and frowned. "There's that, but he pointed out that some of the Bournemouth fans might recognize her and not let her off the train. I knew she'd never go for special treatment, so he had to work it that she's going as Lady Poleski's special guest."

"Margo's going to a match?" Brian was dumbstruck. "Does she even know our colors?"

Mick ignored his sarcasm, although Lady Poleski's preference for shopping in the King's Road to watching her husband's team play was well known. "All the same, I'm glad she's got some protection. Are Connie and the boys coming up?"

Brian shook his head. "No, she wasn't feeling well this morning, so her mother came down to look after everyone."

Mick's eyes widened with concern. "She okay?"

Brian shrugged. "Yeah, just some twinges. It's not time, but soon enough."

"You're awfully cool about it."

Brian glanced at him sharply. "Third time around the block, my son. And the doctor says everything's fine."

Mick considered that for several moments. Brian was a good bloke, but goalkeepers in general were an odd lot, almost like their brains were wired differently or something. But how in the name of God could the man be so unconcerned? If it was Marie-Claire, he'd take her to hospital immediately.

Still, Connie wasn't the sort to complain, and he knew Brian was devoted to her. In fact, they were one of the happiest couples he knew. "How long have you and Connie been married now?"

"Twelve years come August," Brian answered proudly.

"How did you know? I mean, how did you know you wanted to marry Connie?"

"When I realized I couldn't live without her," Brian answered, laughing at the memory. "Literally. We had dated a bit in school but it wasn't serious, and after we graduated she went with some girlfriends to Australia for a holiday. I thought I'd work the field a bit, you know, meet some new girls and sow some wild oats, but I couldn't stop thinking about her. That was a ruddy shock, and I began picturing her on Bondy Beach in a bikini, talking to other blokes.

"I started going mental," Brian continued, "so after three weeks I got on a plane to Australia and ended up having to hunt her all over the bloody continent. Bought a ring in Sydney, found her in Alice Springs, and we got married in Melbourne. Smartest thing I ever did, haven't looked back since."

"Does she ever get upset? You know, about the fans, the groupies?"

The question surprised Brian. "They don't come near me. They know I'm a happily married man. But I guess it's becoming an issue for you now?"

"A bit," Mick conceded. "It feels like everything I wanted before, I don't want now, and everything I didn't want before, I want more than anything now. And the one keeps getting in the way of the other."

Brian nodded. "Then you've got a reputation to change."

"How do I do that?"

"The same way you got it in the first place. Hard work and dedication."

"And how long is that supposed to take?" Mick asked indignantly. Couldn't anything ever be simple?

"Mick, MC is a lovely girl, and good Lord, if she will still put up with you after the hell she's been through, then I say buy her a whopping big ring tomorrow and lock her in a room until she agrees to marry you."

"It's not that easy."

"I know it seems that way, but if you love her, and she loves you, everything will sort itself out."

Chapter Thirty-Four

THE TWO HUNDRED acres Mick bought in January had been neglected for close to half a century. In the tangled vegetation grew handsome elders, tall chestnuts, and groves of oaks and walnut, some probably hundreds of years old. It all needed a good cleaning and careful management, and the forester had laid out a plan that would restore some order while maintaining areas of underbrush as refuges for the native wildlife.

Marie-Claire had taken to the job with gusto and was enjoying clearing the dense scrub while Mick used the chainsaw to bring down scraggly brush. The job was an excellent one for a Sunday, and she had brought a picnic lunch that they could enjoy at a scenic spot near the stream.

They had started at eight in the morning, and by eleven the day had turned warm enough for Marie-Claire to take off her thick sweater, under which she wore a thin, cotton V-neck shirt. Mick immediately lost all ability to concentrate on the work at hand, and was being driven to distraction by her every movement. When she bent over to wrestle with some overgrowth, he saw the generous valley between her breasts and remembered exactly how it tasted. A teasing glimpse of her lacy bra riveted him in place, and a brief gap in the waistband of her jeans told him which knickers she was wearing. They were the pale blue ones, with the tiny ribbon at the top and the bit of lace on the hips. His body reacted ardently. They hadn't been together since the previous weekend, and that, combined with the fresh smell of spring in the air and being on his own land, was making him randy as hell.

"Did you know we weren't favored to win yesterday at Bournemouth?" he asked, hoping conversation would help keep his mind on the business at hand.

"The people in Lady Poleski's box mentioned it," she replied, struggling to pull a large branch toward the brush pile.

He took the limb and tossed it on the pile. "Smithson pulled a groin muscle in their match against Liverpool, but the rest were on their game."

"You played like you were on fire. They seemed a little sluggish, especially that striker with the black hair."

"Antonioni. His brother got married in Milan last weekend and he only just got back from the wedding festivities. One of those big Italian shindigs that lasts for days. We got word he hadn't been sober since Monday and we took turns yelling in his ear."

"That was a bit of luck."

He paused and smiled. "You know what everyone is saying, don't you?"

"No?"

"That you're our good luck charm. That every game you have come to we've won."

A frown settled between her brows as she continued to carry limbs to the pile. "That's ridiculous."

"Is it? You came to the Fulham game, and we won."

"And I caused a riot."

"That was after the game. And a win's a win." He grinned and bent to drop a kiss on her head as she passed. "You were at Newcastle and we won, at Wolverhampton and we won, and then yesterday away at Bournemouth, we won again. That's a streak of four, love, and you're getting the credit."

She thought a moment. "Five, actually. I was at your game against West Ham even though they wouldn't let me in. And you won that, too."

"There'll be no living with you now, will there?"

"Aren't you going to take any credit? All the practices? All the talent? It's foolish to lay it all at my feet."

"Footballers are extremely superstitious," he told her, picking up a handsaw and trimming some low branches. "Yes, we've had a remarkable streak of being injury free, and we're reasonably well rested and fit. But you're the extra bit of magic everyone is focusing on."

Branches dropped to the ground as he worked his way around the tree. "Sir Frank spoke with me after the game yesterday. He's offering to pay for a security detail for you, and Lord Lambton thinks it's a good idea, as well."

"Security...whatever for?"

"They're both worried that you'll be too much of a temptation to the other clubs' fans."

Marie-Claire scowled. "Temptation for what?"

"Don't be daft. It won't take long for the other teams' fans to figure out that if you're not at a match, their team might have a better chance."

"They think someone might try and stop me from coming to a game?"

"Maybe. It's a legitimate concern and I agree with them."

"But no one would seriously try and stop me from coming, would they?" she asked in growing discomfort.

"Someone might. We're playing Chelsea next Saturday. They're sixth, and a loss to us might put them out of the Cup."

"Okay, I won't go to the game then."

"The hell you won't! You'll be there with bells on. We need to win."

"What if you don't win?" she countered. "What if I'm there and you lose?"

"Then you can dismiss the security."

Without warning, a branch he was sawing whipped back and lashed across her bare arm, and she recoiled with a yelp.

He was at her side in an instant. "Bloody hell, sorry. I didn't realize it was going to snap that hard."

He held her arm and examined where a faint line of blood was starting to form.

She winced at his touch. "Ouch! No, it's okay, it's my fault. I wasn't paying attention."

"Let's go to the stream and get some water on it. Sit here." He motioned to a large stone on the bank, and shrugged off his t-shirt, dampening one hem in the clear water and dabbing her arm.

"How's that?" he asked, crouching before her on his haunches, the cloth pressed to her skin.

"Wonderful," she murmured, letting her eyes roam over his naked torso.

Keeping the cloth pressed against her arm, he traced the line of her lips with his index finger, smiling when she bit the tip. His finger followed a path across her chin, dropping to stroke the smooth column of her throat and the delicate nape of her neck. Her eyes closed as he traced further still, to the deep cleft between her breasts and around the edge of the lacy bra.

His hand slipped under the wispy fabric and captured a tight nipple and fondled it, making it tighten even harder. Kneeling before her, he put his lips to the cut and sucked a bit of blood out, his tongue running over the thin line. She pressed against him as he tumbled her onto the blanket spread on the soft moss by the edge of the stream. His lips returned to hers with a vengeance as he covered her body with his, her hair spread behind them on the wool blanket.

She looked so beautiful lying there, a blissful smile on her face, her eyes drugged with desire for him. With sensuous slowness, he undressed her, suckling, nuzzling, licking all the delicious parts of her body. He felt her arch beneath him, her nails biting lightly into his back.

Shedding his jeans, he pressed her against the soft earth and ravenously engulfed the tip of one pert breast, and then the other, till she moaned in abandon beneath him. Slipping a hand lower, he felt her slick and ready for him. He began to rise over her, intent on plunging into the tightness of her body, when she pressed a hand against his chest.

"Mick."

"What, darling?"

"Do you…did you bring anything…"

"What?" he said, his brain struggling to get the upper hand. "No…no, I didn't, but…oh hell." With a dispirited oath, he flopped on his back, his arm draped over his eyes, his breath coming in hard draws.

The sun warmed their bodies as they lay in frustration, a mild breeze stirring up the scents of the earth and forest. Seeing Mick was still painfully aroused, Marie-Claire rolled onto her side and with impish delight leaned over him, her hair brushing his skin. He remained still as she kissed his ear, letting the tender tips of her nipples tease his chest. Dragging his arm off his eyes, he looked at her with bemusement. "Are you trying to torture me?"

"Mick, you're being silly. How could I be torturing you? You're a huge brute of a man and could stop me anytime you like."

He gulped. "Do you have anything particular in mind, or just random teasing?"

"I do have something in mind, but I...ummm...I've never done it, and I don't know how to, but I'd like to try." The smile she gave him was wreathed with innocent ambition. "Are you willing to let me give it a go?"

"Jesus, yes," he agreed, and then gasped as she slid lower and nestled between his legs. Concentrating intently, she began to explore the rough, scarred flesh on the inside of his knee, tasting the warm skin. Her gentle fingers trailed over his sensitive thighs, working their way upward. He lay immobile as she explored the most intimate parts of him, her soft hair draped over him like silken wings, the brush of the soft tendrils sending tingles like prodding sword tips up his spine.

It was the most exquisite agony he had ever felt. She took her time tasting, licking, provoking, her inexperienced touch flaming his desire higher than it had ever been in his life. She nuzzled the root of his manhood, inhaling deeply, and her sigh of pleasure brought him perilously close to exploding.

There had been other experiences before with other women, but nothing like this state of molten pleasure. Her enthusiasm was obvious, but for God's sake, she was being too gentle, too careful. His hands gripped thick folds of blanket, his back arching in agony as she experimentally licked the heavy weights between his legs.

For the love of God, he couldn't take much more. Now she was lapping his pulsing shaft with slow, deliberate strokes of her tongue, her breath fanning the short, curling hairs, seeming in no hurry to reach the sensitive tip. She would take hours at this rate, and he knew he only had a minute at best, perhaps seconds.

She jerked away and he realized the tormented moan he had just heard had come from himself. "Am I hurting you?"

"No, darling, no, God, it's so good, don't stop." He reached out to press her back again and she batted his hands away impatiently, putting them back down at his sides, and started all over again at his other knee.

It was impossible, she didn't seem to realize the frenzied lust she was creating. "Marie-Claire, I don't think I can take much more of this."

"You can and you will. I'm enjoying this too much."

"You selfish wench—oh my God!" He gasped and sat straight up as her mouth enveloped the raging tip, her sweet tongue flicking in hot laps. The gentle tugging, the softness of her breasts pressed between his legs, was too much. This completely naive and inexperienced—Christ, schoolgirl, really —was giving him the most intense experience of his life.

But bloody hell, enough was enough. With a quick motion, he grasped her shoulders and flipped her onto her back and covered her body with his own, his flamingly hot erection pressed against her stomach. Just a moment of contact with her satiny skin released his seed in a series of tectonic blasts. They repeated again and again, keeping him at the pinnacle of exhilaration. Finally, he lay on top of her, careful not to crush her beneath him, spent. His body jerked with the occasional quake, his breath labored against her ear.

"You liked that," she said with a touch of pride, holding him against her, as his breathing returned to normal.

That had to be the biggest understatement he had ever heard in his life. "I liked that a lot."

"That's okay, then." She smiled and he rolled to his side, pulling her with him and giving into the luxury of just lying there, enjoying her. The stream rushed behind them while Scarlet Buntings flew from tree to tree overhead. Holding her in his arms, calm and relaxed, he knew what heaven must feel like.

There was just one thing missing. The urge welled up inside him, unbidden, like a wave he couldn't fight back. The words were out of his mouth before he knew he had said them.

"Move in with me."

He couldn't see her face where it was snuggled against his chest, but he felt her grow very still.

"It's too far from school," she said after a long pause.

"Use the Range Rover. Or the Aston Martin. Or…" Mick rolled her onto her back, trapping her beneath him. "Or I'll buy you whatever you want."

"I don't know how to drive on the wrong side. It still terrifies me."

"I'll teach you," he countered.

"I really like my house. I know where things are, I know the neighborhood, I know how to get around. I'm happy there."

"You wouldn't be happy living with me?"

She sighed in exasperation. "Yes, of course, I would. And the neighbors would be thrilled if I left. But it would be too easy to move in with you, live away from school, start missing studio hours because it was warmer in your bed. Too easy to just be Mick Carr's girlfriend."

"It would be safer. Sir Frank and Lord Lambton are very concerned."

She sat up, her jaw set. "I said I don't want to talk about the future. But I will talk about the here and now. And here, and now, I like living in Putney, with Neve and Raul. I am very safe there, any kidnapper would have to get in line behind the paparazzi. So, tell Sir Frank and Lord Lambton thank you, but no security."

With an oath, he stood up and dipped his t-shirt in the stream and wiped her stomach and chest, his expression thunderous. Then he waded into the cold water and fully submersed himself, coming up sputtering a few yards away.

"Are you freezing?" she asked in concern, putting her clothing back on.

"This isn't the first time you've driven me to a cold dousing," he snapped and dunked under again.

Mick stayed in the water for another minute before jumping out and toweling off with the blanket. He pulled on his jeans and t-shirt and dropped to his knees before her, head hanging down, and wrapped his arms around her midriff. She picked up the blanket and tenderly dried his hair.

"Kick me. Hard," he mumbled against her stomach and she laughed, her hands caressing his neck and shoulders. He enjoyed it for several minutes, and then pulled back. "Next Sunday night, there's a fancy to-do for the charity the club supports. It's a children's hospital in Kingsbury, and this is their big fund raiser."

"A fair?"

"Ah, no. More like a gala. With an auction. It all goes to raise money for the kids. Would you like to go?"

"What's it like?" she asked suspiciously.

"It's kind of fun. Lots of famous people attend, but the parents of the patients come, too, and the doctors and staff. They put on a good dinner and have an auction. Dad and I donate a day's shoot each year, it usually goes for over a thousand pounds."

"Very dressy?"

"Straight-up classy, red carpet, black tie. They sell the pictures to the papers. They're good kids. It's worth it. I talked to Connie," he added, "and she said she had lots of things she can loan you. You're almost the same size, when she's not pregnant."

"That's very kind of her," Marie-Claire said, "but I think I can manage. I'd very much like to go."

Chapter Thirty-Five

WEDNESDAY AFTERNOON, A dozen journalists pressed into the interview corner at Madejski Stadium as Mick tried to find the patience to answer their endless questions.

"Do you think MC's absence in the stands was the reason for Kingsbury Town's loss to Reading today, Mick?"

He glared at the TV sports personality thrusting the microphone in his face. "I think Reading played a good game and deserves the win."

"But you've won the last four games with her there to watch, and today she's not here and you lost. Surely she's a factor?"

"She'd only be a factor if she kitted up and Giles put her in the lineup," he snapped and stalked away. And it's five games, he added to himself.

Back in the locker room, the atmosphere was glum. His teammates shrugged out of their stained and sweaty uniforms, ripping tape off bandaged muscles and slumping, exhausted, on the benches. Reading, facing relegation, had attacked from the first minute of play and never relented, sapping every last ounce of strength from Kingsbury Town. To blame the loss on Marie-Claire's absence was ridiculous.

Mick stood in the doorway and looked at his teammates with disgust. "Well, you sodding lot of grannies, don't blame her. We had our arses handed to us by a hungry team that showed us a thing or two about converting penalties, and thank God Fernando showed up to play because without him, Reading would have gotten their first clean sheet of the season."

Grudging nods of agreement went around the locker room.

"Where is she today?" Lars asked.

"She got an opportunity to go to a private art collection and I told her to go."

"Is she coming Saturday against Chelsea?" Jason asked.

With a snarled oath, Darius stepped into the fray. "It doesn't matter if she does or not, you bleedin' pansies. Pull your panties up, ladies, and figure out how eleven grown men are going to beat Chelsea and get paid for it, regardless of who's in the stands."

The players began to pack up and head to the coach for the trip back to London. Outside, Darius caught up with Mick and drew him aside. "So, is she coming Saturday?" he asked.

Mick rolled his eyes. "Yes. She is planning on coming. For God's sake, Darius, it's just a coincidence."

"Keep saying that, mate."

Mick settled into his seat, secretly knowing he didn't believe in coincidence either. Marie-Claire had cast such a thorough spell on him, the idea that it extended to the entire team seemed entirely reasonable.

Mick Carr had another secret, and a nasty one at that.

He wanted to get Marie-Claire pregnant.

He had never planned anything so underhanded and deceptive in his life, and part of him was shocked he could even be thinking it. Why would he want to do something so unscrupulous? The poor girl was working her tail off trying to achieve her goals and become a serious artist. He should be smoothing her way, not throwing up roadblocks the size of boxcars in her path.

But he was desperate. He knew what he wanted—a home with Marie-Claire as his wife and the mother of his children. He could see the future before him with perfect clarity, and he meant to have it with her.

There would be no problem with her finishing school, he reasoned. She had less than a year left and they could be married and set up by the time a baby came. He had seen some pregnant students coming and going at the Lady Warwick, and they didn't seem fussed. He could afford to give her and their family the best of everything.

Yes, he was trying to trap her. But she loved him, and he loved her, and in the long run that was all that mattered. He grimly proceeded with his plans.

———◦———

A small storage closet off the main studio at school was pressed into service as a fitting room, and Marie-Claire stood on a short stool in her bra and panties while Yvette draped fabric on her.

"Hold still, you git Yank," Yvette said, her mouth crammed full of pins. Marie-Claire held her arms akimbo, afraid to move lest she be jabbed by one of the pins tacking her gala dress in place.

"Don't you think you made the hem a little short?" she asked, glancing down to where the edge of the fabric skimmed her thighs.

"No, it's the design."

"Yvette, how am I supposed to sit down in this?"

"Be on your back after he gets a look at you in this, love," Yvette winked, and cursed again as Marie-Claire shifted her weight from one foot to the other. "Stand up straight."

The revealing halter top didn't seem to cover enough of her breasts. "This top is really skimpy. Are you sure this is going to stay together?"

"'Course it is," Yvette replied in reassuring tones. "Neve going, too? I could whip her up a little number, as well."

Marie-Claire shook her head. "No, I wish she were. Darius invited her, but her grandfather is having surgery the next day, and she wants to be with him."

After what seemed an eternity, Yvette stepped back to evaluate the creation and gave a nod of satisfaction. "I just need another day and it will be ready. Get yourself a cute pair of knickers to go with it, mind they match. You never know if it's going to be windy."

Marie-Claire changed back into her jeans and t-shirt and packed her kit bag. Pulling on Mick's field coat, she started down the stairs to the lobby.

Hugo Auchincloss appeared at her side from nowhere and opened the door to the courtyard for her. "MC, good to see you."

She jumped, startled. "Hugo. What are you doing here?"

"Lady Warwick was a great-aunt of mine. My family is still involved in the school, and the guard knows me." His eyes ran up and down her with bored indolence as he continued to hold the door. "After you."

Marie-Claire glanced towards the gate where paparazzi lenses were focused on them. There were no cars parked in the courtyard, so Hugo must have left his on the street in full view. The pictures showing them leaving together would be worth a mint.

She swallowed and ventured out, her step just short of a run.

"Where were you yesterday?" Hugo asked, easily keeping up with her. "Our first loss in four games."

"We were invited to the Courtauld Gallery for a private visit. I told Mick I couldn't pass that up."

"You're wasted on him, you know," Hugo drawled in his spare, upper-class accent. "He's a bit of a brick. Dropout, did you know?"

"He's told me that. It makes no difference."

The guard seemed to take forever to open the gate. Marie-Claire seethed, sure that Hugo had somehow bribed him to take his time while the cameras clicked at a furious pace.

"You know why he wants you?" Hugo taunted her, the iciness in his eyes belying his lazy attitude. "He's used to chasing tarts, thought it was all he could get. You're something he never thought he could have—a beautiful, educated woman."

The breath was tight in her chest. "He has one now."

"Do you think he's changed?"

"I know he has."

A condescending smile flicked across Hugo's thin lips. "Come on, love," he said loudly, "I'll give you a lift home."

"Go to hell, Hugo."

"Suit yourself." With a gallant movement, he shrugged off his raincoat and draped it around her shoulders, and made a show of holding back the paparazzi as she fled through the gate. He jogged behind her for a block, trailed by the photographers, until she turned the corner.

"Tell Mick I said hello," he called after her, and bent to pick up his coat from where she'd thrown it in a mud puddle.

———————— ❦ ————————

That night, Marie-Claire ran to greet Mick at her front door, hugging him like she never wanted to let go.

"What's the matter?" he murmured into her hair.

She relaxed a bit and led him back to the kitchen. "I just missed you, that's all. Dinner's almost ready but there's a pipe knocking in the basement, would you go and have a look at it?"

"Of course."

She opened the basement door and turned the light on, the air cool and musty-smelling. After he went down, she closed the door behind him, turned the deadbolt and waited, her heart pounding.

A few minutes passed until she heard his footfalls on the wooden steps and the doorknob rattled. "Open the door, love."

Marie-Claire stood on the other side and bit her lip. "I can't. Not yet."

"You've locked me down here."

"Yes, I know. I have to tell you something but I can't let you out until you've heard it all."

There was a long pause. "All right. What do you have to tell me?"

"Hugo Auchincloss came by the studio this afternoon."

"What the hell did he want?" Mick bellowed.

"To give me a lift home."

The tone of Mick's voice dropped to icy depths. "Open this door."

"Not yet," she rushed on. "I didn't go. But the paparazzi got lots of pictures."

"Open the damn door right now!"

"No."

"Marie-Claire, I swear I'm going to break this door down —"

"I'm on the other side. I won't move. You'll hurt me."

"Did he touch you?"

"No. Why did he do that, Mick? Why did he want to stir up more trouble? I thought he had a girlfriend."

Mick sighed. "He does. But there are reasons."

"Why do you two hate each other so much?"

"We've never gotten on, even from the earliest times," Mick explained. "Do you remember when I took you for dinner that first night, I told you there were a lot of things I've done that I'm not proud of? Well, many years ago, Hugo was dating a girl, but he was ignoring her. To hear her tell it, he was still living at home with Mother and had no time for her. They were never seen together.

"One night when we were on the road, she and her girlfriends were at the same club as us. I was very drunk, like I was most of the time back then, and we ended up back at my hotel room. Someone tipped off the paparazzi, and they were waiting when she left. It was all over the papers and caused a right stink. Turns out they were engaged, although I swear she wasn't wearing a ring. I apologized to him, and I meant it, too, but he wouldn't have any of it. We've been sparring ever since."

"Isn't that bad for the team? That you two don't get along?"

"No. Giles likes a bit of tension, keeps everyone on his toes. I think it's giving Darius grey hair, though."

Leaning back against the wall, she considered that information. "I don't want you to go after him. It will just make everything worse."

"And I suppose I'm not getting out of here until I promise not to beat him to a pulp?"

"Yes."

"I'm calm. Open the door."

"You have to promise."

"Move in with me and I'll promise," he countered.

"Promise, and I'll stay with you tonight."

A string of colorful curses were followed by a defeated sigh. "I promise."

—◆◇◆—

Hours later, Marie-Claire lay with her head on Mick's bare chest, their naked limbs entwined, looking at the painting of the mated Canada geese on the wall opposite his bed.

"Why did you move this one up here?" she asked, trailing her fingers up and down the hard muscles of his arm.

He glanced at the painting before returning his attention back to the enticing curve of her ear. "It's my favorite. I like seeing it when I wake up and just before I fall asleep," he murmured before nibbling the tip of her lobe.

"I like the Trumpeter Swan better." She purred as his hand moved to fondle a breast. "The paper stretched well and the glazes are more even."

"Geese mate for life. That's why this one is my favorite."

With an effort, she disentangled herself from his entwining limbs. He reluctantly let her go, watching as she skipped across the room with naked grace before disappearing downstairs.

She reappeared with a black permanent marker from her field kit and turned the bedside light on.

Propping the pillows up behind him, she uncapped the pen, and straddling his torso, began sketching on his chest, her hair falling over him in tangled waves. The scrape of the pen against his skin tickled, and he watched in fascination as she drew for several minutes, her lip caught in her lower teeth as she concentrated.

"Go see in the mirror," she announced, sitting back cross-legged on the bed.

Curious, he went into his bathroom where he was delighted to see she had drawn a pair of mated geese over his heart. They were small, about the size of a half-crown, but perfect. Strong emotion welled from deep within him, and tears rimmed his eyes.

"Do you like it?" she called.

<hr />

A discreet chime sounded over Malbrey Jewellers' entry door and Robert Paulson's head snapped up. "Mr. Carr."

"Mr. Paulson."

"What may I show you today, sir?" He'd bet his hat Carr was there for a ring.

Mick paused. "A ring."

Ah, the sign of a true professional. "A *special* ring, sir?"

Mick coughed and shifted his weight. "Yes."

With a subtle motion, Robert Paulson indicated to the staff that he was not to be interrupted under any circumstances. "Right this way, sir."

Chapter Thirty-Six

"WHEN DO I get to see the dress?" Mick asked again Sunday evening, brushing aside the parking valet and holding the car door for Marie-Claire himself. She was wrapped in his field coat, but as she stepped out, there was nothing between the hem of the coat and her four-inch high heels, except what seemed like a half-mile of gorgeous naked legs.

"In a moment." She smiled mysteriously, which made the anticipation all the greater. The drive over had been excruciating.

"In a moment, I'm going to be pulling you into the bushes and finding out for myself," he said, adjusting himself discreetly. Bloody good thing his tuxedo jacket was a longer cut that covered the protruding bulge he always developed whenever she was near.

She took his proffered arm and they walked towards the red carpet and bay of flashing bulbs. A few steps before, she turned away and unbuttoned the coat.

His breath caught as the coat slid off her shoulders and he saw nothing but bare back. The dress, what he would later remember of it, was gold satin with a short skirt draped loosely over her derriere. When she turned around, a halter top revealed the generous mounds of her bountiful breasts, the two sides of the deep-V halter held together by one thin gold chain. The only ornamentation she wore was the bird's nest on the thin black ribbon around her neck.

He blanched. The delicate chain looked like it could snap at any moment.

She smiled at him saucily and reached up to release the curls piled on top of her head. Her hair tumbled over her shoulders and down her back in lustrous waves. "So, what do you think?"

He swallowed hard, his blood pulsing thickly. "I think I should have brought one of the guns."

She laughed in delight, pleased at his response.

"That chain, is that all that's holding your top together?" He frowned.

She nodded. "Yes. But Yvette was pretty sure it will hold. She said it's stronger than it looks."

"Pretty sure," he repeated.

"Almost certain. I just have to be careful."

"Jesus," he muttered as they moved along the carpet.

A velvet rope separated them from the spectator gallery. "Bet you're glad MC was at the game yesterday, eh, Mick? You needed that win against Chelsea!" someone yelled.

He felt her flinch and wrapped his arm around her while they waited in the short queue to be photographed.

Mick was used to the flash of the cameras, but this was an explosion like he had never experienced. Questions were yelled at a furious pace.

"MC, who made your dress?" one shouted.

Reaching into her clutch bag, Marie-Claire pulled out a piece of paper and stood on tiptoe to whisper in Mick's ear. He blanched when he saw the chain stretch taut, and ducked down to listen to what she said.

Taking the paper, he walked to the cordoning rope and handed it to the photographer. "Make good use of that, mate."

The photographer winked. "You're a lucky man, Mick."

The crowd entering the hall was bottlenecked at the door and she pressed back against him, snuggling her bottom against his hardness.

His teeth gritted. "Marie-Claire, have a pity on me."

Once inside the magnificent ballroom, the crowd fanned out and they were able to mingle. Hugo Auchincloss sidled up, smoothly wedging himself between Mick and Marie-Claire.

"Good evening, my love, may I say you look ravishing," Hugo said in a loud voice. Mick intercepted Hugo's hand as it reached for hers, and with a stealthy motion, bent it backwards at a painful angle.

"Lay a hand on her, Hugo, and you'll be playing for the women's side."

"Mick, Hugo!" Darius interrupted, surreptitiously breaking Mick's grasp on the midfielder's hand and stepping between them. "Like for you to say hello to my mum."

Hugo stalked off, while Darius frowned at Mick. "In company, my son."

More people streamed into the ballroom, sweeping Mick and Marie-Claire into the social current. Marie-Claire was surprised at the number of people who wanted to meet her, and they were parted several times, but Mick kept a watchful eye on her, and Hugo kept to his corner, nursing a drink.

"This is fun," she admitted when they were reunited a short time later.

"I can't take my eyes off you," Mick murmured against her hair. "I can't think straight."

"Good. That was the idea."

"To make me miserable?"

"No, to keep your attention on me. I knew there would be a lot of beautiful women here tonight, and I wanted to make sure you thought I was the most beautiful."

Mick grunted. "Every man here thinks you're the most beautiful."

She pressed against him and pulled his head down to her lips, the side of her bare breast sliding against his tuxedo coat and seeming to burn a hole through it. "I don't care about every other man. I only care about you."

"Right, that's it then." With a smooth motion, he grasped her elbow and piloted her out the of the crowded reception area and down a side corridor, making several turns till he found a door in a deserted hallway. A peek inside showed the tiny sitting room was empty, and he yanked her in after him, slamming the door shut and throwing the lock.

The room was thickly carpeted and furnished with a mahogany dressing table under a tall mirror, a tufted settee, and a potted palm. In an instant, Mick pulled her against him, his mouth finding hers. She responded with the same passion and they kissed with a fevered heat, their tongues stroking soft and hot, his desire matching her own frenzied passion.

With a deft movement, he unhooked the clasp at her neck and the halter dropped away, revealing the ample mounds of her breasts. His eyes feasted on the display, and with a smooth motion, he lifted her onto the dressing table and filled his hands with her smooth, pliant flesh. She gasped as his thumbs teased the already sensitive tips to tight buds, and he bent to claim them, his lips closing on the yearning crests in swift plunder.

It was exquisite torture and she groaned under his onslaught. He settled himself between her legs and dropped his hands to her bottom to press her against the full length of his hardness, the thin, wool fabric of his trousers sliding luxuriously against her skin. She rubbed against him, wanting to feel all of him.

Reaching under her skirt, he hooked a finger in the wispy panties and drew them off, and then began to stroke the aroused warmth and wetness. He controlled her every movement like a puppet master, probing deeper and deeper still, preparing her as she clung to him, her breath coming in ragged bursts.

"Hurry, Mick, please, I need to feel you," she urged, her fingers biting into his back.

With a swift motion, he unfastened his trousers, his heated muscle springing against her intimately. Then he was easing into her, feeling the slippery wetness of her longing for him. She wrapped her legs around him and drew him in, and sensations he never could have imagined swept over him, wave after wave. The intensely sensitive contact sent shockwaves through his body in a sensory overload as he thrust to fill her, holding her hips to steady her frantic rhythm, the sensations acute and incredible, and more exciting than anything he had ever felt in his life.

He heard her moan out loud and plunged into her as far as he could go, and they were truly joined as they had never been before. Her head rolled back as he held her hips so that every sensitive part of her was included in his thrusts, and she moved with his body, her soft gasps punctuated by his own.

He felt every clench of her hot, satiny grasp, and it was too much for him. Her back arched in ecstasy and the breath caught in her throat as he gave up all control and spilled into her with spasm after heavenly spasm. She held onto him for dear life as he spent himself, an exquisite sheen covering her body.

A short while later they left the room and found their table in the ballroom, both of them knowing they hadn't used protection.

———— ◆◯◆ ————

Dinner passed leisurely. Their table included some doctors, a patient's family, and Darius and his charming mother. Marie-Claire enjoyed herself, and basked in the warm afterglow of Mick's passion that gave her skin a faint blush.

As dessert was being served, the master of ceremonies, a popular entertainer with a quick wit, began the auction with enthusiastic banter that drummed up the crowd's interest. Autographed footballs, opportunities to go to training camps, and game tickets all fetched good money while he kept the pace moving at a jaunty clip.

"Next on the block, a day of shooting for four at Hempland, donated by our very own Mick Carr." He paused for a large round of applause and turned to their table. "Mick, will you throw in the services of a lovely beater for the winner?" He leered at Marie-Claire and got a good laugh.

Mick draped his arm around her and retorted with a grin, "No, but I might throw in a good beating for you!" Cheers erupted, and the emcee bowed in response.

Bidding was spirited and finished at twenty-five hundred pounds. Mick was impressed. "It's never gotten so much before."

The items grew steadily in value. "But I've been saving the interesting stuff for last, I know you big spenders still have plenty of cash in those wallets!" the emcee trilled with a gleam in his eye.

"Next on the block, a watercolor painting of a Brecon Buff goose, watercolor on parchment, 140 centimeters by 160 centimeters, signed by the artist..." He paused for dramatic effect, and Mick sat up straight in his chair. When the emcee was sure he had everyone's attention and the room was knife-edge silent, he announced triumphantly, "...Miss MC Wentworth of the Lady Warwick College of Arts and Design."

A gasp went through the crowd, and Mick turned to her in disbelief.

"I dropped it off two days ago," Marie-Claire said. "I thought they might like something to auction off. But he should have sold it much earlier. It's not going to get much."

"I wouldn't be too sure," Mick muttered.

"Who will open the bidding at five hundred pounds?" the emcee squealed with ill-concealed delight.

"Oh no," Marie-Claire whispered.

"And we have five on the floor." He pointed to a hand raised in the corner. "And six. And seven. And eight." He picked bids off quickly, like he was taking roll call. "We are at eight hundred pounds...thank you, ma'am, nine hundred pounds." He bowed to a woman at a front table.

Marie-Claire felt sick. "This can't be happening."

"And nine hundred, and a thousand, and eleven hundred, back to you, ma'am, God bless you, and—"

"Five thousand pounds," Hugo Auchincloss announced loudly over the hoopla. Everyone craned their necks to see him, reclining indolently in his chair at a table near the back of the room.

Mick's eyes narrowed. "Six thousand pounds!"

"Seven," Hugo drawled.

"Ten!" Mick responded.

"Fellas! Fellas! That's my job!" The emcee interrupted, taking out a handkerchief and mopping his brow. The crowd laughed, riveted by the display—everyone in the room knew the painting was the last thing they wanted. The competition between the two men was like watching a tennis match played with knives.

Marie-Claire clutched Mick's hand under the table. "I'll paint you whatever you like."

"I want this one," Mick said, never taking his eyes off Hugo.

She cast a desperate glance to Darius, who frowned pointedly at Mick but was ignored.

"Okay, gents, okay," the emcee recovered, "let's remember this is for the kids! We are at ten thousand pounds for this exceptional painting of a Brecon Buff goose by MC Wentworth. Do I hear eleven?"

"Twelve," Hugo shot back.

"Fifteen!" Mick shouted.

"Twenty!" Hugo replied with venom.

"Stop it! This is absurd." In disgust, she threw her napkin on the table and stood to face the room. With a tremulous smile, she announced, "Mr. Auchincloss may have the painting." She paused, and glanced to where Mick sat, fuming. "And I will paint Mr. Carr a painting of whatever he likes for the same donation to the hospital."

Rapturous applause broke out and she sank into her chair, her legs too wobbly to hold her. From across the room, Hugo blew her a kiss and she had to drive her hand into Mick's leg to keep him in his seat. "I said stop it," she snapped, "let it go."

The emcee slumped into a chair with relief. "That is a record for any auction item here at the gala!"

Chapter Thirty-Seven

MICK WOKE HER early the next morning with two steaming cups of coffee, propping some pillows behind her as she rubbed the sleep from her eyes.

"Good morning, beautiful. Did you sleep well?"

She smiled and yawned. "Sleeping is a waste of time when you're in the bed. What time is your flight to Milan today?"

"Noon from Gatwick."

"How long will you be gone?"

"Four days. We'll be back late Thursday night."

"Is everyone going?"

"Almost everyone. I'm sure Auchincloss has figured out a way to skip it."

Marie-Claire didn't want to hear about Hugo. "What are you going to be doing?"

"We all have an endorsement deal with a sport shoe company, and they're hosting a celebrity match Tuesday. In between, we do signings, meet fans, that sort of thing."

"I'll miss you."

"Not as much as I'll miss you." Nudging the sheet down with his finger, he circled the rosy areola of her nipple, which tightened under his teasing touch. "Last night, at the gala…"

"Hmmm?" she sighed.

"I didn't use protection," he said bluntly. "I attacked you. I'm sorry, you were so beautiful, and I had to have you. I can't control myself around you."

His caressing hand moved to cup a full breast. "You would have stopped," she purred, "but I don't think I could have stopped myself."

He chuckled at the thought. "You were a wild woman. Are you upset?"

"Yes and no. There's nothing we can do now, except be more careful."

He bent to claim her lips. "Come to Milan with me today."

"It's almost end of term in two weeks, and I've got mountains of work due," she said, reveling in the languorous feelings he was igniting.

"How much time do you get off between terms?"

"Mmmm…about six days."

His tongue replaced his finger to flick over the sensitive tip. "You need a holiday. Would you like to go away somewhere with me?"

"Yes," she moaned, reaching to draw him closer.

After a long interlude, he switched his attention to her other breast, spending a pleasurable moment in the deep valley between them. "Where?"

"Anywhere," she gasped, as he gently suckled the satiny tip, "anywhere you want, Mick, just keep—"

"How about Maryland?"

It was like a bucket of cold water had been thrown on her. "Why?"

"I'd like to meet your parents."

Her mind raced for any excuse to delay this stealthy advance towards the future.

Mick waited for her response. "Do you think they should meet me?"

She considered this for a very long time. "Probably."

Mick clasped her shoulders, urging her to look at him. "We are right for each other, Marie-Claire. You know how to handle me. I don't know how, but you can. I am so much better with you. And it's the same for you. Tell me it's not true."

She dropped her gaze to avoid his piercing eyes. "It's true."

"Then when do I get to meet them?"

Wriggling out of his grasp, she skittered out of bed, wrapping the top sheet around her body. "Why does it have to be so soon?"

"It's not too soon."

He watched as she paced the room. "We've only known each other a few weeks."

"I'm just asking to meet your family."

Marie-Claire stood at the window looking out at the park, but seeing nothing.

"Why are you fighting this?" Mick asked in frustration.

"Because it could all change on a dime."

"There's nothing left to happen. Everyone knows we're together. Nothing more could happen."

"Mick, I barely avoided going to prison. Don't you realize there are a lot of people who want me gone?"

"Do you seriously think I'm going to let anyone take you away from me?"

"I believe that there are a lot of people who would be very happy if I wasn't in the picture anymore."

"Like who?"

"Fanta, the dean, my neighbors—" she ticked off on her fingers "—the supporters of every team you play, the Football Association, the Hendon police—"

"Enough!" Mick roared.

———◄O►———

Mick dropped her off at the Lady Warwick on his way to the airport. He parked a block from the school, and they sat in companionable silence, the interior of the Aston Martin like a cocoon from the outside world. "I didn't mean to pressure you about meeting your parents. I'll take you to Barcelona over your break instead."

"Can we talk about it when you come back?"

"Of course."

The mob of photographers in front of the school had grown appreciably since the week before, and cameras flashed rapidly as Mick drove into the courtyard and stopped the car. "They're probably hoping you're still wearing that dress," he said ruefully.

"I can go back and put it on."

"Not bloody likely. You'll be wearing that for my own private enjoyment from now on." With a last brief kiss, he whispered, "I love you."

———◄O►———

Inside the studio, everyone was huddled over the morning's tabloids. Yvette glanced up and waved her over.

"Yah, MC, come see!"

GOD BLESS AMERICA shouted the *Observer* headline, featuring a photograph of Marie-Claire in her gala dress on their cover. They were featured all over the four-page spread, making her cringe when she saw just how revealing the dress looked in print. But the pictures accurately captured the glow of happiness she had felt, and they certainly made a handsome couple.

"Listen to this," Yvette read. "'*MC's dress was an original creation of Yvette Lawson-Davies, another student at the Lady Warwick College of Arts and Design. Miss Lawson-Davies is a second-year student studying textile design.*' I've gotten over twenty messages on my mobile so far this morning. Plus, Marks and Spencer called, I'm meeting with them tomorrow. Can you believe it?"

"I'm so happy for you," Marie-Claire said. "And you were right about the dress."

"What, that Mick would have you on your back before you could worry about sitting down?"

Marie-Claire blushed, knowing Yvette had no idea how close she had come to the truth. "No, about the chain holding."

"Ta, never had a worry."

Sandra met her in the hallway and handed her a thick stack of phone messages. "They're from the receptionist. The sports writers from the *Telegraph* and the *Guardian* want you to call."

"I have no idea what to say to them," Marie-Claire said, dumping the messages in the nearest waste bin.

A second-year sculpting student wearing a Kingsbury Town t-shirt passed them. "That was a huge win over Chelsea on Saturday, MC, think you can pull another one off against Man U this weekend?"

Marie-Claire ignored him and kept walking.

"Jerk," Sandra said as they entered the studio. "Although my dad's a big Manchester United fan and he said he wouldn't mind if you decided to go to Paris for the weekend."

Stephen Ashe's head snapped up from his worktable. "You're going to Paris for the weekend?"

"No!" Marie-Claire said and threw her kit bag on her table, muttering a colorful oath she had learned from Mick.

The dean's secretary popped her head around the door. "MC, the dean wants to see you in his office."

Sandra sent her a warning look and Marie-Claire shrugged. She followed the woman through the warren of hallways till they found the dean's office, a cavernous room that had once been the mansion's dining room.

"MC, come in please," the dean said and motioned her to a chair.

Marie-Claire sat on the edge while the dean took a seat behind his massive mahogany desk. "MC. The purpose of the Lady Warwick College of Arts and Design is to help artists develop their full talents."

"Yes, sir."

"And you are turning it into a trade school!" he sputtered, turning red with ill-concealed rage. "And I will not stand for it!"

"Sir?"

He flung the *Daily Mail* on the desk. **TWENTY THOUSAND BOB FOR A BUFF?** the headline screamed. Hugo Auchincloss was on the cover, holding the painting, a satisfied smirk on his face.

"It was an auction, sir. For a children's hospital. I didn't make any money on the painting."

"No, no you didn't," the dean replied, "but you set your price point. Your paintings are now worth twenty thousand pounds apiece, and you've effectively sold two. That's more than any member of the faculty could ever hope to get for one of their pieces. And for a watercolor! It's unheard of."

Marie-Claire's stomach began to churn. "I can't control what goes on at an auction, sir."

"Oh, really? It seems like you can't control a lot of things in your life. Did you knowingly give that reporter Yvette Lawson-Davies's telephone number?"

"Yes, but just to help her—"

"It's helped her quite a bit." The dean pointed to a stack of slips piled on his desk. "The switchboard has been jammed since eight o'clock this morning with people trying to find out where they can purchase a copy of that…I guess 'frock' is the closest word for that costume you wore. And I understand that Marks and Spencer are anxious to sign her to a short-term design contract."

"But that's wonderful."

"The paparazzi have created a circus here. Some of the students are starting to complain, and the neighbors at your residence, which is owned by the school, have complained of reporters harassing them."

"Sir, I'm sorry—"

"Miss Wentworth, I will not disagree that the media attention you have attracted has brought a bit of notoriety to the school. But this behavior must stop. Do I need to remind you of the conditions of your student visa?"

"I need to be enrolled in school."

"Yes, you do," he snapped. "Please do not give me any more reasons to reconsider your status here."

She sat in the chair, stunned.

"That will be all. Good day."

Marie-Claire raced back to the studio, which was mercifully empty. Classes had started a few minutes before and she unpacked her kit bag. The Kolinsky brush was missing from its usual place in her brush roll, and with mounting despair she emptied the entire bag. She remembered washing the brush and lovingly placing it there the day before, and now it was nowhere to be found.

Her head began to pound as she wondered just how much worse this day was going to get.

Chapter Thirty-Eight

IT WASN'T UNTIL ten o'clock Tuesday evening in Milan, which was an hour later than London, that Mick was able to get through to Marie-Claire. He had excused himself from the lavish dinner the athletic shoe company was hosting for the team and stepped onto the terrace of the Renaissance villa that had been rented for the event. The lights of Milan glittered in the distance.

Broad marble steps descended from the terrace to an expanse of manicured lawn and gardens. A full moon cast golden light over everything, and a gentle breeze wafted the scent of honeysuckle through the night. If Marie-Claire had been here, he would have waltzed her around the wide patio, holding her close against him.

The mobile phone reception was scratchy and the signal weak. "It's beautiful, you'd love it," he told her as he looked at the twinkling lights of the city. "This place they've brought us to, it's an old palace. The food is amazing."

"I'd love to see it someday." Even with the awful connection, he could tell by her voice she was tired.

"I wish you were here now," he murmured. "You sound exhausted."

She laughed when he pointed this out. "How much sleep have I been getting lately, Michael Carr?"

"Good point," he conceded. "Oh, you'll probably be hearing soon enough, Fanta showed up this afternoon."

He heard her intake of breath and rushed to reassure her. "She hasn't given me a second look. She's been plastered to Jean-Georges the entire time. He doesn't look too happy. He didn't invite her, said she just showed up saying it was a surprise and that she was lonely."

"Speaking of bad news," she began, and told him about her interview with the dean.

"Bleedin' bastard!" Mick exploded. "Where does he think he gets off telling you what to do?"

"He gets off because he's the dean of the college."

"That doesn't give him any right to butt into your personal life."

"What personal life? Everything we do is splashed across a dozen newspapers every day."

Mick sighed and leaned against a marble column. "You've got a point there."

"Sorry. Didn't mean to sound crabby, I guess I am exhausted. Tomorrow a few of us are going to the Royal Botanical Gardens at Kew, I can't wait. Margaret's brother-in-law works there, and he's going to let us in early through the employee gate and give us day passes. They've got a pair of Great Crested Grebes, I've never seen them. Then on Thursday, we've been invited to the Tate for the opening of their new exhibit before the public opening. I'm really looking forward to that. And after that you'll be home."

They talked a while longer and said goodnight, and she promised to go home and get a good night's sleep. He couldn't wait to get back to her; the thought of her waiting for him, warm and willing, was almost too much to bear.

Reaching in the pocket of his suit coat, he drew out the small black box and flicked the lid open for probably the thousandth time. The ring was simple and perfect; he'd seen it straight off in the first tray Robert Paulson had pulled out. He'd hesitated, afraid the stone was too big, but the jeweler had assured him it would be easy to clean. Dad was right, he shouldn't have bought an engagement ring, it was truly burning a hole in his pocket. But at the same time, it was like a talisman.

This was what pure happiness felt like, he realized—quiet, peaceful, and calm. The feeling had nothing to do with the raging hard-ons he got just by thinking about her. Happiness was the feeling of peace and contentment, of just being so damn satisfied with the world exactly as it was because Marie-Claire was in it. When people sang songs saying the same thing, they sounded trite, but the songs were true. She was his life.

A smile played around his lips as he stared at the diamond, the moonlight making the facets glitter with dark brilliance.

"Quite a sparkler," Fanta remarked from behind him. "Is it for her?"

Mick spun around at the sound of her voice. Fanta had approached silently, sheathed in a glittering, diaphanous green gown that left nothing to the imagination. Glancing about the terrace, Mick saw that they were alone. Without a word to her, he walked towards the atrium doors that led back inside.

"You're going to propose to her, aren't you?" Fanta asked, raising her voice to carry across the wide expanse.

Mick turned and scrutinized her. "Yes," he answered. God knew it would be all over the tabloids by tomorrow, but rumors of an engagement had been swirling since the first time they were photographed together. Marie-Claire would ignore it.

"They're bringing along another girl on *Willy Nilly*, you know," Fanta continued. "Sasha Glebman, but she calls herself Sasha Simpson. She started six weeks ago and is dating Nate, the producer. Next week she's going to be allowed playful banter."

Mick shrugged. "Sorry to hear that."

"Quite a to-do about the auction on Sunday. MC's got you and Hugo at each other's throats. I wish I had thought of that." Fanta wandered to the edge of the terrace and looked down the steep stairs to the moonlit gardens. "Care to go for a walk?" she asked, with a half-hearted attempt at flirtation.

"No, I wouldn't," Mick replied, and turned to go back into the villa.

"Sorry, Mick," Fanta said matter-of-factly. The odd tone in her voice stopped him dead in his tracks. "I need to get to Hollywood, and I'm running out of time. MC's got momentum now, and I need to use it. You're a nice guy, but a girl's got to do what a girl's got to do."

Glancing down the stairs, she grasped the bodice of her gown and ripped it with a neat movement, the glitter and loose beads sticking to her hands like fairy dust. Taking a deep breath, she let out a blood-curdling scream that echoed like crashing cymbals off the marble walls of the villa. In horror, Mick watched as she threw herself down the terrace stairs, curling into a tight ball and protecting her face, but hitting the stone steps with nauseating thuds.

At the bottom, she arranged her limbs in a broken composition, closed her eyes, and went still.

The terrace was immediately filled with people rushing down the stairs to where Fanta lay prone. Everyone erupted in a frenzy of English, Italian, and French, yelling at each other and no one in particular while Mick stood paralyzed, unable to believe what he had just witnessed. For a few moments, he was lost in the confusion, but soon became the center of attention as it became clear Fanta was not only conscious, but had begun screaming.

"Keep Mick away from me!"

Darius stayed close by his side and didn't ask any questions. An ambulance arrived, followed by the police, who separated him from his teammates. Jean-Georges managed to stay with him to interpret, but the meaning was clear—he was under arrest.

———◦———

Wednesday morning in Putney dawned clear and crisp. Marie-Claire sprinted out her door to Margaret's car, surprising the photographers slouched against the lamp post, drinking coffee. They hastily shouldered their cameras and were able to snap a few shots before Margaret gunned the tiny car down the street.

"They seem more excited than normal," Marie-Claire said.

"What's normal?" Margaret quipped.

The Royal Botanical Gardens at Kew were a green oasis in the middle of the congested city. Margaret's brother-in-law was at the staff gate to greet them, and give them a brief tour before he went to work. As they walked he pointed out the carefully created vistas, ending at the most spectacular one, the pagoda vista, whose view stretched across the plain down to the river.

Marie-Claire was enchanted. "How long has this been here?"

"Over three hundred years," he said, "and we have samples of one out of every eight species of every plant on the planet."

Margaret was there to sketch the riotous, blooming rhododendrons and azaleas, and Marie-Claire set off to find the lake and Great Crested Grebes. On her way through the wooded walk, she was waylaid by an extensive field of bluebells being patrolled by six golden pheasants in the morning sun.

It was too good to pass up, and she sat down on the side of the path to sketch. Hours slid by, her attention absorbed by the fowl, and she barely registered the visitors who observed her painting. At two o'clock, the growl of her stomach told her it was lunchtime. Mick and the team would be leaving for their game soon, and she called him on her mobile to wish him luck. The call immediately went to the recording, so she left a message describing the brilliant birds and the wonder of Kew, plus a kiss for luck. An impersonal beep cut her off in mid-sentence.

The girls had agreed to meet back at the staff gate at three o'clock, and she had to hustle to finish her last value charts and pack up her field kit to get there in time. She arrived five minutes before Margaret, who had also lost track of time, and together they compared their sketches, Margaret's full of vibrant rosy-hued shrubs with deep green foliage.

The day had been wonderful, and she couldn't wait to tell Mick about it when they talked that evening.

"Bloody hell," Margaret cursed under her breath as they approached the school.

Ahead, Marie-Claire saw the gates were blocked by photographers and film crews jostling for position, kept in a tight cordon by police. Her jubilant mood vaporized as Margaret's little car honked and inched through the mob until two policemen came out and cleared a path, which closed back around them like water. The camera flashes almost blinded Margaret as she drove into the parking court.

Neve rushed out and gave her mobile phone to Marie-Claire, her hand shaking. "It's Darius."

Astonished, Marie-Claire took the phone. "Darius? What's going on? Is Mick okay?"

"He's okay, love, Mick's okay." Darius's deep voice reassured her and she exhaled. "But there's been some trouble."

"He didn't fight Hugo, did he?"

"No, no, Hugo didn't make the trip."

Marie-Claire's jaw tightened. "Fanta."

"Clever girl. She's claiming Mick pushed her down a set of stairs outside the villa where we were having dinner last night. Said he did it in a jealous rage."

"But that's absurd."

"Don't we both know it. But she's also claiming Mick was trying to propose to her, and MC, the police found an engagement ring in his pocket."

She swallowed hard, feeling like the wind had been knocked out of her. After several moments, she was able to form words. "Where is he now?"

"He's being held at police headquarters in downtown Milan. We were able to hire a good lawyer and he's already been in to see him and he's okay. Furious, but okay."

At Margaret and Neve's urging, she began walking back into the studio building where they wouldn't be observed. "Where's Fanta?"

"Still in hospital, giving interviews to whomever will talk to her. Snappers, as well. There were no broken bones or even a concussion, and she's supposed to be released tomorrow morning. Her agent has called a press conference for nine o'clock."

"What are they going to do to Mick?"

"We don't know. The lawyer says we have to wait a few more hours to see what charges are filed."

"I'll get on a flight right now."

"No! I know you want to come, love, but don't. At least until we know something. It's already a zoo, they've staked the airport out waiting for you. Mick sent word he wants you to go to his house and stay there, and to be a good girl and not make a fuss. Take Neve with you. Can you do that?"

"Of course, but—"

"Good, we'll get word to him." There was a deafening roar and his voice grew faint. "Look, we're at the match but I will call you afterward and give you an update."

Marie-Claire handed the phone back to Neve, whose face was a conflicting mixture of emotions that spilled out of her in a rapid burst. "That ugly cow! Poor Mick!" She threw her arms around Marie-Claire. "Poor you!"

"Poor us," Raul added, entering the foyer, her overnight bag swung on his shoulder. "It just took me half an hour to get here from the house. They're twelve-deep outside on our pavement and the police have been called in to keep order." He winked at Marie-Claire. "And the neighbors send their love."

"Come and stay with us tonight at Mick's," Marie-Claire implored.

"Ha, no way. I'm going to hold down the fort. Parade naked in front of the windows, put on a show."

Neve had called Raul and told him what to toss in the overnight bag, and armed with that, they made a plan. A cab was a big expense, but the safest way to Mick's house. It waited for them in the lane behind the school and they were able to slip out, but when they got to Fulham, the gates in front of Mick's house were clustered just as thick with people, spilling into the road.

Darius had called ahead. After the gates opened briefly to let the taxi speed through, they quickly shut out the unruly mob behind them.

"What are you two birds then, supermodels?" the driver asked as he glanced in the rearview mirror, and did a double take when he saw Marie-Claire. "MC Wentworth?" he asked, dropping the sarcasm.

"Yes," she answered, opening her wallet. "I suppose you're a Manchester United supporter?"

The driver stopped in front of Mick's house and stepped out to open the door for the girls, putting his hand over her wallet. "Not interested in your money, love. Our Ryan did a spell at the Kingsbury Town Children's Hospital, and they fixed him up right as rain. I figure you've done your part." He pulled out a small notepad and scribbled a number on it. "You lot are going to have to get out of here tomorrow. You call me and I'll see it's done safely," he instructed, and drove off.

"What time will Kingsbury Town's game be over, do you think?" Marie-Claire asked as she opened Mick's front door with her key and disabled the security system.

"Around eight o'clock in Milan, seven here."

Mick's house was peaceful and quiet, and Marie-Claire had a hard time believing she had only left it two days before. In the living room, Neve sat on the leather sofa and turned on the television, and Marie-Claire took the chair next to her.

"Watch," Neve said, gesturing towards the enormous widescreen where a television hostess was relating the news of the day.

"Romantic Italian rendezvous ends in tragedy! Fanta de las Mercedes lies in a Milan hospital tonight recovering from a nearly fatal fall down a steep set of marble steps, thrown there, she says, at the hands of her former lover, footballer Mick Carr. StarPower has the exclusive interview!"

Marie-Claire felt a heavy weight press on her chest. Former lover. Well, that was true, he had hardly belonged exclusively to her. Hearing the words said out loud just hurt.

The coverage switched to a chipper-looking Fanta being interviewed in her hospital bed, a small bandage taped across her jaw.

"We were all out for a meal at the Villa Paola and I felt the need for some fresh air, so I went out onto the patio. Mick followed me," Fanta relayed breathlessly. *"He told me he wanted to get back with me, that he loved me. I told him I was with Jean-Georges, and he became jealous and hysterical. I tried to walk away, but he pulled me around and proposed with this gorgeous solitaire diamond ring. He even went down on one knee and begged me to marry him."* A small tear escaped her eye and rolled down her cheek. *"I said no, and he went crazy. I don't remember anything after that."*

Switching back to the studio, the hostess intoned, *"Police have the ring, purportedly a five-carat solitaire diamond, in their possession."*

"Is there anything else on?" Marie-Claire asked in irritation.

Neve clicked through the channels and came to a stop on the European football network.

"—when earlier today, Kingsbury Town wing Jean-Georges Mayotte visited the hospital before their game with AC Milan. We managed to get a few words with him after he visited Fanta de las Mercedes."

Jean-Georges's grinning face filled the screen, surrounded by hordes of microphones.

"How is she?"

He shrugged, his smile at full wattage. *"She's fine."*

"Why didn't you bring her flowers?" a reporter shouted.

Jean-Georges made a mocking gesture of shock. *"Sacré bleu! I forgot. My bad."*

"You only stayed twenty minutes!"

"Long enough."

"You don't look too worried."

"Worried? Moi? Non."

He blew kisses to the crowd and ducked into a low-slung Italian sports car and sped off.

"He's quite the Romeo," Neve said.

"Mick said Jean-Georges didn't invite Fanta to Milan. She just showed up."

The reporter returned after the commercial break. *"This news just in: Fanta de las Mercedes has checked herself out of the Milan hospital, while Mick Carr remains behind bars in the Central Milan police station."*

The screen was filled with footage of Fanta leaving the hospital wearing a broad headscarf and dark glasses, huddled in a raincoat and being herded into a small sedan. Mercifully, there was no footage of Mick being led into the jail, just an exterior shot of the police building.

"Darius said Mick had an engagement ring with him," Neve said.

"I told him I didn't want to talk about the future." Marie-Claire buried her face in her hands.

Neve patted her shoulder in consolation. "He's mad for you, love."

"But I want to finish school."

"You'll be done in nine months. Plenty of time to plan a wedding."

Neve's mobile phone whirred and she answered, spoke for a moment, and then handed it to Marie-Claire.

"Okay, love, there's good news and bad news," Darius began. "The good news, which is very good news, is that Fanta hasn't pressed any charges yet and the *polizia* are beginning to get suspicious. That, and she's checked herself out of the hospital and holed up in a hotel. So, Mick's lawyer is going to petition for release as soon as possible."

"And the bad news?"

"The earliest that could happen would be tomorrow. He'll have to spend another night in jail."

"Can I get a message to him?"

"Not tonight, but the lawyer is going in around ten o'clock tomorrow morning. We'll know more then."

Darius was right, it was hopeful news. "How was the match?"

"We lost. We needed Mick to break up plays, no one does it better than him. Milan got the ball and you could have set a sundial by how long they kept it."

Marie-Claire thanked him and handed the phone back to Neve, and went into the kitchen to pull something together for them for dinner.

"Darius is a great guy," Marie-Claire said when Neve joined her.

Neve laughed. "Dad and me brothers are smitten. Mum, too. He's been to dinner twice, and I swear I could have left halfway through and no one would have noticed."

"And you?"

Neve tried to keep a straight face, but it cracked into a silly grin that she couldn't control. "I'm smitten the worst of all."

"I think Darius is rather taken, as well. I'm jealous, though, you're handling this a lot better than I am."

"I don't have to deal with psycho ex-girlfriends, MC. And Darius has only had two regular girls, and they married friends of his. They're all pals, and very nice."

Marie-Claire smiled. "Now I really am jealous."

Chapter Thirty-Nine

MARIE-CLAIRE GOT Neve settled in Mick's guest bedroom, and then, feeling like every bone in her body had turned to lead, crawled into his bed, the empty expanse overwhelming her. Where was he now? What kind of bed was he sleeping in? She pulled the covers over her head, trying to block out the world, and within minutes fell into exhausted slumber. It was the longest, most undisturbed sleep she had ever had in his bed.

The girls had breakfast before the television, but there was no news. Everything was a rehash of the night before, with the added speculation about Mick's chances of being back in Britain to play in Saturday's game against Manchester United.

Cameras caught up to Sir Frank outside his offices. *"I fully expect Mick Carr to be in the lineup Saturday,"* he replied to the reporters, his expression grim.

They decided to take the taxi driver up on his offer and he was as good as his word, appearing on Mick's doorstep twenty minutes after they called. "An even bigger crowd today. I also hear the Metropolitan Police have your street blocked off and are thinking of doing the same at the Lady Warwick. You've got patient neighbors," he reported.

They found out how true his words were as they pulled up to the school. "I've got her in the back," he called to the policewoman who waived them through.

Once inside, they made their way to the second floor where the students had gathered to go to the Tate. "There's no way I can go," Marie-Claire said and no one argued with her.

"I'll stay here with you," Sandra said, then added, "I twisted my ankle at a rave over the weekend and I'm not looking forward to the trek."

Marie-Claire had the feeling that this was all prearranged but was grateful anyway. "We'll go next week," she promised.

Raul checked his watch. "Where's Stephen?"

"I saw him this morning," Margaret said, "but not since MC arrived."

"Then we're leaving without him. Let's go run the gauntlet."

Marie-Claire and Sandra returned to their worktables, where they looked through her sketches from Kew Gardens. She had only drawn them yesterday, which seemed like a million years ago.

"MC," a professor interrupted, "you're wanted in the dean's office."

"Again?"

She nodded. "The entire faculty is there, as well. And Stephen Ashe. You can come, too, Sandra."

She wouldn't, or couldn't, answer any more questions, so Marie-Claire and Sandra followed her to the cavernous office. The entire faculty was assembled, as well as the dean and Stephen Ashe. No one greeted them and no one was smiling.

"You wanted to see me, sir?" Marie-Claire asked.

"Yes, MC. Have a seat." He pointed to an empty chair beside Stephen, but she recoiled at being so close to him.

"Thank you, I'll stand."

"I'll stand as well," Sandra added.

The dean gave them a withering look and moved to a nearby easel. He turned a framed painting around, and Marie-Claire was startled to see it was her painting of the ducks from Moorsgate.

"Miss Wentworth, do you recognize this painting?"

She began to laugh until she realized the seriousness of the question. "Of course. It's the Mallards I painted for the Critique."

"Can you produce your preliminary sketches and value charts for this work?"

"No, of course not. It was for the reflected light assignment, I was to paint directly what I saw."

"Did anyone see you paint it?"

"Just my...boyfriend," she said, stumbling a bit over the word, and then continued more confidently, "my boyfriend Mick Carr. He sat with me while I painted it."

"I see. And where is he at the moment?" The dean asked with an innocent air.

"In Italy."

"Oh yes. I remember now. A 'guest of the Italian government,' so to speak."

She bit off a sharp retort and stood in stony silence.

"Still, he is not available to vouch for you," the dean continued. "Did anyone else see you paint this?"

She searched her memory. "His neighbor, Robbie. Why?"

"Because it's time to tell the truth, MC!" Stephen jumped out of his chair to confront her. "I couldn't lie any longer. I had to tell them I painted it!"

Marie-Claire heard Sandra's sharp intake of breath, but it was so absurd, all she could do was laugh. "Don't be ridiculous, Stephen."

"Mr. Ashe, can you prove you painted this?" the dean asked.

"I can. She gave me this in exchange." He pulled the Kolinsky wash brush from his jacket and displayed it for all to see. "I really wanted it, and MC said she would trade it for a reflected light example with some ducks. It was easy to paint, I went out to Long Pond on Clapham Commons and finished it in under two hours. But doing that just wasn't right, I shouldn't have done it. I'm...I'm so ashamed." He hung his head in a pantomime of dejection.

Marie-Claire blanched at the sight of her brush in Stephen's pudgy little fingers. "That's my Kolinsky! It went missing yesterday. You stole it."

Stephen sighed and looked at her sadly.

Seeing he was determined to lie, she spun around and addressed the dean. "Why would I do that? Why would I bribe someone to paint an assignment for me?"

"Because you were desperate to stay."

"Yes, but not that desperate."

"Sandra," he said, switching his attention, "do you see anything in her work that would lead you to believe this painting was done by MC?"

Sandra walked to the painting and studied the work for several moments. "The Prussian Blue. MC always uses that," Sandra said, "and the Alizarin Crimson in the shadows. And the Winsor Orange, straight out of the tube. No one else does that."

"You also saw all of her failed attempts. Is there anything that makes you believe MC is capable of producing a work so radically different from her previous attempts?"

"Love will do that for you, sir," Sandra replied dryly. "I also understand that when she painted it, she had gotten some sleep and eaten more than she had in the previous three weeks."

"Well, supposing you are still in love with Mr. Carr and have had a good breakfast, perhaps you'd be so kind as to oblige us by duplicating this effort." The dean pointed to a blank piece of watercolor paper and a palette with an assortment of pigments, including Prussian Blue, Winsor Orange and Alizarin Crimson.

Snatching her Kolinsky out of Stephen's grasp, Marie-Claire swished the brush in the water, her hand shaking badly. Closing her eyes for a few seconds, she tried to remember the clarity of the scene, the ducks standing on the smooth wet stones, the glittering water, and the brilliance of the reflected light on their glossy white stomachs. With careful, deliberate strokes, she began to re-create the scene.

Stephen painted at the same time but kept one eye on the original, his expression blank. With rapid strokes, he re-created the image almost exactly, while hers was emotionless and flat. Even Marie-Claire could see that Stephen's was the better reproduction.

When they were both done, the dean said, "We'll ask you both to wait outside. Dixon, take Stephen into my private study."

While the two girls stood in the hallway, voices rose behind the closed door to the dean's office, and it was clear there was a heated battle going on. Sandra squeezed her hand as Marie-Claire trembled.

"What is going on?" she said.

"I don't know but I've got a good idea," Sandra muttered.

"What?"

"I think our Stephen found an offer that was too good to refuse. You're going to be expelled," Sandra told her matter-of-factly. "And then you'll have to leave the country immediately."

"That doesn't make any sense."

"Immediately—meaning before the Manchester United game this Saturday," Sandra clarified.

"No."

"I'd bet me mum's house on it."

The door opened and a faculty member gestured for them. "MC, Sandra, please come back in."

One look at everyone's faces told her all she needed to know. "I'm done," she said.

"Miss Wentworth," the dean began formally, "you have been accused and found guilty of academic dishonesty by trying to present another student's work as your own. This is clearly against the rules of the Lady Warwick College of Arts and Design, and you are summarily expelled. Do you understand?"

She managed to nod her head yes.

"I must also ask you to vacate your house immediately," the dean added.

"Do Neve and Raul have to move out as well?" she asked, her throat dry.

The dean shrugged. "If they can afford the rent they may stay."

"Do I get any of my tuition back?"

"Unfortunately not. By cheating, you've forfeited your school fees." For a moment or two, he tried to muster a sympathetic expression but gave up.

Marie-Claire turned to the faculty, who looked horror-stricken. "Thank you so much for all you have taught me. I…" The words she wanted to say became tangled with the tears that threatened to pour from her. Instead, she lurched out the door.

She moved swiftly through the narrow halls till she came to the entrance foyer. The press had the school almost under siege, and the only way out now was through the front door. She doubted she would get to the end of the block without breaking down.

"MC," the receptionist called to her in hushed tones and gestured to a deliveryman standing by her desk. "This is Carl, he delivers for the framers. He said he'd give you a ride in his van, to get beyond that lot." She jerked her head contemptuously towards the pack outside the gates, clearly visible from her desk.

"It's a plain white van, miss," Carl added. "You can hide in the back."

Without a backward look, she followed him out.

The van passed unnoticed through the gates and sped away. "They don't suspect a thing," Carl reported. "Where do you live, miss?"

Good question, thought Marie-Claire. Best to try and get to her house first and pack a bag and then from there, who knew. "Turn right, and down four blocks."

"I'm not getting through there, miss," Carl said moments later. "Police've got the road shut off. I can drop you off as close as I can get, but that's it."

"That's fine. Thank you, Carl, I appreciate all your help."

In the end, Carl parked one block over and Marie-Claire scrambled out and began resolutely walking towards her road.

Turning the corner, she paused, dumbstruck, when she saw the police barricades across the narrow street at mid-block and hordes of paparazzi swarming on all sides.

She was spotted instantly. The mass stampeded towards her, screaming her name, and pure terror seized her. She turned to flee.

From across the street, a black sedan pulled out of a parking spot and made a tight U-turn towards her. The window rolled down and a familiar face craned out.

"MC, get in the car."

Astonishment kept her frozen to the spot. The world had truly gone insane.

"Now, damn it!" Eric yelled.

Marie-Claire did as she was told and in an instant, the car sped away, leaving behind flashing cameras and indignant yells.

Chapter Forty

JEAN-GEORGES BOUNDED UP THE corridor that connected the small jail to the Central Milan police station as Mick's possessions were returned to him.

"Mon frère!" He greeted Mick with a hearty hug, and hurriedly shepherded him towards the front doors of the police station.

"What's happened?" Mick asked. "I think they're trying to tell me that the charges have been dropped?"

"Oui," Jean-Georges told him as they ducked out the doors and into a rainstorm. A car waited for them at the curb while photographers jostled for a shot.

"Nice big smile for the cameras," Jean-Georges muttered. Mick did as he was told, and in six steps they were in the back of the car, which sped away.

"They have returned all your possessions, *non*?" Jean-Georges asked as Milan passed by their car window at top speed. "Including the ring?"

Mick patted his jacket and breathed a sigh of relief. It was secure in his pocket.

"It is for *ma belle* Marie-Claire, *non*?" Jean-Georges winked. "I thought so. She is very concerned for you. Let's go back to the hotel, you get cleaned up and packed. The plane departs at noon, we will be home before you know it."

Good by him, Mick thought. He was exhausted and grubby after living in his suit for two days and desperately needed a shower. Flipping open his mobile, he listened to his messages, the first one being from Marie-Claire. He laid his head back against the cushioned headrest and smiled for the first time in ages, listening to her excitement as she told him about Kew. When the message was done, he saved it and pressed the speed dial to call her. The mobile rang repeatedly and failed to go to her messages. He frowned and tried again, and then cursed savagely when the battery gave out and the phone went black.

At the hotel, he emerged from the steaming bathroom feeling like a new man. His mobile was recharged and he tried Marie-Claire again, but still heard nothing but the endless ringing.

Jean-Georges had turned on the television, which was showing footage from Fanta's press conference earlier that morning. Mick hardly recognized her as she sat at a table wearing a plain brown dress and little makeup, apparently wishing to get the ordeal over with as fast as possible. Elliott, her agent, stood by her side answering all the questions the press put to her.

"*Miss de las Mercedes has no comment. Yes, she has dropped the charges. It was all a misunderstanding. Yes, she remembers falling but it was because she tripped, Mr. Carr did not push her. When she hit her head, she forgot that. Her dress ripped when she fell. All she remembers was that Mr. Carr was showing her the engagement ring he is planning on presenting to Miss Wentworth.*"

Fanta furtively whispered something in his ear. *"And she is here in Milan to visit an aunt. Not to see Jean-Georges Mayotte,"* he added.

The press corps seemed genuinely stymied by her complete reversal and could think of no more questions. Fanta leaned toward the microphones. *"I wish Mick and MC all the best,"* she said tersely, and then stood and left.

"What the hell?" Mick marveled, regarding Jean-Georges closely. "How did you work that?"

The Frenchman shrugged. "You heard her, she hit her head and she forget. She also forget that I did not invite her here, and I remind her that I am trying to get back together with my wife. If she had not remembered...I would have told my side of the story. And parts of her story, *la polizia* were already beginning to not believe. Fanta is not a stupid girl."

<hr/>

Bad news awaited them at the airport. The rain had settled into a steady downpour, punctuated by intermittent flashes of lightning and thunder. The first class lounge was full of passengers from delayed earlier flights, so the team staked out one corner of the room and settled in to wait.

"We're delayed for at least two hours, maybe three," Darius explained when they entered, shaking Mick's hand. "Good to see you out, mate."

"Good to be out. Have you been able to get a hold of Neve —"

Darius's mobile rang and he abruptly turned away and stalked to the opposite side of the lounge.

"He's been going up the fucking walls," Jason said sullenly. "No idea why. I thought we were going to watch footage of the match before the flight."

Darius said a few words to the lounge attendant and left, leaving Mick wondering what was so important. He tried Marie-Claire's mobile again but it immediately went to voicemail, so he left a message telling her he had been released and was on his way home.

"Move off," he motioned to two other players sitting on a long sofa. "You've both had soft beds to sleep in." He lay on the smooth leather couch and was asleep in under a minute, his mobile by his ear.

—◦—

The plane finally departed at three o'clock and after a two-hour flight, landed in London. Darius, who hadn't spoken to anyone the entire time, grabbed Mick's arm as they deplaned. "This way, Mick. Don't need you walking through the main concourse and creating a ruckus"

A gate agent met them and guided them back down a flight of stairs to the tarmac, where an airport truck waited to take them to where Mick's Aston Martin was parked.

"Give me a ride back, Neve picked up my car," Darius said curtly. "And give me the keys, I'm driving."

At Mick's stutter of protest, he snapped, "Look, you're exhausted, and the last thing we need is for you to get a speeding ticket."

"What about the luggage?" Mick asked as they pulled away.

"Someone at the office in Hendon is picking it up and will drop it off."

Darius's face was grim as he maneuvered towards the main highway. "Look, Mick, something's happened."

"For Christ's sake, what else could be happening?"

Darius exhaled. "They've expelled MC." At Mick's blank expression, he continued, "From school. They made her leave this morning. Neve called while we were at the airport."

"They can't have sacked her, she hasn't done anything," Mick said reasonably.

"Stephen Ashe is claiming she asked him to do her painting, the one with the ducks on the rocks."

"That's ridiculous. Of course, she painted it, I sat with her the whole time and watched her. It was brilliant."

"Yeah, well, I guess he's saying he did it, and there's no one to prove any different."

"That little prick!" Mick was shouting now. "I should have beaten that weasel to a pulp when I had the chance." He whipped out his mobile phone and tried MC's number again, and cursed viciously as it went to the answering message again. "Why won't she pick up?"

"There's something else," Darius added joylessly. "They can't find her." Darius glanced in the rearview mirror and smoothly accelerated, passing all the other cars in his path on the M4. "Everyone had left to go to some gallery when the dean pulled her and that girl with the blue hair, Sandra, into his office. When they came back, she had gone. She's not at the house."

"Jesus…" Mick ran his hands across his scalp in despair. "Oh, Jesus…"

They made the trip to Putney in record time. Darius parked three blocks away, and they sprinted down the back alleys to the house, disappearing over the garden wall before the lookouts the press had posted had time to sound an alarm. Neve let them in the back door and threw herself into Darius's arms.

"There, love," he crooned as she gave into uncontrolled sobs. "Tell us, what do we know?"

"Nothing still." She reached out to clasp Mick's hand. "Raul's gone to see what he can find out."

Through the lace curtains in the front room, Mick saw the enormous pack of photographers, bigger than any he'd ever seen. There was even a film crew lurking on the edges attempting to interview neighbors and passersby. Maybe it made sense that Marie-Claire hadn't come back here. He knew in his gut she wouldn't have attempted to wade through that lot. The thought gave him a flicker of hope.

Neve sat next to Darius on the sofa, his comforting arm around her, the week's tabloids scattered on the low table before them. Outside, camera flashes began to explode like daytime fireworks as Raul fought his way towards the house. Mick went out into the throng and pulled him in.

"Right, the dean expelled her this morning," Raul told them. "Then he had her clear off the premises immediately and told her she had three days to leave the country."

"But she didn't fake that painting. I sat right next to her while she painted it!" Mick yelled.

"We know that. But Stephen knew that it was a stretch for her and banked on her being upset and not able to reproduce it. He's a mime, a natural mimic, doesn't have a creative bone in his body. He also banked on you being out of the country and unable to defend her."

"So, where is he?"

"The school has given him a few days off, so I'd say he's gone to ground till he's sure she's left," Raul said. "Sandra thinks someone is paying him to do it. It would be the perfect motive for him. He's always wanting more money."

"But who would pay him?" Neve asked.

"Just about any Manchester United fan," Darius said darkly, "who wanted to make sure MC wouldn't be at our match Saturday. Christ, he could have gotten a million pounds if he had passed a hat. But more likely, he found one fan with deep pockets and settled for that. The question is, where is MC?"

"We don't know," Raul said. "I got here about one o'clock and a pap said they saw her walking towards the house but she never made it. The whole lot was running down the street towards her and she got into a car. Some that got close enough say it was a rental car from Heathrow, it had a sticker on it. A man was driving it, and not very well."

Mick paced the room. "Didn't they even give her a chance to defend herself? They just kicked her out?"

Raul gave Mick a very hard look. "She had been warned. The auction was the last straw, and all the publicity that came with it."

"So, what? What is so bloody wrong with that? She single-handedly raised over forty thousand pounds for a children's hospital!"

"I told you," Raul snapped, "they don't like the cheap publicity. They want to maintain their exclusiveness. Plus, the neighbors have been complaining, and it's just about impossible to get in and out of school. It all became too much, and the dean had been looking for a reason to sack her. You gave it to him."

Mick's eyes narrowed and he took a step towards Raul, his fists beginning to clench. Raul stood defiant but Neve jumped between the two men. "Stop it. This isn't helping us find—"

A loud knock at the door interrupted them, surprising them into silence. Neve went to the hall to answer it, spoke for a few moments, and returned, followed by a man wearing a dark overcoat, suit, and tie. He had a receding hairline and jutting chin and exuded arrogance. Mick hated him instinctively.

Mick drew himself up to his full height, which was considerably more than the man who stood before him. "Who the hell are you?"

"This is Eric Loudoun," Neve answered, "MC's old boyfriend."

For a brief moment, the room swam and Mick saw double. When he could refocus, he swallowed. "Where's Marie-Claire?"

"Safe." Eric sized Mick up. "You must be Mick Carr."

"How the hell did you find her?"

"My secretary read on the internet about some auction in London. I guess you attract a lot of attention," Eric said with derision and Mick's fists began to flex. "I was on the next flight."

Darius moved to stand behind Mick, crossing his arms across his broad chest.

"Thought you had a wife," Mick bit out.

"Ouch!" Eric pretended to wince. "Had is right. It lasted six months, now she's got a house in Georgetown free and clear and I've got my freedom back. And just in time."

"I want to see Marie-Claire."

"She doesn't want to see you," Eric countered.

"The hell she doesn't."

"Actually, Michael," Eric spoke deliberately, like a teacher talking with a slow student, "you've done such a thorough job of screwing up her life that she's done with you."

Mick's gut churned with sickening intensity. "I don't believe you."

"You don't? Gee, that changes everything." Eric paused dramatically. "What will change your mind? Oh, wait, I came back to give you these." He pulled the mobile phone out of his pocket, and Mick's house keys, and, finally, the length of black satin ribbon with the small silver bird's nest on it, dropping them all on the table with a flourish. "You're a big spender, Carr. Were you going to get her the matching earrings for her birthday?"

In a red haze, Mick saw nothing but the arrogant asshole's smug face. He lunged at him, ready to tear him apart, but only got two steps before Darius and Raul tackled him to the ground. Eric skittered out of reach behind a chair while the two men struggled to keep Mick down.

"Mick, he's a bloody lawyer," Darius said, using all his might to keep Mick's arm bent behind his back.

"Where is she?" Mick roared like an enraged lion.

"Lay a hand on me and I'll make sure you actually go to jail this time!" Eric screamed. "She's being deported, you idiot, and she's someplace safe until I take her home." Turning to Neve, he took a thick wad of cash from his wallet and tossed it on the table in front of her. "She wanted you to have this, to cover her part of the rent."

"She can't afford to give us this," Neve said.

Regaining some composure, Eric straightened his tie. "You obviously don't know MC very well. That whole 'poor art student' thing—" his wagging fingers made air quotes "—that she's got going on? Complete bullshit. Her family owns most of Kent County, Maryland, and what they don't own they could buy tomorrow if they felt like it. But she's stubborn and thinks she has to make it on her own. Her grandmother had to pretend she sold two farms to give her a so-called inheritance."

"What makes you think that you can just walk in here and interfere," Raul demanded, still pinning Mick to the floor.

"What did I walk in on?" Eric began, just getting warmed up. "MC in tears, on the front page of every tabloid in this godforsaken country, and having just been tossed out of school. All because some high school dropout couldn't resist parading her around like a trophy to prove he wasn't a Neanderthal."

"It's not like that," Mick bit out.

"Spare me." Eric sighed. "Tell you what, Beckham, you play on that knee till it blows, and then go back to whatever quaint hamlet you came from and trade in on your fame." It was obvious Eric had done his homework. "You stick to your Barbie Doll girlfriends and hot cars, and if you screw up again maybe you can work another plea bargain for probation instead of the jail time you deserved. Because she's not coming back."

Mick had never felt hatred so deep and consuming in his entire life. He hated that this man had known her before him, had been with her, and knew things about her that he didn't. "I need to see her," he said, trying not to beg.

With an elaborate motion, Eric crouched down on his haunches until he was eye level with Mick. "You seem pretty thick, so I'll use small words. I've got her now, and you don't. Bye."

Chapter Forty-One

MORNING SUNLIGHT STREAMED into the bedroom she slept in, waking Marie-Claire. Birds called outside the window as she lay warm and happy, a wonderful dream still lingering on the fringes of her consciousness. She had been lying in Mick's arms and he had been nuzzling her neck while his hands wandered over her body, whispering things that made her dizzy with desire.

But he wasn't here, she was alone, and she had to blink a few times before she recognized the tidy room and remembered where she was. The pain as reality crashed down around her was almost unbearable.

There was a soft knock on the door and Sue opened it a crack. "Ready for some tea, dear?" Lacey padded in behind her, wagging her stubby tail and leaping onto the bed to snuggle against her.

Marie-Claire rubbed her eyes and accepted the mug. "Thank you. I hate to be such a bother."

"You're no bother. Gordon's thrilled to have your help with the poults, he said you're worth three of the lads. And I'm happy for the company."

The corners of Marie-Claire's mouth twitched upwards. "I'm glad I can be useful."

"That man who brought you yesterday, he stopped by again earlier," Sue said with some distaste. "He said to tell you he was negotiating with the school to have your things shipped back to your home in America, and he also said things were square with Heathrow for you to leave tomorrow."

Marie-Claire nodded. "Eric. He's been very helpful."

"Quite," Sue replied primly. "Is he flying home with you?"

"Yes. He bought the tickets." With a clumsy motion, Marie-Claire wiped the tears away that threatened to spill down her cheeks. Which would only add to the ocean she had already cried.

Ah, young love, thought Sue sadly as she watched the poor girl try and keep her composure. They'll figure it out.

——◆◆◆——

EXPELLED! Declared the *Daily Mail* while the *Observer* wailed **WHERE IS MC?**

Across the country, sportswriters were wringing their hands over the effect of her disappearance on the big match Saturday evening. It seemed to Mick like everyone in the United Kingdom was looking for Marie-Claire, which only made the fact that she had disappeared into thin air that much harder to accept. He truly had no idea where she would go because he knew for a fact she didn't know that many places.

That asshole ex-boyfriend of hers probably had her stashed away in some posh hotel. Mick put out feelers, called in favors, and spent hours on the phone cajoling hotel staff who were anxious to help a famous footballer, but who knew nothing. Sir Frank put the staff at the club on the trail, as well.

Saturday morning, the television droned in the background as Mick worked his way through the list of hotels the club office had already called, on the off chance someone had missed something.

Mick's mobile rang and he answered it, his nerves on a hair trigger.

It was his father, who sounded madder than Mick had ever heard him. "What the hell have you done, Mick?" Gordon demanded without preamble. "Christ, son, don't you realize the mess you've gotten that poor girl into?"

"I realize it, Dad, and I'm trying to fix it. It all just blew up."

"Well, you're making a bloody mess of it. What the hell is she going to do with her life now? She's trying to make her own way in this world, and you've turned her into a pariah. She's a real person, Mick, not one of your doxies made of fake parts."

"I know that, but how am I supposed to make it right? I can't find her, I don't even know where she is."

"I do," Gordon said.

"How the hell do you know?"

"She's been staying with Sue and me since they kicked her out."

A huge weight lifted off Mick's chest. Thank God she was safe. "Why didn't you tell me? I've been going insane."

"That's all right. I'm okay with that. Plus, she asked us not to tell you. But she's so miserable, I think she might want to at least say goodbye to you."

"I've got to see her."

"And say what?"

"I need to tell her that I love her."

"It's going to take a bit more than that now. She's being deported, thanks to you."

"Yes, I know. Just keep her there. I'm leaving now."

Marie-Claire sat in the sitting room by the fire, Lacey at her feet making satisfied grunting noises as she got her ears rubbed. Eric paced outside in the courtyard talking on his mobile, or to be more precise, yelling. Snapping the phone case shut, he cursed and stalked back in the house, ignoring everything and everyone in his path. Sue and Gordon stayed in the kitchen to avoid him, Marie-Claire assumed.

"God, what will it take for these people to understand plain English?" Eric said loudly, and then glanced at her with a modicum of apology. "I'm sorry, sweetheart, I'm trying to finalize the plans at Heathrow. It's all arranged, we'll go in through a side entrance and do customs and security in the quiet area. They don't want any more fuss than we do. But your stupid limey school is refusing to refund you the balance of your tuition."

"It doesn't matter," she replied, scratching Lacey's ears.

"That's what you think," he said, rubbing his hands together in unconcealed excitement. "Just let me handle everything. Are you ready to go?"

At the sound of a car in the courtyard, Lacey jumped up and began barking. Marie-Claire's heart began to beat a staccato rhythm as she, too, recognized the rumble of Mick's Range Rover.

The back door slammed and she heard him enter through the kitchen and talk in low tones with Sue and his father. Lacey scrambled to meet him, and then returned immediately to her side. Eric stood motionless, his eyes narrowing, and then moved to stand behind her chair.

Her eyes were fixed on Mick when he came into the room. He filled the doorway, glancing briefly at Eric then settling on her. Seconds ticked by as it seemed everyone in the house held their breath.

"I want to talk with you. Alone," he said to Marie-Claire, his face granite-hard.

As if drawn by a magnet, she stood and moved towards him, but stopped when Eric reached out to grab her arm.

"We have to leave for the airport," he said, holding her back.

The moment Eric laid a hand on her, Mick moved so quickly it was like a blur. She managed to throw herself between the two men before he could make contact. Grabbing Mick's sweater, she pushed against him with all her might, barely stopping him.

"I will be back in a moment," she said to Eric, and turned to Mick. "Let's go outside."

She swept out the front door ahead of him and walked towards the barns, stopping just inside the door to the hatchery. Mick followed, and up close she could see how drawn and exhausted he looked.

They stood inside the dim room, close but not touching. He struggled for words, at a loss. "Dad says you've been a huge help."

"They've been wonderful. I saw Fanta dropped all the charges."

"Yes. Jean-Georges put the fear of God in her. She confessed that she threw herself down the steps to get in on the publicity from the auction, and was ordered to leave Italy and never come back." He paused uncertainly, and then continued, "Raul and Neve told me what happened at school. You did the right thing, coming here."

"I couldn't think of anywhere else to go."

"You can stay here, you know. You don't have to leave." Finally, the emotional turmoil was too much and he exploded. "Damn it, Marie-Claire, I don't want you to leave."

"Your Queen does. I'm being deported. Today is the deadline."

"We'll fight it. Stephen is lying, we both know that. I can hire a dozen lawyers. We can prove you painted those bloody ducks."

"Mick, even if I stay, it's not working. The school is mobbed. I can't get to my house, it's mobbed, too. The neighbors are fed up, and if the other students aren't fed up, they should be. I've been kicked out, you barely got out of jail. None of this is right." She shrugged, defeated. "I'm done. There's no reason for me to stay."

"No reason to stay?" he repeated, flabbergasted. "There's me. There's us. And you might be pregnant. With my child."

A sob caught in her throat and it was difficult to breathe. "I know all that."

"I love you. And you love me."

"I do," she said, "but it doesn't matter, it doesn't change anything. I have to leave. They've given me until today. If I wait any longer they might throw me in jail. There are a lot of powerful people who want me gone."

"Just until after the last game," he implored. "And you don't have to go to the bloody game against Man U! For Christ's sake. It's so not right," he swore, pacing the tiny space. "I'll take you to the airport."

She shook her head. "No. Eric is taking me."

"That bastard has made it very easy for you to leave, hasn't he?" Mick jerked his head savagely towards the house.

"He's helped, yes. Airport security has said the press is there waiting, so he arranged for me to go through a side entrance and do immigration and security privately. If everyone sees you, it will just be another—"

"Circus," he provided bitterly.

"Well, yes."

"Bloody hell. This is so not right." He swept her into his arms and held on to her for dear life. Marie-Claire clung to him, not knowing where she was going to get the strength to pull away like she knew she had to.

Outside, a car horn honked twice.

"Goodbye," she said gently.

"No." His arms refused to yield her.

"Yes. Mick, yes."

"Call me when you land," he said desperately. "Let me know you've gotten there safely—"

Eric honked again. Disengaging him, she went back into the courtyard. Sue and Gordon came outside and stood by the door, and she went to them, hugging them both.

"Thank you so much," she whispered into Sue's shoulder.

"Don't lose hope, lass," Gordon consoled her.

"Please take care of him. Make sure he's all right," she said between sobs, her heart breaking.

She broke away and jumped into the waiting car, burying her head in her hands so she couldn't look back as Eric sped away.

In the end, his father ended up driving him to Townsend Lane Stadium while his Range Rover stayed at Hempland. Giles met him at the locker-room entrance, his face grim. "Don't bother kitting up, Carr. You're benched till we can get this sorted out. Sir Frank agrees. You're not fit for anything."

Blind rage filled Mick. This was the last straw. "How can you not let me play? Our back four will annihilate them."

"Nasser's in for you," Giles replied. "It's what's best for the team."

"You're letting them win!" Mick raged. "You're doing exactly what they want!"

Giles shook his head sadly. "There's naught to do about it, lad."

Manchester United pressed hard from the first minute of play. Kingsbury Town struggled to make adjustments and set up plays, but failed abjectly, and so the defense crumbled, leaving Brian the Keeper to work feverishly while Manchester United's keeper pretended to be sunning himself on the beach for most of the match.

Mick and Hugo, who had been sidelined as well, sat at opposite ends of the bench, separated by two assistant managers who had been put in charge of keeping them as far apart as possible. Mick hated having to watch from there, and after a wrenching ninety minutes plus three minutes injury time, Manchester United beat Kingsbury Town, 3-0. Kingsbury Town fans left the stadium in high dudgeon, the loss putting them out of the Champions League Cup qualifiers and denying them a trip to Europe.

Mick made a brief appearance in the locker rooms to listen to the postgame talk. Afterward, he cornered Darius. "Take me to Heathrow."

"No can do, our Mick," Darius answered, "we've still got two more matches and all practices are mandatory till then. I'm not letting you go AWOL."

"You fucking bastard."

Later that night Mick sat motionless in his living room, staring at her paintings, a light rain beating against the windows. He had been sitting there in limbo for five hours, but it could have been months, or years, for all he knew.

Time passed. A church nearby tolled eleven and then midnight. The phone trilled, the number unrecognized.

"Marie-Claire?"

"Mick."

The connection was horrible, scratchy and practically unintelligible, but it was her. Relief flooded through him. "Where are you?" he shouted to be heard.

"Still at Dulles Airport in Washington." She sounded exhausted. "There was an accident on the Annapolis Bay Bridge and it's closed. We'll have to stay in Washington tonight."

"What? Where will you stay?"

"We were delayed two hours leaving Heathrow," she tried to tell him, her voice choppy.

"Where are you staying tonight?" he repeated.

"I have to go now Mick," she said abruptly.

"No, Marie-Claire, don't—"

"Goodbye," she said and then the line went dead.

His heart turned to ice. Cold, deadly, piercing ice. He held his head, thinking it was going to explode, and heard a whimper escape his own mouth. They had to stay in

Washington tonight? He would just bet Eric's apartment would be remarkably convenient. That idea was something he could not let himself think about, the thought of her staying with another man would drive him mad. Did the bastard have a guest bedroom? He would bet Marie-Claire would insist, but he couldn't stop the movie playing in his head.

Chapter Forty-Two

IT TOOK SOME SEARCHING, but Darius, alerted by a call from an Arsenal player, gathered the team and found Mick at a seedy pub in Hampstead in the wee hours of the morning. He was drunk, very drunk, and already bloody from one fight and ready for another. His teammates got him out of the pub before more trouble broke out, and a thick stack of twenty-pound notes purchased the silence of those involved.

It took four of them to get Mick into Darius's SUV before any reporters could catch up with them.

"You're a nasty drunk, Carr," he said, pitching him on his sofa, where he passed out, Marie-Claire's name on his lips.

It was blazingly hot under the stage lights where the team was assembled later that afternoon. Mick stood in the back row, feeling beads of perspiration roll under his suit, and his tie felt like it was strangling him.

The president of the Kingsbury Town Civic Association stood at the podium of the packed auditorium, his speech droning on interminably. The firefighter seated next to him seemed unaffected by the heat, but then again, maybe he was used to it. Mick almost laughed, thinking he'd have to remember to tell that to Marie-Claire. Then his gut wrenched, and the emptiness came back and threatened to swallow him whole.

The rest of the team stood motionless next to him on the dais before the audience of neighborhood families, civic leaders, and schoolchildren that filled the Kingsbury Town Auditorium.

"…and we welcome to our annual award ceremony Captain Gerald Hawkins of the Kingsbury Town Fire Department. It is my great honor to present him with our Citizen of the Year award for bravery in the line of duty…"

Mick ran his hand over his jaw, grateful he had remembered to shave. Darius had shown up at his house earlier and bullied him into getting cleaned up and changed into a suit, and several cups of coffee had washed the taste of stale booze out of his mouth. Darius had also taken his keys to the Aston Martin, which Mick had to admit was probably a good idea.

"…the rescue of seven Kingsbury Town Grammar School students from a burning motor coach…"

Christ, how long would they have to stand here?

"Thank you to the Kingsbury Town Civic Association for this honor," Gerald Hawkins began, and then stopped as the microphone screeched high-decibel feedback across the auditorium. "Oh, sorry—" he apologized, bending to turn off his emergency walkie-talkie.

Mick's head pounded, and the sweat was getting worse. He swallowed, wishing there was water somewhere.

The firefighter seemed to natter on for hours. Finally, Darius stepped forward, handsome in a tailored suit, to present the firefighter with a Kingsbury Town jersey emblazoned with his name across the back.

Applause rang out and the team shook his hand, and the photographer arranged them behind him for the traditional pictures. The firefighter's wife and beautiful little daughter came out to join them, and the audience clapped politely while everyone smiled and the photographer began to snap.

By an unfortunate accident, Mick was sorted to stand behind Hugo. He had not been within two meters of the bastard since the auction, and in a haze of pain, Mick studied the man's aristocratic posture, his handsome good looks, and impeccable dress. It became crystal clear to Mick that this prick was the source of all his problems—if Hugo hadn't pitched up the bidding at the auction, there wouldn't have been any news for the tabloids, Fanta wouldn't have decided to use the situation for her own publicity, and Marie-Claire's ex-boyfriend would have never found her.

Desperate, uncontrollable fury welled in Mick, and he was not a man built to withstand that kind of pressure.

———————◆———————

People who were present that day would later recall that what happened was like an explosion—a sudden, unexpected release of combustible hostility that fanned out in all directions, with Mick and Hugo at the epicenter. It was also an accurate description of Mick's emotional state, resulting in a detonation of all the rage and helplessness boiling in him, directed at the one person he held responsible.

His fists grabbed Hugo by the throat, and Mick saw nothing but the person responsible for his misery. He felt others trying to pull him off, but he was gripped in a bloodlust and nothing less than the feel of Hugo's bones breaking under his hands would satisfy him.

Everyone agreed that Hugo put up a good fight. Surprisingly resilient for a much lighter man, he fended off direct punches and landed a few of his own until both men were bloody, yet continued to fight on with a ferocious intensity. Chairs collapsed under them as they fell, and rolled over the edge of the stage in a maelstrom of pummeling fists and grunts.

It took the entire team to separate them, and Darius later confided to Neve that he had let the two of them go at it for a while before ordering the team to pull them apart. The damage had been done, and the way Darius looked at it, they needed to blow off some steam.

Mick sat slumped in a chair in Sir Frank's office the next morning, a copy of the *Daily Mail* staring back at him.

NOT IN FRONT OF THE CHILDREN!

The cover shot showed Hugo pinned to the stage floor, with Mick's fist drawn back and ready to smash, his face a mask of fury. Behind them, six-year-old Sally Hawkins, in a pink pinafore and blonde ringlets, screamed while clutching her mother's leg.

Sir Frank sat across the desk from him, frowning, while Hugo sat stiffly in a chair on the other side.

Lord Lambton stood at the tall window staring out at the London vista stretching thirty stories below him. "I say, old boy, you're going to have to pull it together," he began, turning back to address Mick. "What happened to Miss Wentworth is terrible, but we can't have you brawling in front of little girls. It just sends the wrong message."

Mick pressed his fingertips into his jaw and winced.

"You're both to send flowers and a note to Mrs. Hawkins, you know. Barely missed her and little Sally when Hugo threw you into the folding chairs. And I'm handing down a two-game suspension, effective immediately."

"It's the ruddy two final games, sir!" Mick protested. "We're still only one point out of the Cup play!"

"You have to reconsider, my lord," Hugo said.

Lord Lambton was unmoved. "We have no choice."

"I'd bench you both anyway," Sir Frank said. "Carr, you're a walking red card."

"Okay, suspend me, I don't care. But keep Hugo in, at least they'll have him."

Sir Frank shook his head no. "The fans wouldn't let Hugo leave the stadium alive. Until this mess gets straightened out it's the only thing we can do."

"Sir Frank is right," Lord Lambton said. "The Kingsbury Town fans have been screaming bloody murder since MC left, and now you're losing it, as well. We need to get this situation under control immediately."

Mick buried his face in his hands and tried to regain some control over his breathing.

Lord Lambton regarded him carefully and not without sympathy. "There is a way out of this, but we have to move quickly. I think I can help." He shot a meaningful look at Hugo. "I think we can all help."

———— ◆◇◆ ————

Practice had been cancelled for Monday, but Mick caught a cab to St Augustine anyway, knowing he'd just be climbing the walls at his own house. In the old kitchens, the building custodians were watching a rebroadcast of the Manchester United match on a small television. He watched with them, seeing from a new angle all the missed opportunities and senseless mistakes he could have prevented if he'd been on the field. They grimaced in commiseration as he vented his fury on an innocent stack of metal chairs, kicking them around the room with a deafening yet satisfying din, and then refused their help in collecting them and restacking them against the wall.

It was getting dark when he left the building and pulled out his mobile to call for a taxi. A new, blue Jaguar convertible sped in from the street and pulled up next to him, its engine purring with well-bred precision. At the wheel was Hugo Auchincloss.

The two men glared at each other.

"Come back for more, Hugo?" Mick taunted. "You're in luck, I've got the next five minutes free."

"Shut it and listen to me, Carr. I'm sorry about what happened with MC, she's a nice girl and didn't deserve any of it. Now, I think I've worked out a way to make it right, but I need your help. Get in the car, we've got work to do."

Mick eyed him with distrust. "The hell I'm going anywhere with you."

"I said shut it, Carr. I'm trying to do the right thing here, but I need your help and need it now. There's an emergency Regents meeting at the Lady Warwick tonight, and if we're fast we might be able to do something. So, get your arse in the bloody car."

Mick paused a moment, and then, figuring he had nothing to lose, opened the passenger door and slid in. As soon as he touched the seat, Hugo slammed the car into gear and sped out of the lot, barely glancing at the oncoming traffic. Cars honked in protest as he merged seamlessly into traffic, indifferent to their complaints.

"Where are we going?" Mick asked, grudgingly impressed at the man's driving skill.

"Tottenham Green. A club called Charmers."

That crime-ridden section of the city was the last place on earth Mick would imagine Hugo Auchincloss frequenting. "How the hell do you know Tottenham Green?"

"It's a long story, but let's just say I know a chap who's familiar with the area. I put him to looking for this Stephen Ashe, and he found him holed up at this club, blowing lots of cash and bragging to all who'd listen that he'd put the nail in our coffin. I think we need to go have a chat with him."

Chapter Forty-Three

MICK KNOCKED ON the conference room doors at the Lady Warwick College of Arts and Design, and without waiting for an invitation, shouldered them open while Hugo hustled a battered and bruised Stephen Ashe into the room. Hugo's speed had come in handy when Stephen had caught sight of them and tried to flee out the back of the seedy club, but no one could outrun Hugo. And once Mick had caught up, all hope of escape vanished.

The board meeting had obviously already started. Marie-Claire's painting of the Mallards at Moorsgate was displayed on an easel in the center of the room, and the group of people at the table spun around in surprise at their arrival.

"What is the meaning of this?" a well-dressed woman asked from the head of the table.

"This is Stephen Ashe," Mick informed them, shoving the pudgy man forward, "a student here. He has some things to tell you."

"I was brought here against my will!" Stephen protested, dangling from Mick's clutches.

"That's no way to talk to the nice lady," Mick scolded, and tossed Stephen into an empty chair. "Now. Tell her everything you told us."

The woman in charge looked to Mick, and then Hugo, and then Stephen. "Go ahead, Stephen, you've something to say?"

"I was supposed to wait until Mick was out of the country."

"To do what?" the woman prompted.

Stephen's mouth moved soundlessly for several seconds, and then he clamped it firmly shut.

Mick leaned over him, frowning. "Oi! The lady asked you a question!"

"To say I had done MC's painting," Stephen replied, petulant.

The members of the board exchanged glances.

The woman's gaze narrowed. "I think we better start recording this." She nodded to a man sitting to her left, who produced a tape recorder, and then spoke rapidly, relating the details of who was in the room and why they were there.

"And who paid you?" Hugo prompted from behind Stephen, jabbing his shoulder.

Stephen burst into tears. "He'll kill me!"

Mick muttered "He'll have to get in line," and Stephen sobbed and whispered a well-known name that caused everyone to gasp.

"Why did you do it, Stephen?" a man at the table asked.

"For the money. For the stinking money, why do you think?"

The woman put her hand over her mouth in shock, but then composed herself and addressed Mick. "You're Mick Carr, I presume. You said you saw MC paint this picture." She gestured towards the easel.

Mick had been in this position many times before, in a school and answering to an adult in a position of authority. It was odd, he thought, his father was usually there, as well.

"Yes. I sat next to Marie-Claire for the entire two hours she painted that picture. It was at my farm."

"I see," the woman nodded. "We've obviously done a serious disservice to MC. We will need to figure out how to put things right."

"This is the most important thing to her, being here, at your school," Mick continued. "She won't come back, though, if it's disrupting everyone, so I'll buy her a house near here with security, and I'll get security for the school, too. Just let her back in, and I'll leave her alone. Just let her come back."

Mick looked around the room, his voice quiet yet firm. "None of this is her fault. It's all mine, and I'm the only one who can put it right. I love her, but if you take her back, I'll let her go."

The stillness of the room was interrupted by a sniffle from a lady sitting at the end of the table, which she buried in a handkerchief. Several board members found their eyes unaccountably itchy, and more than one reached for tissues. Hugo dropped into a nearby chair and sat, sullen.

"You've played your share in this as well, Hugo Auchincloss." The woman's cold scowl held him. "What do you have to say for yourself?"

"Sorry," Hugo mumbled, his gaze fixed on the floor before him.

"Beg pardon?" The woman sarcastically cupped her hand to her ear. "Didn't quite catch that."

Hugo squirmed in his seat for several moments, and then flashed a defiant look. "I said I'm sorry, Mummy."

———◀○▶———

She hadn't left the farm in over two weeks.

That wasn't hard to do. Their land encompassed hundreds of acres, almost an entire peninsula that jutted into the Chesapeake Bay. Her things from the Lady Warwick had not arrived, and Marie-Claire didn't care. She wouldn't have touched them if they had.

Their neighbors alerted them that British tabloid reporters were swarming over the Delmarva Peninsula looking for her and making a general nuisance of themselves. The farm, like many on the Eastern Shore of Maryland, was remote, and Chase assured her that the locals weren't talking. Still, she felt like a prisoner.

Her mother had picked her up at the airport; Marie-Claire had seen her across the crowded baggage claim area when she was on the phone with Mick. A wave of homesickness engulfed her and she ran to her. Her mother, shocked at her daughter's appearance, briskly thanked Eric for his help and then dismissed him, refusing all his entreaties to carry the luggage or take them for a meal.

She'd taken Marie-Claire to a hotel in Annapolis while they waited for the bridge to reopen. Marie-Claire poured out her heart and her mother listened.

"I love him. I don't know how I'm going to live without him," Marie-Claire said, sitting on the bed surrounded by sodden tissues, comforted by the feel of her mother's arm around her.

"I know nothing is going to solve your problems today," her mother said, "but let things take their path for a bit, they might sort themselves out. You're exhausted and you know you never think well when you're like that. It's good you came home, it's good you're going to get a chance to clear your head. You can decide what you want to do in a few weeks. Dad and Chase will keep you busy in the meantime. Give it the summer."

It was a good plan and the work was endless. There was still planting to do, the first cutting of hay to bring in and a hundred chores a day to occupy her time. She woke before dawn and fell into bed at night, exhausted, but it still wasn't enough.

Mick haunted her dreams. She would wake in the middle of the night, her windows open to the sounds of the wildlife on the Bay, her body vividly remembering the feel of his lips on her skin and the heat of his body where it pressed against hers.

Eric had worked up the courage to come see her once, but she had sent him packing almost before he could get out of his car. She was grateful for his help in leaving England, but she made it clear she didn't want to see him again. He hadn't taken the news well and attempted to follow her into the farmhouse when she walked away from him, but Chase's sudden appearance had quickly convinced him to leave.

That only left Mick, and the faster she forgot about him, the faster she was going to get her life back. What that life looked like, she had no idea.

Saturday was Kingsbury Town's last game of the season, and Mick's flight left four hours afterward. He watched the loss from the sidelines; in fact, he and Hugo sat together. The photo of the two sharing a wry laugh when Kingsbury Town scored their only goal appeared in several papers the next day.

"Mick," Fanta called out to him as he crossed the parking lot at Townsend Lane Stadium, on his way to the airport.

He glanced over his shoulder but didn't break stride. "What do you want?"

"I'm not here to cause trouble."

He barely recognized her. She wasn't wearing any makeup and her hair hung around her face, making her appear years older than she was. "Then why are you here?"

"To apologize."

"Bit late for that."

She nodded in agreement. "I thought you should know I just got sacked from *Willy Nilly*. I'm getting the blame for all of your girl's troubles, and the viewers howled so they canned me. I'm done."

"Can't say you don't deserve it."

"I do. You can let your girl know that. She won."

"I don't think she'd want to hear that."

"It was mean what I did, and I'm sorry. That's all I came to say." She shrugged, and then turned away.

Raul was waiting by the Aston Martin to drive him to the airport. "Was that Fanta de las Mercedes?"

"Yes."

Raul blew his cheeks out in surprise. "She looks a lot different on telly."

———— ◆ ————

A blast of hot air hit him as soon as they got off the plane in Baltimore. At the car rental, he got an SUV and drove it around the parking lot several times, getting reacquainted with driving on the wrong side of the road. He ventured out onto the highway and knew how Marie-Claire felt driving in England; it was a little scary till you got the hang of it.

He drove across the long Annapolis Bay Bridge to the Eastern Shore of Maryland. The map showed he had to go north up the peninsula to find Chestertown, and he followed the main highway until it turned into a two-lane road that wound through flat, scenic farmland.

Miles flew by, and he realized he had no idea where to go or where to look for her. He racked his mind for references—she had gone to college in Chestertown, she'd had an apartment there that wasn't too far from her parent's farm. But for these damn Americans "wasn't too far" could mean fifty miles. He had just driven twenty-five minutes and had passed through exactly one town. He was stymied by the immensity of the place.

Then inspiration struck—he would look up some hunting and fishing shops. They would certainly know her family if they were in the guiding business. Using his mobile, he found the addresses of several that seemed to be local and continued on his way.

The first one was doing a brisk business and the man at the cash register looked up and smiled. "What can I do for you, young fella?"

"I'm looking for a family in the area that does duck hunting guiding. Name of Wentworth."

Every person in the store seemed to freeze, and then became very busy. Gazes dropped, and people around him became very busy elsewhere.

The man's face settled into stone. "Can't say's I know the name."

"Really? Chase Wentworth? They live around Chestertown."

"No." The answer seemed forced. "No, no one around here by that name. Might want to try south down the peninsula. Heard the name Wentworth on the Virginia side of the line." Then he walked away.

Mick read everyone's body language and knew something was wrong, something had changed in a big but subtle way. He left.

Chestertown was a pretty little brick town on the Chester River with beautiful homes and tidy shops. The college was located at the northern end and he got out to walk around the campus. No wonder she was so overwhelmed by London, this place was as idyllic and peaceful a place as could be imagined. People sat on the lawns in groups and strolled unhurriedly along the tree-lined paths, and somewhere a string quartet was practicing near an open window. The place was like something out of a movie.

A sign on a post said Art Gallery and he followed the arrow to a three-story brick building. "Wentworth Hall" was carved in granite over the door.

It was deserted inside and he began to explore. Student work was prominently displayed, and he approved of almost all of it. This was proper art and jolly nice to look at. As he turned into a long gallery, he spotted one of her paintings—an Oldsquaw on the Bay and signed "MC Wentworth." The plaque was dated three years earlier and was very good, but her work in London was light-years better. He stood there a long time, drinking in the painting as if she were there. This was her painting; she had been here.

"Like it? It's one of my favorites," a matronly lady said, coming up behind him. "MC graduated two years ago and has gone on to art school in Europe. We're very proud of her."

"Yes, in London," he said. "I know her from there. I'm trying to find her, can you help?"

The woman's jaw clamped tight. "The gallery is closed now," she informed him briskly. "You'll have to leave."

"But it's only two o'clock," he protested as she ushered him to the door.

"All the same. Thank you for visiting." The door closed behind him, and he heard the latch thrown. What the hell?

Mick sat down on a nearby bench and considered his options. The woman knew Marie-Claire, that was for sure. She was near, he felt certain. But where? A wave of exhaustion washed over him and he realized he should find a hotel for the night and resume the search in the morning. Chestertown had several charming inns, and he chose the one closest to the college. A lady greeted him at the door with a warm welcome, which instantly turned to a hostile chill and "no vacancy" when she heard his accent. The same thing happened at the next, and at the third, he didn't even get in the door before he was tersely told they were full up. At the fourth, no one even bothered to answer the door, even though he could hear a radio playing inside.

The sun was setting over the water when he got lucky and found a room at a seedy motel on the outskirts of town, the Bay-Vu. The desk clerk seemed to take pity on him and said cryptically, "I'm not from these parts, either."

Mick lay on the hard bed feeling exhausted and paranoid. Aside from Marie-Claire, his experience with Americans was that you couldn't get them to shut up, yet on the Delmarva Peninsula no one had two words for him.

Early the next morning, he had breakfast at a small grill, and then drove north and west out of town to the Chesapeake Bay, following miles of cornfields, their bright green shoots sprouting out of the dark, rich soil. Were any of these her family's farms? He had never thought to ask the size of them, but from the looks of these, they were immense, probably hundreds or thousands of acres. The silo complexes staggered the imagination.

At a marina in Rock Hall, he made inquiries and again the initially warm welcome turned to stone-cold silence. An unreasonable frustration gripped him as he stood alone on the dock, the locals having busied themselves anywhere but near him—didn't they know who he was? Although he had always taken great pains not to abuse his celebrity at home, right now he wanted to be recognized, wanted everyone to know who he was, wanted everyone to fall over themselves to be of assistance to him.

But nobody cared that he was Mick Carr; all they cared about was getting rid of him.

Mick drove the winding back roads of Kent County for hours, the sun blazing hotter than anything he had ever experienced. Even though he was checking the map, he could swear he had already driven through these parts before, or maybe he was just getting cross-eyed from the unending flat vistas of wheat, soybeans, and corn. An occasional mailbox would interrupt a stretch of deserted road, and he would slow down to read the name, but none so far read Wentworth.

Around a corner, a large hand-painted sign advertised Strawberries—Pick Your Own. Several cars were parked in the farm lane next to the field and people were busy in the long rows. A woman with a cashbox and a stack of baskets relaxed under a shade umbrella, and with a spark of hope, Mick pulled in next to her.

"Hello, who owns this field?" he asked, doing his best to sound friendly.

Startled out of her nap, the woman's eyes flew open, and with great haste, she grabbed the cashbox and began marching down the dusty lane away from him. In desperation, Mick followed her.

"Go away, we don't want your sort around here," the woman snapped over her shoulder.

"What sort?"

"You know very well. Leave her alone, she hasn't hurt anyone." With a final scathing look, she climbed into a battered truck, gunned the engine and drove off in a plume of dust.

With nowhere else to go, he went back to Chestertown College and sat outside Wentworth Hall in the late afternoon sun, utterly defeated. Defeat was nothing new, it was part of the game. But this wasn't a game. He wasn't going to move on from Marie-Claire. There wasn't going to be another woman after her. He had found what he wanted and lost it, and the crushing reality was almost unbearable. He was past the anger, past the fight. The bitterest part was that everything had been put right, and now she was so close, yet it seemed the entire state of Maryland was intent on sending him packing and casting him into hell for all eternity.

The campus spread before him in that expansive American way, like no one had stopped to think about boundaries when they built the place. A group of guys was kicking a football on a luxurious pitch across the lawn from where he sat. He watched them for a while, and then walked over for a closer look. Without a thought, he took off his shoes and socks, rolled up his pants legs a few inches and went out to join them. They welcomed him with a wave.

He began to play, dribbling, passing, heading a few balls and sizing up their talent. Several were good, two were very good. The slackers soon dropped off to watch from the sidelines, and a few more joined until a 7-on-7 game started. Blowing off steam, and having something fun to focus on, felt good. He couldn't remember the last time he had played a pickup game.

During a break, they introduced themselves as the Chestertown College Men's Soccer team, and explained that they usually got together in the afternoons during the summer to stay in shape. They shared their water with him and then returned to the pitch, drawing more spectators as the play began to get serious. Mick felt his mind settle into the game, his concentration becoming sharp and focused, and everything else faded into the background. He could play all day.

The lads were remarkably fit but still only thinking one or two moves ahead. He called plays to his side, reading the defense, sending signals, and making them play as a team. After an hour, he swapped sides and did the same thing, and found himself enjoying the game immensely.

When another player arrived, Mick gave him his spot and began to coach the entire team, showing them how to set up plays and working on a few set pieces. The lads were eager learners and worked hard. They played for over four hours, and it was only absolute darkness that shut them down.

"Dude, that was the best we've played all year," a tall midfielder named Alex, the team captain, said. "Come with us to the bar, Mick. We owe you some beers and pizza."

They packed into a local pub, and over slices of pizza and freezing cold beer, regaled Mick with ribald stories of away game road trips that rivaled his as a professional footballer. They were a hell of a nice bunch of blokes, genuinely kind and sincere. Just like her.

After five pizzas had been demolished, they ordered another round of beers and turned to Mick with interest. "So, what are you doing here, Mick?"

"I'm looking for a girl, actually."

Howls of laughter filled the bar and he got several approving slaps on the back. "Well, you came to the right place. Omega Pi sorority is having a party tonight, and with that accent of yours you'll be getting all the—"

"A girl I met in London, actually," he added hastily. "She's from here."

This piqued their interest. "Oh yeah? What's her name?"

"Marie-Claire Wentworth."

It was as if everyone in the bar was in a photograph, so completely did they freeze at the mention of her name. Jaws dropped and beers that were held to lips remained motionless. A glass slipped from someone's fingers and beer sloshed on the table.

Several moments passed and the team exchanged frantic looks. "You're the guy who's looking for MC. The guy Chase warned everyone about," one of them dared to utter in hushed tones.

Well, that made a bit of sense, Mick thought. Her brother had warned everyone, and the town had pulled up the drawbridge and locked all the doors. Maybe he was lucky he hadn't had a shotgun leveled in his face.

"I am looking for her. I need to find her. Can you help me?" He looked from face to face. "I just want to talk with her."

Alex wiped his hand over his mouth and leaned forward. "You see, Mick, it's like this. There's been a ton of those tabloid photographers hanging around here for the last couple of weeks, real scum of the earth, all looking for MC. She was involved in some big mess in England that I guess involved you, too, if you're that English soccer player that got her expelled from school."

"I am."

"Premier League?"

"Yes, Kingsbury Town."

There was a round of quiet whistles from the group.

Alex soldiered on. "The Wentworths are nice people and mind their own business. My older brother went to school with Chase, and they're good friends of my family. In fact, most of the families around here know them well. We're mostly local kids." He motioned around the table to the players listening intently and sighed. "A lot of our families work for them."

"Her mom was my Sunday school teacher," a lanky forward said.

"My brother took MC to the senior prom," another added, and then, seeing the fierce look that crossed Mick's face, amended, "just as friends."

"I'm not going to cause trouble," Mick said, hating himself for putting the lads in such an awkward position and promising silently to make it up to them. "I just want to talk with her, apologize at least. There are a lot of people that want to apologize to her."

The team cast uneasy glances amongst themselves, and then the captain stood up and motioned for the team to follow him. "I think we need a team meeting. Excuse us."

They went to a corner of the bar and huddled in discussion. Mick swallowed another mouthful of the icy beer and prayed. These lads were his last best hope.

The huddle broke and the players returned to the table. "Okay, we took a vote and it was unanimous," Alex said. "You're a brother player, and we'll look after you on two conditions. First, if the Wentworths ask you to leave, you will, and quietly. They don't need any more problems."

Mick nodded. "Second?"

"Team picture with us?"

Chapter Forty-Four

MICK HAD TO wait most of the next day before starting out for Betterton, a little town on the Chesapeake Bay about fifteen miles from Chestertown that he had driven through two days before. The lads had told him that her family would most likely be out during the day on one of their farms. Best to wait until suppertime.

The hours had dragged by, but now that he was at the farm, the agony switched to a dread of what she might say. He had to keep hope.

"Mr. Wentworth?"

The tall man turned from the tractor hydraulics he was working on and wiped his hands on a rag. "Yes?"

"I'm Michael Carr," Mick held out his hand to the older man, who let it dangle there. The two sized each other up, the older man's face blank, Mick's tense. The barn they were standing in was cavernous, the quiet broken by the nervous fluttering of roosting pigeons overhead.

"I see," her father said.

A younger man came through the barn, and one glance told Mick that this was her brother, Chase. He was just as tall as his father, but stockier. He glanced between his father and the stranger and was immediately on guard.

"Can we help you?" he asked Mick politely.

"I hope so. I'd like to see Marie-Claire."

Chase's face darkened when he heard Mick's accent. "You're Mick Carr?"

"Aye." He offered his hand to the younger man and again it hung in the air.

"You've got some nerve coming here," Chase muttered, and then hauled off and punched him squarely in the jaw.

Mick took the punch, and for the first time in his life didn't fight back. Chase's punch was a tough, solid hit that took a minute to shake off. "I want to see Marie-Claire," Mick repeated, cradling his cheek.

Chase stood seething, and then exploded with rage and jacked Mick against the barn wall. Marie-Claire's brother was shorter by an inch or two but just as thick and powerful as himself. "You can go to hell, you're not getting near her. Do you understand how much you've messed up her life?"

Again, Mick refused to fight back. "Yes, I do. Beat the hell out of me if it will make you feel better. It might even make me feel better. I won't stop you."

"Chase," her father said, never taking his eyes off Mick. After a few seconds, Chase released him and stepped back.

"Marie-Claire's not here," her father said, his lips pressed in a thin line.

"I actually came to see you. Both of you. I need to talk with you about her."

"She's none of your business—" Chase began, but his father shot him a look and he snapped his mouth shut.

Her father sighed and finished wiping his hands. "We'd better go in. Her mother's going to want to hear this, too."

The house was a large, two-story tidewater farmhouse whose white clapboards dazzled in the late afternoon sun. A beautiful woman, obviously Marie-Claire's mother, met them at the door.

Her father made the introductions, and a surprised light flicked in her mother's eyes, which were so exactly like Marie-Claire's, it wrenched his heart. She offered her hand and a smile played about her lips. "Michael."

"Pleased to meet you, Mrs. Wentworth."

"Please, it's Danielle. And you may call Mr. Wentworth Charles."

He shook her hand and followed them into the house. Several of Marie-Claire's paintings hung on the walls, and his mood lightened just being near them. Her father murmured a few words to her mother, who got him an ice pack for his jaw, which he took with thanks. The family took seats around a large kitchen table, Chase grudgingly offering him one, as well.

"Now what's this about, young man?" Charles asked. "As I've said, Marie-Claire's not here."

"I don't blame you for wanting to throw me out," Mick began, nodding to Chase. "If she were my daughter, I'd want to throw me out, too. And yes, I do understand how much I've messed up her life. But I think I can put things right.

"I'm a footballer," he continued, "sort of like your professional American footballers. At home, I get a lot of press and too much media attention. I first met Marie-Claire when I went to see her paintings. I fell in love with them first, and then I fell in love with her. First time in my life for both. But it's hard, courting a girl like her, when a paparazzo is watching your every move. Nothing went right. She was a champ, though, and put up with it all.

"But I underestimated how it would affect her. I was stupid. I didn't understand how her school worked, and I let things get out of control. It's my fault that they kicked her out. I tried to stop it, and was having some success, but she still left."

"What the hell did you expect her to do?" her brother asked in disgust. "She was being deported—"

"Chase," Danielle interjected.

"No, Mom, this bastard needs to know what kind of hell he's turned our lives into. They followed her here, you know. She can't go anywhere without them chasing her. She says they'll lose interest as soon as you move on to the next girl and leave her alone. So, the faster you do that, buddy, the happier we'll be. That's the biggest favor you could do her."

Mick shook his head. "I can't do that."

"Why the hell not?"

"Because I'm not going to move on. I love her. I want to marry her. I'll do whatever it takes. Retire from football, move to America. If she's not ready now, I'll wait."

Recognizing the solemn intent of Mick's words, Chase slumped back in his chair. "Jesus, you're serious."

"Completely serious," Mick said, and then turned to her father. "But I can't do that without your permission, sir. My intentions are honorable." He took the box out of his pocket and showed the family the glittering contents. Her mother's eyes widened and Chase whistled under his breath.

"What kind of life would you give her, Michael?" Danielle asked, not unkindly.

"I will love her for the rest of our lives. I will protect her, which will be much easier when she's my wife. I admit that I have sowed my wild oats, but since I've met your daughter, ma'am, I have not looked at another woman. No desire.

"My contract with Kingsbury Town has another three years left, and then I'm planning on retiring, it will be a good time to go. I've saved a considerable amount, and I own a large game farm near where I grew up. There's a house on it that I think Marie-Claire will enjoy fixing up for us. For our family."

"What about her being deported? She can't go back with you," her father countered.

"Actually," Mick said, pulling a stack of paper out of his bag, "they want her back rather badly. Nothing's gone right for anyone since she left."

The family paged through the documents.

"The deportation order has been lifted," Mick continued as they passed papers between themselves, "and I have a letter for her from the Lady Warwick, inviting her back on a full scholarship."

Chase snorted. "That'll make her happy. Girl could make a penny scream."

"There's some other stuff in there you might want to read. Her housemate, Neve, saved all of the news articles about her since she left. They're pretty interesting."

The family began sorting through the thick stack of clippings with interest. "And this is just since she left?" her mother asked.

Mick nodded, and then winced when she got to the *Daily Mail* cover with him, Hugo, and the little girl. "It wasn't as bad as it looks," he said sheepishly at her frown, but caught a glimpse of amusement in her brother's expression.

"MC took some girls camping on Kent Island and won't be home until tomorrow afternoon," her mother said. "What are your plans?"

"I don't have any, really. I was waiting to see her before I made any."

"Then why don't you stay for dinner," she said, glancing at Chase and her husband. The invitation sounded more like a statement.

"I don't want to be a bother."

"No, stay for dinner," her father repeated, although Mick sensed he wouldn't be upset if he declined.

"Thank you, sir. I'd like that."

Chase stood and extended his hand to the man he had wanted to tear limb from limb an hour ago, but who now stood a good chance of being his brother-in-law. "Sorry for the hit. No offense."

Mick took his hand and shook it gratefully. "None taken."

Her father offered his hand, as well. "We're going to go out on the water and pull some traps before dinner," he said, "if you'd like to give that a try."

"I would," Mick accepted, feeling better than he had in weeks.

⸺◦⸺

The sun glittered over the Chesapeake Bay the next afternoon as Marie-Claire piloted the small skiff around Jane's Point and headed towards home. With one hand on the tiller, she motored across the still waters, enjoying the peacefulness of the Bay as fish jumped nearby to catch flies in mid-air.

The camping trip to Kent Island had been a welcome distraction. The girls from the neighboring farms had been lively and chatty, and had enjoyed drawing the local wildlife with Marie-Claire.

She tied off the skiff at the dock and set off through the tall grass towards the house. Her mother was in the kitchen and Marie-Claire handed her a bunch of wildflowers.

"To make up for being grumpy," she apologized, giving her a kiss on the cheek.

"*Bon voyage?*" her mother asked. Good trip?

"It was fun," Marie-Claire replied in French, pouring a glass of lemonade from the refrigerator. "Did anything of mine arrive from London?"

"Not from the Lady Warwick," her mother answered, wiping her hands on a tea towel.

Ten minutes later, Marie-Claire stood at the dining room table, working her way through the pile of clippings and envelopes in front of her. A beautiful bouquet of summer flowers was in the center of the table in her mother's favorite crystal vase, a tacit sign of approval.

"He brought them?" Marie-Claire asked, her throat dry.

"Yes."

"Nice touch."

Her mother smiled. "I thought so."

With a trembling hand, Marie-Claire opened the letter from the Lady Warwick and read the contents, and then had to reread it before she understood the offer. "They want me back," she said in shock. "With a full scholarship, retroactive to last year."

"That's very generous. But do you think that's fair? The scholarship money could go to someone who really needs it."

A small piece of paper fluttered out of the envelope. The clipping was from the Times, dated five days prior.

Dean of Lady Warwick To Take Early Retirement

Arthur Albert Hewitt, dean of the Lady Warwick College of Arts and Design, Putney, yesterday announced his retirement, effective immediately, as dean of the school, citing health reasons.

The second envelope was smaller, made of thick creamy paper with an "L" embossed on the flap. She read the handwritten note inside.

Dear Miss Wentworth,

Please accept my most sincere personal apologies regarding your treatment by the press, as well as my regret at your undeserved dismissal from your school. I am assured by Sir Frank that efforts are underway to rectify the situation, and he has every expectation that you will be able to return at your earliest convenience.

If I may take the liberty, I have reason to believe your friend is intending to propose marriage to you. The decision is entirely yours, of course, but on behalf of the Football Association, we fervently hope you accept.

Your friend,

Lambton

"What does that one say?" her mother asked.

Marie-Claire clutched the note to her chest, her eyes wide. "Nothing."

Together, they started to go through the stack of clippings. **MC, COME BACK!** pleaded the *Mirror*. She winced at the cover of the *Daily Mail,* and whispered "Mick" disapprovingly under her breath. Several clippings conveyed despair among Kingsbury Town fans and glee from their opponents. Finally, there was the coverage of the last game that they lost and a photograph of the dispirited players leaving the field.

At the bottom of the stack was a long article that brought tears to her eyes. **WHY I LOVE MARIE-CLAIRE: The First Interview with Mick Carr.** She slowly turned the pages, which showed the first picture of them kissing in Wandsworth, and then random shots of them on the streets, at matches, and a few candid ones that their friends had taken. *"What does the future hold? That's for her to decide. I love her,"* Mick was quoted as saying.

"Is this really what it's been like?" her mother asked in dismay, picking up a clip that showed the mob outside of their house in Putney.

"Most of the time, yes."

"If you go back, your father and I insist you move into a safer house," she said. This caught her attention; her mother had switched to English which meant she was trying to drive home a point.

Marie-Claire slumped into a dining room chair. "I can't go back, Mom. I'll just mess up again. You have no idea how hard it is, what it's like to have every move you make photographed, everything you wear criticized, every mistake you make splashed on the front page the next day."

"You're right. I don't know these things. But I do know you, Marie-Claire, and I know how stubborn you can be. Mick obviously loves you and wants to protect you. This might seem harsh, but perhaps some of these problems were of your own making. He did his best to protect you, but he can only do so much. If you love him, you're going to have to meet him halfway. Do you love him?"

Marie-Claire tried to make order out of all the conflicting emotions that were jumbling inside of her. "I love him very much. But I don't love all the attention."

"Do you love the things that go along with him being famous?"

Marie-Claire grimaced. "Like, sometimes, but not love. I guess I love his farm. But he would still have a game estate even if he wasn't famous, I'm pretty certain of that." She thought the question over further. "He has a reputation of being a real playboy. Or, at least, had. Women still come up and try to give him their phone numbers."

"He mentioned that. Does he take them?"

"No."

"I think that's because he's crazy about you, Marie-Claire. Which means he's a very smart man because you're wonderful. But the decision is yours."

Marie-Claire stared at the evidence before her. He had moved heaven and earth to make things right. "Where is he?"

"He's staying at the Bay-Vu."

Marie-Claire tried and failed to visualize Mick at the run-down motel on the outskirts of town. "The Bay-Vu? Why?"

"All of the innkeepers in Chestertown ran him out because of the photographers and those nasty English tabloid people. Chase offered to get him set up at the Queen Street Inn, but he refused and said he'd actually gotten used to the Bay-Vu and they were being very good to him."

"Do you know where he is now?"

"I believe he said he'd be at the college this afternoon playing soccer with some friends he's made."

"I need to go see him."

Chapter Forty-Five

MARIE-CLAIRE SHOWERED and changed, choosing a simple white sundress and sandals and leaving her hair long around her shoulders, with a few sections pulled back with a thin, white ribbon. At the college, she parked her car near the playing fields, freshly mown grass scenting the warm air. A languorous breeze blew off the Bay, stirring the leaves of the massive oak trees that lined the path to where Mick was playing. Keeping her pace at a walk was torture when she wanted to sprint across the lush grass to where he was.

As she approached the pitch, she saw Mick dribbling the ball up the field amongst the players, calling instructions and gesturing with authority. He'd lost weight, she saw, noting the black shorts and Kingsbury Town t-shirt that was already soaked through with perspiration, outlining his leaner physique.

A group of women stood on the sidelines watching Mick instead of the play on the field. With a stab of possessiveness, Marie-Claire saw some of them were loitering quite near him and smiling. She walked a bit faster.

Mick turned to chase a ball that went out of bounds and then stopped in his tracks when he saw Marie-Claire.

"Hi," she said when she reached him.

Words seemed to form but his lips moved soundlessly. He stood towering over her, panting with exertion, sweaty and dirty, and seemingly paralyzed.

"Hey, MC," Alex hailed from the pitch. She waved back and the team came to greet her, swarming them. They chatted with easy familiarity while Mick stood beside her, mute.

"How long have you guys been playing?" she asked, bewildered by Mick's silence.

"Since two. Mick's been great. He's been running plays with us all afternoon. Tell her how we did, Mick," Alex said.

"Ah," Mick began, taking a deep breath. "They've been... they've done...good. I mean, great. Very nice. Yes."

Alex stared at Mick, confused by his sudden change from outgoing leader to a man fumbling for words, and then followed Mick's desperate expression to Marie-Claire.

"Okay, guys, time to hit the showers," Alex said, shepherding the players towards the field house. "Good workout. Thanks, Mick. Are you going to be around tomorrow?"

"I honestly don't know," Mick said.

"Well, if you are, we'll be here. Good to see you, MC." Alex nodded, and then clapped Mick on the back and said, *sotto voce*, "Good luck, mate."

As Alex herded the team off the fields, the crowd on the sidelines began to disperse, leaving Mick and Marie-Claire alone.

"They're good lads," Mick managed to say, staring at the ground.

She nodded her head in agreement. "I've grown up with most of them. My mom had them all in Sunday school class, and I work with their families."

"They've said." He glanced up at her. "They've been very good to me. It's funny, how they're all like you. They're open, laid-back, and friendly. When I first met you, I thought you were ridiculously naive. It never occurred to me that people could be this way."

That made her smile. "Most people around here are. Although I heard you've gotten the cold shoulder from some. I'm sorry about that."

"It's okay. I understand completely. You're worth protecting."

He seemed unwilling to look her in the eye, so she took the opportunity to let her gaze run over his body. "You've gotten a bit sunburned," she murmured, and then gasped when she saw welting and faint blue marks below his right eye. "Oh my God, Mick, are you all right?"

Reaching out to hold his face in her hands, she examined the deep blue and red swelling. "What happened?"

"I met your brother."

Her eyes widened. "What did you do to Chase?"

"Never laid a finger on him," he assured her.

Her hands gripped his shoulders. "Why did he hit you? What did you say to him?"

Stilling her hands in his own, he said, "He had every right to punch me. We're okay now. We went out fishing and had a good talk."

"What about?"

"Some interesting things you hadn't mentioned."

"Like?"

"Like you were the Maryland State Junior Clays Champion two years in a row."

She had the good grace to blush. "That was years ago. And I hadn't shot in months." At his grin, she added, "You met my parents, as well."

"They're lovely people."

"I think they liked you, too."

Feeling like the conversation was heading towards dangerous territory, Marie-Claire pulled her hands away from his and walked to a bench under a nearby shade tree and sat down. He retrieved his kit bag from the sidelines and followed her, coming to a stop next to where she sat.

"Did you see what I brought you? The letters and the clippings from Neve?" he asked.

She nodded. "How did you make all that happen?"

"It wasn't just me. You have a lot of friends in high places who wanted to put things right for you. The deportation order has been lifted and you're free to go back anytime you like."

She dropped her eyes and changed the subject. "How did your season end up?"

Mick raked his hand through his short-cropped hair. "Things fell apart after you left. The club lost the last three games, and we finished ninth. Hugo and I got suspended for fighting."

Marie-Claire pressed her lips together. "I saw."

"It wasn't as bad as it looks, but I deserved the suspension. And something good came of it at least, Hugo and I are on a lot better terms now." At her skeptical look, he added, "And the little girl in the pinafore has a good start on her university fund."

That made her laugh in spite of herself. Being with him was so good, just being near him made every nerve in her body feel alive. Reminding herself of what she had to do, she tucked her hair behind one ear and tried to get a hold of herself.

The silence between them became fraught with tension.

Knowing it was better to say things face-to-face, she stood before him, her stomach churning with sickening dread. "Mick," she began but he cut her off, his voice rough.

"Have you come here to tell me it's over?"

It was so hard to do the right thing, to explain why he had to move on from her. She tried to control the tears that were welling in her eyes and took several deep breaths to make her voice sound firm. "I appreciate you fixing things, and making it so I could go back if I wanted to. But you shouldn't have come here. You need to move on from me."

"I will never move on from you. Or is it that you've moved on from me?"

"What do you mean?"

"Are you with him? That ex-boyfriend of yours who swooped in and stole you from me? I need to know if you're with him now."

"No, I'm not with Eric," she answered in complete bewilderment. "Why would you think I was?"

"Because the bloody bastard made it very clear you were. Why did you leave with him?"

"I didn't have much choice," she said, trying to understand Mick's blazing anger. "After they sacked me, I tried to go home but the paparazzi had mobbed the house. He helped me get away. I didn't know where to go, so he took me to your dad's, and then went back to get my things. I didn't see him again until we flew home together, the morning that you came up."

"The night you landed, you said you had to stay in Washington. Did you stay with him?"

Seeing the raw pain in his face, she realized what it was costing him to ask these questions. "No." She cupped his cheek in her hand, overwhelmed with regret. "No, my mother had come to pick me up. I saw her when I was calling you, it's why I had to go, I hadn't seen her in a year and I missed her so much. The bridge was closed, so she took me to Annapolis, and we stayed the night there, in a hotel. I cried all night. Did you think I had stayed at Eric's?"

He nodded.

"Never. Mick, I've been over Eric a long time. I guess I was in such shock at being expelled, I didn't question his taking things over, and you were still in jail in Milan."

Mick gave a harsh grunt. "Has he tried to see you since you got back?"

"Yes. He came over last week. I sent him on his way."

She could see the relief flood through Mick.

"Why did you cry all night?" he asked.

"Because I missed you so much. And I had failed so badly and lost everything. I couldn't handle it, couldn't handle being your girlfriend, couldn't handle school, couldn't handle the press. I realize now it's a miracle I had lasted as long as I did. They should have bounced me earlier."

He leaned towards her, putting his hands on her hips and drawing her against him. "Were you happy before they expelled you? Were you happy with me?"

The weight of his question made her shoulders sink. "Yes. But I can't go back," she added, seeing the flicker of hope in his eyes. "Even if they're willing to take me back, I would only end up causing more problems."

She gestured around with her hand. "You've met my family, you've met my friends, and you've seen where I'm from. The glamour, the attention, the money, I just can't do it. It's not going to work, Mick. I love you but you have to let me go."

"For the love of God, woman, do you have no sense?" he swore, pressing her back against the tree. "I am not moving on from you, ever. I know I agreed not to talk about the future, but that's all out the window now as far as I'm concerned, and you need to know this."

His expression was fierce, his face just inches from her own. "I want to marry you. Right now. Tomorrow. I want you with me forever. No other woman, just you. I want you in my bed every single night. I want you to take care of me, and I want you to have my children. I want Eric, and Hugo, and every other man on the face of this earth to know that you are mine and completely off-limits, and I will break their arms if they even touch you.

"I fell in love with you the day I met you, and it was truly love at first sight, just like the day Dad took me to Moorsgate. I can't tell you any more than that because that's all there is. You're all I want."

The simplicity of his words shattered her heart.

"I know I have pushed you and bullied you to be with me, and that I am probably reaching way, way above my station in life to get you. But you're what I want, and I will love you forever."

Reaching into his gear bag, he pulled out a small box and with a trembling hand, placed it in hers. The lid popped open with a small click, displaying the dazzling contents.

The ring literally took her breath away. The brilliant stone sparkled radiantly in the afternoon sun, the design simple and beautiful.

"I told the jeweler that you were a painter and he said it would clean well..." he said nervously as she continued to stare at it.

"It's beautiful."

Dropping to one knee before her, he took the ring and held her left hand. "Marie-Claire, I love you and I can't bear to let you go. I know I've put you through a lot and if you need time, I'll wait. I will wait forever for you because I know that I can't live without you. You're right, the world I live in is a lot different from here, but we're not. We're the same, you and I. We want the same things in life, and that's all that matters. Everything else will work as long as we're together."

Tears streamed down her face at his words, and her heart swelled to fill her chest, making it difficult to breathe.

At the sight of her tears, Mick blanched. "If you don't want to go back, I'll move here." Mick added quickly, "I'll sell Moorsgate and buy a farm around here. God knows I've seen enough of them."

"No, you can't sell Moorsgate. I love it there."

"So do I, but it means nothing if you're not there with me. Will you marry me?"

He was right, if they were together, it would all be okay. She loved him, and they were right for each other. "Yes," she murmured, "yes, I will marry you. There is nothing else I want in the world as much as you."

Pressing against him, she wrapped her arms around his neck and pulled him closer, her knees going weak in his embrace, drinking him in. She had missed him so much.

A wolf whistle echoed from across the lawns. "Bloody Yanks," he muttered, and took her hand in his and slipped the ring onto her finger. The fit was perfect.

"Are you pregnant?" he asked as she admired it.

Standing on tiptoe, she softly nuzzled his ear. "Not yet."

He groaned in heated frustration. "Jesus, Marie-Claire, don't start. I'm trying very hard to impress your family, and if your brother finds out I've been ravishing you on the Chestertown College football pitch—"

Impatiently, she pulled his lips back down to her own.

Chapter Forty-Six

LATER, MUCH LATER, they lay in each other's arms in the darkness of his bedroom at the Bay-Vu, happily content. He had made love to her in a frenzy of passion, and she had responded wildly until they had both peaked in an all-consuming crescendo, and then again more slowly, with tenderness and joy at being together. Then they talked, and he told her about everything that happened since she left London.

"Stephen admitted everything?" she asked, lying in his arms, sated.

"Everything. It's a huge scandal. The guy who paid Stephen is a powerful liquor distributor from the north and not to be messed with. He's a maniacal Man U supporter and didn't want to take any chances on the match."

"But how did Hugo find out? I wouldn't think he knows too many liquor distributors."

"It's quite a story and I'll tell it to you next. His girl is involved as well, but it seems like it's all worked out well."

Marie-Claire sighed happily and shifted to drape one long leg over his. "I'm just glad it's over. Do you think things will be different when I go back?"

"Things will be very different," he assured her. "Hugo gave me the name of a friend of his who does pretty much the opposite of public relations. He's very good at keeping people out of the papers. I've already talked with him, and he's agreed to take us on. Said he always likes a challenge, whatever that means."

She laughed. "I think it means he knows he's going to have his work cut out."

The ring on her finger glittered in the darkness, reflecting light from the parking lot outside. "Do your dad and Sue know that you were going to propose?"

"They've known for some time, and they couldn't be happier. Now I've something to show you," he announced, and she grumbled as he reached away to turn on the bedside light. "Well?" he asked, lying motionless on the bed and indicating his naked body.

"I've seen it all before but I'm always up for another look." She grinned and pounced on him, and he gave her bottom a light whack.

"No, look closer at my body. See if you can find it."

Needing no further encouragement, she started at his toes, examining each one as she kissed and sucked on them, and then started working her way up his legs. "Hmmm..." she murmured, her tongue running along his sensitive inner thigh, "I don't see anything yet, I must be going too fast..."

With a Herculean effort, he pulled her up beside him. "It's above my waist."

She pouted, eyeing his rampant arousal. "Are you sure?"

With an oath, something about tempting the saints, he grabbed her hand and placed it on his chest. She brushed aside the thick mat of hair, her face screwed up in concentration as she hunted. Then she saw the ink drawing she had done of the geese over his heart.

"But how are they still there? They should have faded a while ago."

"I had them tattooed on. The night you left. The guy followed your lines, they'll be there forever."

"You were awfully certain of yourself," she murmured, examining the artwork.

"Yes, I was. I also sold my house in Fulham and bought one in Putney, a few blocks from the Lady Warwick, on East Hill."

At her shocked expression, he continued, "There's four bedrooms, and a large sunroom off the back. There's even room for Raul if he wants to move in."

Marie-Claire sat there, astounded. "And Neve?"

Mick smiled. "I think Darius has other plans, and he can buy his own house. We're not running a hotel. Now come here."

Epilogue

LATER THAT SUMMER, *Country Life* magazine ran the following on their "Girls in Pearls" page:

> "Mr. Charles Wentworth of Betterton, Maryland, New World, announces the engagement of his daughter Marie-Claire to Mr. Michael Carr, who owns a large game estate near Aylesford, Hertfordshire. Miss Wentworth is a watercolorist."

The portrait was of Marie-Claire sitting in front of the painting of Liza.

"I must say, this is the first time *Country Life* has ever scooped the *Daily Mail*," the editor-in-chief mused in delight.

About the Author

MARINA REZNOR lives with her rugby-player husband and their two Labradors in Birmingham, Alabama. She became interested in English Premier League football (or soccer as she occasionally slips up saying) when American television began broadcasting matches and she realized there were almost no commercials.

Impressed by the players' agility and stamina, Marina began following their exploits off the field. As fiction authors know, the start of a good book often begins with "I wonder what would happen if…" From the first chapters of *Fowled*, the characters formed themselves and wrote their own story. Marina swears she just wrote it down as it happened.

In the course of researching English football, Marina fell in love with Hendon Football Club, a semi-professional club based in West Hendon, in the London Borough of Brent. The Kingsbury Town Football Club series is dedicated to their spirit.

Visit Marina at her website, marinareznor.com, and join her on Twitter @MarinaReznor and Instagram @MarinaReznor.

While you're at her website, keep in touch with Marina by

joining her charming, interesting, and very infrequent newsletter. Infrequent as in "My goodness, is the next ice age here already?" Sign up at https://marinareznor.com. She doesn't share and she doesn't spam.

Made in the USA
Middletown, DE
25 November 2023

43517881R00258